To my wife, Angela, who has allowed me the time and freedom to pursue my dream.

Adrian Lee Baker

APOK

The Birth of Đavo

AUSTIN MACAULEY PUBLISHERS™
LONDON • CAMBRIDGE • NEW YORK • SHARJAH

Copyright © Adrian Lee Baker 2022

The right of Adrian Lee Baker to be identified as author of this work has been asserted by the author in accordance with section 77 and 78 of the Copyright, Designs and Patents Act 1988.

All rights reserved. No part of this publication may be reproduced, stored in a retrieval system, or transmitted in any form or by any means, electronic, mechanical, photocopying, recording, or otherwise, without the prior permission of the publishers.

Any person who commits any unauthorised act in relation to this publication may be liable to criminal prosecution and civil claims for damages.

This is a work of fiction. Names, characters, businesses, places, events, locales, and incidents are either the products of the author's imagination or used in a fictitious manner. Any resemblance to actual persons, living or dead, or actual events is purely coincidental.

A CIP catalogue record for this title is available from the British Library.

ISBN 9781528907101 (Paperback)
ISBN 9781398426382 (ePub e-book)

www.austinmacauley.com

First Published 2022
Austin Macauley Publishers Ltd®
1 Canada Square
Canary Wharf
London
E14 5AA

Lyndsay Purdie, thanks for your help during the early stages of *Apok*. Catherine Dunn, for your outstanding skill, incredible feedback and making me believe I can do it. Carol, my biggest fan. I'm just so glad you liked the story. Sarah, for always asking about the story I was writing. Your enthusiasm and belief was invaluable.

Prologue

Apok: No prisoners – death to all – spare no one…

To fully appreciate *Apok* and what it is, you must first understand where it comes from and its concept.

Apok is an abbreviation taken from the Ancient Greek word *apokálypsis*. It is also where the word apocalypse originates.

An apocalypse (Ancient Greek: ἀποκάλυψις *apokálypsis*, from ἀπό and καλύπτω, literally meaning 'an uncovering') is a disclosure of knowledge or a revelation. In religious contexts it is usually a disclosure of something hidden, 'a vision of heavenly secrets that can make sense of earthly realities'.

In the Book of Revelation (Greek: Ἀποκάλυψις Ἰωάννου, *Apokalypsis Ioannou* – literally, *John's Revelation*), the last book of the New Testament, the revelation which John receives is that of the ultimate victory of good over evil and the end of the present age, and that is the primary meaning of the term. Today, the term is commonly used in reference to any prophetic revelation or so-called end of time scenario, or the end of the world in general.

But what if humanity has got it wrong? What if apocalypse doesn't mean the end, and in fact, means something quite the opposite? What if it means a new beginning? What then…

Is humankind ready for such a concept?

And just suppose that this new beginning doesn't lie in the hands of the world's greatest powers but, like all radical thinking, is locked away deep in the minds of each and every one of us. Something that is so frightening, so formidable, modern society has done its utmost to bury it, suppressed as though it is the most fiendish of prisoners, entombed in the darkest innermost recesses of the human psyche. But this is where the answer lies. It is where the answer to all our problems has always been, standing next to you in the street, in a shop, at work, whenever you see family or friends, or behind the face that stares back every morning from your bathroom mirror; everyone carries a tiny piece of the puzzle, the complexity and vast multitude of which, when brought together, will combine to shape a revolution that will change the world forever. It lies in that innate part of us that has always challenged convention, the part that wants to flip John's Revelation onto its head by asking: Where exactly on this earth is good winning the fight against evil?

It's just that no one can see it! And, what's more, the great powers that control our day-to-day lives want it to stay that way. To them, the status quo is everything; it is to reign with absolute supremacy. From the laws they impose to the relentless plethora of advertising, their master network is an apparatus so entrenched in the collective consciousness that it has the dominance to affect dreams, and in turn it can coerce our moods and behaviours, working its divine magic 24/7. It covertly dictates what we read and what we watch, the food we eat and the beverages we drink, the clothes we wear and the vehicles we drive, right down to the toothpaste that is best for us and even the holidays we go on. All of it is decided by a faceless, nameless master race, the secret elite who don't want the masses to know that we, as individuals, are each perfectly capable of playing our own part in rescuing humankind's future.

The year is 1991, the beginning of a new decade. There is no let-up for the warmongers as they regroup after Operations Desert Shield and Desert Storm to heighten the rhetoric between Croatia and Serbia. Not content with stirring up the Middle East, they are threatening war in Europe for the first time since World War II, their appetite for power and destruction insatiable in the spectral twilight of yet another millennium. The phantom cries of wars past heckle the victims of the devastation yet to come.

As intellectual beings, we never learn from our mistakes. That's why history always repeats itself. I suppose, if nothing else, the aggrieved can seek revenge for previous injustices. Our conceit and narrow-mindedness are so ingrained, it seems that every person who is either eligible to vote or capable of carrying a gun is willing to cut off their nose to spite their face in settling past grievances, as though we can only find true happiness in the idea of hurting others, whatever the cost. Einstein said, "I know not with what weapons World War III will be fought, but World War IV will be fought with sticks and stones."

It is frightening to think of what, if left to the secret elite – a bunch of egotistical, pseudo-Aryan billionaires who aspire to fill the shoes of God, playing 'chicken' with their Scuds and Tomahawk cruise missiles – they will one day leave us.

Not that God cares. He would waste no time in having us press the button. To Him, we are a burden, nothing but an unwanted scourge ruining what should have been his magnum opus. Yet here we are, the most ungracious and belligerent of pests, as arrogant as ever, like an old Victorian schoolmaster rubbing God's face in our technological success as science continues to debunk His credibility.

So, it is no wonder He has left us to perish in a flood of our own making, the deluge slowly but surely overtaking us to pollute land, sea, and air, placing our species in jeopardy for the first time in its short but extraordinary history. What's more, leading scientists have conceded that the data proves that this thing *they* call 'the great human experiment' is at serious risk of failing. It's showing no signs of slowing down.

At a recent climate technology conference, a guest speaker broke protocol and grabbed the headlines: "As a scientist, I was never inclined to pray, but perhaps now is a good time to start." A tabloid newspaper's front page read: "Surprise away win! Science 0, God 1." The 1980s saw consumerism explode and individual expectation skyrocket exponentially to movie dogma and pop culture mantras. The audience soaked up quotes like 'Greed is good' and 'Sex and horror are the new gods' and took them straight to heart, their hunger voracious and impatient, the youth movement, in the time it took to sling on a pair of headphones, replacing the old gods of tradition, hard work and the quid pro quo of due reward, with the easy fix of glitz and glamour, fast food and an even faster life, with everything on tap at the mere flick of a switch.

It was a decade ill-equipped for the demand. Everyone was having too much of a good time to notice the glaciers melting and the seas rising, as animal species fell off the radar in unprecedented numbers to warming temperatures and increased deforestation. It was a period that defined a new era of haves and have-nots, a super-breed of super-wealth generating an ethos devoted only to furthering the new hierarchy of worldwide commerce and high finance, the latest in a long line of emerging deities favoured by the secret elite. They cared not for the gods of old, not because there was a clash of interests but out of sheer apathy, which played straight into their hands. They let the wars rage and allowed biblical famines to flourish unabated, starving millions, just as they were equally indifferent to the diseases that plagued entire continents. Death's icy grip reigned supreme as the Four Horsemen smiled and looked on, as they always have, with the same patient optimism. Where the 1980s finished with the ongoing conflicts in Kashmir and Afghanistan, the Romanian Revolution, the US invading Panama, and civil war in Liberia, the 1990s upped the ante in the Gulf and, with the death tolls in Rwanda and the Balkans, the international stage was set yet again for genocide.

Croatia had always been considered a melting-pot of centuries-old prejudices bubbling away, festering like an invisible contagion of the deep subconscious. Its roots stretch back as far as the fifteenth century and the Ottoman Empire's expansion into Europe. It sparked a brutal struggle in the region that for the next few hundred years, with only a few brief respites, saw no let-up. By the late twentieth century, it left in its wake a time-bomb, a tightly interwoven incendiary mix of 'us' versus 'them', the social map like that of a prison yard, confined and intense. Its multiple factions were always in sight of one another, no one giving an inch, old wounds never forgotten, scornful in its conceit, in the backhanded scowls and abrupt conversation of daily life. Common courtesies were voiced to friends and merely nodded to others, people looking down their noses, the hurt and disdain always there to the discerning observer.

Having trained with the Croatian military for months as part of an international influx of volunteers, Andrew is one such observer, an adventurous 23-year-old who, after embarking on an extraordinary journey of discovery, found his true meaning and purpose serving as a soldier in the nation's new emerging defence force. He knew the hate had never gone away. Those outsiders who thought it had didn't know the people of the region. After World War II, they had simply learned to bide their time.

It was a kind of self-imposed selective mutism to avoid direct contact; a discriminatory form of social distancing – 'If you can't say anything good, don't say anything at all'. But the sentiment was so callous and so obvious, it didn't so much suppress the ill-feeling as concentrate it, driving social divisions underground, firmly putting a lid on the communal pressure cooker.

However, it only takes one person to see the situation for what it is, to lift the lid, to see the potential and how best to tap into it. Now, that takes one hell of a keen eye and an even keener intuition. It was this inexplicable ability that allowed Andrew to see the darkness behind the glowered looks, the layers of hatred and the social complexities these layers represented. He didn't know how; he just knew that he could. But, more than this, he could see it wasn't just one faction of the prison yard which hated all the rest but a dire dichotomy where every faction hated the others with equal intensity, placing each side on tenterhooks, nearly at one another's throats.

It was this same ability that allowed him to see the dark for what it was, just like he could see war, horror, fear, hunger, pestilence, and death for the gods they are and the domains they rule. To Andrew, they were fantastical creatures who had learned to co-exist alongside humankind, albeit at our continued expense.

But some gods exude more dread than others, their reputations never failing to precede them. The master of terror and the most formidable monster of them all is the dark; the domain in which all evil prefers to dwell.

Andrew could see war's pace gathering momentum, the darkness pervading people's lives, trending on televisions and across news media the world over, but this time to a global community divided, screaming out for a non-complicated solution to ever more complicated issues.

Andrew saw the decline and found it uncanny. He could feel the horror as though it was reaching out. His dreams provided dark conduits to the screams of bombed convoys and strewn bodies scorched into the desert sand along Kuwait's Highway 80 and to the slow grind of stone on steel as the Hutus sharpened their machetes to the radio message of 'Cut down the tall trees'. But now Andrew is in war's theatre, training, and preparing. As graphic and horrifying as the conduits were, they darkened still further allowing him to see Croatia and its people rapidly transforming from a brooding tinderbox of social unease to a case of dynamite sweating under the midday sun, its volatile beads of nitro-glycerine trickling down the thick greaseproof wrapping to drop and snap-crackle on the floor, ready to set Europe and the world on fire, just as the Balkans had done seventy-seven years ago on 28 June 1914.

But as much as he saw the problem as being global, Andrew knew that Croatia and whatever it led to would be the guinea pig, a litmus test of things to come.

With war imminent, Andrew knew instinctively that the time was finally right to put his plan into action; a plan which, once hatched, would spread with war's lightning speed, its relentless barrage of hateful paranoia preying on those centuries-old prejudices, prising open ancestral wounds, unresolved feuds and unwelcome family alliances, casting doubt and suspicion, turning neighbour on neighbour and brother on brother. It would unlock the minds of all who touch it, like a super-malevolent virus, its vehemence unparalleled and its course unstoppable.

In Andrew's mind, if humankind was ever going to get a glimpse of heaven, it must first go through hell. Everything has its price, and the admission to utopia is the highest there is – your soul. To enter the light, you must first cross over to the dark in order to prove you have what it takes to survive the forthcoming revolution. However, not everyone who crosses over will come out on the other side. Like all monsters, the dark will have to be fed, leaving its mark; that is the only definite outcome. In the months to come, there won't be a community, family or individual that doesn't bear the hideous scars of war's merciless wrath and the dark's insatiable appetite.

Andrew could see a nation heading for calamity, its people already subservient to the dark's subliminal call. He knew that, given the current climate, if you gave two hungry Croats a chicken leg and a knife, one would end up dead while the other feasted. He saw the darkness affecting human nature, dividing, exposing innocuous cracks, then flipping them to create vast differences, separating what used to be cohesive into opposing adversaries, forcing them to compete. But Andrew wanted to take this concept a step further by giving them a knife. What would happen then? To this game-changer, Andrew thought he knew the answer; just like the food, the knife would not be shared, and one would still end up killing the other. In this way he saw that, as a species, we are deeply flawed; our survival instinct, that primordial part of us, is too powerful, overriding our reason in a nanosecond. And it is exactly this that the dark relies on: Our intrinsic human frailty, the characteristics we cannot shake.

The human mind is already a dark place without anything darker invading it.

In Mary Shelley's *Frankenstein*, Captain Walton is quoted as saying, "There is something at work in my soul which I do not understand."

This quote is true of everyone regardless of age, gender, colour, creed, or era. It is a curse inherent in mankind; a darkness that dwells within us. As individuals, we all battle our demons; the struggle forces us to make choices we hope are good and that put our minds at ease. But what Shelley's really doing is asking the reader this: When it comes to choosing, which one do you favour? Good over bad; yourself over others? Do you think of yourself as a good person, or are you cursed as well?

Andrew sees this curse as the madness that drives us to do evil things and individual acts into collective actions. To him, it captures the very essence of what it is to survive, to kill, to do whatever it takes. He wants the people of the world to wake up and decide: Is life meaningless and cheap, or is it the most precious commodity we have? He wants them to go through the pain barrier to places once thought inconceivable, flipping minds, and playing with their addictions, and personal fallibility the result of not being able to kill. He wants everyone to ask themselves: Can addiction make us stronger and better able to survive? And on a spiritual level to ask God: What are your thoughts? After all, throughout the Bible's text, does *He* not promote ruthless ambition and blind devotion – qualities not a million miles away from addiction? But if you're asking God, it is only right to ask the Devil how he might reply. Because what is good for the goose, I guess, is good for everyone else. There is a lot to be said for a level playing field. Parity is the greatest weapon there is in fighting inequality. It's how the mighty fall!

For it is this curse that will outdo the gods and the powers that be, giving rise to the most hideous of beasts, the dormant monster that lies within each and every one of us, the darker primordial half that knows only kill or be killed and the barbaric art of survival.

A curse that was intended to be humankind's downfall, a kind of self-destruct mechanism God slipped into our DNA when He fell out with us, will now act as our new guardian angel, with its army of monsters led by a new redeemer. Who said the next messiah would be from heaven and that the second coming hasn't already happened? And what if the fate of humankind is not yet decided; if the gods have left it for us to fight it out among ourselves? What if the real battle for our species' survival is just about to begin?

Chapter 1
The Spark

Abandon All Hope Ye Who Enter Here; A Message Etched Deep into Every Fitful Sleep...

Spontaneity is the craziest thing. Not thinking, not rationalising, just doing what you've got to do, like it's the only thing that matters but you don't know why.

Not knowing if you're acting out your ultimate fantasy or something you've always wished to do but have put off for too long, but in your heart of hearts you're confident it will be the most decadent thing you will ever do – a moment of pure selfishness, where whatever you do will be for yourself and only yourself and nothing else; a moment that will see fear and consequences fall by the wayside, leaving you free to take the plunge and see where the *rabbit hole* takes you. Have you ever been compelled to challenge yourself in such a way, to do something extraordinary in a place no one would believe, that is incomprehensibly out of this world? I have. But not only did the experience affect my outlook, it made me completely re-examine who I was and where I wanted my life to take me. Talk about giving life to a monster!

It was like being hit by the proverbial diamond bullet. My mind expanded in a million trillion directions all at once, as if something godlike had whispered the true meaning of life into my ear.

But ask me to remember and I can't – just snippets in the wee dark hour's past midnight, the recurring night terrors my only recollection, like it never really happened, though my battered and scraped body told me otherwise. It's as though during the day my amnesic mind spares me the trauma only to go looking for it once I'm asleep. My sleep is a place of Death's shadowy vileness, populated by the fantastical beasts that carry out its bidding. It is a domain of chaos, where legends are born, and the foolhardy brave are slaughtered in their quest for notoriety. The gods lap it up in the darkest and most violent hell, *Jahannam*, has to offer: The ruckus.

How I found it I'll never understand; I'd never even heard of it. I was led by a casual encounter, a faceless, hooded street urchin, through a maze of tiny, cobbled alleys and covered courtyards that somehow bypassed the main thoroughfares, as if *Jahannam* was a puzzle to solve and a prize to be had, lost at the centre of some elaborate labyrinth. But once there, I knew my mystery friend had taken me to the right place. For *Jahannam* is a realm without comparison, without an equal; an ancient palace of sorts that descends deep into the earth, its layered tyranny dedicated to the gods of old and the power they still command.

There, decadence knew no bounds, and horror became my dearest friend. In the sickening imagery that haunts me to this day, the ruckus is an ultra-violent maelstrom of bloody torrents and flesh boiling and bubbling to acid-red froth, fizzing to melt a virgin's butter-soft complexion. It is a self-contained world of jaw-dropping amazement and gut-wrenching terror, where sight and sound combine to awe-inspiring effect. It is the roaring rage of sadistic exhaustion and the almighty medieval clash of steel on steel as maces and axes bludgeon through armour, as weapons of old compete to drown out the two-stroke motors of chainsaws, and their high-revved buzz as they slice sinew and bone. It is a pair of desperate hands that claw to grab a face and the snapping teeth that pluck out its eyes. It is the insanity of a speckled-red ghoul biting into a still-beating heart while parading the offal of its victim around its shoulders like macabre bunting. It is a world like no other, a world turned on its head, where elderly gimps rape child-like nymphs, and infant siblings are coerced into slitting older siblings' throats, drinking their blood hot from its source. Sons are forced at gunpoint to pleasure fathers, and daughters are forced to pleasure everyone else. It is a place debauched beyond darkest depravity, where only one mandate rules: *Lasciate ogni speranza o voi che entrate* – abandon all hope ye who enter here; a message etched deep into every fitful sleep. I know that when I close my eyes the rabbit hole will take me back. It always does, back to low-lit caverns and the dull clank of heavy manacles and thick chain, to gibbets swinging, to petrified faces of stammering tears, smeared with snot and puke, the pathetic creatures within screaming in incoherent delirium to the whir of power tools and the revving of industrial disc cutters.

My dreams never fail to regurgitate the bread and butter of my sleep's toil: The bashing in of someone's face, pulling at teeth and gums with pliers, the cutting out of a tongue from a toothless face and the pouring of acid to dissolve a person's features. I see flash segments of battle and hear the sharp noise of limbs being severed and brains dashed out. I catch a glimpse of a cannibal butcher sharpening his cleaver, his gluttonous chops salivating to the splash of arterial spray and the slop of spilt guts hitting a hard floor. From the gloom, fiendish mutations growl and snarl with glowing eyes that track your every move, fighting over body parts and discarded foetuses. A new mother slumped against a pile of cadavers struggles to stuff her stillborn baby back into her mutilated C-section, in an attempt to save it from the circling beasts.

It is horror personified, as though your very essence gets swept up in a crowd of other dreamers, all out of their depth and all trying to escape. Prostitutes, sex-loving freaks and sex-hating fiends, sodomites, cannibals, sadists, masochists, rapists, torturers, murderers, mass murderers, serial killers, mutilators, and devotees of bestiality, urophilia, coprophilia, paedophilia, and necrophilia – everyone has bitten off more than they can chew in a mad crush, buffeted around in each other's crazed dreamtime, hoping they'll wake up. But when you don't, the horror continues its freak show; a gore-fest to suit every perverted mind. Fingernails and toenails prised up with red-hot needles, then ripped from their root only for the bloody digits to be amputated and the stumps cauterised with naked flame. Dungeons bellow with the sound of elbow and knee joints being drilled as freshly made monsters, unable to blink, cry into dirt-speckled mirrors, their eyelids, lips, nose cartilage and ears cut away, the titbits left for the worm-like sludge that inhabits the floor, a writhing secretion alive with millipedes, centipedes, and all manner of bugs. But violence alone can't satisfy all.

There are those who seek more.

They want high heels, seven-inch Louboutin's stamped through cheek and mouth, pinning their quarry while the other shoe is used to excite the prostate to the point of prolapse.

I've seen virgins thrown to the wolves as they pick their way through a minefield of studded leather and shiny PVC locked in death-defying duels; livid females clawing and scratching, biting and gouging, doing whatever it takes, armed with greased up strap-ons and macabre dildos. The losers, hung by their hair, are fisted, brutalised, and left to bleed out as other floor-dwellers, enticed by the lure of fresh offal, scurry around everyone's feet in a race to mop up the hysterectomy scraps. I've listened to the mock wedding bells and screamed echoes of twisted erotica, seen a beautiful blonde slumped across a butcher's block, her partner reeling at the soggy crunch of a spit-roasting pole as it enters her rectum to travel the length of the spine and exit through the neck against the side of her delicate jaw. It is where the morbidly obese are waited on by salivating anorexics, and starved vegans, bound in carnivorous servitude, convulse, straining vacant stomachs while serving stillborn calf fillet tartare.

And still, this is just the tip of a very dark and enticing iceberg. For me, it was the spark that started my fire burning; a rage that has been intensifying ever since. I remember a newscaster quoting a terrorist: "I am the spark that will burn down the forest." And although I recognised that this man knew he wouldn't see his plans through to the end, what he did know was that regardless of him being alive or dead, the fire would keep on burning. And then it struck me – what an adversary! What an inspiration! How do you fight someone like that? How do you even counter an enemy who will willingly die for their cause? The thing is – you don't. The best-case scenario is that you get to die alongside them. For the terrorist, it's win-win, and this was what the *Jahannam* faithful represented – a hardcore throng that would do anything to satisfy their next fix, let alone live out their dreams.

It was the most despicable of wombs, a melting pot of what should not be, yet there it was, hell's abyss and the darkest recesses of the human psyche spliced in perfect harmony – the ultimate fusion of soulless contempt. Where on that fateful night, not one, but two evils were conceived, a spark igniting two fires that began to grow. Two evils that complimented one another, both destined to be inseparable. They were identical twins of the foulest marriage. A union that should have never been allowed, but the gods – they wanted to play.

They were two evils that reset the axis between right and wrong, light, and dark, the surface world and the underworld, tilted in favour of the latter. Two evils whose names, Đavo and *Apok*, were but a rumour whispered in the dingy bars of back streets amongst the lower classes and seen as daubed graffiti in alleys by delinquent kids. Yet the stories inspired all who heard them, despite their myth and fantastical boasts, the onset of war fuelling their impact.

They were the kind of tall tales told in bars that would go quiet on the main door opening, only to pipe up again, but staying quiet to strangers. Hunching around tables, hushed groups in fervid excitement would regale the latest saga in a series of ever more lurid Chinese whispers as they went around the houses –

Đavo, the ultimate psychopath and his superhuman exploits. He was seen as a peoples' champion, a warrior-king, invincible, who relished the heat of battle and revelled in its carnage. However, *Apok* was a different tale to tell, in that, it was not about a person. *It* was more of a concept, an ideal described as the ultimate addiction – the vice of killing. But however hard folks tried to grasp the nuts and bolts of it – what it is to kill and enjoy the act of killing – the more insane their chatter sounded and the more like killers they became. And so, having fought my first ruckus, I left *Jahannam* under a new name and for the very first time, had given myself meaning and purpose, albeit whispered. But again, ask me to remember – and I can't. Not until the next time I sleep.

Chapter 2

A Baptism of Fire

Wars Are Like That; They Attract All Sorts…

They're coming around. Everything needs to be ready. It has to be perfect, all my props in their rightful places ready to tell the story, for this is a rare treat indeed and hopefully a taste of things to come. Excited, I take two syringes from my trouser pocket, one labelled 'Mr' and the other 'Mrs'. Now is as good a time as any to inject, on the basis that it will cause less stress to the abductees, plus stop them from moving, which for this particular exercise is the whole point.

I inject the man and the woman with their respective syringes, choosing a fleshy area between the back of the neck and the shoulder, aiming the thin plastic tube like a dart and jabbing it in, slowly pressing the plunger to a scowled retort. If looks could kill…

Good. They're prepped. I usually give an intramuscular injection roughly a minute to take full effect, depending on the drug being used. Anyway, I'm in no rush; all the hard work's done, and it will give me time to get properly set up. I push four large, lidded plastic boxes into position. Two blue and two white stacked two boxes high, the lids sealed airtight with duct tape. I place a spindly metal-framed chair with a wooden seat and back carefully beside a zipped sports bag about an arm's length from the stacked containers, making sure it is roughly in the centre of the room. Sitting down on the chair, I pick up a piece of dog-eared A4 off the floor where I'd left it and scan the handwritten notes scrawled hurriedly in blue ballpoint. Terence and Paula Childs, home address, occupations, relevant work addresses and contact phone numbers, ages forty-eight and forty-six respectively, parents of three: Daniel, twenty-two; Tracey, nineteen; and Stuart, fifteen. Not the most detailed of dossiers, but it's all you need. In fact, it is far more than you really need, but that's me, insistent and demanding, a stickler for detail despite the work involved to obtain it. To be honest, I've seen less talented folks than myself find the proverbial needle in a haystack without so much as a glimmer of hope and only rumour and idle gossip to go on. But I make no apologies; in my work I like to be thorough, and the results speak for themselves. Why make it difficult when it doesn't have to be? I shuffle in my seat to the aged creak of metallic stress on worn wood, a reminder of school assemblies and how uncomfortable twenty minutes could be on such austere furniture. I click my fingers towards Mr and Mrs Childs and, happy that they are both conscious and alert enough to properly listen, I read out the penned information in full. A formal introduction to what promises to be a most interesting get-together.

I wonder if they know that their son had the same wide-eyed, dumbstruck look on his face, that *is-it-really-him*-cum-*is-this-really-happening* gawping stare, for it is a stare I have seen many times, a stare born out of long-term naivety when fate inevitably catches up with the very people who can least afford to gamble against such devastating odds. As if fate has anything else to do. Like death, it is something only fools tempt; a timely reminder of one's poor choices on the Blood Red Road to Boz.

Even though the Childs weren't with their son when he decided to cross that forbidden line and they hadn't seen his subsequent descent, in the eyes of the gods who dictate the road's toll, they might as well have been. My guess is that they don't even know its name, the Blood Red Road, or that of Boz, but in the minds of those looking down casting judgement, it no longer matters – they're here! And if you are here, that's all that matters.

With the formalities out of the way, I take a lighter from my jacket pocket, one of those cheap fluorescent jobs you can buy at any petrol station and put a gentle flame to a corner of my A4 dossier. I toss the flaming paper calmly to the floor and watch silently as it curls, eventually blackening and then extinguishing, burning itself out, followed by a waft of grey smoke not that dissimilar to blowing out a candle. I lean to twist my foot on top, reducing what remains to a black smear of nameless ash. All Mr and Mrs Childs need to know for now is that I know exactly who they are, to give the crushing impression I have the right people, despite the acutely absurd surroundings they find themselves in. Believe or not, at this point saying less is scarier than getting straight to it. I don't get it myself; I'd rather whip out a chainsaw and have these two piss themselves, scare them senseless, yet bizarrely this 'killing them softly' approach does seem to add a certain gravitas to the tension.

I give the couple a few extra minutes to acclimatise. Everything is going to be a blur to them, my voice a booming tannoy, the room and its contents irrational, their situation one of those nightmarish dreams that feels a little too real for comfort. But as soon as the adrenaline kicks in to counteract their high cortisol levels, their senses will become razor sharp in a matter of seconds, producing a moment of the utmost clarity as their pupils dilate to saucers, the sluice gates blown wide open to the sheer horror awaiting them.

"Don't worry about the grogginess. It's just the Devil's Breath, *Aliento del Diablo*," I say with a lazy swat of my hand, as if it's an everyday occurrence. "A substance called burundanga, very similar to scopolamine, derived from the borrachero tree in Columbia. Leaves you a little woozy and confused, but that will pass, if it hasn't already done so." I click my fingers once more to gauge their reaction. They're fine. "It's a drug that allows for folks to be manipulated more easily, as well as loosening their lips when it comes to divulging secrets. You might say it's a 'one hit does all'; something it seems us kidnappers these days just can't do without!" I laugh involuntarily at my own realisation: I've unknowingly become considerate in my abducting. Well, who'd have thought? It wasn't so long ago that I would have had to use a Taser and drag their sorry arses to the van. Now it's simply a matter of a few deep breaths and with the help of one of my associates, I walk them out holding their hands. Everyone's a winner!

Scared eyes bulge in lazy expressions at my every movement, waiting on each deliberately pronounced syllable for a clue as to why they are here. Despite the Childs not being able to turn their heads to see or acknowledge one another, each is intensely aware of the other. This I find sweet in married couples, almost endearing. But I know that inside they're desperately trying to patch together the hazy dreamscape of masked men, sudden panic and having to look down the barrel of a gun while being told to take a whiff of gas. I shrug my indifference. So what? Needs must! Abductees can't have it all! Like my old C.O. used to say: If money talks, violence shouts. It doesn't 'alf speed up the process. The prelude to war soon teaches you this most valuable of lessons: Violence is the tool that supersedes all other forms of negotiation. The proof being that I haven't met anyone yet who hasn't been fully compliant after five minutes being blow-torched and having their digits pulled and snapped with pliers.

I'm a simple man who follows a simple set of guidelines. War and the intricacies of war don't have to be a complicated business; extracting information or exacting punishment ain't exactly rocket science. It's just knowing how best to administer an abrupt form of cruelty. From picking up a hammer, a blowtorch or an electric power tool – you simply beat, burn, or drill the fucker. It couldn't be easier!

Apprehensive, wanting this to go well, a sudden wave of paranoia kicks in to set off my OCD, and before I'm even allowed to think, I find myself triple checking my prisoners' restraints, nylon zip-ties mercilessly pinching skin and body to similar metal chairs to the one I'm sitting in, only theirs have armrests. I applied the zip-ties at the ankles, knees, wrists, and elbows; their necks and heads held in place by steel wire wrapped around metre-high wooden planks, secured vertically to each chair like two lone posts on a firing range.

Everything is okay; the restraints are secure; the drug is in full effect. I don't know why I even had to check; I just know that for peace of mind I had to. Now that I'm reassured, I can move forward, hence my fastidiousness.

"Oh…and that stiffness you're feeling, as well as being zip-tied and held with wire, which explains why you haven't flopped to the floor, it isn't the burundanga; its pancuronium, a non-depolarising curare-mimetic muscle relaxant. Basically, it means you're paralysed from the tips of your toes to the hairs on your heads, every muscle fixed as it is. Yes, you can still breathe; your heart can still pump, but that's about it; you won't be able to move, period, which, for the point of this exercise, will give me your absolute and undivided attention. And to ensure this remains the case, I have given you both the recommended dosage of sixty micrograms per kilogram of body weight, guessing you're what, a little over twelve stone?" I say, looking at Mr Childs, whose fixed gaze glares back, the strain rendering his eyes bloodshot. "And you, my dear, a more feminine nine – nine and a half maybe?" I add, rocking the palm of my hand to my guesswork. "Either way, it means for the next hour at least you won't be able to move anything except your eyeballs. And even that reaction will be painfully slow. And just so you know, though you can't move, please understand you will still be able to feel pain. Is that clear? Good. And as you can probably detect, due to the coolness of this room, you are both naked. For both your sakes, I don't want this to be any more unpleasant than it has to be. So, listen carefully. My advice for you both is to clear your minds fast and tune the fuck in to the message I have come here to deliver. You got that?" I ask rhetorically, their replies a sense of extreme agitation behind fixed expressions. "I know you're worrying about your kids…of course you are…so let me assure you there's no need to worry…both Tracey and Stuart are close by, waiting for you to join them. Now, what could be better than that? And all you have to do to ensure that happens is just sit there, do nothing and listen. Your role here is not an active one. You're not here for your input; you're merely here to listen to me talking to you. So, relax if you can, and please try to take in what I have to say."

Realising that I have begun to pace the room, I sit back down and fold my arms with one hand resting over my mouth and chin, hoping I didn't waffle on and that those looking in didn't notice if I did. It's a big day today; there's a lot at stake. No wonder nerves are seeping in like the dark I see slipping and slithering along the room's nooks and crannies, adding shade to edges and recesses. Shadows are building, mould creeping, its ever-so-faint yet distinctly crisp rustle crackling in my ears; the creatures of the dark are close by, their ruling gods closer still, the room suddenly charged with a greater presence, an invisible monster laying siege to my visual mind, a surreal blitz of comforting terror, of rolling tanks, soldiers marching. The sound of thunderous explosions curdles with that of girls and boys at play, some alone, others prancing about in small groups, all happy and smiling and carefree and full of energy, gaily dodging tracer bullets and shrapnel till one gets hit and the fun stops – the game wasn't meant to be dangerous. All run for cover amid the torrent of mayhem that comes pouring in, all except one little boy, who sits cross-legged amongst the massacre still smiling, still looking up for his friends to continue their game. The Dan I knew, the son of the proud parents who now sit before me, was that little boy; a boy-cum-man, caught in a perpetual struggle with his demons, and he always wore that fixed smiley face like a cheap Halloween mask whether he was happy, sad, or plagued by murderous indifference, as if cursed by a predetermined emotion. His smile was a clown's façade for the malevolent turmoil festering inside. The rabbit hole can take you many places, but *Wonderland* was never going to happen for the Childs family. Daniel took care of that. Dan was always a little off-beat even at the best of times, but when drunk, he would literally unravel this tortured soul, the slivovitz peeling him layer by awful layer via a myriad of tortured voices, each an ever-decreasing level of despair at how his mother scorned him for her 'troubled' pregnancy that *spat* out, in her words, 'a troubled boy', and being the focus of his father's disappointment, because of his lack of interest in almost everything put before him. Even his school shunned his endeavours to conform, once using the term 'freak', for the entire experience bore no qualifications, no friends; in fact, nothing to say he'd even attended except ever-worsening reports and growing concerns about something being not quite right.

But among the international contingent at Vojarna Tuškanac military base, Zagreb, Dan at first barely stood out at all, let alone as 'troubled'. There were plenty of recruits who, for one reason or another, arrived not quite right: In fact, too many. The base was an asylum of sorts, catering for the disturbed and the dysfunctional. I guess rubbing shoulders with such diverse criminality had its effect; Dan could finally relax, be himself and become the person he had always wanted to be. It was one drunken night around a campfire when Dan decided to confess all, a declaration of how troubled he really was. It was the night he truly popped his cherry, came out of his shell, first regaling his childhood and adolescence and then professing an inkling of what was to become his nemesis – a self-destructive *ménage à trois*; an affair between his beloved slivovitz, violence, and the totally unadulterated, decadent spoils of war. But what struck me most about Dan's confession was how he described his last official day of school. On the night when everyone else was celebrating at their end-of-exams graduation party, he professed with all his heart that, being the only one not invited, if he could have curled up and died, he would have, but in his piteous state he just didn't know how. "I became something rather than someone," he said, describing that moment. "Something of no value, considered less than nothing…something invisible…something already forgotten." They were words of neglect and abuse, the corrupt ingredients of someone wanting to prove their ability to the detriment of all other things.

Dan was a silent bomb on a hair trigger. I remember not long after Dan had joined our squad, while on night patrol, he lit up a cigarette, the biggest of cardinal sins. He was pounced on in nanoseconds and beasted for days by the other squad members. But throughout the many punishments that the lads dreamed up, Dan nattered on regardless about how he used to get the blame for everything at home, despite its pettiness, even as an adult, taking it day in, day out, week in, week out, wherever he happened to be. Whatever he did, nothing was ever good enough. No wonder he ended up in Croatia, full of bullshit and steroids after a couple of years dossing around gyms pumping iron. So much so, the lads called him Walter, as in the fictional character created by James Thurber in the 1939 novel *The Secret Life of Walter Mitty*. Dan had such potential, but instead he fell into a trap of his own making, ending up a delusional mess whose inept talent for compulsive lying was only matched by his continual cowardice in bringing up the rear; a glory-hunter the lads called him, who wanted no more than to dip his toe into the grim pool of war yet reap the spoils and bragging rights. He saw it as a platform from which to re-launch and, I guess, re-brand; a way to put himself on the map once and for all. But for most, me included, despite our closeness, he was just another meat-head war tourist brainwashed by Rambo films and badly dubbed German porn, hell-bent on popping his battlefield cherry without so much as firing a shot. Such was his reputation, despite him seeing a little action. As the lads put it, 'someone who needed to be watched, who you could never trust'. That's what a mercenary war gives you; an army of Walters whose families and countries no longer want them. Wars are like that. They attract all sorts. But now I'm digressing. I've inadvertently slipped into a parallel narrative, and I happily drift along until I'm jolted back to reality by the scream of an infant tugging at its dead mother. I pull my wandering gaze back to drill once more into the Childs' psyches. Wonderland! In your wildest fucking dreams!

I'll give you fucking *Wonderland*, a version so far removed from normal convention you'll be begging for the Devil's wrath.

A penny for your thoughts, my inner voice quips in regard to the absolute panic that must be in overdrive, if not meltdown, somewhere behind those two pairs of glaring eyes, windows into petrified souls, their minds in a flap of unconditional freefall, the ripcord snapped and the ground rapidly approaching. The Childs know they are in trouble. But they have no idea of its seriousness. What I'm about to say will be the ground hitting them harder than they could ever imagine. You see, the Childs are no longer in their cushy world where problems get solved and rational mediation prevails; the damage is done. There's no going back; things aren't going to get corrected, because they can't be. The loss is irretrievable. As far as the Childs are concerned, no one will get to live happily ever after, considering the amount of water that has flowed under this bridge. They're in my world now, and this isn't a negotiation, it is a reckoning.

I bet Mr Childs is thinking that if they can only hold on till the pancuronium wears off, he will somehow be able to talk them out of this situation, racking his brains for answers I don't care for or ways of funding a ransom. "It must be about money," I hear him sigh, thinking he has the solution, that money solves everything. Not in here! There is only one currency within these four walls. Dan knew; it was what he lived for. If the Childs had taken the time and effort to get to know their son just that little bit better, they too would have known that this room is a place where no one wants to wake up: The ultimate Room 101, where nightmares are made real; an insurmountable worst of the worst from which there is no coming back.

This room is as bad as it gets; life doesn't get any more evil than this.

"Follow the Blood Road, follow the Blood Red Road, follow-follow-follow-follow, follow the Blood Red Road," I chirp to Dorothy's dulcet tones in 'Yellow Brick Road'.

"Ring any bells?" I ask to blank faces. "Fair enough. I guess Dan thought he was better off keeping that one to himself. How about this? I know you'll recognise this" – I continue – "Oh Danny Boy, the pipes, the pipes are calling. How about that? I don't know about you, Mr Childs, but I can hear him now, singing away, seeing all that hate fill his eyes to the very words that tormented him from birth, the same words he sang when committing so much atrocity. And when I say atrocity, I mean the rape, torture and murder of innocent women and children, girls, and boys, especially girls, and any other poor defenceless fuck that happened across his path." A tear rolls down the man's cheek, over stubble, to course the lines around his still mouth to the jawline. He knows why I'm here. She may not, but there's no shadow of a doubt that he does. "You see, Mr Childs, I have a theory that Dan could've been avoided – not cured, that would have been asking too much of any parent, but made to feel 'loved', certainly. Even if you didn't mean it, what's a little white lie in the greater scheme of things? Little lies are nothing, just inconsequential comments. The odd word of encouragement, praise for a job well done, mere snippets that take seconds to say but last forever in a child's mind; it's that everlasting note of fatherly recognition which makes all the difference. If only you had, Mr Childs. That's not to say you're blameless in this, Mrs Childs. You really want to know why I took this job? It wasn't simply to see you get what's coming. I took it because I wanted to see for myself the two people responsible for creating such an inexcusable monster; someone so broken, death came as a welcome relief." I smirk at the Childs' seething paralysis, the dual ironic glare hollering "Who the fuck are you to call our boy a monster?" I pause to let the death of their eldest son sink in, despite it feeling like news they've been expecting for years.

"Y' know, your son had that same dumb fucking stupid look on his face, just like you had earlier, as if he'd seen a ghost. Though he wasn't drugged and strapped to a chair, stripped naked like you. He was standing upright, but you could tell by his eyes that I was the last person he expected to see. He thought I was some kind of apparition, hoped I would pop into thin air and disappear. 'Behold my hands and my feet, that it is I myself: Handle me and see; for a spirit hath not flesh and bones, as ye see me have'," I quote, leaning forward to slap Terry's bare thigh. "Now, doesn't that feel real to you? Do you know your Bible, Mr Childs? That passage comes after Christ's crucifixion and subsequent resurrection, Luke 24:39, a test offered by Jesus to his disciples. It doesn't matter if you don't. It's just that the New Testament, at times like this, sums up experiences like this so damned well. John 20:27 says, 'Then saith he to Thomas, reach hither thy finger, and behold my hands; and reach hither thy hand and thrust it into my side: And be not faithless but believing'. You see, Mr and Mrs Childs" – I pause to eyeball the teary, statuesque mother nose-to-nose, her inward screams deafening, her fear crippling – "especially you, Mrs Childs; I need you to believe that when I last saw Dan, it was me who put my fingers into his side. I need you to believe it was me who crucified him naked on a little girl's bedroom floor. I need you to believe it was me who cut out his tongue and watched him choke and drown in a sea of his own foul blood. And above all, I need you to believe it was me who cut off his genitals to daub 'Nikada nemojte misliti da ćete se pobrkati s tim' across the wall. Roughly translated, it means 'Never think you are going to get away with it' in Croatian. Now you see, Mr Childs, the scary man in your boy's war stories, the one called Đavo, he's real, not a ghost or a figment of his disturbed mind, but alive and well and sitting before you. Yes, Dan was full of shit. Tell me something I don't know. But when it came to me, believe it or not, as fantastical as it may have sounded, he was telling the truth. Thing is…you already knew he'd been to Croatia, didn't you, Mr Childs? Dan confided in you; shared the burden, so to speak. Perhaps he didn't share specific details, but what serial murdering rapist of young children would? But you knew he'd been up to no good. That's why the two of you concocted the story of him working in Disneyland Paris. And why not? It spared your wife and Dan's siblings, and life carried on as normal. But were you so naive that you believed a day of reckoning would never arrive?" I pause to clear my throat, my mouth a little dry before the big reveal. "I know Dan spoke of me, probably more about my exploits than our relationship. We started off as FNGs, fresh-faced and not a fucking clue what we were getting ourselves into, but we loved it all the same. He was a good mate. Hell, I even considered him the brother I never had for a while. We did everything together, but that was until I came to realise why he was really there." I shake my head. "Like I said, I knew he had issues – we all knew. It was no big secret; once Dan had opened the floodgates, there was no stopping him. That's why the Croats kicked him out. I wasn't surprised to see him in the bus queue. I stood with him and kept him company, saw him off, happy that he was still in one piece and going home. At least, that's where I thought he was going. But like all bad pennies, he couldn't help himself; he had to turn up one last time, a hopeless addict hooked on the juice that kept him going. So, when the brass at Vojarna Tuškanac finally had the evidence to justify bringing him back for trial, they sent me looking for him, both here in the UK and back in Croatia, as did others, but no one could find him. We thought he was probably dead. I kind of hoped he had managed to turn a corner and was living a quiet yet decent life somewhere. Then one day word had it that a crazy Englishman was travelling around with a rogue unit of HOS extremists, paramilitary nutjobs who tear-arse around the hard-to-get-to rural fringes of Croatia looking for isolated villages to cleanse. And because these communities were so far off the beaten track, their silence was easily enforced by the threat of total, instead of partial extermination. I remember tracking them for some days, keeping to the rustic back roads, heading west following the Sava, the river that denotes Croatia's southern border, then up and around the Una-Sana bump of northwest Boz in the wake of murder and mutilation; a trail of horrid breadcrumbs, of butchered bodies, smashed heads and quiet communities left in utter shock. Eventually I caught up with him close to the Boz border, on the main route to Bihac. When I say, Boz, I mean that's what we call Bosnia. Anyway" – I pause to sigh – "It was a few weeks since I'd seen him riding off in that bus. But it might as well have been a lifetime because who I found looked like Dan, *it* wore his shell, but behind that dumb smile of his was something truly deranged, a monster I had not anticipated, that I hadn't thought was possible, yet there it was, glaring, basking in its vile glory. Our final meeting defied all probability; it was never meant to happen, but there we were. It was one of those weird quirks of fate, a reunion that, when I dwell on it, I find inevitable – who else was going to find him? You could call it karma, I guess; what goes around comes around. Before he'd even turned around, I knew it was Dan. There was no mistaking him, the outline of his physique, his noise, his breathless voice, that distinctive northern accent, and the fact that I had caught him red-handed raping a girl, her parents already dead. I had had to step over their bodies on my way to the girl's bedroom. From her diminutive figure she looked no more than eight; he'd beat her little face into her tiny skull while literally fucking the life out of her fragile body; blood haemorrhaged from between her legs. She was bleeding out, yet the poor little mite somehow still managed to cling onto life. Dan, on seeing me, just got up and stood there, brazen, tunic unbuttoned, combats draped around his ankles with a hard-on that looked as if it had been dipped in a can of bright scarlet paint, smiling his gormless, idiot smile that he always smiled, which on that day had an extra curl of detached lunacy. I couldn't save the girl. She was too far gone. I shot her in the head. Seemed like the kindest thing to do. I shot Dan as well in both legs and feet before knocking him unconscious with the butt of my rifle. In crucifying your son, you would have thought I'd use nails – wrong! I used these long screws I found in the girl's father's tool shed. He had one of those battery drills with a screwdriver attachment. It was brilliant – so easy! The screws went through flesh and bone like a hot knife through butter. I screwed through his hands, wrists and elbows, his feet, ankles and knees, even a few into his face, through the bones of his cheeks and jaw. I made it as painful as I could for the families he had destroyed. I am truly sorry, Mrs Childs, that you had to find out this way. Your husband should have told you long ago. If he had, perhaps it might have been the catalyst that would have put a stop to this madness, because as time has gone on, your boy's debt has accrued some interest. The pipes are calling Mrs Childs, and they're calling to be paid in full. Some of which, I'm glad to inform you, has already been paid." I tap the nearest of the plastic containers. "Like I said, your other two children are close by. Stuart is in the blue boxes and Tracey is in the white." I point out the two contrasting colours. "I did try to get pink for her, but apparently the range of colours available in polyvinylidene fluoride tubs is rather limited. And I'm afraid it is these specific tubs I need, as they don't melt when you pour in acid."

If the Childs' initial bout of clarity didn't have the desired effect, this is going to hit like a fucking freight train. *C'mon you can do it! Cry for me! Let it all out. Show me your pain.*

Glossy corneas involuntarily well up to spill their overriding psychosomatic reaction to the shocking truth of my visit's actual cost, the tears their only means of communication. I feel their hearts sinking beyond their bodies like the infinitely dense singularity of a black hole, eviscerating every last scrap of hope, their sadness and grief accelerating from barely manageable to outright incalculable; a quantum leap into the abyss freefalling straight to *hell*. I stand to retrieve the sports bag, its weight obvious from the metallic clanking inside. I unzip the bag, pull out a small two-stroke petrol chainsaw and place it on my seat, along with a pair of branch loppers, secateurs, pliers, and a claw hammer.

"You're looking at the tools." I knew this particular moment would up the ante from panic to unconditional terror. It is one thing telling someone their children are dead, but it's quite another when they are faced with the instruments of their own impending demise. If they weren't quivering jelly before, they're certainly racked by phantom nausea and cramps now. "These aren't for me. I'm off in a few minutes. You see, Mr and Mrs Childs, these" – I circle my index finger above the assorted tools – "are presents I've brought for someone else. After I leave, two men will enter to get what is still owed; two men to whom Dan owes a great deal. But before I do, I need to know what it was that made you hate Dan so much. What was the trigger? Something started this, and that something occurred in his early formative years. C'mon, what snapped? We know Dan was different – his inability to show love or gratitude, socially interact, to adequately problem-solve on a generic level, to interpret other people's actions – so what gave? Was the one-way relationship too much; nothing but thankless drudgery? Who cracked first?"

I point at the Childs in turn. "In my experience, it's usually the mother's frustrations that lead to Dad disengaging and becoming resentful. Is that it?" I raise my voice to Mrs Childs. "One buckled, then the other thought, why not? Let's kick the kid while he's down and keep him there. If the little fucker is going to make it hard on us, why not return the favour in duplicate?" I shout, shaking my head in disgust. "Let me tell you what Dan had to say on this matter…shall I? The point where all this mess began. He forgot the day, even how old he was when it happened, but the incident in question stuck with him for the remainder of his life to taunt the very legitimacy of his existence, even during his death. He remembers swearing at a neighbour's daughter, a mere slip of a girl – not on purpose, he said it just kind of popped out, the B-word, as you used to call it, Mrs Childs. A silly error of judgement from an ill-equipped child suffering from learning difficulties over some innocuous petty squabble, the type kids constantly bicker about without even being aware that an argument is taking place. Yet without hearing Dan's side of the story or giving him a chance to make amends, on hearing the news via another parent, Dan said that in front of the whole road with everyone watching, you bellowed, 'And don't forget it's you that's the real bastard!' Of all the things a mother could say! What a way to treat your child, letting others think he's adopted. You knew the stigma attached and the hurt it would inflict, yet you did it anyway."

I pause to exhale my aversion, looking down at the tools, then lifting my chin to glare at the Childs. "I get it. You found him hard to handle. He let you down, disappointed you – what child doesn't from time to time? It's a prerequisite; they learn through their mistakes. You should know that. All parents should know that! But to counter such a minor blunder by branding him publicly, humiliating him before what he considered to be his whole world…you didn't only break the poor boy's heart; you simultaneously crushed everything he ever held dear. The one person he thought he could always count on turned out to be the most evil. From that moment on, what good lay inside of Dan began to implode into something very negative and very dark. Just like you two, working through the gears from confusion, panic, anger, grief to where you are now – despair. You both have that impassive stare of dead fish. It's like looking into the eyes of Myra Hindley and Ian Brady. Because to me you are them – two monsters in your own right: Two people responsible for the birth of so much wickedness. Can't you feel it, the evil in the room, its blackness creeping along the room's edges, extending the shadows, seeking you out, getting closer, becoming stronger, longing to devour your soul?" I stand there, lost to past horrors and catcalls of spectral shrieks and screams, with Dan across the room from me, naked and blood-splattered, beaming back his usual dumb grin, eyes glazed over. I hear a soundtrack of children crying, begging for Mama or Papa to come and save them.

"I'm beginning to understand now" – I say, lowering my tone through a wry smirk – "Have you ever witnessed a true cry for help? Do you even know what it looks like?" I pause, wishing now that they could answer, as I brood, baiting the Childs. "I wonder…guessing that was something Dan never did, considering the two people he wanted so much to help him, to love him, were the ones doing all the harm." My sarcasm was scathing. "Was he the meek silent type that would just sit there and take it, so you kept on dishing it out?" I growl, picturing a boy shivering with fear, vehement mouths bellowing point-blank at his screwed-up, scared little face. "Makes for a trouble-free life, doesn't it? As soon as your patience is tested, it's an excuse to let tempers fray. You lash out; it feels good, taking the edge off your own stress, plus an added extra of rendering Dan a virtual mute. I mean, why change a winning formula? Your anger and hate worked a treat and, I guess, in some warped way it restored a semblance of peace, as false as it was. But if you had just stopped, even for one second, to look at it from his point of view...out-numbered, out-manoeuvred, and out-gunned, day on day, from when he woke to when he went back to sleep. To answer back was futile, not to mention he was afraid. Did it ever occur to you that from your little boy's perspective, being bullied by the very people he thought were there to protect him was the scariest thing ever? Why do you think throughout his growing up he said as little as possible, never really taking an interest in anything? He was damned if he did and damned if he didn't, a beating always one wrong move away. The poor kid lived his entire childhood on tenterhooks. The family home was a fucking minefield for him."

I pause again to shake my head in disgust. "I get it, you both got a taste for it – why not? He was the bane of your lives, and violence can yield such good results, plus it has therapeutic qualities. I should know; I'm a psychopath myself – what's not to like? Yet despite the pleasure it gave you – and it must have given you a lot, considering the status quo it upheld – you both knew you could only get away with physically abusing Dan for so long. That's what I find so unforgivable, more than the abuse itself – how calculating you were, that you had it sussed, had a strategy you worked to. You knew the traceable marks it left, the bruises, the grazes, the fact that parts of his body hurt to the lightest of touches and that he'd flinch at the most innocuous of gestures. Combine that with Dan's sombre outlook and his lack of confidence, esteem, interest, motivation, that he never appeared happy and was always alone, no wonder you were frightened people might take notice and talk. Who knows? Perhaps they did, teachers or other parents, but instead of intervening, they put his frailties down to the woes of an accident-prone kid on an unlucky streak. It's easily done when the narrative can be backed up by a mother's fake concerns. My guess is that you swapped tactics when Dan reached secondary school, making punishments more psychological than outright physical, designed to have a much deeper and longer-lasting impact. In other words, Mr and Mrs Childs, instead of simply lashing out, the two of you became cruel." The thought agitates me. I clench my teeth as the synapse impulses start to zap throughout my brain, the rage building. I despise cowardice in any form. I get up angrily and begin to pace left, then right, then left again, stamping my feet like a soldier on sentry duty. I don't know if this is a sudden wave of empathy, because I am not entirely sure I know what empathy is, but being made to feel wrong, having others always criticise your actions, going back to that 'damned if you do and damned if you don't' analogy, this feeling of inadequacy that was forced upon us is something that Dan and I share; such scorn can be the making of monsters. All my life I have had to put up with friends, family and perfect strangers, picking fault, pointing out the supposed errors of my ways and then, in patronising, supercilious fashion, laying siege, dictating how I should act, spitting their ill-founded, arrogant bullshit at me like I was some hopeless imbecile that didn't know any better; then, if that wasn't enough, after rattling the hornets' nest, they'd try to claim the moral high ground, afraid of the angst and ferocity they'd stirred up.

Yet I don't think such people can help themselves; it's just another example of the vicious, divisive circle that is the human condition, in the same way as Dan and I can't help ourselves. The two of us are caught in our respective traps, sinking further and further away from the types of people our supposed loved ones wanted so much for us to be. The crux of this whole sorry mess is that when Dan and I needed help, for our cries to be understood, all we got was hindrance; nobody wanted to listen as we bore the brunt of a perpetual blame game.

Mr and Mrs Childs are no different. If they were given the chance to explain, they would do the same – stake out their moral superiority in selling their eldest son down the river, claiming it had nothing to do with them, that it was all down to Dan, down to him being so awkward and obtusely different and having fallen in with a bad crowd. His crimes and the atrocities I described, they would argue, were the result of having been coerced; wild acts of desperation in a crazy world where he didn't belong. Perhaps secretly they even blame me; anyone except themselves, their blinkered narrow-mindedness instantly settling for whatever option is easiest or creates the greatest distance. They are stereotypical of how parents these days shun responsibility; anything as long as the spotlight isn't on them.

"You really didn't have a clue what you were doing, what you were creating and the possible consequences further down the line, did you? *Did you?* And you sure as shit didn't anticipate the possibility of someone like me standing here, explaining to you how your children had to die in such appalling circumstances in order to set the balance right – now did you?"

I stop pacing to take a long hard look at the Childs.

"You idiots! You could've stopped this at any time." I pause involuntarily, as I can't help but laugh at what I am going to say next. "It's irrelevant now, but some months ago, I found out Dan was seriously thinking about killing both of you. When I saw him in the bus queue, I quizzed him about it, and to my surprise, he told me of his plans. I asked him: If you do go ahead and kill your parents, who will you have left to blame for your lack of achievement, your weaknesses, and failures? You know what he said in reply? He said, "You're probably right, 'cos after the shit I've done, someone's gonna come looking wanting some recompense." He knew long ago that this was on the cards; if not by me, then by someone else." I glare, nodding, as if his exploits were some grisly means to an end, a grotesque cry for help: "Look Mom, look Dad; see what I can do – I can skin an infant as easy as pulling a pelt from a rabbit carcass."

"To tell you the truth, I'm convinced he wanted to kill you but lacked the guts. In his own twisted mind, he just worked out a way to kill you the only way he knew how. He played a shrewd long con, knowing that the odds, however slim, would always come up trumps. It took a while, but he got you! He knew the cards were stacked against him and had been since birth; it was just a case of learning how to rearrange the deck so that he became an integral part of the card trick instead of the trick being played on him. And he also knew it would cost him his life and the lives of his entire family – anything to break the cycle. What a price to pay! Perhaps it is this sentiment that sums up Dan's desperation most. So, there you have it! Sorry to be the bearer of bad news." For the Childs, this will be the end of a long, sordid road; as for me, it's just another unbridled excursion through my pre-war preparations. Though it does seem like the more Hydras' heads I lop, the more replace them, the death machine's infectious tendrils still managing to grab at my ankles and pull me under into the mire.

With hands on hips, I pause…breathe deeply…and relax.

That went well.

I think I included everything. Yes, I'm sure I did.

I take stock and look around the room; a moment to twirl and fling out my arms in exultation. I snake and weave in weightless relief to a devil's dance celebrating a job well done.

As a parting gesture I impersonate Dan's stupid smile, thinking of the times I'd sent the dumb fuck marching on ahead because of the threat of a mine, or a sniper's bullet. But it never happened – the luck of having Irish heritage, I guess, hence the smile and the blissful ignorance. "Oh, before I go, my *father* says he'll see you on the other side," I quip, laughing. "Now don't tell me Dan didn't let you in on our other little secret!"

Chapter 3
Slatter

Neil wanted him dead, and I wanted him to suffer, though in the end, the most sadistic punishment came in the form of letting Slatter stew in his own paranoid, paedophilic juices…

All great plans have humble beginnings. 'I have a dream', I hear a man cry, a good man with good intentions, his dreams shot down like a dog to the howls and moans of the flesh-eaters closing in. The grim spectre of war passes overhead, pulled across the sky by *ninety-nine red balloons* as the warmongers and power-brokers scoff at Kennedy's ineptitude at not being able to push the button. I want to tell this man that I too have a dream; a promised land that I may or may not get to. For my dreams are most people's nightmares, my sleep a newsreel of barren landscapes, wastelands scorched by fire and left to freeze over, waiting for nature's sweet return. Night after night I relive the storm that Noah fought, the pain he felt and the agonising torment of his responsibilities weighing down on an already burdened pair of shoulders.

I know the rains will come again. I just don't know what form they will take. Whatever the outcome, the deluge will start with one drop; one drop that, like toppling dominos, will set off a chain reaction, an unstoppable master plan that will eventually correct the failings of humanity over the past century. And all it takes is one drop followed by another and then another…I guess all such master plans start so unassuming; a million miles away from what they end up being. Mine started by being trapped in a room screaming and racked with fever. Blurred shadows held me down and gouged my eyes with exposed white-hot filaments of broken lamps while forcing my fingers through the cogs of grinding machinery. I would be crushed, my extremities pulverised and minced into paste, only for everything to be somehow miraculously put back together and crushed once more. As a child I dreamt of different monsters, ones from an innocent conscience. They were conventional yet thoroughly frightening, shadowy ghouls that would crawl out of the walls and ceiling, black effigies, slender and branch-like, blocking any means of escape, their threat alone enough to make me quake where I lay. Now I find myself dropped into another world and left to drown in the disease and mayhem; the nightmare is complex, as if bespoke, testing me to see if I have bitten off more than I can chew. It is a sinking feeling that pulls me down through the floor into a hellish realm where horror's greeting kiss smacks of blood and guts, the whir of buzzing chain and the revving of a two-stroke engine. Every night, the demon doctors in their beaked plague-masks wait to treat me, my medicine a diet of cancerous gruel that infects my mind. My dreams are tiered hell overwhelmed by numbers, an evil calculus that represents the path I have chosen, where I watch a digital clock displaying millions accelerating into billions. Cells replicate exponentially like tumours that have emerged from thin air to grow and swell, taking up all the available space in the room, consuming carpet, furniture, food, water and, last but not least, breathable air. The abhorrent mass presses me into the wall, its caustic surface eating away at my clothes, seeking the flesh underneath and my organs beneath my flesh as I slowly asphyxiate, claustrophobic and panic-stricken, my final screams pathetic, hope desperately fading. The solution is there somewhere. Each time I wake I think I have it. I know I'm close; just a few more nights and a few more trips to hell from realising my dream. But once my dream and I are properly acquainted and I have unravelled its code and embraced the guidance therein, I am under no illusion that I will need help from like-minded people who share a similar vision. It is these people who I need first. Then and only then can I proceed.

***

 It's funny how you can suddenly see things shape up, like fog lifting to unveil a lifetime's worth of dreams; years of sculpting, tapping gently at the chisel, chip by careful chip, working blind till finally I can see my muse take form as the dross falls away – and by muse, I don't mean a person or something of material value; more of a concept, an ideal representing a perfect state of being.
 The only way I can describe it is that it is a *darkness* in the light of day, like a black sun pulling me towards it. The closer I get, the darker it is, and the darker it is, the clearer I see.

With my epiphany still lucid in my mind, I wrote the following two letters post-Easter in anticipation of full-blown war breaking out. It is the only remaining component I require for my plan to spring into life, and one that seems more imminent day by day; a catalyst from which all else will be born thereafter. Even if the war doesn't last, as long as it gives me a few weeks to fully immerse my new bastard breed in their future roles, that'll be enough.

Letter One:

To: Pork Chop

From: The man with the plan.

Re: *Apok* }:-)→

Surveillance operation urgently required. This is to be an overt op; the more open it is, the less anyone will suspect an ulterior motive. Form an official investigation involving your superiors and colleagues and string out the case till I arrive back on 17 May. Intel gathering only – no arrests are to be made! The subject in question needs to operate freely. This is imperative.

Subject is Michael Slattery, a.k.a. Slatter. He is of white British origin, has light brown hair, brown eyes, is approximately 5 feet 10 inches tall and of medium build; age 25 years approximately. Last known address: Flat 2a, Lodge Court, Shakespeare's Cross, Solihull. Occupation: Computer analyst/programmer. Employer: UK Telecommunications.

For your investigation, note that the subject is believed to be in possession of and distributes extreme pornographic material, i.e., this investigation is the result of following up on an anonymous tip-off suggesting child pornography is most likely involved.

Please have the subject's dossier fully compiled by 10 May latest. I will contact you when I'm back.

Burn this letter after reading.

Keep up the good fight, and thanks again, your loyal comrade in arms }:-)→

I've known Pork Chop since I first arrived in Zagreb last year, our paths forever crossing, first at Vojarna Tuškanac military base, then on many subsequent operations along the eastern corridor through Bjelovar to Virovitica and on towards Osijek. Working the snatch squads and on patrol together, we soon formed a tight bond, our trust in one another firmly assured, and for a copper, he totally broke the mould of any prior preconception I had about the police.

Our friendship during the initial months was a learning curve for us both; mine was an insight into the political chaos of modern policing and the breakdown of a beleaguered workforce whose frustrations are born out of the hate and distrust of the people they are trying so hard to protect, countered by the view of someone always on the receiving end.

He even proposed his own nickname. "Pork Chop! Why the fuck not?" He said on first declaring his profession. "Pigs are pigs! They'd sell me out as much as any one of you. It's part of the reason I'm here. At least there's honour amongst thieves. My lot would shop their own grandmothers if they thought it would get them a promotion."

Abso-fucking-lutely! Of course, they would. The golden rule, in law as in crime: Trust no one. But here, trust keeps you alive. It's all we've got. When shit goes down, there is no time to check the man next to you or those around you. You trust they know what to do and when to do it and that they have your back. If all you've known is looking over your shoulder waiting for someone, anyone, to trip you up, at the mercy of both colleagues and the general public, seeking solace amid a band of eclectic killers is as far removed and yet refreshingly radical as any remedy.

Pork Chop, though I knew his real name, never once referred to his UK identity, his family or friends. He arrived a broken man, overworked and undervalued, looking for something different on a fortnight's annual leave; a disillusioned police officer who'd been seconded to vice, which in turn came under the Serious Crime Squad. You couldn't get more of a contradiction, but if you want a rebel with a cause, Porky, as he's affectionately known, is it. He just wanted to break the mould and draw a line from where he could reinvent himself.

Letter Two:

To: Key-man

From: the man with the plan

Re: *Apok* }:-)→

I have R&R scheduled for May, from Friday, 17 to 31. This might be the last chance for us to talk for a while. Something's brewing – don't know what, but it looks big!

Make the necessary arrangements for me to meet your computer friend on Saturday 18, day or night – doesn't matter. I'll attend the meeting alone and take it from there. Remember – be careful! You cannot be seen with him. Contact via payphones only. The situation is too risky. You need to remain anonymous at all costs. Thanks again, your ever-faithful friend }:-)→

It is always wise to have a friend outside the loop. By this I mean somebody who, despite how hard someone might try, cannot be linked to you in any way. It has to be someone you can unconditionally trust, a person with no family connection to you whatsoever; someone outside of all known friendship groups, including schools, colleges or any work-related activity; someone who has no affiliation with the area in which you grew up, where you currently live or anywhere you've ever lived. If you know such a person, then anything is possible; they are your skeleton key to the world – hence Key-man, his loyalty as fierce as his boundless generosity. A true friend: Someone I do not deserve, yet have. Affectionately known as Welsh Neil, originally from Newport in Monmouthshire, he has been an absolute stalwart of a friend since the mid-eighties. Though we met via a mutual acquaintance, Mac, an old school friend and semi-pro bodybuilder, the vital link Mac represented no longer exists, as he recently died; an infection, by all accounts, complications of liver and kidney failure attributed to a sustained abuse of anabolic steroids. Though we thought of Mac as being super-healthy and invincible, his death does mean that Neil is now the perfect candidate for what I have in mind.

***

I had a lot of time to think on the drive back from Zagreb, twenty hours and over 1,100 miles to suss out how to lure Slatter. I am going back to where it all began, and though I have been back a few times, this time is different. I am on the verge of my dream becoming reality. However, the next forty-eight hours will be critical. Stuck behind the wheel watching day become night and then day again, I thought of nothing else except how to tell Slatter, how do I pitch my idea to him when I can't even tell my parents, Neil or my closest friends what goes on over there? I tell them snippets, watered-down anecdotal half-truths to liven up an otherwise boring conversation, but not what really happens. So how do I broach something as sensitive and controversial as my dream when I have trouble owning up to it myself? Since I wrote the letters, the big question has always been: How do I entice a socially inept off-the-chart intellectual who happens to be hopelessly addicted to extreme porn? Then it struck me while having a drink on the ferry's upper deck bar. I watched the drunken antics of a returning hen party, the girls brazen and delicious, still dolled up from the night before, tottering precariously, reapplying foundation and lipstick while keeping a keen eye out for any buff passengers that fitted their brief. The offer of what I can do for him needs to come before the sales pitch and way before I try to close any kind of agreement or deal. The answer lies not in what Slatter can get, but in what he can't. He is, after all, a resourceful fellow, and he will always be able to put his hands on more porn, however extreme, but not on a woman, therefore switching the currency of my proposal from the virtual to the actual experience. He needs to get laid; masturbation is a poor substitute for the real thing, and with who better, than the hottest piece of pussy in town – Mandy. I remember Neil telling me that in the four years they shared a flat, as well as sharing the same employer as IT analysts, he never once saw Slatter with a woman or heard him mention any female friends, not even in passing conversation, let alone caught him engaging with one in or out of work. He described Slatter's aversion to females as a phobia, similar to an acute fear of heights.

Neil and I, with our 1980s' naivety, thought his closeted attitude might be down to him being gay, repressed because of his sexuality, afraid to come out due to the stigma of AIDS, adding insult to an already bygone list of injuries. But on finding his secret stash, we released that was probably not the case – a wardrobe full of magazines and videos depicting lesbian gangbangs, interracial threesomes, fist-fucking, bi-sexuality, mocked-up rape, rimming, fetishes, trans people, dildos, anal, cum-shots, squirting, orgies, bestiality…from the world over, you name it, he had it. The collection showed a gradual timeline of increasing desire till we came across a large red, tin container with a handle, similar in size to those used to store LPs, the chrome latch of which was locked.

The lock was cheap, like the ones you get on suitcases that can be picked with a hairgrip. And that's what Neil did with some adapted copper wire, spilling the contents in the process: A dozen or more VHS video cassettes, not one labelled and all with their tags broken off so they couldn't be recorded over. On playing the first tape, it took us about thirty seconds to work out the nature of what it had to offer before pressing eject; a young girl, a mere child no more than ten, sitting on the edge of a bed. After verifying all the tapes were of a similar type, we put them back, locked the tin and placed it exactly where we had found it – on its own special shelf. As the weeks went by, Slatter knew he'd been rumbled, his stash gone through, and his most closeted secret found. At the time, we toyed with several ideas. Neil wanted him dead, and I wanted him to suffer, though in the end the most sadistic punishment came in the form of letting Slatter stew in his own paranoid paedophilic juices, forever on tenterhooks at the thought of being turned in, worrying to the point of vomiting whenever he saw a flashing blue light or heard the sound of an approaching siren. And it worked! Hence Neil and I agreed not to get the police involved as long as he behaved and kept clear of kids. As a result, we never did confront him about the tapes, and Slatter biding his time, never owned up to having them, so an awkward stalemate has existed ever since.

***

By the time the ferry docked at Dover, I must have gone over my plan a thousand times, chopping, and changing, till I'd finalised what I thought would work, impatient to get a move on. Everything hinged on me being able to speak to Pork Chop.

As soon as the huge cargo doors open and the slow queue of vehicles begins to disembark, I speed off into the town, pulling over at the first available payphone. To my relief, he answers, and I give the call sign. "Mission statement: Alpha-Papa-Oscar-Kilo," I say over the hustle and bustle of Dover's morning rush-hour. His instant reply bursts out of the earpiece with excitement. "Goddamn, it's good to hear your voice."

"And you, my friend," I answer, my heart leaping at the enthusiastic greeting, my trust which has been put in a good man whom I haven't seen for weeks, vindicated beyond a doubt. As the hungry payphone eats through my change at a rate of knots, I ask if the Slatter dossier is ready; he says yes as I apologise in advance for adding to an already weighty request. "I need some other stuff," I say. "No problemo! Name it and I'll get it," Pork Chop replies, taking my order in his stride as if I've just asked for a cup of sugar. "Thanks," I reply in turn, the sentiment as genuine and as emotional as I have ever felt towards another human being. After all, he is risking everything – family, friends, and career – effectively passing the point of no return on home soil, and in my world that means an awful lot. It's as much as a person can give without putting their life on the line. "Got a pen and piece of paper ready?" I ask, waiting to the crackle of the poor connection. "Okay, go!" Comes an urgent shout. "I need three hundred pounds in cash for expenses, preferably in fivers and tenners; fifty to a hundred grams of cocaine, whatever you can get your hands on; and at least ten one-gram individual measures wrapped in paper and sealed. I also need a junkie's heroin kit – syringe, spoon, cotton wool, lighter, length of surgical tube elastic and enough gear to cook up a hit. Plus, all the drug paraphernalia has to look like it's been well used. You good with that?" I ask.

"Like I said, this will be no problem to get hold of," Pork Chop says. "When do you need it for?"

"Tonight." I anticipate an "ouch!" In reply, but it doesn't come, the man not flinching one iota. "I'll call you at nine. Be in and be ready."

"Don't worry, boss, I'll sort it. Look forward to hearing from you later," he says, signing off.

"Roger that!" I reply. "Over and out!"

***

Other than the expected slow going up to Canterbury on the A2 due to the volume of freight traffic and the usual tailbacks at the Dartford Tunnel, the journey back to the Midlands goes without incident. But before heading to my parents' house, I make a small detour to see Welsh Neil. We greet each other, hug, and exchange pleasantries. Neil immediately puts his finger to his lips and points towards the kitchen. "Olivia's in," he whispers. "Just be careful."

Olivia is Neil's fiancée; a tall slim brunette, as elegant as she is gorgeous, but comes with one hell of a temper. Her mood swings are almost bipolar. It's the main reason why Neil is punching way above his weight in the beauty stakes. He has often confessed she is out of his league, but who else would put up with her daily tantrums?

I knew Olivia would stay out of the way, preferring to stick to the chores rather than say hello. She's shy in that respect, always in the background, looking absolutely ravishing yet meek, as if lacking self-confidence, a demeanour which I find ironic considering she is so pretty.

"Put the kettle on, Liv," Neil shouts to no reply. "To what do I owe the honour?"

"You got the letter?" I say.

"Yeah." Neil nods.

"So…is Slatter okay to meet?" I ask.

"Tomorrow morning at his flat," Neil confirms. "Any time after nine thirty."

"Good work, mate." I pat him on the leg as Olivia comes out of the kitchen with two mugs of steaming tea. "Keep your hands off my fella," she snaps with a playful smile.

"How are you?" I enquire.

"I'm good" – she says – "An' you?"

"Yeah…I'm good too." Her expression, as always, gouges out my eyes with disdain. It's not that we don't get on – we do, but more as two like poles of opposing magnets whose relationship repels as much as it wants to attract, nullifying virtually anything said to the point where we simply don't bother. "Don't mind her." Neil swats his hand, ushering her back towards the kitchen.

"You still got the keys to your old flat?" I ask, knowing Neil is a stickler for having an extra, undeclared set of keys cut, whether for a house, flat, car or his place of work, just in case a situation arises where unauthorised access is necessary.

"Yeah, sure!" He confirms. "You want 'em?"

I nod. "Then I'll go an' get 'em." He gets off the sofa to go upstairs. "You know there's stuff still in there," he says, on his return, handing me the keys.

"Such as?"

"I mean, if y'need it as a shagging pad, the kitchen is clean and it's tidy, and it should still have its curtains, but all of the down and upstairs carpet had to be removed" – he explains – "When I helped Slatter move out, we left the old armchair and sofa downstairs, and I think there's a mattress or two in one of the bedrooms. But that's y'lot. As far as I know, it was never re-let, 'cos our dual lease agreement only ran out a couple of months ago if that! I know Slatter used it right up to the death. He had stuff boxed up that he stored there, due to his new landlord not wanting the extra clutter or something like that." Neil shrugs to show that he couldn't care less. "Cheers, mate, and thanks for the tea. See you, Liv," I shout through to the kitchen to a muted reply of "Yeah, yeah."

Neil walks me out to my car, but I can see he is concerned. He hasn't seen me in an age and then all of a sudden, I'm on his doorstep asking for the keys to his old flat, no questions asked. Of course, it looks suspicious. He knows me too well. I'm going to have to tell him. "Look, mate, I've something in the wind; something I've been planning for a while now," I say, treading carefully, knowing that what I have to tell him will come as a burden, never mind the shock of being suckered into the mêlée. "And it involves Slatter."

"Something serious?" Neil asks.

"Yeah…it's serious" – I reply – "Though it will mean you'll get a grilling from the police at some point, due to you having lived with him and, of course, your working relationship."

"You're not kidding, are you?" Neil looks me square in the eye. "I thought your letter sounded a tad dramatic: 'Be careful' – 'don't be seen with him' – 'use payphones only' – 'the situation is too risky' – 'remain anonymous at all costs'. I've gotta tell you, it has had me thinking."

"When they come, just act naturally. Tell them the truth – that you vacated the flat eighteen months ago and Slatter kept it on for another twelve to fourteen months. Tell them you helped him move out to his new flat but leave it there. And if they mention any links to paedophilia, you remember his red tin?" I nod knowingly. "How can I forget it," Neil snarls.

"Act surprised, as though you are truly shocked, but don't overdo it." Neil nods briefly. "You'll do all right. It will just be a case of hanging in there till the Old Bill are satisfied."

"And Liv?" Asks Neil.

"What about her?" Surely, she can't be a complication.

"Will the police want to speak to her?" Neil asks.

"Why would they? Did she ever know him? Did she ever meet him? Did she ever go to the flat? Does she know about the spare set of keys?" I list the potential snags.

"No! None of those!" Neil exclaims.

"Then you have nothing to worry about; any police involvement concerning Liv will be minimal, merely routine. She'll be quickly ruled out. But you, my friend, will need to be strong. When Slatter's gone and I've got him where I want him, I'll clue you in to the bigger picture. And these keys, once I'm done, I'll get rid of them. You never had them. Is that clear?"

"I get it. I do," Neil says, reassuring me. "You said in your letter about something brewing. I take it that means something bad; something other than what you have planned."

"Don't say anything to anyone, not even Liv, but there's gonna be war, and I wanna be there when it happens," I say.

"But you might be…"

"Might be what? Killed? So fucking what?" I counter. But in fairness, how can I expect Neil to understand? You can't understand unless you have been over there, confronted with death and injury, seeing those around you hit, then falling, as you wait to be hit yourself. For death has scant regard for combatants; the narrow escapes are many, with casualties random and bloody, gored by bullets or shrapnel, death taking its toll of your comrades and innocent bystanders alike. How can they know what it's like, to attack or be attacked, the rush, the adrenaline, the fear, and desire? For me, this is the event of a lifetime; the ultimate game of survival, a no-holds-barred free-for-all, and he thinks I'm gonna miss that! I booked my place long ago.

"One day I'll show you what you're missing," I say. We hug and pat each other's backs.

"That's what I'm afraid of." He laughs.

"See you later. And remember the police visit. Though you might think it arduous at the time, the line of questioning will be purely routine." I get into my car, my mind checking and triple checking the plan: Pork Chop, Neil, Slatter and Mandy; their roles, what they have to do and what can go wrong, like a looped computer program going around in circles. Heading off, despite obsessing over every detail, I know that Neil will acquit himself perfectly, as will the others when their time comes. He continues to wave till I'm around the corner, and I smile back via the rear-view mirror, feeling guilty for using Neil in such a cold, calculating way, wondering when I'll see him next, if I ever do.

Chapter 4
Home in the '90s

If the '80s were about excess, the '90s are going to be about sheer gratuitousness; a pure shit-show for the established order…

Standing in the Saracen's Head car park, I watch the red brake lights of Dad's car merge with the rest of the evening's traffic. He left troubled, as he always did whenever I told him of my adventures. But despite the burden this dark news put upon him, I was happy Dad knew, and out of respect I had told it like it was, enough to paint a rudimentary picture without being patronising, leaving out the gory details. But even then, he changed the subject, afraid for my future and what I was getting myself into, similar to how he used to worry about me falling in with the wrong crowd at school or when I was out playing with my friends. I have always been open with Dad, yet recently when we talk, I feel the dark inch a little closer to my heart like the poison from an infected wound. I feel it now seeing him drive away, the infection reacting to his anxieties, feeding off them, their cumulative pressure fuelling and heating this black virus within me. But if I told him, I see monsters, what would he say then?

Best to take it one step at a time…

To think I am losing my mind is one thing, but for my dad to say I am crazy is quite another! I can settle for him being worried, but to push him over the edge, that's not fair. Because if he goes, so will Mom; the truth would simply crush her. Happy that Dad is out of sight, I go into the pub, call the taxi firm, and wait outside. To my annoyance, the taxi overshoots where I am standing, leaving me to run ahead to where it has stopped. I jump into the passenger seat, preferring it to the back, abruptly telling an over-apologetic driver, "I want to go to the city centre," explaining that I will decide on a specific destination – that is, a street name – once we are nearer. I get the driver to drop me off at the Bullring. I pay him, a small Asian chap, happy and overly chatty, who didn't let me get a word in edgeways for the entire fare. He told me of his two sons, Barsha and Sabbir, praising Allah every few seconds for his good fortune, and he told me that he was planning a trip back to his beloved Bangladesh. He had this tremendous aura of family togetherness about him, one I wish I had. This man is a rare commodity, not just in his profession as a taxi driver but in general, content with his lot, a person free of worry, all of the negatives expunged, leaving a kind radiance that I found almost holy, as if I'd just experienced the purest karma; the living embodiment of the Golden Rule, Matthew 7:12 – "Therefore all things whatsoever ye would that men should do to you: Do ye even so to them: For this is the law and the prophets." He is a person who makes perfect sense in an ideal world. I mean, what idiot wouldn't give his right arm for such heavenly bliss? But where we find ourselves is far from any utopian dream that any belief system may have us envisage. Still, it is comforting to know such people exist. I never get tired of walking down Smallbrook Queensway; the memories, the parties, the decadent laughter, my rendezvous ahead as I mull over the chance encounter. Why, tonight of all nights, on the eve of the most defining moment of my life, should he, a shining beacon of hope, pop up to interrupt my dark flow? Is it to remind me that there is still good in the world; a weird curveball to illustrate that good just takes more effort to find? God, I wish there were more of you out there, like the hippy in my dreams preaching *I am him, as he is me, as we are one together,* then I wouldn't have to set this dark ball rolling. Or does it mean the darkness is within us all?

I don't know! I guess we shall see…

I'm sorry, whoever you are, and to your two sons. Don't think for a second I'm not, because I am. Please believe that, an inner voice pleads, my conscience's apology as profound as the note of sincerity. But from my viewpoint, society's ills far outweigh its virtues, and year on year it'll get worse, hence the irredeemable price of waging war. This bubble humankind is in has to pop if we are to survive as a species. The pious and the self-righteous will call it a reckoning; the poor, a comeuppance; the rich, an opportunity; and the rest, as always, will go with the flow to see where the mayhem takes them. But, like all great endeavours, it must start with the first step, or in my case with a phone call.

Aware that I need to call Pork Chop in the next few minutes, I duck into a busy bar where I know the payphone is located out back by the toilets.

The payphone is an old grey wall-mounted model. I dial the number and wait to push the coin into the slot on hearing Porky's voice.

"Alpha-Papa-Oscar-Kilo. Repeat. Alpha-Papa-Oscar-Kilo. We good to go?" I ask. 'Papa-Charlie receiving', comes Porky's call sign. "We are good my end. Repeat, good to go," he confirms. "Good to hear. Well done. Meet me in the city centre; the corner of Gough Street and Ellis Street off Holloway Head at ten thirty. Got that?" My lips are pressed right up to the mouthpiece as I try to make my voice as clear as possible above the ambient noise of the adjoining bar.

"Roger that. Corner of Gough and Ellis. Got it! See you ten thirty. Over," he replies, signing off.

***

As the bar sings out to James's 'Sit Down', I push open an adjoining door to people linked with arms around shoulders and beer glasses held aloft – *"Oh sit down, oh sit down, oh sit down, sit down next to me"*; the revelry of today's exploited youth celebrating the passing of yet another week at keeping their noses to the YTS grindstone. I watch the alcohol free inhibitions and the dark creep into the evening's expectation as eyes glow red and mouths thirst for more, desire taking over from the day's responsibilities, a whirlpool of individual vices mixing to rebel against the established order.

"Thank fuck I'm no longer one of them," I whisper under my breath, toasting the fact with a sip of my first pint of the night. The lager may be a tad tepid, but Christ, does it taste better when you're not in bondage to the ill-founded initiatives that are the government's youth training schemes. I make the drink last, scanning the tightly packed crowd as I wrestle my way through the crush, and there, all of a sudden, like a goddess in her place of worship, under the bright neon, surrounded by drooling onlookers, is Mandy. I haven't seen her in four years but, creature of habit that she is, I knew exactly where to find her.

I could say things have changed, and I'd be right, but she hasn't; still in her standard Friday night attire: Black lycra mini-dress, black patent six-inch stilettos and sheer black stockings, with her Debbie Harry bleach-blonde hair and make-up, the lads cheering her on as she sways hips and body to gyrate and bounce her femininely wiles to the music.

"You can take the girl out of the council estate, but you sure as hell can't take the council estate out of the girl," I remember Anna used to say. Polly-Anna to her mates, a pet name her mother would call her in front of friends, including boyfriends. No one knew why, but the name stuck. Yet despite her opinion, Anna adored Mandy. The two of them were inseparable, despite their chalk and cheese personalities. So much so that for a time they shared a flat together as well as working at the same veterinary practice, not to mention their reputation as a man-eating duo around the city centre's pubs and clubs. I check the time – nearly twenty past nine. I bet at half past she goes over Pagoda Park with whoever she's duped in here to pay for her entrance and drinks; that's if they still do happy-hour two-for-one cocktails before ten. It's been a while! With another slightly younger girl and the gang of cheering lads, Mandy leaves the bar right on cue, her old itinerary no doubt indelibly imprinted via years of repetition. I give it a minute, then follow, careful to linger at least fifty yards behind. With one eye on the prize and the other window shopping, I walk past the exclusivity that's now on the periphery of my pay-packet: A row of glass-fronted boutiques and outlets displays the latest in hi-fis, videos, TVs, leather jackets, designer brands and exotic holidays, my involuntary drooling enhanced only by the reflections of the BMWs, Mercedes and Jaguars that cruise past, their glistening bodies golden under the orange street lights, all of them icons of how success is measured, a living trophy cabinet of sorts; a trophy cabinet my parents wish I had. Yet only a couple of days ago I was measuring success in terms of surviving a reconnaissance mission near the Serbian border, my trophy a full clip of ammo, not having fired a single shot, my reward no more than a pat on the back and a warm bottle of Osječko, a local Croatian beer.

Though in fairness, there is something unnerving about how absence does make the heart grow fonder, as if comparing lifestyles and currencies of two contrasting worlds, excitement and bullets versus boredom and hard-earned cash.

In Croatia, during my spare time between training and missions, I'd thought of little else but reacquainting myself with the girls I once knew back home, imagining them grown-up and sophisticated in office skirts and blouses, flirting with their newfound sexual confidence. The fantasies were enough to see me through, but now I'm home, I daren't ask Mom and Dad about my friends, because as soon as the subject of girls pops up, I know what my mom's first words will be: "Are you seeing Anna tonight?" She loved Polly-Anna, as most people do. But even though my mom misses her, the great homecoming fuck fantasy, unlike my comrades back in Croatia, is not my idea of R&R – rest and recuperation. Holidays, like girls, are meant to be fun. Anna's more like hard work, similar to most girls I know; each beautiful in their own right but complicated by existing friendship groups and shifting fads. Me being one of those fads. However, in Croatia, I find relationships are simpler. Croatian girls require little or no chatting up; the understanding is simple – you are either attracted to one another or you're not. That philosophy also applies to the buying of goods.

Croatia in its national incertitude has become an almost cash economy, with the black market growing daily, like any economy when certain commodities are in short supply. There are no credit checks or payment plans; it's just a case of have you got the money or not, each transaction based on a straightforward, no-nonsense bartering system of mutual understanding and respect. You either want it or you don't; either way, there's no hard feelings. But that same simplicity doesn't apply here. How can it when most of Britain, mortgaged up to their eyeballs, is living on plastic, disposable incomes decimated by direct debits and standing orders, cash as rare as being fully solvent? No wonder everyone is on the lash getting slaughtered, turning to cheap booze and drugs, trying to forget about the shitty week they've just had. Everyone is blinkered by the night-time's glitz and on the look-out for an easy lay. Not having been here for a while, it is interesting to see the drink scythe through the politics of romance; politics that I still don't understand today. I, too, in my early days of trying to attract the opposite sex, drank to stem my nerves in the hope of bypassing the initial inhibiting shyness that usually led to a stream of awkwardly articulated chat-up lines and a courtship ritual I dreaded, as my usual bullshit would always have consequences – consequences of intrigue where the truth was rarely told, meaning that lies had to be told in order to cover up more lies. It seems my two contrasting worlds are not so different after all. It's insane how we live, how I live, inhabiting these two worlds that on paper are considered polar opposites; one whose people fear repossession and bankruptcy, and the other where they fear total collapse under the looming spectre of war. Yet in either land, I realise, glancing from shop to shop and hearing the smooth growl of straight-six engines whoosh by, I wouldn't want to be without those things that make me the happiest – fast cars and even faster women! It's shallow, I know, on a par with killing without emotion. But it is a decadence that is in itself a beauty that deserves a place alongside the horrors of a country soon to disintegrate; expendable goods worth fighting for – worth dying for! The love of a country and its cause spurned for desire, the battle forsaken so that a nation's youth, hooked on the latest brands, can loot and rape, hopelessly obedient to the false idolatry of post-eighties consumerism.

"We want it all, and we want it now!" I hear the kids of today shout. And why not? After all, it's there for the taking. If the eighties taught us nothing else, it taught us it's a dog-eat-dog world where it pays to be the dog with the biggest teeth – tenacity and ferocity winning the day.

"If you can't beat them – join them!" I hear the revellers yell, their army growing drink by drink, their patience wearing thin.

You know what? I might just do that, a voice inside me says. *I'm sold!* As the wealth swirling about me calls back for me to join it. *You may not need them, but boy, you sure as hell want them!* My inner voice adds. Ain't that the sorry truth! And that's the crux of the problem. It's how *they* get us, like giddy bees in search of the sweetest nectar, lured by the bright city lights, drawing us in to the honeypot of all honeypots; a banquet boasting so much variety, no bee can refuse, me included, which makes me hate it all the more. For on the other side of the glass is an enemy I don't think I can kill. But what I find even more bizarre, almost eerie, is the live-for-today-fuck-tomorrow attitude; the bars are buzzing and the streets echoing to the familiar pent-up anger and dissent, the drink fuelling the ethos from whence I came, as if both nationalities are inexplicably joined, heading in the same direction towards their own versions of civil upheaval. The atmosphere is odd in how it regresses me to the mindset of World War II Britain and the weeks leading up to D-Day. Every night was party night for those who were set to storm the beaches, knowing that soon they'd be aboard landing-craft waiting for the tailgate to fall, partying to the absolute finish as they prepared for the onslaught.

It's faint, but you can feel that same sense of dread here, the onset evident in the guise of heavily discounted prices and 'best ever sale' signs, 'everything must go', the whole ugly façade adding to an underlying air of doom and gloom. The noise of tonight is the relief of one week finishing, but between the laughter there is equal contempt, the futility of knowing that another will soon start. It's as though the city is counting down as one, uncertain of its future and therefore putting on a brave face in the hope that next week will be better, postponing the inevitable spark that'll ignite the touch-paper. That would be weird, coming back to find your own country at war. Like they say: *Never say never!* One tax too many is all it will take. Turning my attention back to Mandy, I wait till both she and her exuberant friends are past the scrutiny of the club bouncers before approaching. I jog gently up to the pink neon of Pagoda Park's entrance, panting, trying not to overact.

"All right, gents," I gasp to the mute response of two pairs of piercing eyes. A towering duo in black ties and three-quarter length Crombie coats decide to shuffle shoulder to shoulder, blocking my path. "I'm with the group that have just gone in." I attempt to change my gasp to a less sarcastic wheeze.

"Oh yeah," one of them says.

"Yeah! I was held up at the cashpoint. Tried to catch 'em up, but they got in ahead of me," I say, pleading my case as the two goons in their mock penguin get-ups deliberate.

"Go on, then. Just this once, mind, an' no trouble, okay? We'll be watching," the other explains, bolshie in his address, as though practising for when it gets busier. The two of them grin like village simpletons as though mocking me is a job well done.

Reluctantly canning my displeasure, I slip between the two humungous bookends before doing something I might regret. As if I look like the type that would give them trouble – patronising pair of meatheads! I hate being stereotyped. At least in Croatia I'm treated with respect, trouble or not. What you have to remember, though, is that to the average nightclub doorman I'm just Joe Bloggs, another scrawny punter half their weight and therefore half their strength and ability. What it is to be stupidly ignorant. The training camps are full of them. I wonder what Đavo would do, given a different time and place. If an automatic pistol were to be shoved underneath one of their noses and press a knife to the other's throat, would they be so condescending then? I think not. At least they didn't put me through the undignified procedure of patting me down. I am thankful for that. That would have pushed me over the edge.

Inside the club, it's not difficult to locate Mandy and her younger female friend. Maintaining my distance, I keep an eye on them from the far end of the long upstairs bar as, with expert deftness, having got their drinks, they ditch the gang of lads, promising to meet them later. A couple of them get their prize of a slow, lingering kiss, copping a good feel of breast and arse as they do so. But the girls don't mind; it's what they're used to: A kiss here, a quick feel there, a hand-job, blowjob, perhaps a fuck in the toilets, if need be, anything so long as the cocktails and champagne keep flowing gratis thanks to a good-looking and gullible benefactor.

With about fifty minutes to kill before meeting Pork Chop, I get myself another pint and find a seat where I can keep an eye on proceedings. I lounge, stretching my feet out, and hug the armchair-style seat, taking full advantage of the respite in what has been a very busy and long day. Though, on the downside, I'm left once again to dwell on the demons that set me on this path and the day's only disappointment.

***

I knew better than to romanticise about my homecoming. I dared not, even before the ferry, scared that if I actually allowed myself to look forward to something, it might jinx my fortnight in paradise. But since Dover, despite the fated outcome, I have done just that, duped for no other reason than being on home soil, the passing blue motorway signs, hypnotic, snapping me from the murk back into the light, exorcising the final stresses of conflict, like friendly milestones counting down my journey to safety. I know I'll soon be home; the drive is a twenty-hour plus decompression from brooding menace to a place where I could literally float away. In my naivety I didn't expect much. I never do. I'm not one for banners or any extravagance; just a few folks to welcome me back; a kind of not-so-much-of-a-surprise party for when I walk through the door, that sort of thing. Even as the bonnet of my car tipped over the brow of the hill, I still hoped to see the driveway full of guests' cars. But, alas, when you are well out of sight, you are also well out of mind; that is, very low on the list of priorities.

Needless to say, I arrived home to an empty house. My mom, as she later explained, was out grocery shopping, and Dad was playing golf, having switched his usual morning round for a less busy afternoon slot, both knowing I was to be expected mid to late afternoon. But in hindsight it didn't matter; my time was usually filled telling lies of some description; playing down rumours of atrocity for my parents and my sister, keeping conversation to "Oh what stunning scenery there is" and "What a wonderfully cultured people they are," to hyping up the blood and gore content for my uncles, who'd always trade ale for tall tales of explosions, firefights, and outrageous body counts. You couldn't win. No one wanted the truth, just the version that suited them. My stories range from the monotonous, to be forgotten, to the outright ridiculous, to be regaled down the pub, but it keeps everyone happy and, bizarrely, begging for more.

But earlier this evening I settled for good old boring scenery and a cultural dish called Zagrebački Odrezak, veal steaks stuffed with ham and cheese, then breaded and fried. It seemed to do the trick, veal being Mom's favourite.

It felt good to break the ice and not make an issue over their absent protest. I took the gesture as a blessing; it meant I had less time in which to lie.

I wanted to spot something different about them, an improvement – a slightly altered hair style or new clothes, a tan, new jewellery – but both were pretty much how I'd left them, my dad in his Pringle jumper and golfing slacks, my mom with her hair tied back in a bun, dressed in her gardening clothes, jogging bottoms and a thick woollen cardigan.

They'll never change. Though I wish they would, for their sakes, like I have.

My mom was the first to notice I had altered. On my first visit home, as soon as we locked eyes and spoke, she knew something was wrong. She's good at that, spotting subtle differences, slight nuances of a person's character, to the point of being a running encyclopaedia of friends' and family's personal histories. But such is her double-edged nature; she is also not afraid of letting you know. Mom later described it as a glaze, something different in my eyes, something missing, something sad, as if the dreams she once had for me had suddenly gone up in flames, the person standing in front of her no longer the son she used to know.

My mom is a very grounded person and, like me, knows better than to romanticise, afraid that the fall back down to earth might be one disappointment too many; her dark side is pessimistic and generally distrusting of anyone who doesn't fit her antiquated remit of post-war decency.

Mom wanted nothing more than for me to become Mr Andrew Brown, family man. I can't see it myself; never could. I'm not really drawn to the safety of belonging, being part of something bigger, more established. Though I do have this peculiar job, which, I guess, is part of something bigger, but still, it is nothing to offer a wife and child. She knows I'm not perfect, but then again, who is? Certainly not my scrutinising mom, who in anger called me a bastard in my time of need, and not, I guess, Dad either; he neglected me for his love of golf and freemasonry, leaving my teens mostly devoid of his presence.

So much for the tortured thoughts of an empty house.

After a shower and a much needed sprucing up, I ordered Chinese takeout to save Mom cooking, and in turn she set the main dining table and we ate as a family for the first time since New Year. During tea, I kept my stories to long meandering walks along the Danube through the wetlands of eastern Osijek-Baranja County and the fascinating wildlife I never encountered, throwing in a black pudding dish for Dad – krvavice, a mixture of dried blood, mildly spiced minced pork and kaša, which is buckwheat. Once we had finished eating and our conversation had tailed off to one-word, one-syllable replies, I could see Dad growing impatient, and as predicted, he offered to drive me to the Saracen's Head on the Stratford Road. That's where he presumes, I am spending the evening with friends. The fact is, I never get taxis from my home address, not even when splitting up a journey. Cabs these days are too easy to trace; such is the efficiency of modern taxi firms in keeping track of their drivers.

As soon as we were in the car, he said, "So what really happened?"

These are the conversations I always dread, and this one was no different.

"Depends on what you want to know."

"Did you really walk along the Danube?" He asked, all dad-like, his tone taking me back to my mid-teens, when he would quiz me to see if I'd done my homework.

"Of course, many times, whilst on patrol." I smirked. "But I'm not gonna tell Mom that."

"Don't be cocky," came his usual rebuke. "What about your friends Mark, Darryl, and the other one, Doug, I think it is?" Dad asked, expecting a straightforward answer. "Have they come home too?"

"Well, that's the thing. I wasn't gonna say anything, but since January we've taken some heavy losses." Dad squinted at me. "They're dead."

"What?" Dad barked – out of sheer shock, I guess, at having heard something he thought he would never hear. "But…but…there aren't any hostilities…you said…"

"Not that you'd know. It's more brief skirmishes along the border areas."

"What do you mean, 'skirmishes'? Who with?" He exclaimed, pulling rank, his double-barrelled question a clear demand to know the truth.

"With the enemy – the Serbs – who do you think?" I answered. "Look, there's nothing to worry about," I added.

"There clearly is!" Came Dad's retort. "You just said your friends are dead." Dad paused to puff and blow, frustrated at not being able to understand my apparent calmness. "God knows what your mom would say if she ever found out."

"They're just short exchanges which last seconds, if that, no more. So, what if some of the guys have been unlucky? Stuff happens!"

"'Stuff happens'? Listen to yourself! These are people's lives we're talking about; they are your friends, friends that your mom and I have met, that you introduced to us. Don't they mean anything?" Dad asked rhetorically.

"Of course, they did. I've had time to get used to it, that's all," I replied solemnly.

"What about their families? Have they got children?" Dad asked, a note of this-could've-been-you in his voice.

"I dunno for sure; got their addresses, though. I suppose I'll have to make the effort to visit sometime in the next two weeks. To explain, I guess." My answer was very matter of fact, which didn't help Dad one bit in coming to terms with their deaths. But I thought it was best to pre-empt the inevitable question. "Doug was hit by a sniper back in Feb. Hit in the shoulder. But the bullet, a high-velocity round, deflected off a bone – the top arm joint, I think – causing it to travel back into his body. He didn't last five minutes. Mark trod on a mine late March, most likely a Soviet TM-46; didn't leave much. He wouldn't have known much about it. And Dazza, along with a few others, got taken out only a couple of weeks ago; claymores strung up on tree-trunks waist high attached to a tripwire. Half a dozen men cut to pieces in the blink of an eye. But if you think that's bad, we've had a lot go missing."

"Missing?" Dad's tone was almost sarcastic, hiding the real question: How do you lose a fully grown man, let alone men?

"Captured by the enemy," I replied. "I know it sounds strange, but even on deep patrols out in the sticks, when we know there's a chance of enemy contact, folks have a tendency to wander, and some don't come back, never to be seen or heard of again."

And war hadn't even broken out yet; my friends' deaths were the result of the friction when two hard bodies famed for their stubborn ruthlessness suddenly clash, neither backing down, the first to react usually being the ones who live to tell the tale.

It was better that Dad knew the score, and I told it like it was, just in case I never came back, leaving out what the enemy really does to those it captures, the torture and mutilation, figuring that was too morose. Those details were best left for another day when he'd be better prepared.

We chatted on, Dad quickly changing the subject to football and politics, his two favourite subjects, in particular the poll tax riots and Maggie. Our conversation was rudely cut short when Dad announced we had reached the Saracen's Head.

It felt good to talk, to be father and son, to listen to his voice, a voice of reason and compassion despite our differences. It was like we hadn't spoken properly in ages. It was a private moment to savour amid the madness, reminding me that when I'm next home I must make a concerted effort.

Dad never really had the stomach for war. He loved war films and watched news reports, but when it came to discussing the real thing, he wouldn't do it; the truth was too gruesome to visualise. Not necessarily spectacular, the way my uncles prefer to hear it, but there's an accuracy of detail in authenticity that leaves the squeamish almost paralysed with fear, having to double-take, pinching themselves at the knowledge that bullets are capable of amputating limbs, and bombs, from falling ordnance to buried mines, are capable of turning a person inside out in less than a second.

I don't blame Dad for not wanting to know. Who would? It's vile what one person can do to another. Whether pulling a trigger, twisting a knife, pressing a button, or using a rock, the results are the same, the wounds grotesque and obscene, and the pain is screamed a thousand times from a face unrecognisable from when it was alive.

I guess when you put it like that, I don't blame anyone for not wanting to know.

Chapter 5
Mandy

I bet she looked hot, perhaps too hot in her high heels and some of Mandy's clothes, which I know she used to borrow back when I knew her; a favourite outfit was a black mini-skirt with a laced-up split at the back, a strapless corset-style top and black suspenders, and stockings…

I have got fifteen minutes. Fifteen minutes before I must leave to meet Pork Chop. Fifteen minutes in which to convince Mandy and her friend to meet me at the Dome nightclub. My entire operation is in the balance. The next fifteen minutes are critical if I'm to wage war on those who deserve it most. The club has filled up considerably since I arrived; More girls than lads. But if you want to run a successful club these days, that's how you do it. Gone are the good old days when clubs relied mostly on the revenue generated by large groups of beer-swilling lager-louts. There are a couple of places that still cater for us rowdy types, but they're spit 'n' sawdust by comparison; the mood has shifted towards quality, not quantity; the owners are savvy to past gripes and what the punters of today really want: Sophistication with bells on! It's not just a drink, a dance, perhaps a little romance anymore. They want it all: Glitz, glamour, fucking, the lot! Things have changed; the good times are all about the experience and about being phoney rich for the night. If the '80s were about excess, the '90s are going to be about sheer gratuitousness; a pure shit-show for the established order. I can't wait!

Yet the downside of glitz and glamour is that they cost money to set up. And in order to recoup that expenditure, you need to create the right kind of atmosphere that attracts the right kind of affluent person. Hence my ordeal at the door with bouncers trained to be selective, thus reducing violence and maximising profits, where the thin veneer of designer labels and looking good has replaced the etiquette of good manners in order to gain entrance, and the flash of cash pushes you to the front of any queue.

It's all about what you have, not who you are; the virtues and values of decency, like a banana republic's super-inflated currency, are made worthless as consumerism continues to erode our once gracious empire. For it is a brave new world fuelling a new brazen revolutionary for a revolution I haven't even started yet. I'm a spark in a tinder box and no one but me can see it. I catch Mandy's eyes scanning the crowd and give a brief wave to grab her attention. Seizing the opportunity, I leap from my seat and make for Mandy's table, calling over a waitress as I do so.

"Hi, how are you? Mandy, isn't it?" I ask, trying to be modest.

"Yes. How'd you know?"

"Don't you remember me?" I bat back, not meaning to be cryptic. The other girl can't help but burst into laughter, anticipating one of those embarrassing moments when you are confronted by a disgruntled ex.

"Err…I think so." She grimaces to focus. "Hang on. Don't I know you?" She clicks her fingers to point. "Don't tell me, don't tell me, I'll get it. It's…it's…"

"I'm Andrew, Anna's ex-boyfriend. Y' know – Polly-Anna," I say, noticing both of the girls' glasses are nearly empty. "That's it. Of course! How are you?" She exclaims. "This is my sister, Sharon. You remember her."

"Oh, wow! You've grown up. What were you, sixteen or something the last time I saw you?" I'm mesmerised by how girls can suddenly fill out. This carbon copy of her older sibling has opted for a pallid salmon-pink dress and matching heels, her hosiery a natural sheen showing off an underlying false tan, a tasteful bronze, the tone accentuating the colour of her dress and her strawberry-blonde hair.

"Yeah," Sharon replies, her attitude all but blowing a bubble of pink gum and giving me the finger.

"Can I get you girls a drink? Champagne, perhaps?" I ask, the question rhetorical. Both girls raise their eyebrows.

"Get you, Mr Champagne Man!" Sharon blurts. "You can come again!"

"Champagne's fine," says Mandy.

"Two mini bottles of champers, the Moët, and I'll have a bottle of Pils lager. Thanks," I say to the waitress hovering at my shoulder.

"Anyway, what brings you here? I haven't seen you in ages," asks Mandy.

"To be honest, a couple of gorgeous girls, but it looks like I've been stood up," I reply. "They should've been here by now. In fact, they're long overdue."

"Still unlucky in love?" Mandy gives me a knowing look. "Yeah, aren't you the one who tried it on with me that once?" Sharon butts in. "I wouldn't say you walking into Polly-Anna's bedroom and finding me still in bed constitutes 'trying it on'."

"Yeah, you say that. But you were gagging for it. I could tell. Still are by the looks of it." Sharon can see straight through my bullshit. That's because I am gagging for it. It is why I walked over to you, struck up conversation and bought champagne. It ain't rocket science. She knows. Sharon may play dumb, but her intuitiveness is sharp like that of a well-honed grifter, the bimbo guise perfect for giving her the edge. Even if told, you would never give the mind behind her crass mouth the credit for being that of such an extraordinarily cunning con artist, able to fleece the most obstinate of marks right under their very noses, her skills handed down by the best, her sister.

"You're right on both counts," I reply, holding up my hands, thinking, *yeah, you're probably right; given the chance, I would have fucked you, and Mandy too, come to think of it. But hey, that was then, and this is now.*

"See! Told ya!" Sharon nudges her sister whilst giving me a cheeky wink.

"But if truth be told, right now I am gagging for two girls; two potential employees that I am meant to be interviewing."

"Employees, eh…going up in the world," Mandy says as Sharon gives a sly 'oooh' to accompany her sister's comment. "I'm impressed" – she adds – "So, you're a boss," interrupts Sharon, talking over her sister.

"Hoping to be, if they ever turn up, which is getting more and more unlikely." I look at my watch for effect.

"I like bosses, especially those who dish out free champagne. Got any more?" Sharon is shameless in her approach. "Yes, lots more. But not here, over at the Dome," I say. "I've got a private booth booked in one of the upper VIP bars. You know, the roped-off sections overlooking the club."

"Yeah, we know, don't we, sis?" Sharon elbows Mandy's arm as Mandy gives her approval, nodding ever so slightly.

"Why not?" Her smile broadens at Sharon's sudden enthusiasm.

"We could come and work for you instead," Sharon adds in jest.

"Yes, you could," I reply, laughing, my tone soon turning more formal. "You are both very welcome to join me. It would be a shame to let it go to waste. By the way, do you still see Polly-Anna?"

I couldn't help but ask. Since I'd sat down, the question had been niggling away at me, like the onset of a sneeze irritating my nostrils, threatening to let loose, till out it came, sending my line of conversation on an unexpected tangent.

"Err…no! Haven't you heard?" Mandy tone changes to one of concern.

"Heard what?" I ask, thinking she might have died.

"Obviously not, then," says Mandy, her voice deadpan. Sharon shakes her head, knowing full well what's coming next. "When did you last see her?"

"In terms of romance, about a week or so before Christmas 1987. After that, she came around my parents' house a few times, always unexpected, as though she needed to pop in for a quick chat, like we'd never been apart. Then she would disappear," I explain.

"Yep, that's Polly all right – always running away. And it all started after she left you," Mandy says. "Believe it or not, looking back on it, you were good for her."

"Yeah, thanks. But what do you mean? I thought she was happy with that vet guy."

"Well, that all fell through." Mandy spoke with an I-told-you-so tone of sarcasm. "She ain't cut out for two point four children and having tea ready day in, day out; never was, never will be! He already had a kid – wanted to play happy families, but she wasn't having any of it. Walked out 'n' before you knew it had shacked up with some footballer. Nice fella, good lookin' an' all, but he got her into coke. One of these *Playboy* flamboyant types. She couldn't handle it or him. It was a right mess, with Anna's mom and stepfather disowning her for a while."

I don't doubt what Mandy is telling me, but something doesn't add up. This is not the Anna I remember. Okay, we split up, but it ended up being quite amicable to the point where she found it hard to really let go of me, and when I last saw her, she was dead set on marrying this man she had dumped me for this man of her dreams. She envisaged domestic bliss, spoke of children and a long and happy life together; a pretty far cry from what Mandy has just described. To say I'm shocked is an understatement. I want to say something, but I daren't interrupt. Now the story has started, I want it to finish.

"Stop beating around the bush; tell him," Sharon urges her sister. "It's bad enough as it is without you stringing it out."

"You mean there's more," I say as the plot thickens.

"Yes." Mandy nods. "I don't know what to say. None of it's good."

"Just say it," I implore, trying not to sound too anxious.

"How can I put it? The Polly-Anna everyone sees isn't the Polly-Anna that's inside her head, that tells her what to do. You know the saying 'seven-year itch'; well, in Anna's world seven years are seven days or weeks. I mean, at veterinary college she boasted of fucking a different boyfriend every week, as though it was some kind of popularity contest. Even when you and Anna were an item, she cheated on you. It's what she does; she can't help herself; she implied it stems back to her father and has something to do with why her parents' divorce was such an acrimonious ordeal. Anna didn't say outright, but I think her father abused her and her mom found out. Hence why her mom burnt her wedding dress and destroyed all of the family photos." Mandy pauses to take a long slug of her champagne. "Some nights, after we'd been out, I would find Anna downstairs in our flat on the sofa, knees tucked up to her chest, sucking her thumb like a baby, with her eyes wide, staring into the darkness. Sharon used to describe it as a waking coma, didn't you?" Mandy looks at her sister.

"Damaged goods, that one!" Sharon says as though delivering the punch line of a tasteless joke. "Don't get me wrong, nice girl 'n' all, good fun, but something inside has gone. Do you get me?" Sharon taps her finger on her temple. 'Crazy', she mouths, as if saying it quietly is meant to soften the blow. "Tell him!" She insists, not letting up.

"And then…" Mandy's voice suddenly fades. "That's when it happened." Her face dips changing from smiley to solemn in an instant, her stare from under lowered eyelids a warning of *you are really not going to like this*.

"What? Come on, Mandy, what happened?" I exclaim, my manners for a split second forgotten in demanding an explanation.

"Just so you know, I've nothing to do with this, so don't shoot the messenger, okay? After all, it was nearly three years ago," Mandy explains. "I'd been out with Stuart. You remember him, the plumber." I nod in acknowledgement. Stuart was a good lad, decent. I liked him. "Anyway, it was the weekend. We'd been out drinking, got back late, and I guess the next thing I knew, I was being woken up by noise coming from downstairs. Stuart was still fast off, and knowing it had to be Anna, I went down to see if she was all right."

As though a switch has been flicked, Mandy stops speaking. She swallows nervously, reaching for her champagne. "Go on," I say.

"C'mon, it'll do you good" – Sharon whispers into her ear – "She lost her job, y'know, 'cos no one believed her. Fucking stepdad! Dirty old bastard! All 'cos he was shagging someone else on the side."

"Was it Liz?" I ask, already knowing the answer; a forty-something dusky brunette with a figure most women in their twenties would kill for.

"Yeah" – Mandy purrs – "She fucked it up for everyone; her and Anna's stepdad. He tried it on with all the nurses; even had to give him a hand-job once to get myself out of trouble – bastard caught me dipping into the petty cash. But such is life! I wouldn't be surprised if he didn't try it on with Anna. She was in a mess. She would have done anything."

"So, what did happen in the flat?" I say, bringing the conversation back to the matter at hand.

"Like I said, I went down to see how she was. Even though the flat came with the job, only she and I had keys, bar her stepdad who owned the place." Mandy is trying to stave off the inevitable explanation. I remembered the flat's layout. Mandy's bedroom was the boxroom directly at the top of the stairs, the single flight coming down to a long narrow hallway by the front door. The kitchen was then immediately to your left as you turned, as though entering via the flat's front door, with a built-in under-stair's cupboard to your right; the hallway had a single door at its far end, which accessed a large lounge spanning the entire width of the property. Even if Mandy had tiptoed tentatively – which in this case let's suppose she did, not wanting to unnecessarily disturb Anna in case she did have company – it would have taken no more than thirty seconds tops to reach the lounge door.

"As soon as I got to the bottom of the stairs I could hear men's voices, and I could hear Anna as well, but…" Mandy's voice tails off again, and she rolls her eyes.

"Don't stop now," I snap.

"It just didn't sound right. It didn't sound like the Anna I knew. Yes, knowing what I saw, and, of course, what I know now, I should've gone in. And yes, I should've stopped it from going any further, but I was scared, okay?" Mandy exclaims. "I'd never been more frightened for myself or for anyone else in my entire life."

"Even with Stuart being upstairs?" I ask.

"You don't understand. There were five of them, including her footballer boyfriend, all boozed up and coked up to the eyeballs, Anna more than any of 'em, like a woman possessed, calling on anyone who had the balls to fuck her. It wasn't like this was rape; she was asking for it – begging for it! I'd never seen her like that. I was speechless to the point where I could hardly breathe. You see, the door was slightly ajar – a few inches or so; it was all I needed. I wanted to walk in, I did! I was plucking up the courage, but then it was all too late. The men had their clothes off in seconds and…and…" Mandy pauses, her gaze staring right through me. "First, they took it in turns, then two at a time…you know…one at either end. She loved it, goading the lads to do more, be more outrageous, saying she wanted three cocks inside her." Mandy gives a shrug. "I'd never seen anyone used so cheaply," she adds as I contemplate the irony of her comment – the pot calling the kettle black, "as though she were pure trash!"

I shake my head at the stark realisation that this is Polly-Anna Mandy is talking about. But as much as the story shocks me, I feel no sympathy for Anna's fall from grace or empathy towards Mandy, whose guilt trip is clearly still evident.

Instead, Mandy's account reminds me of stories the guys back in Croatia tell when recalling tales of women who'll do anything rather than be arrested and detained; yet another close comparison that my two worlds have to offer.

I try to put myself in the room with Polly-Anna on that fateful night. I can picture her now, strutting around the lounge, teasing provocatively, flaunting her body as she played her dangerous game, thinking that she was in control. I follow her every move and gauge every sexual taunt, the men egging Anna on, not wanting the free sex show to stop. I bet she looked hot, as she usually did, perhaps too hot, a perfect image of wanton lust in her high heels and some of Mandy's clothes, which I know on occasion she used to borrow; a favourite outfit was a black mini-skirt with a laced-up split at the back, a strapless corset-style top and black suspenders, and stockings.

But what was she thinking to put herself in that position; a position she knew she would not be able to get out of? It had an element of suicide about it. If not literally, it signified the killing off of the old Anna and, I guess, the emergence of someone new.

"But that's not all of it," Sharon says to my shaking head as an inner voice sighs, *why am I not surprised?* "She went completely off the rails; started hanging around druggies, owing money, giving blow-jobs for taxi fares, the cheap skank." Sharon, in her own bull-in-a-China-shop style, continues Mandy's story. "Word had it she was over at Newtown fucking for drugs and a roof over her head. That's right, innit Mand?" Sharon nudges Mandy.

"Afraid so! No one knows for sure where she is. Someone I know said they saw her once in the Elbow Room; another source swears blind he drove past her standing on a street corner in Balsall Heath's red-light area. Like I said, no one knows for sure. Anna's mom and stepdad have even had the police looking for her, the situation's that bad," explains Mandy as we both sigh at the sorry tale. "Don't look so glum. It's all in the past now," she adds.

"I just wish someone would have told me, that's all. I could have helped her."

"You say that. But she was beyond help; still is – somewhere." Mandy gives my arm a reassuring squeeze.

And just like that, Polly-Anna is a thing of the past, a sad story to be told to younger teens – 'Don't end up like poor Polly-Anna', people will say, a girl who had everything, yet threw it away, and for what…? It just goes to show how life is a minefield and what can happen when you tread where you are not supposed to, unless it is exactly where Polly-Anna meant to tread; her way of crossing over from the light into the dark. Scanning back to when Polly-Anna trod on the mine that diverted her path, in my mind's eye, as her exhibitionism grew wilder and her words turned to demands, it dawns on me that she had no intention of staying in control; in fact, she desired quite the opposite. She wanted her bluff to be called. She wanted to be abused by design and didn't care for the outcome, as if experimenting with her newfound freedom, similar in a sense to how I cheat death on patrols. I am free, freer than I have ever been, and yet I put myself deliberately in harm's way.

My two worlds are getting closer still.

Perhaps at some point they might merge…

Suddenly realising the time and that Pork Chop will be waiting, I get up and make my excuses. "Oh shit! I've gotta go. I'll see you later, okay?"

"I hope this hasn't put a kibosh on the champagne," Sharon says. "I'm gasping!"

The three of us laugh and finish our drinks.

"There's no need to worry. The champagne will be waiting." – I pause for effect. "Anyway, it looks like those other girls are a definite no-show. So it's their loss and your gain," I add, rubbing my hands.

"We're going as well. We need to line our stomachs before the main event." Mandy smiles as the three of us get up to leave together.

We head for Holloway Circus, and I leave the girls at a kebab outlet overlooking the busy road junction. I give Mandy a tenner to cover the bill for her and Sharon's food, plus another twenty so they don't have to fork out any of their own money to get into the Dome nightclub, knowing full well the gesture will keep them sweet and go a long way in securing their place at that VIP table.

"I'll see you in half an hour. VIP suite, don't forget" – I say – "And I'll have the champers on ice waiting."

"Looking forward to it." Mandy blows me a seductive kiss as she turns to join Sharon, who is already ordering.

"Doner meat 'n' chips; plenty of mint sauce and chilli," she shouts to the man behind the counter, pointing at the overhead menu.

"Thank God for that," I sigh. That's the bait sorted; now to put the mechanism in place that will put this plan into action.

Chapter 6
Nightclubbing

I mean nightclubbing with a bat – rampage style! Still carry one in the boot…

On the other side of Holloway Circus, the mouth of Ellis Street beckons like a corrupt councillor offering me the keys to the city.

From the grounds of a residential tower block on my right, to a patch of fenced off waste ground opposite, I scan the street metre by metre for anything that doesn't belong, a rule of thumb I was taught when using night-vision equipment. For example, when on sniper duty I'd look for rounded or abrupt silhouettes among the more random arrangement of forest shapes. "If it doesn't belong, pull the trigger," I was told, because in the monochrome green imagery of infrared, that is what the enemy looks like.

My kill ratio went up after that tip.

But even though this is an urban environment, the same applies; people loitering where they shouldn't or hunkering down inside parked cars, or passers-by that take one too many glances in your direction: All reasons to abort.

I give a cursory glance back towards the bright fluorescence of the distant kebab shop and its unwary prey enjoying their penultimate night, then I turn back to look up the slow, straight incline of Ellis Street towards the red taillights of my co-conspirator, Pork Chop.

The road is pretty much as I remember it, approximately 120 metres long with limited parking zones and gutters lined in prohibiting double-yellow; the buildings lining the pavements on either side from beginning to end offer few hidey holes for individuals and zero cover for any waiting vehicle. Hence Pork Chop at the top of the street sticking out like a sore thumb.

Feeling the need to make haste, I walk calmly yet steadily, keeping to a set of railings on the right that are over-shadowed by tree branches, throwing a stretch of pavement into a gloomy yet concealing strip, as I follow the tower block's perimeter, constantly on the look-out. After forty metres or so, the gloom ends where I emerge to hit the exposing glare of streetlights and the concrete of a multi-storey carpark, its bleak structure offering very little in the way of concealment. If possible, I need to reach Pork Chop's car unseen. For my peace of mind, it will be one less complication. I look behind, then ahead and behind again. The road is still clear, and I have only seconds to go.

On approaching a black Ford Escort, I can tell its Pork Chop from a mile off; not because it's parked where I told him to meet me, but due to it being an RS Turbo sporting a limited-edition metallic paint job, tinted glass, silver 18-inch alloys, rear boot spoiler and large bore exhaust. He probably has it chipped underneath the bonnet too; definitely a senior vice cop's must-have piece of kit – that and watching too much *Miami Vice*.

Pork Chop, otherwise known as Detective Sergeant Darren Space, age 40; a husband to wife Jeanette, 38, and father to David, age 9, and twins, Sophie and Stephen, age 4; height 6 feet, medium to large build, muscular, approximately 14 stones in weight, brown eyes, reddish-brown hair, and beard, neatly cut and trimmed, with a fair complexion. A person who on the surface appears well organised, coming across as a career-motivated, family man, but underneath is a raging torrent of pent-up anger; a man who feels caged in, smothered by his life and those around him, torn between desires, just begging for a chance to prove himself.

I clock him eyeing me up in the driver's side wing-mirror, probably cursing my lateness.

"Quick – drive!" I say, jumping into the passenger seat.

"Phew! Thank fuck for that!" He snaps. "Thought I'd fucking missed you."

As a stressed Pork Chop blurts out his relief, he slams the car into gear, the wheels screech at our sudden acceleration.

"Yeah, sorry for that," I say, somewhat repentant. "Tomorrow's bait required more grooming than I thought. If you can go to Irving Street around the back of the Dome, that'll save us walking more than we have to. You got the stuff?"

"Absolutely!" He sounds excited.

"Any problems?" I ask.

"None whatsoever," Pork Chop declares, laughing. "In fact, I dropped on somewhat."

"Explain!" My tone switched in a nanosecond to that of an impatient headmaster. The phrase 'dropped on somewhat' immediately rang alarm bells.

"The dealer I went to see, someone I've known for years, suddenly thought he could blackmail me," Pork Chop explains. "I knew you wouldn't want any loose ends."

"Too fucking right, I don't. And where is he now?"

"Still in his flat." Pork Chop smirks wryly. "Well, when I say flat, technically speaking his head and hands are in the fridge and his body is sitting in an armchair enjoying whatever's on TV this time of night, with 'доносчик' carved into his chest. It means informer or snitch in Russian; something to throw off the police. It'll keep 'em guessing for weeks."

"Nice one, Porky, and good thinking with the Russian angle," I say. "Did you enjoy it?"

"Fucking right I did," he roars. "Took me right back to those interrogations we used to do in the forests. Only thing is, I didn't know I missed it that much. Goddamn, those were good times."

"Weren't they just!" I pat Pork Chop's arm.

"Oh, and I robbed his entire stash; had to wreck the flat, mind, but I thought that would add to the effect," Pork Chop quips nonchalantly, as though he'd forgotten an item on a shopping list, the comment sounding more like an adlib than a serious remark.

The chat causes me to lose track of our progress, and before I know it, the car is slowing down as Pork Chop pulls over, yanks on the handbrake and turns off the engine. "Right, we're here," he chirps, having reached our destination. "The Dome's just there on your left." He points, assuming his night's work is over.

"Cheers, mate, but I need you to come in with me. We've got a long night ahead of us," I say to a nodded reply. Porky Chop's response is as mute as it is surprised, yet I can tell he respects my judgement call. "By the way, not that it's any of my business, but how much did that dealer's stash come to?"

"Nearly thirty-seven grand in untraceable bills, two kilos of ninety percent pure cocaine, five hundred grams of uncut heroin, plus various bags of pills and what I got for you," Pork Chop gloats as we laugh, whoop and holler in celebration, punching the roof of the car.

"Good for you, man," I shout. "Don't you fucking know it! And watch the interior," he shouts back, "I've only just started paying for it." We continue to cheer, stamp our feet and beat our fists on the dashboard in a crazed celebratory drum-roll.

Although I have very few feelings, if any, I'm glad it's Pork Chop I chose. I guess what I am trying to convey is that, in my own way, I missed him too. And now we are together once more, re-united like two young runaway lovers, I can see how happy he is, what it means to him, and that my choice from here on in is vindicated. I've never seen him this happy.

I'm glad he was able to let go, that he found a release; the visit to the dealer did him the world of good just when he needed it.

"Here, have this!" Says Pork Chop, waving a stack of bills. "I know you asked for three hundred, but here's five, okay?"

"Thanks," I say, taking the money. The thick wad of fives and tens requires both of my inside jacket pockets, weighing the cloth down a little so it bulges under each arm; the look of a gangster wearing twin shoulder-holsters, ready for a St Valentine's Day massacre all of my own – I wish! "What it is to feel rich, eh!" I mock, lifting my arms to flap them, the cash all but falling out.

"I know. Fucking gorgeous, isn't it?" Pork Chop exclaims, his mojo cruising on cloud nine. "The other things you asked for are in that carrying case on the back seat. The dossier on Slatter is in its own wallet, located in the outer zipped section; in the main section you'll find a sealed cellophane package containing a hundred grams of high-grade cocaine, a tin containing twenty individually wrapped one-gram measures of the same quality cocaine, plus a black leather, zipped wallet. This contains all the drug paraphernalia you asked for; two pre-loaded ten-mil syringes of heroin, freshly cooked and ready to inject, one very burnt and recently used bent spoon, a length of surgical elastic, an old Zippo lighter, some cotton wool, ascorbic acid in the form of vitamin C sachets, and a small plastic pouring beaker for water. Plus, some spare gear wrapped in cling film."

I look over my right shoulder and reach for the bag. Leaving the dossier and everything else well alone, I concentrate on retrieving the tin. I remove its lid and examine the contents – twenty individual paper wraps, each wrap sealed again by a layer of cling film.

"Keeps it fresh," Pork Chop says, raising his eyebrows.

"We better not keep the girls waiting, then." I open the passenger door.

"C'mon, let's do it," Pork Chop replies in true police fashion, showing off as he locks the car's central-locking system via a key-fob.

"You're paid too much," I joke.

"That much I still have to rip-off dealers!" Pork Chop's sarcasm hits the who-gives-a-flying-fuck nail right on the head.

Boy, has he come a long way since I last saw him!

***

I watch the night-crawlers cruise, the plethora of unlicensed taxi-drivers and anonymous prowlers running errands that don't exist; any excuse to get out there, closer to their dark desires; the majority are wannabe sex-fiends with their side windows wound down, anything to get a closer look. The night is young to them as they peruse, licking their lips and rubbing their loins at the candy flesh, sounding horns to flimsily clad girls who, in party shoes, totter along towards their chosen Friday night Mecca. The passing cars are a dystopian lottery, a menacing counterbalance to the good times. It's impossible to predict which one has the chloroform-soaked rag and duct tape at the ready. For sure, one of them will go missing tonight. You can feel it, even see it, the cogs of horror slowly turning, putting into place an innocuous chain of events invisible to the untrained eye that will eventually lead to someone on a back seat, gagged and bound, heading to a disused building or a patch of isolated waste ground, only to be found a day or two later dead or wishing they were. I think of Polly-Anna in the hope that she is okay, not exactly pain-free but alive, as a little pain never hurts; good for the soul, as they say. A period of sufferance is the perfect tonic in atoning for one's accumulated sin, and, judging by Mandy's story, poor Polly-Anna has been making up for lost time. But what interests me most is what pushed her over the edge. I don't doubt Mandy's account, but she insinuated a lot; being sexually abused as a child, a possible sexual incident with her stepdad, as well as the other promiscuities. That was not the sweet, bubbly Polly-Anna I knew, that I can pictured and relate to. That girl, it seems is dead, snatched by the very reassurance she clung to and whittled away till hollow. She's out there somewhere, totally off-grid, surviving the only way she knows how, probably no more than a numb husk by now, functioning on instinct and muscle memory, her face aged by the deeply etched trauma, her demeanour mistaken for the dead-pan stiffness of Parkinson's – that look of fixed hopelessness, or perhaps the desperation of a woman accelerated far beyond her years and her tolerance of suffering.

Like I said, a little pain doesn't hurt. But a lot will maim as cruelly as polio cripples, the scars all too apparent; a physical labelling that you are broken. I've seen it. I know what it looks like, the ugly flipside of rape. They are never the same; the horror is irreversible. As a police commander in Osijek once put it, "Nikada ne možete vidjeti ono što vidite." – you can never un-see what you see. Absolutely goddamn right! But what the victim sees, they also feel, as does the perpetrator, evil glaring into innocence and vice versa, the two trading a simultaneous experience, doubling the dreadfulness of it all. Hence victims often voice disdain at being spared. Death is considered more compassionate than being left to relive the terror over and over. Looking at the white, yellow and red flashes of passing traffic, I wonder which of these drivers have already taken advantage of Polly-Anna's predicament and her subsequent vulnerability and which are yet to take advantage, and who amongst them, if anyone at all, would do the decent thing and refuse such a gift-horse baring promises of the flesh for so little. But there again, that's not the world we live in, except for my Bangladeshi friend. He would do the decent thing. In the name of his sons, Barsha and Sabbir, and his god, he would help, driving her to safety in the hope this sweet child could be set free from her pain. Wherever my driver friend is, I hope it is he who finds Polly-Anna, though watching the circling hyenas and vultures amass, it looks like hope is all she has. It's sad how the odds of success always favour the worst outcome, as if somehow bad news is the only news that society expects. No wonder I am what I am – society expects it! And what society is expecting – society gets! It has helped shape me. It wants someone like Đavo. And who am I to shun the wants of my *maker*? Certainly no one who'll disappoint the expectation bestowed.

As advised, I linger on the pavement beyond the range of the club's outdoor CCTV cameras; the plan, though very ad hoc, is for Pork Chop to first gain entrance and convince the club's manager, whom he knows from previous police investigations, to have both the outdoor and indoor surveillance cameras turned off under the pretence of protecting the sources of a covert sting operation. Then, via an emergency exit, Pork Chop and a member of the club's security team will let me in, and from there they'll escort me to the VIP section.

Pork Chop is taking a while, and I'm growing bored with counting down the minutes when a metal-clad door suddenly swings open.

"Hey, hurry up," Pork Chop shouts, waving me over. "Quick! Inside! This is Vinny."

Vinny, a six-foot-seven, twenty-stone giant of a man, sticks out his gorilla of an arm to shake my hand.

"Nice to meet you, Vinny," I say, purposefully not introducing myself. The solid fire door slams behind me.

"Likewise," Vinny's booming voice replies, his eyes squinting with an air of distrust, like a mighty silverback that hasn't seen a lion before but instinctively knows what it is capable of. "C'mon, it b'gin to jam up in dare," the big man adds, turning to climb a flight of stairs, obviously unhappy at being asked to help a police officer and his surprise guest; a guest who's not opened to using the front entrance like everyone else but prefers the shadows.

"What part of the Caribbean are you from?" I ask, detecting a familiar twang. "Don't tell me – Bahamas."

"New Providence," Vinny booms back, smiling, giving me a sideways glance as if to say, "How the fuck did you know that?" – "Y' know it?"

"I'm no Conchy Joe, if that's what you mean," I say, and he gives a thick bass laugh. "I've worked with a few Bahamians in my time, so I got a feel for the dialect." I continue. "The phrase 'jam up', for example. It's a clear giveaway."

"Blurd-clart!" Vinny exclaims, eking out the syllables, shaking his head. "You one clever English!"

Pork Chop stays quiet as Vinny and I chat fishing, boat-planes, and Bahamian women, laughing at one another's misuse of language as my colloquial English meets his repertoire of Bahamianese idioms. I like Vinny. He has those genuine attributes that immediately grab you and a friendly smile I find infectious, even though his misgivings about me are all too apparent.

The stairs lead to a corridor which in turn spits us out, via another safety door, at the far side of the famous domed dance floor. We skirt the magnificent structure, the crowd parting for the big man as Pork Chop and I tuck in behind, climbing through the different levels of bars and revelry till we reach the VIP section that overlooks it all.

A rope between two waist-high brass poles; the symbolic nightclub tool that separates the so-called VIPs from the dross, an elite few from the bread and butter that week in, week out, keep this place running. Vinny gives a nod to his colleague and the rope is unclipped. I reach up to tap him on the shoulder and slip fifty quid into the palm of his huge hand. "It was good talking to you," I say, thanking him. Vinny's broad smile acknowledges my gesture.

"The cameras are off till twelve. It's all I could get," Pork Chop explains. "They rarely get any trouble before then, so it was an easy sell, but that is our deadline," he affirms with a stern look.

"Twelve should be enough," I say. "Anyway, looks like the girls aren't here yet, so I'll get set up. You okay your end?" I add, checking Pork Chop isn't going to wander too far, just in case an emergency crops up.

"Yeah, no prob; got it covered. The manager is a new guy; young, too. He seems quite excited we're conducting an operation on his watch, so I'm anticipating no real issues," Pork Chop says, coming into his own; a glint in his eye tells me he just lives for this shit! "I'll be in radio contact with Vinny, and he'll keep an eye on proceedings from a safe distance, making sure you're not interrupted. As for me, I'll be in the security suite ensuring those cameras stay dark. We good to go?"

"Yeah, let's do it," I say with a clap of my hands as we all assume our positions; Pork Chop heads off towards the security suite, Vinny is in his overseeing role, and I'm in the VIP area, where a waitress directs me to a semi-circular booth of my choosing; the one furthest away in the corner where the light doesn't quite hit. That'll do nicely. I take my seat in the centre of the booth. I can see the bar, the roped-off entrance, and every other booth. Strategically speaking, it's perfect.

The low-lit ambience exudes exactly the kind of opulence it is there to cater for, an inviting yellow haze mixing with white neon to give a golden glow. One has to pay just to breathe the luxury on this side of the rope.

With the waitress hovering, I order two bottles of champagne. "We've Lanson Rose or Moët & Chandon Imperial," says the waitress.

"Moët it is, then," I reply, thinking, *why change a winning formula?* "And can I have three champagne flutes? I'm expecting guests. Thank you."

"That'll be eighty pounds," comes her automated answer. I hand over the money in equally robotic fashion.

The ice buckets arrive minutes later, the foil already removed from the bottlenecks. Anticipating Mandy and Sharon at any second, I twist the wire of the nearest bottle and gently ease the cork with a muted pop and fill the three tall flutes. Then, as if fate couldn't be more prompt, I hear Sharon call, waving her arm above her head as though attracting a helicopter on an airlift rescue. "Hey, Andrew, we're here!"

"It's okay, they're with me," I shout over to Vinny, who instructs his colleague to let them through.

Sharon in her eagerness leads her sister, giggling like a silly schoolgirl at the sight of two laden ice-buckets and me standing with a champagne flute in either hand, as Mandy, a diva to the last, struts behind, working her stuff, to quote her weekend ethos, as though each entrance made, however inconsequential, is the result of her putting on a show after some camera assistant with their clapboard has shouted *lights, camera, action!* A set of behavioural traits I find rather shallow and pathetic, but in here, superficial is all you need.

As they take their seats on either side of me inside the curved booth, I realise once again that I'm on the clock, my curfew twelve-midnight. With a string of disco and '80s' remixes sending the club into dancing overdrive, I let the girls soak up the atmosphere and a couple of glasses of champers before making my move.

"You still like a bit of Charlie?" I say, leaning towards Mandy.

"Charlie who?" She replies, missing the point entirely.

"Cocaine Charlie!" I say. "Do you still like to party with it?" She glares back at me, her sassy arrogance faltering, suddenly stuck for words.

"W-w-what you trying to say?" She mutters, fluttering her eyelashes, half trying to deflect the comment, down-playing it while doing her level best to stay cool and weigh up whether my question is some kind of faux pas or the actual offer of a Class A drug. I note the brief tell-tale sign of her tongue running along the inside of her upper lip in anticipation of something she's been missing.

"Depends on who's asking," she bats back, the mere mention of cocaine putting her ever so slightly out of kilter.

"I'm asking. 'Cos if you do, I can help." I produce the tin and offer her a cling-film square under the table. "That's a gram, ninety percent pure."

"No one can get ninety percent," she snaps.

"I can," I reply. "Have a taste. The cling-film might be fiddly, but that's so the paper doesn't unwrap. Go on – it's free! I've plenty more."

Mandy's long red fingernails make short work of the tightly pressed cling-film, scoring it open to unpick the paper parcel. Daintily she scoops a nailful of white powder and snorts it, rubbing what's left into her mouth, the narcotic an instant pupil-dilating, lip-smacking hit.

"Fucking-hell, that's good," growls Mandy like a bitch suddenly in season, dipping her head to snort straight from the palm of her hand, one gram not lasting thirty seconds as she licks the paper clean, brushing her teeth with what minuscule granules remain on her finger.

"Enjoy that?" I ask rhetorically.

"Oh…my…God!" She gasps, taking her first breath for about a minute. "You weren't fucking kidding. Wow!"

"Can I have a try?" Sharon says. "Bin ages since we've had good shit, innit, Mand?"

I hand Sharon a wrap, and in similar fashion it is tasted, snorted, and licked clean in seconds flat, the two orgasmic in their approval.

"How do you feel now?" I smirk.

"Like I can drink all day and fuck all night," Sharon purrs.

"And you?" I look at Mandy, who my question was originally for.

"For that, very grateful," she replies in one lazy exhale.

"The rich side of life tastes good, doesn't it?" I reinforce the message. "Champagne and coke – does it get any better?"

"If this is what it's like, the only thing missing is a beautiful set of pecs and abs to sniff it off. Know what I mean?" Mandy's tone is a blissful hum of unadulterated contentedness.

"Sure do, sis," responds Sharon.

"I've been working out," I joke, patting my stomach and flexing an arm.

"Careful, Andy; she might hold you to that." Sharon laughs.

"Another gram of this shit and I will," cackles Mandy.

"Think I'll join you," howls Sharon. "Feeling kinda horny as it is."

As we laugh, tucking in to the second bottle, I'm reminded, as the narcotic's demon-like excellence works its awful magic, elevating its recipients to new euphoric heights, of babies eating chocolate for the first time, going from sterile jarred food to sweet, creamy opulence, the addiction instant, their eyes widening to saucers as smiles broaden, ear to ear; little faces that if they were happy before the chocolate, after are the happiest they've ever been, positively beaming, their eyes, once the first piece is consumed, fixed only on the next piece. And as a pusher of the finest candy going, Mandy and Sharon know they only have to ask, and they shall receive. They are mine!

"Remember I said I was here to conduct interviews, hoping to recruit two employees," I say. "Well, this is the product I wanted my so-called employees to sell. Whaddaya think?"

"It's good; perhaps too good," Sharon replies, wiping her brow, looking flushed. "You could cut this a little and still get a nice hit."

"And I think I want to hear what you have to say," Mandy adds, proving she's as shrewd as her younger sibling, if not shrewder.

"Thought you would," I say, topping up their glasses. "But I wouldn't cut it." I direct my comment towards Sharon. "You see, it's the quality, not the quantity, that's in demand. I already have a customer base, therefore making the business model simple: A good-looking, quality product sold by an even better-looking sales team that know the product; a team that might as well be two sisters than anybody else," I explain as Mandy and Sharon, just like the babies, fall in line, transfixed by the next piece of chocolate.

"For instance, you'll be travelling first class between cities like London, Manchester, Glasgow and Edinburgh, stopping in top hotels, with your expenses paid, and earning bloody good money along the way, all because the demand for my product has, quite inexplicably, sky-rocketed." I pause to take in the girls' reaction; both are mesmerised by how too good to be true it sounds. For all they're hustlers, I've got them eating out of the palm of my hand. "And to ensure everyone's safety and well-being, the product will be paid for in advance, so no money will change hands, keeping the risk low, meaning there will be none of this snooping around back-alleys, doing dodgy deals in the dead of night, or lone meetings in anonymous hotel rooms. I guess what I'm trying to say is that you're the delivery service with an after-sale, customer provision attached. The money side of things and preparing the product for delivery is my job, as well as making certain everything runs smoothly. It's the kind of bespoke yet discreet catering my clients are used to. I don't want to lose them. Not to silly mistakes."

"As it stands, we are definitely interested," Mandy remarks.

"Yes, we are," Sharon chips in, as though shouting a last-second bid across an auction room to steal the bargain of the century before the gavel strikes for the third and final time.

"You see, my clientele are hand-picked; all are from high-level professional backgrounds, the top earning tier of society, doctors, lawyers, business owners, bankers, judiciaries and the like; the kind that like to throw lavish corporate functions and exclusive parties; swimming pools, drugs, booze, sex and money. It's how the elite like to let their hair down and play. Plus, it's a chance for both of you to sample the lifestyle you've only seen in *Hello* magazine, free of charge." Realising that about now is the right time to take a strategic pause, I call over the waitress to order a third bottle of Moët, giving the girls a couple of minutes to digest what I have said.

"Did I mention this job comes with its own flat?" Sharon all but chokes on her champagne – *did he just say what I thought he said?* – Her gawping gaze quizzical as Mandy pulls my face around so we're nose-to-nose.

"What do you mean, it comes with a flat?" Mandy shakes her head in disbelief, thinking my generosity too cynical to be real; the joke is finally exposed.

"Not straight away. It needs sprucing up first. But it does come with a flat, located just a few miles from where you are now. Again, it'll go down as an expense, with no rent to pay. You'll just need money for utility bills and food," I hope I've sold the idea as a genuine yet realistic proposition. "And if you girls have got time, tomorrow we can go an' see it. Strike while the iron's hot, so to speak," I add, with my best salesman's-pitch smile.

"I dunno." Mandy grimaces to pangs of suspicion.

"What's to think about? Fuck it! I'm in even if she's not," Sharon counters from behind my head.

"Look, it's a lot to take in, I know. You haven't seen or heard of me in almost four years, and here I am suddenly offering you this incredible opportunity. I get it. It's freaky! But us bumping into one another like this, I think its fate. I think it's meant to be – don't you?" I put the ball in their court, hoping they'll accept.

"You can fucking say that again," Sharon exclaims. "Tell him, Mand!"

"Yeah, you're probably right – why not?" Mandy says, planting a soft kiss upon my mouth, her sudden melancholy lifting. "We'll come and see the flat. But it better be good."

"Of course, it'll be good," says Sharon, refilling her glass. "It comes with perks!" The 'perks', as Sharon puts it, being Slatter popping his cherry. All I'm doing is fattening up the goose – or rather geese – up for the main feast.

"Don't worry, you'll see the potential," I say, winking at Mandy and tapping my watch. "Look, I gotta go. I didn't realise the time. There's a meeting I have to attend," I say, making my excuses.

"Is it about product?" Mandy whispers.

"Kind of," I whisper back. "More about keeping everything on track. Here's another sixty quid for some more drinks and to cover your taxi home" – I add, handing Mandy a folded wedge of tenners – "You still in the same flat?"

"More's the pity." Mandy shrugs. "Hopefully not for much longer."

"Well, if all goes swimmingly, that's the plan. Is seven o'clock okay?" I ask, smiling. Mandy nods energetically in reply. "Good. Seven it is. I'll be in a black Ford Escort parked up below your balcony outside the newsagent. Listen out for a couple of bips on the horn. If you can come down to me, I'll take it from there. And dress to impress. After seeing the flat, I'm thinking we might celebrate – go for a meal, a bar or two, perhaps take in a club – cocktails. Who knows? We'll see how the mood takes us. Anyway, I'll see you tomorrow at seven. You got that?"

"You fucking bet we've got it," Sharon bellows, standing up to give me a peck on the cheek.

"Already looking forward to it," mouths Mandy, her parting kiss wet and sloppy. She drags her tongue across my cheek to probe my ear. "Leave us some gear" – she whispers – "and I'll make it worth your while."

"Sort me out tomorrow, okay?" I say, tossing them another couple of grams the way a zookeeper throws fish to seals after they've jumping through hoops.

With my work done, I call over Vinny and let him escort me through the crowd down whence I came, past the domed dance floor to where Pork Chop is waiting by the fire safety door that leads to the exit corridor.

"C'mon, Cinders, time we left the ball. We're cutting it fine," he shouts. "Get done what you needed to?"

"Yeah! All's good," I reply, and Pork Chop gives me a thumbs-up.

Vinny, like the true gent he is, sees us out, and I slip him another fifty quid. "I was never here, okay?"

"Mudda sick, man," Vinny says, his voice a cool slur of calm and collectedness.

"I mean it! I was never here," I repeat in a slightly more forceful tone. "That money you've accepted means we've entered into a contract whereby I do not exist. Understand?"

"Sure I do. I know you're not dem." Vinny flicks his head towards Pork Chop, referring to him being police and me not. "I know da real ting when I see it."

"Good for you, Vinny," I say, reaching out to shake the big guy's hand. Our eyes meet and exchange a mutual expression of the utmost sincerity, mighty strength paying respect to fearless resolve. I give a slight bow in recognition.

We walk away and quickly around the corner, making for Pork Chop's turbo-charged dream machine, its black finish reflecting the night lights in full movie Technicolor.

"Where to now?" Pork Chop asks, knowing me as he does whenever he sees that devilish glint in my eye. He knows I'm far from finished for the night, that I've other irons in the fire; his mind is racing, scanning through the possibilities of which red-hot poker I'll grab, and the direction it'll take us in. He also knows that whenever we are together, especially when expectations are high, whatever the course of events, it usually culminates in one celebratory activity – a rampage!

"We're going nightclubbing," I answer.

"So, what was that?" He remarks sarcastically, pointing back towards the club.

"I mean nightclubbing with a bat – rampage style! Still carry one in the boot?" I say. Pork Chop claps his hands and punches the air.

"Fucking knew it" – he roars – "I knew you were saving the best till last."

"Don't I always." I smirk.

"I knew it! I knew it! I knew it!" Pork Chop continues, dancing his last few steps to the car door like he's just scooped the Pools.

"Thought that would cheer you up, you fucking poser," I say as Pork Chop waves his key-fob with an exaggerated thumb-press, the car bleeping like something off *Nightrider* with a subsequent low whir of releasing locks. "Hope you've been practising your swinging arm, 'cos you're gonna need it for what I've got in mind," I add, laughing.

Chapter 7
Rampage Style!

A period of violent and uncontrollable behaviour; moving through a place in a violent and uncontrollable manner…

Once in the car, I direct Pork Chop to head north out of the city centre. The man is brimming with animated anticipation, tapping his hands against the steering-wheel to the music pumping from his in-car stereo.

There's a fascination in how music intimately intertwines with one's desires, the two inexplicably linked yet complementing one another like an indecent marriage of the perfect drumbeat fuelling the darkest taboo, one lost without the other; an unstoppable driving force; a bond so strong and passionate it has to be acted on in the heat of the moment. And that moment, I have decided, is now!

"So where to?" Pork Chop shouts, competing to be heard over Blur's "There's No Other Way."

"I need you to listen; turn the music down," I say. Pork Chop reaches across the dashboard console for the volume control. "In fact, turn it off altogether. This is important."

"What's up?"

"I've decided to call in your debt," I explain. Pork Chop squints, nonplussed. "You know – the pledge you made in Osijek – remember?"

"I remember," he answers solemnly, narked at how his jubilatory bubble has just been burst. "You wanna do that now?"

"The timing's perfect," I reply. "I realise it's a big ask, but I'm gonna say it anyway: Papa-Charlie activate Alpha-Papa-Oscar-Kilo protocol, execute."

"You're not kidding, are you?" Pork Chop says. I shake my head. "I mean, don't get me wrong, I'm not having second thoughts. If you want me to do 'em, I'll do the fucking lot, rampage style 'n' all. It's just come as a surprise, that's all."

"Remember, this is what you wanted above all else. I respected your decision then, as I respect it now," I explain, clarifying my expectation that it's time to pay the piper.

"But—" His stabbed interruption, more of a nervous reaction than a counter to my request, ends abruptly, as though halted by a silent stammer.

"But nothing!" I shrug, adopting an 'it'll-be-alright-don't-worry' tone, trying not to sound too nonchalant. "Your time to prove yourself has come. Just think – you will be the first; my first proper recruit and the first, in my eyes, to prove himself beyond reproach. Anyway, it's not as if you're going to be doing this alone, now, is it?" I smile and pat his arm as though I'm the 40-year-old detective and he is the one racked by the inexperience of youth. "C'mon, it'll be fun. Like old times. You remember that roadblock we set up south of Bilje and that car which didn't stop? How many were in it?"

"Seven in total," replies Porky, his eyes suddenly distant, reminiscing, feeding off past horrors. Although Pork Chop can't, I hear the car creak like a deep submarine, the dark's outside pressure building. It knows what we're discussing, and so do the demons carried on its ill-wind. Unwittingly, we are teasing with only the thinnest of safety nets between us, as if wetting their appetites from within the cage. They want to get in, their poised voraciousness picking up on our conversation before you can take your next breath, their parallel world too close for comfort.

"It'll be just like that," I say.

"You reckon?" The corners of his mouth begin to twitch, forming an ear-to-ear grin.

"Of course!" I bellow. "You're a natural. After all, you're the only one I know who has used an AKM as a baseball bat to bludgeon a carload of people to death. It may have taken a whole magazine to stop the vehicle, but I'll tell you now, you sure as hell didn't leave anything else to chance. You smashed the absolute shit out of them."

"I did, didn't I?" Pork Chop answers. "Smashed them to hell!" His voice is slow and deliberate, as though reciting the mission statement of some divine affirmation; the stern word of God rubber-stamped by the Devil's merciless mandate, the ultimate partnership of warped love empowering and energising, a love embraced by my psycho buddy.

***

When Pork Chop and I first met at Vojarna Tuškanac military base, I can't exactly remember how or when it was, but from the off we talked and acted as though we were old friends. Even our fellow comrades couldn't believe that we had only been recently introduced, and because of this, our instant bond, the Croats teamed us up. We bunked, trained, and worked together, our friendship growing day by day till we were like brothers, brothers in arms who gladly trusted each other with our lives. It's funny, 'cos I grew up trusting no one, not even family or friends, as they inevitably had a tendency to let me down. But in this stranger whom I got to know so well, I developed such a level of trust, psychologically speaking, that I felt safe around him. I could unburden myself, talk to him without the pressure that I would be judged. It came as a huge comfort and one hell of a support mechanism. Hence, we were selected for high-risk details with special police units, like the snatch squads rounding up political dissidents and covert border patrols along the Danube. During our downtime, if either of us had an issue, we would always talk it out, with no subject off limits. We would chat for hours, often burning the midnight oil with a few bottles of local pivo and a final nightcap of slivovitz; a kind of make-do, tit-for-tat therapy exercising the theory that a problem shared is a problem halved. But although Pork Chop is seventeen years my senior, it was I whose wisdom had the most profound effect. He, almost a generation older, listened to what I had to say, never questioning the age gap or my limited years of experience, always respecting my judgement as if I was an equal.

No one had ever done that before.

I loved that about him – not that I'm an egotist or vain. It was more about supporting one another, making sure our demons didn't get the better of us, hence our path into war's conception; an atypical baptism to absolve any good that still remained. But there lies the problem: Good versus evil. You would think it was clear cut, but how wrong you are. The evil in which Pork Chop and I found ourselves, soon became the food we ate and the air we breathed, as pure as the driven snow and as innocent as a new-born babe, its character exact, able to differentiate in a heartbeat what matters and what does not. We came to know it as a force of nature, as it came to know us, enveloping our very existence. The madness was an inescapable maze that we transported back with us to infect those we love most; not content with putting ourselves in harm's way, we must include everybody else. It's a cancer that, all credit to its ingenuity, never fails to filter homeward like an antibiotic-resistant virus picked up on a cut-price holiday, sold on the too-good-to-be-true, picture-perfect pretext of the perfect family relaxing on the perfect beach, a Xanadu we are all told as young adults exists. In reality, the end of the rainbow, the sun, surf and sex we're promised, is no more than a lacklustre, unsanitary landscape of used condoms and syringes and a dose of pox. I know what first took me to Croatia. I wanted to unlock the real me, to truly find myself for the very first time. But when I tried to think what line Pork Chop was sold, I could only guess at what made a person want to reinvent themselves. "Come to sunny Croatia, pick up a gun, fire some bullets, be a new man and you'll never look back!" By my reckoning it was something like that. Many who took the bait were misled. Croatia isn't *Westworld*, where the robots cannot hurt you. The enemy is real, firing real bullets that kill real people. Death has a face and stares you right in the eye.

But try prising the truth out of folks about why they went and it's like trying to get a straight yes or no answer from a politician. But these are the kind that wield their bullshit kangaroo-court politics in such a way that if riled, they'll probably smash your head in, or at least give you enough grief that you'll never ask again. After a few heated exchanges, I gave up asking, no longer caring why they were there, just so long as they had my back as I had theirs. And while on operations, this was the case; we all looked after one another, no exceptions. But back at base, all the bullshit made for a house of cards; everyone was living a lie.

Like the victims I saw on a daily basis, when I looked around the barracks I saw victims of another kind, with that same look of irreparable damage, staring off over yonder. It was a refuge for broken souls where nobody cared. Everyone preferred the bullshit default narrative of wanting to prove how tough they were, instead of being more transparent; their lives back home were collapsing due to mortgage arrears and mounting credit card bills or their marriages failing due to acts of unfaithfulness, or they were simply on the run from the authorities. Whoever it concerned and whatever the pretext, all you heard was the customary bravado, like it was expected; anything else was taken as a sign of weakness. Though if you listened closely, behind the show and bluster, you would notice that each exaggerated sentence and every overly emphasised, profane statement was delivered with a snarling undertone of misogynistic hate, a hate projected on a tidal jet-stream from one land to another and back again, transporting their misery to inflict yet more on a people who had no idea of the sheer amount of woe coming their way. However, despite the chaos of the madhouse, Pork Chop was the exception regardless of his victim status; he wasn't afraid to ask and admit that he needed help, even from someone considerably younger than himself. He welcomed free speech and the sharing of ideas; his style was considered odd by his peers, a tad too hippy-cum-love-thy-neighbour for some, yet amongst the men this idiosyncrasy was tolerated and sometimes even adopted due to his strong character and unquestionable bravery under pressure.

So, what brought such a man to such a hellhole?

Her name is Jeanette.

***

Forever the cynic, I always saw the sanctity of marriage as some great conspiracy; the church aisle lined by everyone you know is God's pact with the ruling classes to get the two of you to the altar so you can pledge allegiance to Jesus and the endless possibilities marriage offers – the great new beginning and everything that comes with it; a house, children, nursery fees, school runs, family holidays and, to top it off, university fees. Let alone all the other crap in between, but no more church! Most of us only go to christenings, weddings and funerals for the free buffet, and that is more out of habit or to save face than because of any faith we might have. Yet it was a life Pork Chop craved. All he ever wanted to do was pay his bills and be a good dad.

When we first met, he and I would argue, he in the married corner and I in the singles corner, where he ardently spoke of marriage in terms of having purpose, a meaning, and a legacy. I, on the other hand, saw it as a cul-de-sac, a stifling no-way-out that offered no adventure and nothing to look forward to. So why would you?

"To fulfil God's purpose," he would say. And there started our next debate – God! Does He exist; doesn't He? If so, where? Pork Chop used to be adamant He did, saying I couldn't prove that He didn't, while I always countered by saying 'You can't prove He does'. If nothing else, during those early days it was nice to see Pork Chop as the person he wished he could be and not the broken wreck he embodied. If ever a person deserves to be saved and set free, it's him, just like I hope to save and set free the rest of the world. I remember the moment he told me. We were on a deep reconnaissance patrol, way out in the sticks north of Vukovar, bivouacked in earshot of the Danube's increased wash after a day's heavy rain. It was a huge outpouring of pent-up emotion and anguish whispered in the dead of night, as Pork Chop relived the tragic circumstances that had brought him to my side.

With one ear listening for the enemy and the other tuned in to Pork Chop, I played the part of a calm yet reassuring shrink to a tee, as my new friend spilled his life story; a story that flowed like a chapter from some trashy romance, as though he was reading straight from a book. But the crux of the story was not so much about him as it was about his wife, mother of his three beautiful children – Jeanette.

"I love her to bits, yet she's the one who has hurt me most; more than you could ever believe," he said, the moonlight reflecting off his glazed eyes, his voice dry, overcome, as if already grieving for someone he had lost.

Having never met the woman or even seen a photograph, Pork Chop's description of a petite blonde with a bubbly, flirtatious personality full of verve said it all. As much as he loved her for it, the persona these qualities created was also her undoing, as irresistible as it was infectious; a crazy, playful combination of angelic porcelain features and a slim physique which, he boasted, had remained perfectly proportioned; a honeypot to any passing bee, hence his pet-name for her, Honeypot. I don't know why, but at the time it reminded me of *Pussy Galore*, perhaps the name to end all femme fatale names. Honey-pot kind of said it all – like bees around a honey pot – but do the bees get a taste? Surely all that buzzing deserves some reward.

"Men just love her. It's like they can't get enough," he said. "That's why, as a couple, we have so few friends; Jeanette is always inviting male attention, whether they be husbands, boyfriends or fiancés. She plays the field like a pro, always the belle of the ball and talk of the town. Needless to say, every woman I know hates her." A trait of every woman, I think. Especially if they are anything like the few girlfriends I have known, a species unto themselves and catty enough at the best of times, but give them something personal to bitch about, like an unwarranted intrusion – say another attractive woman coming onto their man, innocent or otherwise – and their scornful envy will character assassinate the threat in seconds. And woe betide any comebacks.

Hell hath no fury like a woman scorned! – Or women scorned, for that matter; the wives' club casting out Jeanette like a bad omen, their sixth sense united like a compass needle pointing towards her looming immorality. Little did they know of Pork Chop's demons and the precious light his friends were shutting out, a light that was keeping the darkness at bay; a darkness that had spread to family and friends, the evil enjoying its mischievous play. It was a sorry tale that Pork Chop had to tell; a lonely one that had a recurring theme of distrust and a family in denial trying desperately to paper over the cracks. But these were no superficial breaks that could be quickly patched up; he admitted that their existence signified major subsidence.

But the longer their friends' boycott lasted, the more the darkness took over and the more frequent his trips were to Croatia. "I think I see monsters," Pork Chop once said to me. "They wait for me at night." As most peoples' monsters do. His expression was that of a frightened child lost tin a waking nightmare, God clearly forsaken in his search for a new fix. But the biggest surprise was how his sudden lack of popularity affected him. "I've always been popular" – he confessed – "at work, in general, even as a kid." The sense of loss was unfathomable in his mind, as though he had lost a limb. How could this happen to everybody's best buddy, a man who adored his friends and who thought they loved him back?

How fickle friendship is when the funniest joke of the night is on you!

With little choice but to spend more time at work, Pork Chop's state of mind deteriorated. He grew estranged from both his wife and his children and from the friends he no longer saw, a downward spiral, that week by week, took him to an ever-darker place, the increasing isolation fuelling terrible thoughts.

But on the surface, it looked like Pork Chop was managing – until he confided in me how even her own sister, Judy, kept her distance, having once accused Jeanette of trying it on with her then husband, now ex. He said no one knew what to make of it at the time. Most people simply laughed off the possibility as totally absurd. But Judy, knowing her sister better than anyone and being a solicitor, knew there wasn't any smoke without at least a little fire. Hence it was the beginning of the end for Judy's marriage. As for the rest of them, including Jeanette's parents and extended family, they all chose to ignore it, because the alternative didn't bear thinking about. It would have torn their family apart, ripping the guts from its very core.

It was then I knew that I had to take Pork Chop under my wing properly, not just as a mate, but to give him a whole new reason to live, to turn his darkness into something positive, into something that would give his marriage a defining purpose, meaning and legacy. But for Pork Chop, who had managed to keep a lid on his feelings, the rumours of Jeanette's infidelity persisted. They would crop up when he least expected it – brief comments whispered too loudly in a pub from one concerned friend to another, snippets of gossip that never dispelled his fears but fanned the flames of scandal, always starting with someone who attended Jeanette's gym.

"She was forever complaining. Her latest gripe was that I looked different," Pork Chop said. "'What's wrong? Why are you looking at me like that?' She'd yell. But by that time, it didn't matter. I didn't care – I'd switched off!" Of course, he did! That's what you do when you become different – switch off. Because let's face it, what's the alternative? Discuss the intricacies of combat and how you contributed to the torture, mutilation and killing of others? I think not!

Thing was, Jeanette was probably right. Her husband would have looked different and not acted like his usual self. On his first visit to Zagreb, within a week he had one confirmed kill to his name, with another two to be verified. A man – a husband, a father, a career policeman who wanted to be reinvented – had been reinvented! For Pork Chop was born-again hard. It's one thing to stray off the reservation, but quite another to adopt your new surroundings as intensely as he did, then return to civvy street without so much as batting an eyelid. That level of discipline takes some doing. But despite Pork Chop's best efforts, there was no disguising what horror does to an individual – seeing it, participating in its wretchedness, forever having blood on your hands and guilt in your heart, reliving the moment you thrust a knife or pull the trigger. I don't care how tough folks think they are, the fact is, you are never quite the same again. Whether addicted or repulsed, it will stay with you for the rest of your days, as will the monsters that death and killing attracts.

Jeanette saw the change. If she had known the reason why, she would have packed her bags, grabbed the kids, and run the moment he walked back through the door. But she didn't, how could she? Pork Chop was shrewd, telling Jeanette he was needed for an ongoing investigation that required him to work in London, while informing his commanding officer that he was taking advantage of time owed in lieu so that he, Jeanette, and the kids could finally go on that long-awaited holiday. It was a simple subterfuge that fooled everyone on both sides time and time again; a perpetual three-way chess match Pork Chop juggled in order to keep the status quo. Meanwhile, he had persuaded a former colleague from vice, turned private investigator, to join Jeanette's gym on a full membership. It was the move that sealed her fate. She had thought the gym was her sanctuary, never to be infiltrated. It was tough on Pork Chop. He knew it was make or break. I told him not to sweat it and go with the flow, and so he did, day by day, week on week, as the reports gradually accumulated and grew, piece by illuminating piece, till the picture, conclusively and ironically, favoured the gossipmongers' sordid conjecture above his own wished-for outcome.

"They were right all along," I remember Pork Chop saying, his expression one of utter deflation, with a frown that screamed, "How did they know her better than me? She's my wife, for fuck's sake!"

But Porky Chop's PI had pulled out all the stops. He had timed and dated video footage, photographs, taped conversations between him and Jeanette, plus extensive witness testimony. It made for a compelling case and cringe worthy reviewing but fell short of proving she had been unfaithful; it just highlighted the intent of a woman seeking attention and a possible way out of her own.

"I chose Mac 'cos I knew he'd be her type," Pork Chop said. "You know, surfer-dude-cum-man-about-town, chiselled jaw, blond hair and a tan; a rugged Val Kilmer – Brad Pitt cross with Patrick Swayze moves. The guy's a walking fanny-magnet for crying out loud! What is there for a woman not to love except that he's gay? Not that he's gonna tell her."

In the pitch black, I remember trying to can my laughter as we bit our knuckles like two silly, sniggering kids trying not to attract attention in school assembly.

But the picture Mac had painted was sobering. It was a torn picture of humdrum day-to-day, of being married with kids versus the excitement of being free and daring to dream the unthinkable, of a woman whose body language yelled 'I'm available' and whose dialogue only ever used singular terms like 'I' or 'mine' never 'we' or 'ours'. Jeanette erased her family from any conversation, never admitting to having a husband or partner, let alone three children. The very thought of them cramped her style, like her non-existent wedding and engagement rings, and when she used her maiden name, Harriot, when applying for the gym membership.

No wonder Pork Chop's sneering laugh tailed off into a lingering sigh of slowly released negativity; it was the sound of a man rejected, coming to terms with his loneliness and with being unloved.

Not that I can directly relate to missing someone's love. I understand love – what it looks like, what it sounds like – but to miss it I need to have felt love. I guess in the same way I don't grasp what it is to be unpopular – or popular, for that matter. I know a lot of people and they know me. I don't see it as being popular or think about whether they like me; I just know that I am part of a larger network in the same way as an ant is part of a larger colony, with everyone having their place, where I consider no one more special than any other – except those who have a legacy to leave, a kind of farewell epitaph that bucks the trend in punching home a message, whether a simple inscription on a tombstone, an inspiring piece of art or a trail of dead bodies. Pork Chop deserves such an epitaph. That was where the night was heading – towards a final solution. I just needed Pork Chop to see it for himself.

And on that note, under the stars' eerie luminescence, I saw the cogs turn which sealed her fate as Pork Chop revealed the bombshell, the bit of Mac's investigation that he had saved till last. "And if all that wasn't enough, she's got a friend," he said. "A special friend. A fella she's been seeing for months. Apparently, they go running together and have been seen in local cafés having cosy chats over tea and cakes. She would never in a million years suggest we do that, so why is she doing it with him? What has he got that I haven't? I try, I really do, but it's never enough. I'm at my wits' end, to the point where things only make sense when I am here."

"And what would you do if he were here?" I replied.

"I'd kill him!" Came Pork Chop's stone-cold response.

"So there's your answer," I said. "Kill him."

***

"Pull over, just over there on the right," I say. Pork Chop squints curiously as he brings the car to a stop and kills the headlights. "Do you know where we are?"

"We're at his house, aren't we?" He replies, his voice cracking ever so slightly with nerves – stage-fright as Act One of his debut looms one step closer.

"We certainly are!" I say emphatically. "You okay?"

"Yeah," Pork Chop murmurs, nodding.

"Nervous?" I ask.

"A bit," he replies, all of a sudden looking rather meek.

"Just remember, this is the man you told me about, the man you wanted dead, your sweet Jeanette's special friend, the one she has kept secret for months, who she arranges to meet, week in, week out, come rain or shine. Someone who she chooses to spend her free time with, above you and your kids; someone I'd say she loves very dearly; a love so strong it has all but destroyed your own family,"

I say, stoking the embers that I know will soon rage into a blast furnace of destructive fire. "Remember what the word 'rampage' means?"

"How can I forget?" Pork Chop immediately responds, his voice growing in confidence. "A period of violent and uncontrollable behaviour; moving through a place in a violent and uncontrollable manner."

"Exactly! This is what it has all been leading up to; your adventures in Croatia, Mac's report, the snatch squads, the abductions, the killing, the torture, the training, everything getting you ready for this very moment – your moment of truth – because after this there is no turning back," I say, ensuring my explanation is succinct and energising enough to give him the final push he needs. "So, what you waiting for, soldier? This is your call to arms, *apok*, death to all, no prisoners! Go 'n' get 'em!" Most people believe we have free will, that we all choose our path. For some, the path is clear, and for others, not so much, where every journey has twists and turns that have the potential to alter our course. But it is the choices we make when reaching forks in the road that truly define who we are. Pork Chop is at one such fork. But his path is clear, as long as it is me who guides him; everything prior a practice run to see who prevails – family man or killer. Though technically, if he does choose to enter this man's house, the ensuing act of familicide will make him a serial killer. I look at him as though I'm from mission control – T-minus ten seconds and counting – nine – eight – seven…the clock almost up, the decision for lift-off not yet finalised, Pork Chop shaking out the last of his nerves…six – five – four…huffing and puffing, letting go of those final constraints; a nod and a thumbs-up…three – two – one…then in a flash he's up and out of his seat, the driver's side door opening and shutting, the whole manoeuvre around to the rear of the car one fluid motion as the boot opens and his trusty baseball bat, Old Faithful, is retrieved. It's named after the famous Yellowstone geyser, Pork Chop alludes to its use as a good way to let off steam.

Like Pork Chop, I get out of the vehicle fluidly, the street so quiet you can hear a pin drop. I scan left, then right, for anything or anyone who may disturb us; there's nothing except for the distant echo of traffic washing over our heads like the sound of the sea when you hold a shell to your ear. It is a soothing sound and a familiar sound from my childhood, but not for a nanosecond do I let it lull me into a false sense of security. With the car boot left open, I watch intently as Pork Chop wastes no time, trotting up the front path and across the lawn to the main lounge window, his footsteps light and noiseless. The flickering blue light of the television inside captures his silhouette; a dark, predatory figure of cop turned perp tapping lightly on the glass as he presses his police ID against the pane. I wait by the car to observe, my involvement totally prohibited. Less than a minute later – and much to my surprise, considering it's twelve-thirty, pitch black, and there's a total stranger with a police badge knocking out of the blue – our gullible victim eases the front door open to a whispered "What's wrong, officer?" I hear the instantaneous dull thud of Pork Chop's bat. The man falls without so much as a whimper.

Again, I quickly sweep the street, left, then right, keeping look-out, turning back to watch Pork Chop step over the semi-conscious body and pull it inside. I see him drag his quarry across the letter-box vista of the lounge window only to drop him midway in full view, like a killer in a low-budget flick exploiting his passion, swinging his blunt instrument over and over to splatter the camera lens as if the silver screen is turning red from the inside out.

I know Jeanette's friend has a family: a wife and two children. Like all who die on my watch, I would have learnt their names if I hadn't already deemed them irrelevant, details superfluous to requirements. The family, regardless of names or titles, are sacrificial pawns, no more than a means to an end, useful props to get Pork Chop where I want him. It's cold but necessary. Otherwise, I run the risk of sentiment infiltrating my decisions, and that I cannot have, not at any cost, especially at this stage in proceedings.

Tracking Pork Chop's progress, I watch lights turn on and then ten or fifteen seconds later turn off. Each illumination sheds light on death's ugly face, the face of a madman with bat in hand; no words are exchanged, and no recognition is shown, just a bloody awful end. Looking at my watch, I note it has taken my friend and protégé only a couple of minutes tops to dispatch the rest of this would-be adulterer's family. He leaves the house as unceremoniously as he entered, dumps the baseball bat in the boot, closes it, and jumps into his car to puff a huge sigh of relief. I take another long hard sweep of the street as the monsters in the shadows draw in to clutch the house of death, raising it like a trophy amongst a sea of disappointing mediocrity. I'm still not used to the strange things that stalk me. But I am glad, all the same, that they recognise the effort. Not that they scare me. It's more that I know they could if they so desired.

All I know is, it's better they are my friends than not. Satisfied that no other residents have been disturbed, I leave Pork Chop sitting, staring through the windscreen, holding the steering-wheel with both hands clenched tight, looking absolutely whacked, to soak up the moment and regain his composure. It is a huge step he has just taken, surrendering himself to his inner darkness, but now, as his teacher and mentor, I need to see how well he's performed. Approaching the house, I take out two elasticated polythene shoe covers from my pocket, slide them over my shoes and don a pair of latex gloves before entering to assess the damage. The porch is an untidy mess of both kids' and adults' muddy shoes below a mass of too many coats hung on too few hooks; hardly my minimalist utopia, and a perfect reminder of why family life, and kids especially, should be avoided. Once in the hallway, I turn right into the lounge to see Jeanette's secret friend laid out, her dream lover battered with no features above the lower jaw, the rest of the head a shadowy blur of blood, brain, and clumps of hairy scalp. I switch off the TV at the socket and draw the curtains before going upstairs. His wife lies naked, curled up on the bedroom floor, her skull smashed open, and ribs pulverised into the chest cavity. In the two smaller rear bedrooms, the same horror greets me: A splash of arterial spray across Thomas the Tank Engine wallpaper – My Little Pony in the girl's case – with cranial debris littered over their pillows and bed clothes. Both, by the positioning of their little bodies, were fast asleep at the time of impact. As far as I am concerned, it is a job well done. Pork Chop has passed my test with flying colours. But horror like this, despite its normality to me, terrifies your average western populace. They do not know what to make of it, unable to see the bigger picture and comprehend where all of this is heading. They don't get that men like Pork Chop, dark tourists with a few hours' trigger-time and perhaps a kill or two to their name, dream of bringing the horror back, knowingly or otherwise, as though possessed by a horrid fantasy, wanting to let the true light of day expose their darkness and the stark abnormalities to which they have become accustomed.

    Pork Chop is now a changed man, as am I. We all have to cross over at some stage, and tonight it was his turn to make a friend of horror as I have made a friend of him. To me and my cause, Pork Chop is a hero, my first proper recruit, but all the world will see is a man gone mad, someone who has just bludgeoned a whole family to death for no other reason than one individual's supposed infidelity, an act I think you will agree no normal person would even consider, let alone undertake on a whim. This is the imbalance of horror. No one said it was easy; its oppressive all-or-nothing nature is like an indelible wretchedness that permeates to the core, corrupting good thoughts into bad, turning love into hate and caring into murder, to the point where there is no difference between home-town suburbia and the battlefield; the darkness transforms into addiction, taking control in filling the void conflict leaves, so all you are left with when the craving hits is to relive the moment – in Pork Chop's case, to see and feel the warm splash of blood and brain. Pork Chop often said that adrenaline to him is like manna from heaven. Anything else is superfluous; atrocity is his heroin of choice. But, knowing him like I do, I would have said he is more fetishist than out-and-out killer. The conditions have to be right for him to truly enjoy an optimum experience. Pork Chop embraces my ethos: Why do it unless the moment is going to blow your mind? He likes his bells and whistles; it's what makes the difference!

For the layman I equate it to sex: What would you prefer, the missionary position with no thrills and the lights off, or the eroticism of seamed stockings, high-heels and talking dirty as your partner brings you to orgasm with his or her mouth whilst looking you in the eye?

The art of truly enjoying something is all in the detail.

No wonder Jeanette saw a change in him. Horror not only affects your behaviour in how it corrupts your sense of value, but it also alters your entire appearance, your demeanour, your facial expressions, how you talk, what you say and how you think, till ultimately you are a completely different person altogether. Jeanette could see the difference – it's what my dad sees in me. But what she failed to see was the monster I made, the revised version I sent back; a ticking time-bomb waiting for me to return so I can light the fuse.

You see, Pork Chop is a man who has always struggled with his identity and his role in life with not having a purpose; the family-man-cum-police-detective is a façade shielding a man who knows he is different and is uncomfortable with it. Because he feels different, he needs to prove he is different, to show-off almost, to exhibit the new skills he has learned but at the same time expunge the ghosts of his past. To him it is a way of moving forward, putting his newfound talent, as he interprets it, to good use and justifying his decision to go down this road in the first place.

Personally, I liked that I looked different. I needed no justification. It set me apart, gave me confidence and respect and a standing amongst my peers that had never before existed. Like Pork Chop, it is exactly the reason why I went, and I have tried to instil this belief in him. But unlike Pork Chop, I am sure of my role in life, and I have a clear purpose, two distinct qualities that despite my beginner's luck, have enabled me to rise above the mayhem. For me, there is no looking back and no ghosts to liquidate, and even if there are, they know to keep a low profile. I shut the front door behind me and walk slowly to the car, sweeping from left to right and left again, scanning from house to house and window to window. "Its Green Cross Code road safety for murderers," I remark to myself, smiling, still scrutinising the nearest houses for curtain-twitchers the way a spider feels for the slightest of vibrations and that instant when a fly has been ensnared in its web. But the street, as though stuck in time, is silent and still except for my muted polythene footsteps. I take one final look back at the house of horrors, ticking off yet another important milestone on my journey of discovery as yet another sweep of the street's nooks and crannies concludes there are no flies to be had.

"Come on, let's go." I slide into the Escort's passenger seat. "And take it easy. Less noise the better."

Despite the exhaust's growl, Pork Chop eases us into the night's gloom. We move as discreetly as we are able from suburb to suburb, keeping to side streets and away from main thoroughfares and their invasive traffic cameras.

"Where to now?" Pork Chop asks.

"You can drop me off near town," I say. "But straight after, you are going home. You've a score to settle and a mission to finish. Remember what you signed up for. Tonight's the night!"

"Roger that!" He exclaims, turning from one road into another, each road under the intermittent orange glare of staggered streetlamps, looking much the same. I sit back, thinking *so far so good*, but it's what's next that will truly test my dear Pork Chop.

"Pull over. I can catch a passing taxi from here." I point at a bus lay-by as I scan for security cameras on a neighbouring row of shopfronts. "Okay – all's clear. Remember, once you are done, pack a case with all of your belongings, two if need be, whatever you need to take, and leave no clues regarding where you have been or where you are going. Got that?" Pork Chop nods. "Good. I'll see you on the flip side tomorrow morning outside Slatter's flat. Oh, and one more thing. You remember that story I told you about that colonel chap who took me shooting in his orchard?" Again, Pork Chop nods. "Uh-huh! Sure, I do," he answers.

"Well, just keeping thinking about that orchard when the time comes. Focus and discipline – that's what will get you through the next couple of hours."

I leave the bag of goodies Pork Chop acquired for me in the car, after replacing the tin of coke wraps, I'd taken for the girls. Its contents are safer there than with me, but I take the dossier so I can get up to speed, for tomorrow is already here. I wave him off, slightly anxious, like a proud dad seeing his only son depart for his first day at work. I know things should be okay and will be okay. I have every faith in him. It is one thing to kill four total strangers, regardless of gender or age; however, it is quite another when you are facing your own wife and children with the exact same intentions in mind.

Chapter 8
The Orchard

"I think they are ripe for the picking – that's what I think," I replied, in the hope I sounded just as resolute…

It is the morning I have been waiting for all my life. For today is going to be the day I reveal my plan, with one of its two beneficiaries being a total stranger. It is the variable I haven't been able to fully determine. I just hope Mr Slattery sees it the way I do and that I'm not forced to exercise Plan B, meaning I would have to kill Slatter straight after he declines my offer, and somehow recruit Welsh Neil with his crazy partner, Olivia, breathing down my neck.

Mom got up early to make my breakfast. It was kind of her, but I overslept by half an hour. I make my apologies to Mom, and she tut-tuts as I slurp my hot tea, eating the toast on the fly. Dad is already waiting in his car to drop me off at yet another pub car park. In no time, I have a taxi pick me up. In the ten minutes it takes, I thumb through Slatter's dossier, not so much reading it as going over how I intend to pitch such a wild idea to such a logical and intelligent person.

I get the driver to drop me about a mile from Slatter's flat. I curse the morning chill, the booze, bolstered by my tiredness, not yet worn off. The cool air licks my face and hands till they are cold to the touch, its stark freshness a sobering reminder of spine-tingling dread, the kind I would get on a dawn patrol when wading through the fog, knowing that if I ran into something, I wouldn't know till I was right on top of it. It was a weird mix of pre-bereavement nerves and post-loss shock. With it would come the icy, non-negotiable clutches of death's finality, and feeling its merciless hand drift by brought home the impending doom of one's own demise, as though on every patrol I would, in my mind, confront my own grave, freshly dug, the date on my tombstone yet to be pencilled in. It's hard to explain, but these feelings when they hit – and they can come at any time, any place – are difficult to shake off. This one I blame on the conversation I had with Dad the last time he gave me a lift. All that talk of people dying, with the irony being that the real fighting hasn't even started yet. God help him when it does! I know war is in the offing, but despite the cold and its cruel touch, the thought of my own mortality doesn't alarm me. Instead, it invigorates, exciting my expectation. For me, whether I am to survive the upcoming conflict or not is not the issue. Truth be told, I'd press the button right now and sacrifice it all if I could, and let every metropolis disappear in a global spectacular of blinding light. That would be job done. But I can't! The upcoming war is the best I can hope for. I don't care about myself, of that I am sure, as though everything, whatever the outcome, will be all right. If I am to die, thoughts of Mom crying with Dad alongside her, distraught, both arm in arm as I'm lowered into the ground, don't bother me in the slightest. If anything, their significance only drives me on, a nitro fuel injection of the meanest, most pitiless rage. My parents, like all parents, are weakened by sentimentality. For they and their kind are traditionalists, slaves to family continuity and the indoctrinated modus operandi each generation have been charged with, bettering themselves by definition, the process gradual and hard fought for. Yet I see tradition from a traveller's perspective: The more arduous the journey, regardless of distance, the greater the sense of achievement. It almost sounds religious in that there is no gain without pain. I guess that is why I am not a traditionalist or pious in nature or, for that matter, wholly dependent on family or friends. I have never taken pain personally, nor has it defined any objective as being worth the struggle. Pain for me has always been a sensory and not an emotional experience, hence my tolerance for physical distress. You cut out the emotional and psychological affects and pain, like horror, soaks in as one aberration cancels out the other.

Yes, my body has physical limits. I shout and holler just like anyone else when hurt badly. But I have no fear of it. Pain cannot be used against me to scare or deter, like it can with the vast majority of folks.

If life and its illustrious history have taught us anything, it is that people thrive during adversity. Pain is the subliminal catalyst, as though when our lives get too comfy, we crave upheaval, a new purpose to fight for, a new enemy to defeat. So if fighting is the popular choice, my revolution will have to give people something to fight for; something that will keep all traditionalists and revolutionaries happy – a common enemy; an enemy that doesn't distinguish between sides, that knows no boundaries, just the willingness to overcome and conquer. It's hard to fathom, but in talking to past generations, I've heard no one speak more fondly of life, of how rich and rewarding it can be, than when it has been lived in a time of war, a time when people come together from all walks of life, galvanised in fighting a common threat. It just goes to show, if you threaten an individual, no one cares. But threaten the masses and a nation will rise up in unity.

In World War II it was the Nazi regime, then it was the Soviet Union during the Cold War, and now it is Iraq, which, last year, under the leadership of arch-villain Saddam Hussain, invaded Kuwait; the latest media baddy is threatening our way of life, his weapons of mass destruction grabbing every front page as the Balkans is left to its own devices, smouldering away. The world is changing; the powerbrokers are carving up the global map as they see fit. They say Saddam has WMDs, chemical weapons, nerve gas, phosgene gas and anthrax and intends to use them on neighbouring states. I doubt that. Saddam Hussain is the glue that holds that area of the Middle East together. Take him away and it will be a free-for-all reminiscent of the American Midwest and the white-settlers' rush to claim land supposedly unoccupied and vacant.

Even kids watching old Tom and Jerry cartoons get the principle of painting someone to be bad, but they also understand that the cat, although often depicted as the main troublemaker, isn't always to blame. Which begs the question: Who is?

This is why my revolution will aim to hold everyone to account. I won't tolerate all the smoke-and-mirrors politics, the riddles and deception; our elected officials are no more than third-rate illusionists spinning plates who try to fool us that the plates are still spinning when we know for a fact they're not!

My revolution is going to do away with all that. Gone are the stagnant days of tradition, granddad rights and jobs for the boys. A new day is soon to dawn; a day that will favour the brave and where personal merit will mean everything and only the fittest will survive.

But now I have to focus.

Still tired and hungry, the few hours' sleep and one slice of toast not nearly enough, I pick up a brisk pace and scowl at the overcast sky. *"How dare it be so glum on such a glorious day?"* My inner voice snarls, as if disgusted at the gods for not allowing the sun to shine. With Slatter's dossier tucked safely inside the warmth of my hoodie, I pass an apathetic and languid world waking up; a world whose populace expects their milk, orange juice and daily newspaper to be already waiting on their doorsteps, their hunter-gatherer origins just a vicious rumour of some ancient species they no longer relate to. I glance at their dishevelled attire of ill-fitting pyjamas, moth-eaten dressing gowns and sagging joggers, the sight of pride and purpose long lost reflected in the bottles of last night's empties as they totter to hide the tell-tale evidence in their recycling bins. Sensing my intrusion, they squint back, hung over, their eyes pained, attuning to the light of yet another day of doing as little as possible, each a Luddite of the modern era, reinforcing why A*pok* is so important. God, they need a shake up! Perhaps one day *Apok* will have someone do it for me – *vive la revolution!*

Wandering on in my daydream, I smile at pastures new and wonder if my dear Pork Chop considering my parting advice and lived up to his potential.

***

The 'orchard story' was born out of a recent event, where a colonel of the regional police division invited me to go shooting on his family estate, an ancient, sprawling mishmash of fields, both lush pasture and arable, overlooked by terraced vineyards and punctuated by interconnecting fruit orchards, all neatly separated by centuries-old dry-stone walls and crooked gates. Though I never entered the main house, a splendid example of *opus Francigenum* probably built during the late Gothic period, the place oozed old aristocracy and the arrogance of knowing that, come what may, nothing, not even war, will dare disturb this perfect and established symbol of Croatian nobility. Its impregnable aura, for some reason, reminded me of the Berghof, Hitler's mountain residence in the Bavarian Alps, a tyrant's retreat where other tyrants come to play and form dastardly plots so they will always remain king of their respective castles.

The colonel, at the time of my visit, was certainly king of his castle, and by the afternoon's end I understood why.

Although it came as a shock, I knew the purpose of my visit, or so I thought; it was the summons of an employer who wants to know his best performing employee better, curious to know who this guy is and whether the stories are really true – is he as good as they say? But just like the test facility in the Cotswolds and my experience as Candidate 29A in the Welsh Black Mountains, it was a test to see how far I had actually come and a chance to let the powers that be see what Croatia had taught me. In a nutshell, my time with the newly formed Croatian Defence Force had taught me how to survive and how to make it back from each patrol when others didn't. But the colonel already knew that.

What he didn't know was why. Why did this young man with no prior military experience survive an ambush when everybody else within a ten-metre radius was literally shot to pieces? The colonel's emissary who personally delivered the invitation spelt it out. "There were eighteen of you in the patrol spread out over approximately thirty metres from the man on point to the rear guard."

"That sounds about right," I replied.

"It's after midnight; you are using night-vision to navigate your way along the bank, a route your comrades have used many times; then someone trips a flare, and your section immediately comes under fire from the other side of the river."

"So what?" I remarked.

"So you should have been killed – that's what! You were caught in the middle of a firefight which lasted five, maybe six, seconds. The enemy fired something in the region of eight hundred, to a thousand rounds into a concentrated area where you were standing, fully exposed with no time to run and nowhere to hide. Those around you were cut to pieces. How many was it – nine? Ten?"

"Something like that," I confirmed.

"Where you didn't receive so much as a single scratch. In fact, our investigators found a patch of untouched earth, an effigy in the shape of a human figure, directly behind where you were standing. I can't explain it, just like the investigators can't and those who were there can't. And God knows we have asked them. Our intelligence units have even picked up radio chatter from the Serbs about a bulletproof man who stares death in the face. It seems you made quite an impression on both sides. This is why the colonel wants to meet you." I remember the opulent crunch the Mercedes' tyres made on the twisting mile-long gravel drive leading up to the main house. If I close my eyes now, I can hear it, the exquisite noise of *old money*, its infectious din awash throughout my senses like a relentless looping message…join us…join us…join us…join us…join us…*Why not?* I thought; the car's interior was a microcosm of absolute finery, a taster of a world I wish for, of soft leather that perfumed the air, accelerating one's ambition like a glass elevator through the roof as I watched myself climb the social ladder nearly to the top in the time it took to reach the drive's end. But I also noticed that when the car passed the gates to enter the estate, the driver, whom I hadn't taken as the religious type, crossed himself and mumbled a private word of reassurance. His demeanour was nervous, jittery almost, as though he expected something bad to happen.

I didn't get that foreboding the driver obviously felt, though I certainly took the visit as a gamble. Everything you do in Croatia is! Long gone are the state's guarantees: Personal safety and welfare are as arbitrary as its policing. But once there, on the estate's grounds, I felt the randomness of destiny replaced by a new set of house rules; rules that had fixed odds of success and failure, and a defining path instead of having to tread your own, not knowing if you are right or wrong.

I liked it, for I had nothing to lose, unlike my driver, who I guess had.

Two men were waiting for me as the car drew up outside the main house; both were smartly dressed in country attire. One had a rifle slung over his shoulder, the other a gun-belt and holster. The chauffeur, though very professional and polite, stopped for not a second longer than he had to; just enough for me to get out and shut the car door behind me. As the car sped away, the two men, whose broken English was more than adequate, greeted me, standing to attention, then bowing courteously when I got out of the car. We engaged in friendly conversation, discussing the fine weather and the beautiful setting of the estate, as they escorted me to an adjacent courtyard, where an elegant table for two was set alfresco. Its germane beauty was perfectly positioned at the stone floor's focal point, where all contours seemed to meet, drawing your line of sight to a smooth, almost marble-like centrepiece resembling a Maltese cross. The early afternoon sun gleamed off the table's immaculate silverware. The courtyard was like a Teutonic horseshoe, skirted on three sides by a pillared arch colonnade, the shaded walkway it protected regularly punctuated by dark stained glass and an occasional darker doorway of deepest brown and black iron bracing. Despite the pomp and ceremony, I admired the colonel's sense of the theatrical. To me, it echoed respect and was far from what I had expected.

In seconds, the colonel appeared with an arm outstretched. He shook me firmly by the hand, grabbing my shoulder. "Thank you for coming," he said, beaming.

"The pleasure is all mine," I told him. Our personalities gelled like old friends reuniting after a winter break.

I couldn't believe how well we got on. He was more than twice my age, if not three times, but the gap was immaterial. It was as though we were father and son catching up on old news. The conversation flowed effortlessly. He talked of his history, being educated first in Germany, then England to carry on the family name, and he told me of his love for all things American. Bathed in sunlight, he confessed his cowboy addiction over a light lunch of figs and goat's cheese wrapped in Parma ham followed by fillet beef carpaccio, appropriately washed down with a vintage Provence Cru Classé rosé.

"Do you know anything about wine?" He asked. I shrugged.

"Not much! I know what I read on the label."

"Well" – the colonel continued – "take this wine, for example. It is a blend of Grenache, Mourvedre, Syrah and Cinsault grapes. A method known as saignée is used to make it, which involves bleeding off roughly ten percent of the juice from red grapes during the winemaking. It is this drained juice that is then fermented into rosé wine. All quality rosé wines are made this way, each a work of art, complex and beautiful; a wine as underestimated as it is understated; a wine of honour and respect, as I, at my table, honour and respect you." As much as I graciously lapped up the colonel's high opinion, I knew it was an exercise in sweetening the palate before introducing the bitter dessert. But I didn't mind. I went there with my eyes open, already knowing there's no such thing as a free lunch.

After we had eaten, the colonel led me via one of the doorways through a long livery stable, boasting of its pedigree; the interior of high stone arches, ornate carpentry and intricate ironwork was as impressive and imposing as any description in a Victor Hugo novel. It was truly jaw-dropping except there were no horses to be seen; no hay, no pitchforks, no tack, no saddles, nothing; just a very beautiful stable, albeit bereft of anything equine. As we neared the large open doors at the far end, the two men who had initially greeted me were waiting by a long table on which three rifles lay on cushioned foam, each neatly placed and polished so they gleamed in the sunlight.

"And what is more American than their guns?" The colonel boomed as he introduced me to a mere snippet of his collection. "I thought these would do for this afternoon," he added, picking up each rifle in turn. He handed one over, something he called a 'plinker', implying it was an American term. "You can carry that," he said, going on to explain the rifle itself. Because it had a resin stock, it was very light, even with a scope and silencer fitted, and therefore very accurate due to there being virtually no recoil.

"Perfect for small prey," he roared. I wondered what prey he was referring to, taking nothing for granted. As the colonel chattered on, he described the specification of the rifle I had been given, a Ruger 10/22 semi-automatic, the 10 denoting its magazine capacity and 22 its .22 Long Rifle calibre. His exuberance got the better of him as he went on to explain with cringe worthy enthusiasm, I guess the way only diehard Americanophiles can, the details of the other two rifles. To me they looked typically Wild West, a cowboy's must-have, both sporting an under-lever action; the kind of law enforcement film prop John Wayne was never without. But to the colonel they were the dearest of relations. He adored his guns. The one he had slung over his shoulder was a Marlin .357 Magnum/.38 Special Model 1894C, a gun he said he once took to Africa on safari to hunt wildebeest. It had a scope attached. He said this was possible due to the Marlin's side ejector. The other, which had no sling and was therefore cradled like a baby, was a Rossi .44 Magnum carbine with a 16-inch barrel, which ejected its spent shell casings via the top of the receiver, hence no scope, just its original open sights. Later I discovered the Rossi wasn't as American as I was led to believe. The colonel admitted it to be of Brazilian origin, made by a company called Taurus.

I liked the colonel's obsessive attention to detail; we had that in common, that giddy school-boy fixation, as well as admitting the truth like he did about the Rossi. He knew from his background check that I was an honest, straight-talking kind of fellow who took no bullshit yet knew how to toe the line, and that a lie, however insignificant, would eventually surface and possibly discredit any further dialogue between us. It was another show of respect, of wanting to make the right impression.

But this was a working lunch, and, putting our familiarities aside, I decided to keep quiet and go with the flow, following my host's lead as instructed. "Put these on," he said, handing me a pair of tiger-striped overalls, which, without question, I put over my clothes. I removed my shoes to don a more suitable pair of rugged boots. "You're looking good," the colonel added with a wink, almost breaking out into a "yee-hah" and slapping his thigh.

"May I ask where we are going?" I enquired.

"We are going on safari," he replied, smiling. "Is that okay with you?"

"Sure!" I answered, not knowing if he meant a safari as in hunting animals, hence the rifles, or a country walk over the hills. But if it was just a walk, why take the rifles – or were the grounds of his estate that dangerous? The colonel had me confused, but by then my attitude was that if I was in for a penny, I was in for a pound. We must have walked for an hour or more before coming across a small wooded copse that sat on the crest of a long sloping orchard that ran for a hundred metres or so down to a track that traversed the visible panorama.

"Be quiet," the colonel whispered, ushering me with a waving arm to lower myself. "They are here as I hoped."

"Who's here?" I whispered back, both of us now stooping as we reached the orchard's boundary wall.

I wondered what he was looking at. *Is he mistaken?* But still the colonel insisted, making me think he had some kind of eagle-like awareness to spot whatever it was, because for the life of me, I couldn't. With eyes like saucers, I scoured frantically.

"Look! Follow the line of my arm" – he said, pointing into the heart of the orchard – "about halfway down. Do you see them? Use the scope on your rifle."

I looked and looked, sweeping each line of trees, hoping for a glimpse of what he saw, scanning for pheasant, guinea fowl or maybe wild boar. Unsuccessful, I altered my position several times before realising what the colonel had meant by 'small prey'.

Approximately halfway down the slope of trees towards the orchard's centre, four boys, the eldest no more than ten years old, were picking fruit; two of them were up separate trees, clinging on for dear life as they each dropped their precious spoils to a boy below, who in turn placed the fruit into a nearby basket.

"They are like pigeon," the colonel snarled under his breath. "They do not look a threat but give them time and they will clear this entire orchard. And though you cannot see from up here, at the bottom of the orchard is an old, disused farm track, once used to access this side of the estate. It heads south to a road which links the two closest towns. Down there, out of sight, will be the dastardly man who uses this track to trespass on my land and bring these pests. He knows not to enter, but he does, year on year. No one else dares except him. I give to the local communities. I give a lot. But he is a greedy pig and renowned for it; someone who is never happy, who always takes more than his fair share. In my eyes, he is nothing but a coward, because he uses children. He sits there while they work, taking all the risk. He knows what I will do if he is ever caught again," the colonel explained in a hushed voice, as if forewarning me of his wrath.

"So why don't you?" I replied, "We've got rifles! We could do it now; march on down and turn him over to the police."

"The law is no good here. Like everywhere, it favours the small-time criminal. He will get a fine and then return with more children. His type always does, like a cornered rat that, despite all your best efforts at trying to get rid of it, will disappear for a day or two only to pop up when you least expect it, more determined than ever." The colonel was ardent in his explanation.

"So, what are you going to do?" I asked.

"'So what' indeed, my friend," the colonel whispered, upbeat. "He knows what he is doing. He is goading me, seeing if I have what it takes. To get where he is, he would have had to cut the lock off the gate and pass the 'Private Land – Do Not Enter' signs and the new one that states, 'Trespassers are at risk of being shot!' He understands," the colonel said, spelling out his intentions.

That was the moment I learned what he meant about 'going on safari' and what the rifles were really for.

"But they're kids," I replied, knowing full well what the colonel wanted me to do, but not the reason why.

"They are pests!" The colonel exclaimed, trying to keep his voice down. "Your Ruger has a full magazine – ten shots! I want you to shoot the children."

"You're serious?" I asked.

"Very!" The colonel replied. "Two shots per child. Wound them in the lower quarters if possible, so they are not killed outright."

And there laid out before me, as clear as day, was the crux of the day's activities, a test of scruples where I had to hit four moving targets with ten bullets, their nature to incapacitate rather than liquidate. But then again, I should have known better. The colonel wasn't interested in incapacitating anyone; he wanted things to stop, not be put on hold.

"Back home we call stealing fruit from trees 'scrumping'," I said.

"Did you, do it?" The colonel probed.

"Of course! We all did as kids. It was considered a rite of passage, gaining your stripes. We saw it as harmless fun, not stealing as such. Anyway, there was more than enough fruit to go around. They weren't gonna miss it."

"But to me this is not harmless fun. This is a matter of honour and a sworn adversary taking liberties where it is forbidden to do so. 'Scrumping', as you call it, maybe harmless fun in England, but in Croatia it is theft, plain and simple; once a thief, always a thief," the colonel spat. "Like it says in the book of Mark: If thy right hand offend thee, cut it off."

"Or alternatively shoot them!" I quipped sarcastically.

"Exactly!" The colonel insisted resolutely. "What do you think?"

"I think they are ripe for the picking – that's what I think," I replied, hoping I sounded just as resolute. But, bluffing aside, I still had to shoot the kids, because how else was I going to make it off the colonel's estate alive!

Bullets swerving around me from a distance is one thing, but from point blank I hadn't tried and didn't want to try.

"I am glad you think so. We are not so different, you and I" – commented the colonel – "But know this: Everyone in life has choices, even children. You know the story of *Oliver Twist?*" I nodded. "It is just like that. Down there in the vehicle, you have Fagin, a loathsome reptile who is too lazy and too much of a coward to steal himself; that's why he gets children to do it for him, picking my prize plums as though they are picking money straight from my pockets. Those children also know only too well that they are trespassing, that they are stealing, and yet they do it regardless. The youth of today care little for the consequences of their actions, and it is a disease that's getting worse. There are no innocents in that orchard. This you will understand in the months to come," the colonel whispered, his tone hard and his words more prophetic than I realised at the time.

"But surely if we just took out Fagin you would achieve the same goal," I said. The children's deaths could be deemed by some as unnecessary; that is to say, a step too far.

"What? And leave his marauding brood, once trained, to keep on thieving – I think not! Young thieves grow up into older thieves, who in turn train young thieves; the cycle never ends. They are a cancer, a disease so cunning they have learnt to slip through the cracks in society to spread unnoticed like rats running through the sewers." The colonel paused; his growling tone was vehement to the point where saliva flailed from his mouth. Aware of it, he wiped his sleeve over his lower face, then grabbed me by the arm. "When I studied in England, there was a phrase: If you can't beat them, join them. If the thieves and degenerates of this land are training their successors, I am going to train mine. This is the lesson you have to learn, but with a twist. It is why I have brought you here. You see, this problem isn't something that can be surgically removed, some clearly defined malignancy to neatly cut away. That time has passed. And long gone are the analogies of cutting off the head to cure the headache. I'm afraid, as a nation, we have reached our last resort – we need to destroy the host completely until there is nothing but ash – that is where we are! You have to see this as a war; a war on theft and the perpetrators of theft, a blow dealt to those who seek to destroy our way of living. This country needs to be cleansed, as does the world. And though I don't have it in me to achieve the latter, you and I can surely start the process in this orchard."

"Look, I've no qualms about what you are asking. Is it regrettable? Yes. Could it have been avoided? No. It's human nature. I see it every hour of every day. Man will always fuck over his or her fellow man. Our species can't help it; it's who we are. But at your request, I'll do it. I understand your argument. It's just that I wanted to hear it explained," I said, appeasing my host's sense of pride as I tried to rationalise what I was about to do. "You see, in my country there is an expression: Possession is nine tenths of the law, meaning that ownership is easier to maintain if one has possession of something and difficult to enforce if one does not; the phrase is born out of the term 'possession' satisfying nine out of eleven factors that constitute 'absolute ownership' – a bullshit decree from a bullshit era. It isn't even law. I've always despised this rule of thumb, how the weak adhere to its hypocrisy and that it is always the troublemakers in society who take full advantage of it. Like you, I have had enough. Don't worry; leave Fagin and the kids to me." Feeling somewhat justified in what I had to do, I slipped over the crumbling dry-stone wall and crawled into the orchard commando style. Approximately twenty metres in, I kept to a prone position in the camouflaging grass and sighted the first of the children via the Ruger's scope; a boy precariously balanced on a branch that bowed under his meagre weight. Zeroing the scope's crosshairs on one of the boy's legs just below the knee, I pulled back the bolt to chamber a round, thumbed off the safety and then fired. The single shot spat like a puff of angry air. He fell with a yelp, hitting a branch and then another on his way to the ground. But before he even landed, I had the next boy in my sights. With long wavy hair way past his shoulders, he stood with his back to me about ten metres beyond his falling friend, below the next tree in line. Again, I took careful aim, targeting the lower legs, but just as I was about to fire, the boy turned at the noise of his friend falling, just in time to witness the awful impact at the tree's base. Caught in that split second of indecision – seeing his mate fall, who now lay dazed in a crumpled heap amongst a shower of floating leaves, with the other boy on the ground frozen in sheer disbelief, standing over the fallen kid – I knew he was going to run. It didn't matter why, whether out of pure fright or to raise the alarm and fetch help. All that mattered was making the shot, so instinctively I tapped the trigger twice, feeling the barrel slightly rise on the second shot. I didn't know exactly where I'd hit him; the boy collapsed instantly out of sight, though to my immense relief I could hear him squealing amongst the knee-high smattering of meadow grass that grew beyond the shade underneath the tree canopies. Still alive, thank God! This left two: The boy nearest on the ground, who, after shaking off his initial scare, was now tending to his injured friend, and a remaining fruit picker still in his respective tree panicking to get down.

The boy tending to his friend I got when he was kneeling, slap-bang centre of the right calf. The one in the tree I shot in the hand as he hung from a branch attempting to drop to safety. He hit the ground awkwardly as he landed.

With my every sense preoccupied, devoted only to the task at hand, I was totally unaware that the colonel had crept up alongside my position. I sprang to my feet with a start when he bent down to tap me on the shoulder.

"Good! Now take this," the colonel ordered as he snatched the Ruger from my grasp to hand me the Marlin. "It's Fagin's turn. And whatever you do, keep low. I'll see to the pests," he added as we skulked in the grass, crouching from tree to tree until we reached three screaming kids, the fourth clearly audible in the long grass where I had seen him fall. Unsure about what came next, the colonel waved me on down the grassy slope. "Go! Go!" he shouted. "Shoot the driver! Shoot the driver!"

The orchard, despite being one of the oldest on the entire estate, was typical of its ilk in that it was planted in a precise grid system, with avenues of plum trees running in perfect alignment the length and breadth of the walled gradient. With only one thing on my mind and the colonel's instructions ringing loudly in my ears, I ran down the grassy slope hunched and low on the blindside of one such row, the modest tree-trunks shielding me like an organic woodland divider till the gaps could hide me no longer. Using a tree for cover and its naturally formed V where the main trunk had split into two to rest and steady my aim, I kept my distance at least thirty metres from the only vehicle I could see parked on the track, a beat-up and very dirty Renault van. The vehicle was facing me, and, remembering it would be left-hand drive, through the dusty driver's-side window I made out a white-bearded figure. I settled the crosshairs at what I thought would be chest height and central on the person inside. Pushing the rifle's under-lever down, I watched inside the receiver, pulling it up slowly to check a round was being chambered. The driver's door suddenly opened. Thinking I had been rumbled, in knee-jerk fashion I fired instantaneously, deafened by the rifle's thunderous report as the driver's-side window shattered and a body fell half in, half out of the vehicle. With the door preventing me from taking a second clear shot, I broke cover and walked forward, chambering another round as though I was a seasoned ranch-hand seeing off a band of marauding cattle rustlers, only to find an old man already dead, his clothes bloodied, and his face squashed into the dirt; a man who reminded me of the colonel if life had taken a less prosperous path. And so, I shot the old man again for being just that – second rate; a head shot, not to make sure he was dead, but more out of a gratuitous sense of the macabre and to see a head come apart, since I hadn't used a .357 calibre weapon before. Its awesome reputation almost precipitated my urge. I left the old man where he was and retraced my steps towards the tree to collect the spent shell casing I had ejected. I pocketed the second from the rifle to be on the safe side. I had seen too many murder mysteries to leave such incriminating evidence in the hands of someone I had only just met. I hiked back up through the drooping boughs laden with purple fruit. I remember taking my time getting back to the colonel, taking a moment's solace in listening to my boots brushing against the long spindly grass and a soft breeze that sounded like gentle waves lapping. The odd bee buzzed across my path, wiping its brow in preparation for yet another busy summer now that the orchard's plentiful bounty was all theirs. The orchard was truly picturesque, its charm mesmerising, definitely worthy of Constable's keen eye or Monet's deft touch, for it held an outstanding natural beauty all of its own; the way the light picked out and accentuated both new and old, the colours like a visual history of God's perfection, made complete by the waft of lush air that circulated the most wonderful fragrant smells. It was a magical place, one of purity and innocence; the kind of place where, if you closed your eyes and imagined, you would see a young Disney prince proposing to his beloved or the von Trapp's enjoying a family picnic, if it hadn't been marred by such a horrific event. And now, just like Eden, it had been spoiled forever. But if my experience of using the .357 Marlin was a pivotal moment, the .44 Rossi was a beast by comparison. It was like trying to control a cannon after you had cut your teeth on a peashooter; the recoil shook me to the very core, and its mighty blast was like God's damnation delivered in person. Never before or since has a gun scared me so much. But as I reached the colonel, he literally threw me the rifle. "Now finish them off," he barked as he took back the Marlin and slung it over his shoulder.

    I said nothing. There was no point. The time for talk had lapsed; the colonel wanted decisive action, not lily-livered hesitation. This was it, my moment of truth; the start of a revolution, and not a single second to waste. *It is now or never. Do you have it, or don't you?* All of it I could hear running through the colonel's mind. On my return, he already had them sitting, albeit slumped over, in a line approximately three feet apart. I noted from the scuffed ground and the boys' renewed anguish that each had been forcibly dragged to a sunnier, less shaded spot and beaten into unwavering submission. The colonel stood over them, repeating 'Ostani mirno ili umri' – stay still or die. The boys were scared witless into blind obedience. They lay dithering as though it was deepest winter, still clutching at their wounds with heads bowed, sobbing 'Mama i Tata' – Mommy and Daddy – in the hope they were coming to save them. I remember humming the tune *"If you go down to the woods today"* to keep myself on track. I had no intention of faltering. I knew I was in the sights of one of the colonel's assistants, if not both. And just like that, I took a deep breath and got on with it. Just as I did with the Marlin, I pushed the under-lever of the Rossi down and slowly pulled it up again, looking into the receiver to check the huge .44 Magnum round was being chambered.

"Hold it very tight into the shoulder," the colonel advised as he began to walk away. When I asked him where he was going, he replied, "This is between you and them, my boy! You and them! I'll be over here waiting. And shoot downhill! You don't want any ricochets." His instruction was like that of a past master, and I took up position instantly, walking around the snivelling kids till I could see the van in the distance.

"Gore! Gore! Na koljena" – *Up! Up! On your knees* – I shouted. "Sada! Na koljena" – *Right now! On your knees* – I yelled again, grabbing each kid in turn under the armpit to help them up. Except that the long-haired kid on the end to my left, who, it turned out, was in fact a girl, couldn't, due to my prior inaccuracy with the .22, which had clipped her in the right thigh and buttock. So, I left her lying face down, crying into the dirt. Everything up to that point seemed so straightforward, but what the colonel had neglected to say was anything about the sheer power that the .44 Magnum cartridge produces. He'd said to hold the rifle tight, but I wasn't prepared for such a thumping jolt of recoil and booming discharge. I had felt nothing like it; an AKM on full auto was no more than a sedate Sunday morning stroll in the park compared to this monster. My ears rang on each pull of the trigger, disorientating my senses to the point where I needed a rest between shots, as if temporarily knocked out of kilter. For the three boys who knelt, despite their tearful protests, the bullets hit like a freight train hurtling straight to hell with an earth-shattering noise to match. Measuring five long paces, I stood and aimed for the centre of the sternum, unprepared in that I was naive, perhaps a little full of myself after using the .357 Marlin, if I thought I was ready for the rifle's untamed ferocity. As I pulled the trigger, the Rossi's butt pounded my shoulder, the orange muzzle-flash of flame fleeting, the roaring boom thunderous, my head swimming as I witnessed the phenomenal force, I had unleashed lift each boy up off their knees to slam their little bodies so hard against the ground that they bounced back up at least a foot before coming to rest. The third in line bounced so far, he flipped onto his front to roll a full three-sixty degrees. Each sorry face, despite all having initially closed their eyes, gawped a fixed expression of complete and utter devastation, with slack, open jaws and saucer-like gazes that bore testament to the .44 hand of God that had just swiped them into the black world beyond. The girl, however, had managed to crawl and haul herself up between the fork in a split tree-trunk nearby. I walked over and knelt before her. I smiled and she smiled back as I angled the rifle's barrel towards her chin, the blast taking the wee waif clean off her feet, the body thrown through the fork in the tree to land a few feet on the other side. An array of cranial debris pitter-pattered around me like thick rain. It was weird, seeing the girl fly back with her head blown wide apart. I was no stranger to killing. I had killed before on sniper duty and in the heated exchange of firefights whilst out on patrol. But they were all combatants, shot from a distance at night. You never saw them close up, injured or dying; they just fell down out of sight. It was not like the orchard in the cold light of day, where I was able to feel the range of emotion and nagging doubt creeping in, and they certainly weren't children. That was new to me, a game changer, the lesson the colonel told me I must learn. I had never felt so detached, so bereft of feeling, of everything. It felt as though I was the long arm of Death itself, my thoughts, and decisions an extension of its cruel desire, a fury that knew no bounds, and it hammered home the realisation that if you think you have a grasp on horror, that you know what it looks like and feels like – you don't! As many veterans continue to tell me, "Things can always get worse, and in war they often do." I remember the boys, how they lay crumpled, a clean hole from sternum to exploded vertebrae that stuck out like jagged spines, the girl spreadeagled, flat on her back, her soft face deformed by the heavy bullet and the phenomenal scorching muzzle blast that had ploughed through the tip of the lower jaw up into the nasal cavity to exit, blowing the top of her head off. The features of who she once was, were unrecognisable. The middle of the face churned inside out, skull fragments dangling on flaps of skin entangled in a matted auburn mess of hair, blood, and brain.

"You done?" I heard the colonel shout, his loud voice just audible above the ringing tinnitus.

"Yeah…I'm done!" I replied as I took stock of what I had done. Again, I picked up the spent shell casings, my trust in the colonel still far from assured.

Mesmerised by their little bodies, I stood there, blinded by a moment of singularity in which I caught up with myself at having done the unthinkable and crossed the defining line that transforms the abyss into somewhere more familiar, as though all of a sudden, I could see in the dark, and the monsters of fear, chaos and wrath, who always used to plague my dreams, welcomed me with open arms.

If you can't beat them join them!

So that's what he meant by a lesson with a twist…"Come on. It's time to go. My housekeeper will have tea ready soon," the colonel shouted, waving me over. "And don't worry about the mess. I will have my men clear it up later," he added, probably to emphasise how cheap life really is in war and how soon the dead are forgotten, their bodies nothing but anonymous litter after the event. I could see I had made the colonel happy. For his work was also done, and with it, a new protégé was born. In Pork Chop's case, I used the 'orchard story' as a motivational tool, a fable of sorts to get my point across, the tale as anecdotal as it was meant to be inspirational, highlighting the importance of focus and discipline and how key they are to achieving what may seem the most insurmountable of tasks, despite the pain and hardship they will inevitably bring.

***

Reaching Pork Chop's car, I open the passenger door and unceremoniously dive in, slamming it shut with equal vigour.

"How'd it go?" I ask, bypassing the usual pleasantries.

"Not bad." He doesn't break from staring out of his windscreen towards Slatter's flat.

"Is that it? Is that all you're gonna say?" I'm chomping at the bit for details.

"I've just killed my wife and children. What do you want me to say?" Pork Chop answers, though in sombre reflection, he adds, "It went like clockwork – it was just how I had envisaged it!"

He's right, of course, – don't push the issue. It will come of its own accord. I'm just glad he found the grit and determination to go through with it. There is no going back now. I've got him! Not that Pork Chop had a choice if he wants to start afresh. His family was the barrier holding him back; a living, breathing and most of all visible reminder of the awful lie he had been living for the past fifteen years, since he and Jeanette first met. But the premise he had first sold me of being overworked, undervalued, and disillusioned, compounded by a promiscuously minded wife, was only a part of why he wound up in such a godforsaken dilemma. Pork Chop had admitted that if it was just that, he could have learned to forgive her licentious nature. Yes, it would have been difficult, but in his mind, it would have been manageable; anything to keep the status quo. Yet as the years went by, a nagging doubt grew to fester, haunting his nights and days till he could bear it no more. I wonder who first coined the phrase 'curiosity killed the cat'; could it have been the same person who came up with 'the straw that broke the camel's back'?

In Pork Chop's case, it was three straws that snapped his spine clean in two. Curiosity was his downfall; in the same way, its burden was eventually his salvation. In spirit, Pork Chop and Jeanette had left one another long ago. Insanity is a funny thing to bequeath a man, but that is exactly what Jeanette did, though it was done unwittingly; the psychosis was drip-fed during every family activity – at breakfast, at evening meals, days out, birthdays, Christmases; whatever the day and whatever they did, the nightmare was there, growing hour by hour, day by day, till inevitably he reached rock-bottom, a stage he had to face before he was able to start rebuilding himself.

What Pork Chop told me on that dark night by the Danube, he said quite categorically: "No other living person, bar Jeanette, knows about this; not her sister, her mom or dad, her closest friend, any of her past lovers it might concern; no one." As far as he was concerned, Jeanette thought she had been successful all these years in keeping it to herself, a series of secrets so bad she dare not share them, skilfully tip-toeing around the dreaded dominos for fear that if one tipped, it would lead to a discovery, an irreversible catalyst that would set off a chain reaction of total destruction, which is ironic considering the path her secrets helped create was her own demise. Another hurdle towards my own version of Armageddon, successfully cleared.

About a year ago, Pork Chop was a man on the edge with nowhere to turn, plagued by demons that were both fantasy and real, demons that were taking him to the brink of murder and suicide. He was questioning his strength as a father and the very legitimacy of his own children; he was drowning in paranoia, where nothing made sense anymore. He was a desperate man seeking desperate solutions, obsessing over his suspicions till one day, as a shot to nothing, he collated DNA from each of his three children and sent the samples, together with his own DNA for comparison, to three independent laboratories to test for paternity, so no two children were tested at the same test facility, despite knowing the impact of what a negative result would do to him. But never in the sum of all his worst fears did he anticipate that all three would come back negative. The tests in each case clearly concluded 'Excluded as the biological father', with the probability of paternity at 0%. It was at that point Pork Chop hit rock-bottom. Needless to say, he was crushed by the news. It broke him, both body and soul. The man whose mind was once thought unbreakable was reduced to the most delicate glass; a mind that had been dropped from the top of a thirteen-storey tower block onto the hardest concrete and left for me to sweep up the pieces; a million, trillion shards of varying distress that, when glued back together, were never quite the same. As the saying goes, the damage had been done; there was no going back. But like all damage, it is just part of a bigger and even more vicious circle.

Sitting in Pork Chop's car, I pretend to look over the dossier, waiting for him to break the silence.

"I did it!" he whispers. "I actually fucking did it!"

"Did it meet your expectations?" I ask, almost salivating in anticipation of his reply.

"I'm free" – he says, turning to look at me – "like the heaviest of weights has been lifted off my shoulders, as though I am reborn to live my life how it should have been, with no house, no wife, no kids, no anything except what I have in this car…including you, my friend."

"I'm proud of you," I reply, shaking his hand – the hand of a winner, of a survivor, of someone who knows what it is like to make a friend of horror and then have horror embrace you as an equal.

"Thanks. That means a lot coming from you. If only you could have seen me. I was magnificent." Pork Chop gloats like a Cheshire cat who has just inherited a cream factory.

"So…indulge me." I gloat back, waiting for my psycho protégé to impress like it is his final graduation.

"I used Suxy, just like you taught me," he starts.

"Succinylcholine: The mark of a professional," I remark, and Pork Chop smiles; a torturer's fail-safe when in for the long haul. It is a depolarising neuromuscular blocker that renders its recipient temporarily paralysed while allowing them to be conscious and able to feel pain.

"Dosed 'em up while they were asleep – intramuscular injections, three to four milligrams per kilo of body weight – it was pure textbook stuff," Pork Chop explains in a calm, monotonous fashion. "Like I said, I felt free for the first time in years. It's funny, I thought she wouldn't be able to move so much as an eyelash, but when I explained to Jeanette how Danny was in fact a private investigator working undercover for me, the years of insinuation, the betrayal I always felt but didn't have the stomach to confront, and, of course, the paternity tests, I was convinced I saw her eyes slightly widen to glare, the way she always did when about to take the moral high ground." Pork Chop pauses to smirk, gently shaking his head at the irony of how Jeanette never missed an opportunity to turn the blame on him, as though it was her favourite pastime. "Then, after the big reveal, I arranged them in one room so they could see each other for one last time, zip-tied their hands and feet, and one by one wrapped their heads in cling-film, finishing them off with a hammer and screwdriver."

"How? I'm intrigued." I'm curious about the destructive finale to what seemed like a good clean operation.

"Remember that doctor guy we once saw performing a lobotomy, hammering that long silver spike into the tear duct?" I nod, racking my brains to trawl through countless torture sessions, vaguely recalling the doctor in question. "Well, just like that, but without the finesse," Pork Chop continues in a nonchalant tone, smiling as though he doesn't quite know what he is smiling at.

"Did the orchard story help?" I ask for future reference.

"A bit…" he replies, drifting into deep contemplation, "but now I have an 'orchard story' all of my own, a legacy to pass down to my successor when the time comes."

"Yes, you have" – I say, reassuringly – "and you've earned it! Now we need to deal with Slatter and get him on board. You ready?"

"Too right I'm ready! You just try and stop me," Pork Chop exclaims.

"As if I would," I joke.

"And if he refuses to go along?" Asks Pork Chop.

"Then we kill him and move onto Plan B."

"As long as your Plan B doesn't involve any paedophiles," Pork Chop snarls.

"No, it doesn't!" I fire back.

"Good! 'Cos I absolutely fucking loathe paedophiles!"

Don't we all! But in Slatter's case, it is needs must, and I need Pork Chop on his best behaviour in order to pull this off. I have the bait – Mandy and her sister – the venue – Welsh Neil's old flat – and an accomplice – my dear Pork Chop. Now all I need is a manager of operations, an architect of sorts who will design and run the infrastructure of my upcoming project.

Chapter 9
Slatter's Offer

Let's just say your refusal at this stage is not an option you want to choose, considering we have in good faith revealed our hand, so to speak. Surely, Mr Slattery, you are not going to betray that good faith…

Pork Chop has parked his car in a pub car park across the road from Slatter's flat; the two of us sit, watch, wait, the tension palpable. Nine-thirty comes and goes; my OCD kicks in like a back-up generator to ratchet up a host of niggling anxieties. Growing fidgety, I dig my fingers into the palms of my hands, trying not to grind my teeth, as though I'm walking a tightrope and have encountered my first serious wobble, my sense of occasion a stickler for punctuality, with any deviation sending that unwelcome hit of butterflies racing through my abdomen. If nine-thirty has been agreed, nine-thirty it must be! "C'mon, it's twenty-five to, for God's sake. What we waiting for?" I exclaim, like a petulant brat being held back from opening his presents on Christmas morning.

"Be patient," Pork Chop replies. "Anyway, in the original brief you did say 'any time after nine-thirty'. There they are. That's who we've been waiting for." He points.

"Who's that?" I snap, watching a middle-aged couple emerge from the property, my impatience hurrying them on as they fuss about their car, putting shopping bags in the boot and wiping the night's precipitation from the windows.

"That's the Turners. They own the property. Mr and Mrs Turner are Michael Slattery's landlords. About this time every Saturday, give or take ten minutes, they do their weekly shop at Sainsbury's, half a mile away. Over the past several weeks I've timed them. Their shortest shopping trip was one hour and twenty minutes. So, I guess that is how long we have to convince Mr Slattery of your master plan," Pork Chop explains, holding up his index finger to emphasise a further point. "And…it just so happens that at present Slattery is their only tenant, occupying Flat 2A, which is sited at the rear of the property on the first floor, guaranteeing us privacy. It's all in the dossier," mocks Pork Chop sarcastically. He thinks I'm slipping, taking my eye off the ball when it is needed most. But that couldn't be further from the truth. I did read the dossier and I do recall its contents, despite a lack of sleep. It is just my nerves getting the better of me, a touch of stage-fright, hoping that all goes well and neither of us fluffs our lines. Tired, I smile, pre-occupied, like a revved-up greyhound running on fumes, pressing its overeager nose against the starting gate, dumbfounded at why it hasn't been let go.

"Any second now," I say to myself, pulling the hood of my sweatshirt over my head in preparation. As the Turners finally reverse off their driveway after what seems like an age, my pent-up irritation catapults me up and out of the passenger seat. I stride over towards Lodge Court with no care for passing pedestrians or traffic. My subconscious starts the stopwatch before the Turners' car has even left, counting down from one hour and twenty minutes, with Pork Chop trailing behind, cursing my zeal. I beat Pork Chop to the front door, but on pressing the doorbell I wonder what we'll do if Slatter, on seeing me, doesn't open the door. I had always assumed gaining entry would be a given, that Neil's word would be enough to allay any doubts he might have. But what if this stranger in a hoodie who wants to meet so badly, who has another unexpected guest in tow, causes him to have second thoughts and scares him off? That is something that had slipped my mind, a variable with no contingency plan, and the doorbell has already been pressed.

Thinking back to last night and how Jeanette's secret friend was so easily swayed into answering his front door, I nudge Pork Chop forward to take the lead. "Show him your police badge," I say. Pork Chop nods and edges that little bit closer to press the doorbell again, with me standing literally on his heels. "And when we are in his flat, ask to have a look around – see what you can find." Again, Pork Chop nods, my instruction received and understood.

"Hello. Are you Mr Michael Slattery?" Pork Chop asks, adopting his working voice, a lower-than-normal tone, formal and flat like that of an undertaker.

"Yes," Slatter answers.

"I am Detective Sergeant Darren Space from the West Midlands Serious Crime Unit, and this is my associate. Would it be all right if we could talk inside?" Pork Chop suggests. He puts his foot across the threshold, holding up his police credentials.

"Yes, of course, Officer," Slatter replies, conceding with a slight bow. We walk past him into the hallway. "May I ask what this—" he croaks, but Pork Chop ruthlessly interrupts his enquiry.

"All in good time, sir," Pork Chop says with the confidence being a police detective gives you. "Is there somewhere we can talk in private?"

Slatter looks jittery, as if momentarily stunned, and I can't blame him. This isn't the smooth start I had hoped for. His eyes are continually darting from Pork Chop to me, no doubt wondering what the hell is going on. *There was no mention of police when Neil originally arranged this meeting, otherwise I would not have agreed to it,* screams an expression that could slay me a thousand times over. I quickly shut the door behind me in case Slatter bolts. An awkward calm ensues. "It's okay, Michael; everything is okay. Detective Space is just here to explain something for your benefit. That is all. I assure you there is nothing to worry about. But we do need privacy, as there is a lot to go through. All will become clear. Just hear us out," I say, indicating with my eyes that 'up' means the seclusion of Slatter's flat. "Shall we?" I add, shepherding both Slatter and Pork Chop up a flight of white-glossed balustrade and freshly vacuumed carpet, the air fizzing with furniture polish and the faint citrus scents of cleaning products. "She keeps it spick 'n' span, I'll give her that," I remark, wiping my finger along the banister checking for dust.

"Mrs Turner prides herself on her cleanliness," Slatter says as he unlocks his flat and casually flings open the door, standing on the inside like a Beefeater on guard, his mouth purposefully upturned like that of a scolded child in protest at the intrusion, knowing he has no choice but to welcome us into his humble abode.

"Nice place. It's bigger than I expected," I say, hoping a compliment might lighten his mood.

"It is actually made of two interconnecting bedrooms that span the entire width of the main house. In here is the seating area, as you can see, 'n' in there is my bedroom, plus an en suite." Slatter points out the various features as though Pork Chop and I are prospective tenants.

Resigned to the situation, Slatter shuts the door and takes a seat on a nearby sofa. I join him, pitching up at the opposite end. Pork Chop remains standing.

"Do you mind if I take a look around? It's a lovely flat," Pork Chop remarks. Slatter throws his arms wide open, the kind of involuntary reaction a movie gangster gives when shouting "I'm unarmed; don't shoot." But in Slatter's case it was more like 'Be my guest'. After all, not wanting to give the game away, what else could he say? "And what d' you pay for this?"

"Five-hundred on the first of every month."

"Pricey, but you're getting a lot for your money." Pork Chop's curiosity is pricked.

"I pay in cash, plus they are holding a month's rent as a deposit. They're happy. They ask no questions and I'm as regular as clockwork with my payments." Slatter shuffles awkwardly as Pork Chop goes into the bedroom.

"Look, I'm sorry if the whole police thing came as a bit of a surprise. I didn't plan for it to happen this way, it's just how things have progressed," I say in an attempt to sound at least a little apologetic.

"Progression in itself is its own worst enemy, regardless of where you are heading," Slatter says. "Each stage of achievement ups the ante till failure is not an option. Sound familiar?"

"You're very perceptive," I reply, playing to his ego, aware that he is assessing me as I am assessing him; our gazes are locked in a pre-courtship prelude to me revealing my plan.

"Progression and its pitfalls are universal to us all and have been since humankind learned to walk on their hind legs, differentiating themselves from their fellow apes. We all share its inevitability in our endeavours, as everything is a gamble; the better you get at something, the higher the investment and, therefore, the greater the risk. It's simple maths; the trick is to know when to stop before it all comes crashing down. But isn't that the very essence of life, the thrill of living it and the intelligence that underpins the whole process?" Professes Slatter, his confidence growing and a smile slowly forming across his face. "Or else what's the point – be nine-till-fivers, working for the *man*, with two-point-four children? No, thanks! That was my dad and his dad before him! He looked the same as a man as he did as a boy, my dad." Slatter continues, gesticulating like an excited lecturer. "A sign that he didn't take life up on its perpetual gamble. The way I see it, life should make you look different, with your experiences designed intentionally to take their toll in ageing and adding character; time should do that to a person, before the decay sets in. Everything has a shelf life; people, planets, animals, ideas, till eventually they die. Carpe diem," he finishes, whispering the last two words in Latin, which mean *seize the day*, clapping his hands the way a bandsman would strike a pair of cymbals against one another, ridding them of dust and years of conforming to social benchmarking.

Understanding Slatter as an academic, I get the vibe he is trying to put over: That of a man who has clearly had enough, who is fed up with the status quo, who wants something very different from what he previously had and probably from what he currently has. It appears he is a person evolving, much like me. I didn't know what to expect, but it's like having a mirror talk back to you, except this time my reflection is a soon-to-be-wanted sexual pervert with a passion for paedophilic material. Am I the same as this man? It is scary to think I might be, as I'm unsure how far our respective addictions separate us, but fellow addicts we definitely are…

"All sin tends to be addictive, and the terminal point of addiction is what is called damnation," Slatter articulates. "It's a line from, *A Certain World* by W. H. Auden. Rather apt, don't you think?"

"Then we are both damned," I reply, baffled, and yet impressed at how Slatter managed to capture both the moment and the two of us in one succinct quote.

"I used to go to church. I don't know why." He shrugs. "Something to do on a Sunday, I suppose. But the more I went and learned of God's will, and the more war, famine, and misery I saw on TV, the more it made me think, are *we* really made in God's image? And the conclusion I came to is that if so, God is just as culpable as the Devil for how we have turned out, if not more. Our kind are caught in a perpetual pincer movement between heaven and hell. The serpent may have coerced man in taking a bite of the apple, but in God's Garden it was one of *His* trees, the tree of knowledge, that grew it to put temptation in man's way. You see, you cannot have one without the other when one *is* the other! No wonder man is cursed. We've been eating apples ever since, hence our inherent nature to be evil and do evil things; as the saying goes, you are what you eat," Slatter explains. I ponder the latent defect inside each and every one of us, a ticking time-bomb waiting to kick in to deny *us* an otherwise peaceful existence. "Needless to say, shortly after my revelation I stopped going." He coughs a nervous laugh and shakes his head. "But instead of leaving Sunday School re-educated and somewhat rehabilitated, I left with the reinforced blessing that it is good to sin, to like what I like and not be ashamed of my fallibilities, knowing that I am in fact on the righteous path, albeit seeing its irony." Slatter pauses, distracted by Pork Chop clonking about in the bedroom. "Do you ever feel the

Devil has had a bad rap over the centuries? The bible is an early form of media propaganda to hoodwink us into thinking *God is good! God is truth! God is beauty! Praise him!*" I recognise the hymn 'God is Love', a staple of my morning school assemblies. "We might as well have been shouting 'Sieg Heil' and hailing our Führer for all the good it did! Or perhaps that was its intention. Let's face it, Führers do come in all shapes and sizes." Slatter laughs.

"They certainly do," I say, concurring wholeheartedly, aware that I am listening to a man unravel, the way quietly reserved men do before the moment of their undeniable exposure. "Neil said you're clever," I add, buying Pork Chop a little more breathing space as he continues his search.

"Clever! I hope he said more than that." Slatter laughs, his mood lifting. "We both got firsts with honours in our MScs in computer science. But unlike Neil, while working at UK Telecommunications, I went onto get my PhD."

"Impressive" – I reply – "What was your research in, exactly?"

"Networking systems and future applications, networking on a larger scale, microwave communication technology, etcetera" – Slatter explains, waving a hand towards the ceiling – "Y' know, geeky, boring stuff."

"Got it at last! Secret compartment behind the dresser," Pork Chop exclaims, coming in from the bedroom to slam a locked metal carrying container and a wine-case-sized cardboard box on the coffee table in front of me and Slatter. "You look awfully calm and collected for a man whose life is just about to change Mr Slattery." Pork Chop sneers, the simple copper inside mocking – *'not so fucking clever now, are you'*? He glares, to a noted drop in Slatter's brimming confidence. "Looks like I hit the jackpot, Mr Slattery. Whaddaya think – did I?" Pork Chop gloats rhetorically. "And there's more on the bed: Two shoeboxes, one stuffed with money, the other full of kiddy porn – photos; nude poses, action shots, you get the gist. Plus, an assortment of books and magazines, including a journal containing names, addresses and phone numbers with amounts of money pencilled in alongside a column of dates."

"So, what happens now? Are you going to arrest me, Detective?" Slatter answers, without so much as displaying an ounce of emotion, as if he already knows the answer.

"Under normal circumstances I am sure he would, but these are not normal circumstances, are they, Detective Space?" I say, interrupting before Pork Chop goes too far in riling Slatter. "We are here to talk to Mr Slattery, not give him a hard time. Isn't that so, Detective?" I add, looking Pork Chop in the eye while trying to be as reassuring as possible towards Slatter, amazed at how outwardly calm he is, though quite possibly not on the inside.

"You're all right, Mr Slattery; nothing is going to happen. I'm not here to arrest you. In fact, my involvement is to do the opposite and help free you," Pork Chop says, grinning for effect. "But before we come to that, I would like to ask one question if I may. The ledger you have in your possession, you wouldn't be selling this stuff, would you?"

Again, Slatter shuffles in his seat, indicating a reluctance to respond.

"It's okay, you can answer. Just think of it as though you have immunity," I say. "Believe me when I say you can trust us; whatever is said in this room will stay in this room."

With that said, Slatter slumps back and relaxes, interlinking his fingers to rest his hands in his lap like an old professor preparing for class.

"You would be surprised at how lucrative child porn is. Those tapes are like plastic gold," he starts with a slight cough. "Depending on quality, availability and customer demand, the eight-millimetre stuff regularly goes for a hundred apiece, with the longer-running VHS cassettes reaching anything up to five-hundred, as they are usually more gratuitous," Slatter explains like a bored salesman, as though he has already explained it a thousand times to a thousand different customers. His candour is a clear sign that he trusts me. "Even single photographs are a tenner, and they usually sell in bundles of tens and twenties. Good child porn is hard to come by; what do you expect?"

"The VHS tapes; gratuitous in what way?" Porky snaps back.

"Torture scenes, maybe some *snuff*; you never know what you are going to get," Slatter replies nonchalantly, as though saying he likes sugar in his tea. Pork Chop scowls.

"So, what's in the boxes?" I add, curious about the extent of what will be revealed.

"In the cardboard box they're mostly Handy Cam V8s. They are smaller eight-millimetre cassettes used in handheld cameras – amateur rape tapes, home recordings; they're standard fare," Slatter explains.

"And the other one?" I point towards the metal container.

"Yeah, well…" Slatter's voice fades, hesitant, as though trading the lowest diving board for the highest. "That's all your juicy stuff, VHS PALs, like I just told your friend. It doesn't get any worse than them!"

"Didn't it used to worry you at all, having all this stuff in your flat? Because it would have worried me, knowing I could be caught red-handed any moment," Porky says, his tone still snappy and eyes glaring as he leans forward, wishing if only for a minute that life could be how it was before, and he could arrest Slatter and wipe that smug, comfortable look clean off his face.

Aware of Slatter starting to show a more defensive posture, I butt, in motioning with my hand for Pork Chop to wind it in a little. "Please forgive my friend; he's had a rough night. He doesn't mean to be an arsehole, do you, Detective?"

"I guess not." Pork Chop coughs and offers a conciliatory handshake, which Slatter tentatively accepts.

"You think I thought this day would never come?" Slatter suddenly pipes up, getting a second wind of self-assurance. "Of course, I did. It is like we were saying: Why fight the inevitable? The system always wins."

"You say it like you are proud of getting caught." Pork Chop shakes his head.

"No one's proud of getting caught. That is the whole point of getting caught – you lost, the other guy won. But I am proud that I got away with it for as long as I did," Slatter boasts as he slumps back onto the sofa.

"You're a piece of work, I'll give you that." Pork Chop gives a mock salute to a man who on paper he detests but, in the flesh, actually finds quite mesmerising.

"It isn't me; it's the system – how it shapes you, conditioning you for the day it will eventually catch up and destroy you. The best you can possibly hope for is to throw up an anomaly – a spanner in the works, so to speak. But in order to do that, one needs the right spanner." Slatter points into thin air, as though he'd thought of something important only to forget it a second later.

"And have you got one?" I ask, seeing he is being so candid about other related topics.

"To be honest, gentlemen, I don't rightly know," Slatter replies. "You tell me. Have I?"

"Interesting," I hear Pork Chop mutter, playing to see if Slatter's cool façade will crack, his police senses sniffing out weakness like a shark detecting blood ready to home in for the kill. "So if you don't rightly know, what do you think you know?" He adds in a more constructive tone.

But where Pork Chop sees a man ready to falter, I see a man still in control.

"Now, that's not for me to say, is it?"

Pork Chop shakes his head, annoyed at Slatter's Teflon resilience.

"He's right in that respect," I say, looking towards Pork Chop. "It isn't. It is for me to say."

"It is indeed," agrees Slatter with a curt nod. "What's the use being a novice poker player thinking you can out-bluff your opponent's when you are sitting at a table with two seasoned pro card-sharks?" He shrugs and shows the palms of his hands, acknowledging his moment of surrender.

"Thank you for not trying to bargain when there is no bargaining to be had," I say, reciprocating his respect as well as highlighting his precarious position. "And to answer your query – have you got what I am looking for? – Yes, you have. In fact, you have up your sleeve one hell of a 'get out of jail free' card. How's that for a novice poker player? It seems Lady Luck is on your side." I toss over the dossier. "Go ahead; read it. It's all about you: Who you are, what you are, where you go and what you do; a documented record of your activities over the last few months. You see, even though the police are well aware of your comings and goings, we are not here today representing the system; we are here on a pre-emptive mission to offer you an alternative to what surely will be, come Monday, a very bleak future indeed. Detective Space if you could please explain the procedure." I hand over to Pork Chop.

"Yes, of course." Pork Chop picks up where I left off. "Mr Slattery, despite you already being very open with us, the evidence accumulated during the past months is pretty conclusive and very damning. It not only mentions you but implicates you as part of a paedophile network. As you can see, this network, or 'paedophile ring', as they are otherwise known, and its members are clearly identified, providing a detailed account of who supplies, distributes, and buys such extreme material, including that of a paedophilic nature, which I highlighted for your attention. Everybody named on that list is going to have their front door kicked in come the early hours of Monday morning. And if they are not where they are supposed to be, then they will be hunted down. There will be no escape!"

"That's when the system will catch up with you," I say. "And once you're in it – you are in it for good! It's like quicksand; the more you fight it, the deeper you go, and if you decide not to fight, you sink anyway. It's what the system is – a one-way ticket."

"Plus, Mr Slattery, you have to take into account the quality of evidence collected; its validity, sufficient quantity, authenticity and reliability. That their file which you are holding represents many hours of good solid police work, and because of this, you must understand that most, if not all, persons contained within will face definite prison sentences. As it stands, for possession of indecent photographs of children under the Criminal Justice Act 1988 Section 1, the sentence is five years. But given there are videos that will surely depict rape and the wanton sexual exploitation of children, the CPS will probably try to implicate you in the making and further distribution of these films, bringing into effect the Sexual Offences Act 1956; the sentences that I can recall offhand are anything from ten years to life. And trust me when I say this, the CPS will see this as a landmark prosecution. They will make examples of you all, regardless of your level of involvement. Of that I am certain." Pork Chop wraps up his explanation.

"You'll be hung out to dry for the nation to see and despise – trial by media, and that's just for starters!" I say. I can't help but add, "But in prison they'll rip you apart. And this new life the system is so keen to provide begins Monday."

"How do you know it won't start today or tomorrow?" Slatter spits out nervously, feeling his toes creep ever nearer to the precipice's edge, scared to look down in case he loses it altogether.

"Because I am the police officer in charge of coordinating the arrests." Pork Chop laughs. "Me! I'm the guy behind this…"

"Whereas I am the guy behind everything." I butt in.

"Yeah…I didn't mean it like that." Pork Chop apologises, looking down at his shoes in mock disgrace.

"I know. But our friend here needs to know who's who." I point to Slatter, then to me.

"Like who is in charge? I know it is you. That was obvious from the outset" – Slatter smiles – "despite the age difference and job title. What's your name again? You never introduced yourself."

"Andrew Brown." I try to give my name's ordinariness a tone of grandeur.

"Yes, I remember now. Neil used to speak of you with great fondness and admiration. It is nice to finally put a face to someone he often referred to as a legend. He also said you were not to be messed with, that you could be dangerous," Slatter recalls with a squinting expression, as though weighing up how dangerous I could possibly be. *Is this man on my sofa a tiger readying himself to pounce or a cobra lying in wait?* Perhaps I'm a bit of both; a worst-case scenario if you are someone like Slatter.

"Dangerous, eh!"

"Yes, he did, though not the kind who is impetuous or callous, but someone whose skill-set and ambition possesses that certain *je ne sais quoi*, an audacious flair which Neil said captured his imagination, posing more questions than it resolved. Yet he described a coldness that chilled him to the bone. Yes, Mr Brown, seeing you, I believe you are a very dangerous man indeed, but also a man of your word, and therefore you have my trust, despite my being at a disadvantage," says Slatter. "Neil loves you; you know that."

And I him, in my own psychopathic way!

In bagging my second recruit of the day, I can't help but beam with pride, my thanks going out to my dear friend for the introduction.

"Neil's a good man," I affirm, nodding.

"He is indeed," Slatter concurs. "It is because he fits in where we don't. Whatever his pleasures, he is able to mask them, where we have nowhere to hide ours."

"And of this morning neither can my dear friend here, Detective Space; the simple fact is, we don't blend in. We want to, but it's not in our nature, hence your law of inevitability. But what if I told you there is a place that accepts the likes of you and me and Detective Space, a place where strange ones go to find acceptance and purpose, a place currently beyond reproach and legislative restrictions? What then…?"

My pause hangs like a waiting noose.

"Sounds exotic, like we're running away to join a crew of pirates on a voyage of discovery," ponders Slatter, sliding the dossier back towards me. "And if I refuse for any reason? I mean, it is a lot to process."

"Let's just say, your refusal at this stage is not an option you want to choose, considering we have in good faith revealed our hand, so to speak. Surely, Mr Slattery, you are not going to betray that good faith?" I say sternly.

"All I'm saying is that it's a lot to take in." Slatter sighs heavily.

"That's why you must rise above it and be strong," I say in an attempt to balance out the negatives with a positive outlook. "Yes – it's a big jump, but you can do it, because come Monday, it is all over. They will crucify you, publicly and without remorse; vilified, made out to be a monster, and left to rot in whatever godforsaken shithole they send you to. Society doesn't want us, and they will do anything to get rid of us. They're scared; scared of sex-fiends wanting to fuck their kids and petrified of murderers wanting to kill them all. We simply don't belong! So, in order to stand a chance, you have to get out. But you have to do it now, and I have a sanctuary that will take you. Do you understand?"

Slatter pushes himself to the edge of his seat and slumps back once more, huffing and puffing and blowing his frustration, flexing then stretching his arms in nervous panic.

"To be honest, what alternative do I have?" Slatter replies with the resigned look of wanting a cigarette or brandy or both to stem the shock, except that he neither drinks nor smokes, left helpless as the dark begins to seep into his sallow gaze.

Chapter 10
Deal Or No Deal

Either way, we loveless people need a place as loveless as us if we are to make it in this world. So whaddaya say now you've heard my plans? Do we still have a deal?

"So where are we going?" Slatter asks.

"Somewhere which, compared to here, is a bountiful Eden – a heaven of heavens – where the trees are plentiful and the apples taste as decadent as sin itself." My words dance to the sound of a serpent's enticing hiss.

"Don't worry, you'll love it," Pork Chop adds, giving his new comrade a nudge. "It's like Disney World for the deranged." And, just like magic, a common bond forms, a spark igniting the unlikeliest of friendships, the distrust and revulsion forgotten, favouring a mutual attraction towards a new life in a new land, as though I had surreptitiously uttered a sacred incantation to expediently resolve our differences. However, I'm conscious that there is still a lot of ground to cover before Slatter is fully sold on my idea.

"Take Detective Space, for example, or, now we are more formally acquainted, Pork Chop, or Porky, as he is affectionately known by the men. He started out a lost soul who didn't care if he lived or died. Now he is a colossus amongst men, a mighty warrior who has gained the strength to bring closure to his past, vanquishing the very demons that threatened him in the first place," I explain. Pork Chop shakes a fist in triumph across from me. "Now he's my first proper recruit." I give Pork Chop a wry grin and top it off with a salute.

"When you put it like that, it sounds rather dramatic. What Andrew says is true. I would be dead long ago if it wasn't for him," Pork Chop says, backing up my sentiment.

"How long have you known?" Whimpers Slatter as his last protective veneer finally peels away, leaving him utterly exposed for the very first time.

"I've known ever since I first found that tin box of yours."

"I knew someone had been in it, either you or Neil" – says Slatter – "but it didn't stop me."

"How could it? You were addicted; it's how it takes over, the thrill factor sending that adrenaline rush coursing through your body. Nothing can stop that," I explain. "I should know; it takes one to know one." My candour gets a nod of respect.

"But that's just it! Sometimes I wish I had been stopped. It is like no one else sees it, this thing I have. Even I didn't at first. And then one day it was there, like I had woken up with the blood of stone-cold guilt on my hands, indelibly stained, not quite knowing how it got there." Slatter, taking a brief pause to compose himself, lifts his head slightly to look me directly in the eye. He doesn't have to say it; I know how the darkness finds people and how they never fail to fall prey to its demons. "The metal container and cardboard box on the table, that isn't who I really am; those things do not dwell within the eyes you are looking into. They are just a means to an end that another version of me clings on to in a desperate fight for survival; a figure I only see in the dim light of reflected shadows; a Mr Hyde of sorts who stalks my every waking thought. Whenever I see him, this other me, I wonder how many others there are suffering, trapped like a prisoner of this parallel darkness and its depraved personality. I don't want to succumb to paedophilia any more than I want to go to prison." Slatter takes another breather. "But it does make me examine where I belong. I don't belong here, as you have quite rightly explained. I've known that for a while. So, I guess it is time to decide where I do belong."

"And where do you think that might be?" I ask.

"It seems I have no choice but to accept your offer of a bountiful Eden, given what that dossier contains. After all, you did say you could cure me." Slatter gives me a cheeky grin.

"The cure comes with knowing the patient. You are no more a paedophile than Porky here is a loving family man," I say. Pork Chop lets out a sudden burst of laughter. "And I know that because I can see it in you, like I know you are still a virgin, unable to make the jump from fantasy to reality; whether it be a woman or a child, consensual or not, you are dependent on how the TV screen separates you from them. But with that said, you can only stay a voyeur for so long. The urge will eventually get the better of you. But you already know that." Slatter nods. "So, what do you propose?"

"I propose you get laid, and the sooner the better. How's tonight sound?" I say invitingly.

"Sounds good to me," Pork Chop adds, giving Slatter a thumbs up.

"So, you are proposing I get laid, as in having sex?" Slatter replies, a little confused.

"Yes, Michael – actual sex with an actual woman; not a child, but a proper woman." I nod my confirmation. "Well, two women, in fact. They're sisters!"

"You lucky bastard!" Pork Chop blurts out. "I get sent on a killing spree and he gets a threesome. You can tell who's got the brain and who the brawn is," he adds sarcastically.

"Call it an introductory offer," I joke to Pork Chop's wry smirk and Slatter's bemused smile.

"And this is the cure you spoke of?" Asks Slatter.

"The first stage of it – yes! And hopefully the start of something new; a new life for a new you," I say with gusto. "You see, Michael, I've seen a lot of people in your predicament; intelligent, ambitious people who find it difficult for one reason or another to form friendships, let alone anything meaningful or romantic. Instead, you withdraw inside yourself, opting for the safety and convenience of porn, where fantasies are preferred to reality, with your inability to bond. Like I said, the cure comes with knowing the patient, and in your case, I need to coax you out of your shell, hence I arranged this experience for you."

"Will it be like a date? I've never been on a date before. I wouldn't know what to do," stresses Slatter, shuffling in his seat again.

"It will be okay. Michael, all you will have to do is be yourself. The evening can go any way you want it to go: It's your night, your rules," I say.

"My night and my rules?" Says Slatter.

"That's right."

"For your first time I wouldn't let you do it any other way. I'm here to support you, guide you. I can see how lonely and isolated you are, despite the intelligent façade; for all these years you have been shunned into a corner where your dependency on porn has grown till only the unthinkable extremes, a place you thought you would never end up, can satisfy your urges. You're caught in that vicious, downward spiral all addicts eventually find themselves in, unable to wean themselves off the thrill of being on the edge, the fix always heading in the wrong direction, stronger, harder, till there is no turning back, and you've crossed the line of no return." I stop with deliberation and pause to gauge where on the sliding scale of addiction Slatter lies and where he thinks he is, which in most cases are completely different.

"The thing is, did you cross the line?" Pork Chop asks, adopting his low police voice. "Because I know all the details of your last purchase. Barney fessed up everything."

Barney, otherwise known as Richard Barnett, is the proprietor of an adult book shop in the city centre, a slimy yet charismatic chap who has been supplying Slatter with pornographic material for years. Needless to say, Barney is at the centre of Pork Chop's investigation, a fiend in his own right who has his sleazy fingers in many unsavoury pies.

"Good, old Barney!" Slatter sighs. "Never was the reliable type given a little arm-twisting."

"I watched a couple of those tapes myself." Pork Chop chips in again, putting his hand up to cut me off before I can speak, his innate police-dog mentality finding it hard to let go of the bone. "Just wondering if you can shed any light on why you bought those tapes in particular."

"Porky has a point. Tell me about your last purchase, and I mean every detail," I say. Pork Chop leans over, pointing at the dossier with a strained stare as if to remonstrate once more about me not properly reading his diligently prepared dossier. Shaking my head in reply, thinking I had already cleared up this misunderstanding, I spell out my reason for wanting an explanation. "For the benefit of clarity, I just want to hear him say it. So please, Michael, indulge me…"

"Like I said before, you don't know what you are getting with these tapes; their contents are something of a lucky-dip, hence our name for them – 'lucky-dips'. It's half the fun, the not knowing. You don't mind, 'cos whatever's on 'em you know it's gonna be bad!" Slatter over-emphasises the 'bad'.

"Barney said he gave you the heads-up on this batch, even offering you first refusal." Pork Chop adds, "Said they were right up your street."

"That is true – he did. But it wasn't until I got home and scanned through the opening few minutes of each one that I knew they were war-zone snuff films – extreme hardcore; in fact, the worst I had ever come across." Slatter whimpers. "Are you aware of what the Congo is like?"

"I know friends who have been there," I reply.

"So if you were to watch those tapes, it wouldn't shock you?"

"I have no doubt it would make grim viewing, but I'm no stranger to atrocity. I know what goes on."

"I must admit, in both videos I watched – it doesn't get more graphic than that!" Pork Chop agrees with Slatter's original summation.

"And you had never seen material like this before?" I indicate Slatter, who shakes his head.

"No – not like that," he replies. "I mean, I have seen my fair share of rape tapes, but this stuff is in a whole different stratosphere."

"So, what did you think, besides your initial shock?" I change tack.

"What – about women and children being gang-raped till dead, then mutilated like pieces of meat; the castration of men and boys, their heads smashed in, then dismembered with machetes or chainsaws, or strung up to be hung, drawn and quartered?"

"Yes – that," I say.

"I guess in the darkest recesses of my mind I have always known it is out there. I guess, similar to believing in urban myths. But I never thought for a minute that it was actually real." Slatter's naivety underlines the bubble in which he has so far lived; a bubble that later today I intend to burst.

"Oh, it's real all right," I declare. "It's as real as you will ever get! But honestly, was it what you expected?"

"Honestly – it was so much more! It should have appalled me, but instead it provided a sort of clarity that watching sex failed to deliver," says Slatter.

"How, exactly?" I ask.

"It was weird, like an intensity I had never felt before, as though I began watching those tapes lost and by the end had somehow found myself; the experience was akin to looking into an old, misted-up mirror that, minute by minute, clears to reveal a darker version of what you once were, that dark version being my true self, the part of my psyche that stayed hidden for all this time. But in doing so, those tapes also showed me how I don't fit in and never will; my days are almost numbered," Slatter says, in a matter-of-fact tone. "And when the opportunity to move on arrives, grab it with both hands."

"And do you think that opportunity lies with me and Porky?" I say with fingers crossed.

"I believe it does." Slatter coughs, his nerves apparent at having to make the final decision.

"Are you sure?" I ask, reiterating the seriousness of what he is about to do.

"Yes, I am – and that is final. I'll come with you and Porky if I may call you that?" Slatter looks over at Pork Chop.

"Now you're in the gang you can." Pork Chop leans over to shake Slatter by the hand.

Now there's something you don't see every day, the lead investigating officer welcoming a key suspect, a budding paedophile and sexual predator, into his fold!

Watching the unlikely duo bond, I wonder if I'm doing the right thing relying on someone so fallibly prone. But there again, that could be said of Pork Chop. I suppose we'll see. After all, who else has the skill-set I'm looking for and can be blackmailed into working with me? In that sense he is perfect.

"So, let's talk about this PhD of yours and how you can help me," I say. "If you can give me a brief rundown of your expertise, that will be great."

"Like I previously explained, my research centred on networking systems and future applications, expanding organisational intranet systems to network on a larger scale, focusing on microwave communication technology instead of hardwired fibre optic cabling," Slatter explains.

"That's the future, and when we have the funds to do it, we will, but what about now?" I ask, not having a clue about IT and tech systems, let alone a computer.

"That's no problem. Any current business application you wish to install I can set up easily as long as you have access to the right equipment" – Slatter replies nonchalantly to my shrug of indifference – "For instance, if you had premises, I could set up a network where the computers, say you had one in every office, would be able to talk to one another. That is, send information to and from any terminal to any other. And on these computers, there would be a suite of features offering service packs to facilitate word processing, finance, auditing, data management, intranet communications, security; that is, different authorised access for different uses, plus a review of any software updates, if you get my gist."

"Yeah – sort of – I think." I grimace at the complexity of Slatter's explanation.

"Sounds complicated in theory, but in practice it's relatively straight forward," says Slatter.

"But that's an overview, as impressive as it sounds. I want to know what your actual computing knowledge is, if you don't mind."

"As in what do I know, rather than what can I do?" Slatter asks. I nod in confirmation. "That's easy, I'll give you a rundown. So, I cut my teeth on BASIC, FORTRAN, ALGOL, COBOL, and IBM RPG during my school years, becoming more or less a self-taught expert in all five languages by the time I went to university. Once at university I was allowed to spread my wings; they had access to everything I previously couldn't get hold of, language paradigms like C, which is systems programming, Prolog, ML, Pascal and Scheme. I was in computing heaven, where I excelled beyond everybody's expectation, my knowledge even extending beyond that of my tutors. It led to an unprecedented exchange visit with the Massachusetts Institute of Technology, a first of its kind and quite a coup for the university. But working for UK Telecommunications, they put me on their developmental division, where I worked with C++, Objective-C, IBM RPG for the new AS/400 system, and other functional languages like Erlang, Perl, Tcl – coding styles that I'd previously overlooked – and more latterly Haskell, a purely functional programming language with non-strict semantics and strong static typing."

"I'm glad you stopped to take a breath. I'm worn out just listening," I quip. "Wow! And here's me thinking all computers speak the same language, when in fact they are just like us: Different dialects, different professions that require different terminology; each a language of its own like the countries of the world. I was impressed before, but now I get what Neil sees in you; you're a fucking off-the-charts genius! This future you mentioned, your research; how far away is it?"

"Glad you asked because we are in it. Computing is moving at such a pace. Give it six or seven years, maybe sooner, and everyone will be able to talk to each other on their computers. The whole computing industry is talking about scripting languages, dynamic high-level general-purpose languages, such as Perl and Tcl, and how they are going to influence programming over the next few years," Slatter announces as though he's prophesying the *second coming*.

"And this is where you see computing heading," I add.

"It's the only way computing is heading. The military are already harnessing the versatility of microwave tech incorporating the use of space satellites. It is only a matter of time before the rest of us are using it," says Slatter, his zeal positively overflowing.

"*Computers, machines, the silicon dream.*" I purr Hazel O'Connor's prophetic yet deliciously appetising lyrics.

"And that's what it will be, except we need a machine which will not get upset," Slatter jibes, making the valid point that a system will need to be robust and secure, one that cannot be corrupted and hurt by external influences; a system loyal to its master and obedient to its creator.

"And so, we shall have one, but all in good time," I say. "In the meantime, I have an idea to get the ball rolling; something based on my experiences in Croatia."

"Isn't there meant to be trouble brewing over there?" Asks Slatter.

"I certainly hope so. I'm counting on it," I exclaim.

"But they're talking of war, and you want this to happen?" Asks Slatter almost rhetorically, as though momentarily lost to another one of his light-bulb moments. "That's pretty radical – I like your thinking. But you're not after a war – are you?" He adds, sounding me out. "It sounds to me like you want a revolution, war being a means to an end, a vehicle by which to propel your own ideology. It's brave stuff. I guess every movement starts with humble beginnings."

"There's that incredible perception again," I say with raised eyebrows, wagging my finger in his direction. "I've been over there, on and off, for some months now. You could say it has become something of a second home to me. And that feeling you said you had whilst watching those tapes, I felt that exact same feeling on my first visit to Croatia; an enlightenment, a freedom of expression where finally I was able to be myself and, more importantly, accepted by my peers. And so will you, as long as you understand one basic concept about where you are going."

"I'll certainly try."

"You'll do more than that!" I demand, lowering my tone. "Imagine Croatia as a game, one big game where the stakes are life or death." Slatter nods, his gaze fixed on mine. "Now imagine two sides, the Serbs to the east and the Croats to the west, both sworn enemies who will do anything to win. And when I say anything, I mean anything; theirs is a level of hate that is evil personified – you get me?" I say. Slatter's gives a slow, accentuated nod. I point to the metal container of video tapes. "Because that in there, my friend, is nothing compared to what these two heavyweights are capable of," I continue, poking mock fun at his closet collection to ramp up the anticipation as his eyes widen to saucers. "I'm talking about a clash of the titans, something Europe hasn't seen since the 1940s, and I for one want to be there when it kicks off and the games begin."

"You make it sound like the Olympics," jokes Slatter.

"In a way it is. And for the Croats it will be played out on home soil. But they will have no home advantage. The Serbs are a force to be reckoned with, and the Croats are too stubborn to back down. Conflict is imminent, the flashpoint most likely Vukovar. It will be a bloodbath, to put it mildly," my comment causes Slatter to raise his eyebrows. "However, the media choose to phrase it – a dispute, an insurrection, war – it will be nothing more than an elaborate game of chicken," I pause theatrically. "Whether it is a collective atrocity or an individual act of barbarism that wins the day, each side will be relentless in trying to go the extra mile to out-do and out-shock the other; it's a war of attrition where the victors will be the more horribly creative of the two. Because if this game is going to have any winners, it will be fear that claims first prize. For fear is the greatest weapon in any army's arsenal. So, I thought, why not create a game of my own – *Apok*?"

"*Alpha-Papa-Oscar-Kilo*. Fuckin' A!" Pork Chop remarks, his interruption drawing a wry smile across my face as I glance over at his reciprocated grin.

"So what is *Apok*?" Asks Slatter.

"Good question," I say, rubbing my chin. "As it stands, *Apok* exists on two different levels: Its primary use as a radio call-sign and what it has rapidly evolved into. You see, when I first thought up the term *Apok*, around late January, I did so as an experiment to readdress the gulf that exists between us and a much more formidable foe, considering our lower numbers and limited resources, not to mention inferior weaponry. It was a tactic more than anything, a way to hit the enemy hard and strike fear into their ranks. Basically, *Apok* is an order that, if given on an operation, supersedes all other commands. But it is an order that has proved to be very popular. Like I said, since I first used it, *Apok* has given us a fighting chance."

"And what kind of order does that?" Asks Slatter, chomping at the bit.

"One that says no prisoners shall be taken; all enemy personnel are to be killed and no one in the kill zone is to be spared," I reply.

"I can see how that might work," says Slatter with an exhaled puff of disbelief. Even though in his eyes the horror of hearing it rings loud and true. "And the second level of *Apok* is…?" He braces himself for what I might say.

"The second level is my game" – I say with raised cheer – "and because the term has become so synonymous with killing and those who police the eastern border, I thought, *why not?* It's perfect. It has reputation, infamy, gravitas, everything an addict craves, like it was always meant to be. All I have to do is slot the players into our day-to-day routine of patrolling the area and the rest takes care of itself."

"A game where you kill someone?" Slatter, sounds unsure.

"Or people, depending on preference and appetite. But you are correct. *Apok* is a game for people who want to kill other people." I pause for a few seconds so Slatter can psychologically catch up. "Look, its simple. Each player in the game is there by invitation only and therefore thoroughly vetted, plus their killings will be filmed and kept as a safeguard against any loose talk."

"And if they do talk?"

"They will be killed, as will their family," I say. "But these dangers will be made clear in their invitations."

"So if it sounds so daunting, how do you sell it?" Asks Slatter.

"Easy! Believe it or not, the game almost sells itself. I just have to add my pitch: You give me any man, together with a choice of weapon, and I will reveal the monster within, hence *Apok's* distinctive selling point and motto – no prisoners – death to all – spare no one!" I explain, reeling off my slogan like some smarmy news anchor-man.

"Your mind is a weird and complicated place, Mr Brown. You have subplots weaving into subplots. It's ballsy, I'll give you that. Do you think the Croats will put up with it, your game piggybacking off theirs, as it were?" Slatter shrugs. "After all, you would be hijacking their initiative, technically speaking, of course, using their resources and flying your flag in their name."

"Once the war kicks off – yeah! I expect a few teething problems, it's only natural, but their hierarchy will come around, given the extra manpower it will provide and the money it will generate. But for now, I have connections in Slovenia, Slovakia and Hungary; the kind that has remote facilities where torture chambers and execution sites can be easily set up and dismantled without a trace." I watch my explanation slowly sink in. Slatter rolls his eyes back and forth, holding his chin.

"And the choice of weapons?" He enquires.

"For beginners it will be between a knife, a hatchet and a pistol," I answer. "With the punters charged accordingly depending on what weapon they choose and how many people they want to kill. I already have a waiting list!"

"Why, are you already up and running?"

"No! Not really. The waiting list is still waiting. But what is interesting is how effectively through word-of-mouth alone *apok* has spread; especially, it seems, amongst a niche sector of the business community. Take that waiting list, for example. Everyone on it came off the back of helping some guy, Austrian, I think, a few weeks back. He's the friend of a colonel I know. But that's another story. Anyway, all I knew was that he was in Zagreb for the weekend, rich and seeking some extracurricular activity off the reservation, so to speak. So, we were introduced and in a further private meeting between him, me, and his bodyguard, I agreed, after successfully pitching *apok*, where he chose all three weapons, to set up a scenario for him to play out at a total cost of twenty thousand US dollars. He literally threw the cash at me there and then. So come the next day, I take him and his bodyguard out to a house whose owners, a husband and wife, I knew to be Serb sympathisers and therefore wouldn't be missed, even if found. Sure, it was a gamble, but isn't that what life is…taking that leap of self-belief?" Slatter's face lights up at his own truism.

"What happened to them?" Chirps Slatter, unable to contain his excitement.

"What *apok* guarantees – they were not spared." I answer.

"But how?" Insists Slatter.

"Simple! I explained to the Austrian that, when political dissidents are questioned, as police militia we first interrogate, then torture, and finish by eliminating the suspects. These people would have died anyway, give, or take a few more days. So that's what the Austrian asked for, to be a bad-ass militia man for the day. And I gave it to him with all the bells and whistles he could handle. You wanna know what happened – fine! Because I tell you, that man certainly knew what he was doing, and he was damned if anyone was going to tell him otherwise. I just let him take charge, and as he grew in confidence, the bodyguard and I withdrew to the room's edge, our pistols at the ready just in case. But the Austrian didn't need us. Like I said, he was no stranger to the role of bad cop. He was a bad dude who liked to take his time. He shot them in the feet and once through their stomachs, used the hatchet to break and dismember limbs and the knife just to stab over and over and over. At one point about halfway through, he even made the husband watch as he fucked his dying wife, only to flip her over to fuck the exit wound in the small of her back. But whatever he did, however deplorable, I didn't interfere; in fact, I didn't make a sound. And to put the icing on the cake, I let him burn the bodies, a sort of freebie thrown in for good measure. He fucking loved that; like a giddy boy scout making camp, he couldn't get enough. Are those the kind of details you were after?"

"Yes, they are – thank you," Slatter replies, his gaze somewhat studious. "A perfect balance of sex and horror, so one does not counteract the other – that's clever; whilst maintaining full control and keeping the player at the centre of the experience. Some might say you've hit the jackpot."

"Though there are some that wouldn't," says the psycho-purist behind my smile, wanting to be heard. "But if a little sex is what's required, who am I to argue? After all, any sector of the service industry will tell you that it is demand-led; the customer is king, and it's hard to say otherwise when 20,000 US dollars are thrown at you."

"And there are some that would," Slatter replies in a reflective tone. "I think there are some who would go as far as to say you are a man ahead of your time."

"Whereas some may say I'm just picking up where others left off," I counter with a smile. "Either way, we loveless people need a place as loveless as us if we are to make it in this world. So whaddaya say? Now you've heard my plans, do we still have a deal?"

"Absolutely – after your pitch, my mind was never in doubt." Slatter remains seated to lean over and shake my hand. "I'm ready to move on; to be honest, I have been ready for a while. So what's next?"

"What's next is that you need to pack your bags, because time is running out and it won't be long before the Turners are back," I say with an air of urgency. "'Cos if they get back before we leave, the deal's off! So, how quickly we get out of here is entirely up to you. Now, what do you have in the way of bags or cases?"

"I have a large hold-all and a couple of smaller sports bags." Slatter gets up and walks towards the bedroom.

"Perfect!" I get up and follow. "You need to empty your wardrobe and drawers of all clothes, underwear, shoes and socks and any personal belongings; anything that is precious to you. Plus, pack your toiletries, and remember, you must leave nothing. Make it look like you're going for good, okay? Porky, help him, will you? I don't want anything left that doesn't support him fleeing the coup. Got it?"

"I'm on it," Pork Chop snaps with blind obedience as he disappears into the bedroom. "Come on, mate, let's get this sorted, shall we?" Pork Chop bellows in good spirits like a drill sergeant dishing out chores to a new recruit.

At the bedroom doorway I put on my gloves to supervise the clean-up, with Slatter immediately showing haste to retrieve a large black hold-all from the top of the wardrobe. He fills it with neatly folded stacks of assorted shirts, T-shirts and trousers, diligently wrapping pairs of shoes, both formal and sportswear, into polythene shopping bags and emptying drawers of Y-fronts and boxer shorts, ironed layers of military precision, and socks rolled into pairs, everything as fresh and neat as when it was bought, each item noted and audited before Slatter tucked them away in the large black sack.

"That's the en-suite done," Pork Chop confirms, walking out into the living area with one of the sports bags zipped up.

"How are the clothes going?" I ask Slatter.

"The wardrobe is done," he says, placing several suit carriers on the bed. "I have just the drawers to double-check, and that's it."

"What about under the bed and behind the furniture? Have you got any more secret stashes?" I say, grilling Slatter one last time, his hesitation indicating that he has. "C'mon, where is it?" Still, he hesitates, unable to maintain eye contact. "Michael, you have to trust us. Porky and I are here to help. Under the circumstances, we are the only ones who can help, so tell me where it is."

"Under the bottom panel shelf in the wardrobe," Slatter confesses, pulling up the thin wooden panel to reveal a shallow hideaway spanning the entire length and breadth of the wardrobe's base.

"You sneaky fucker!" I hear Pork Chop snipe as he walks back into the bedroom. "I missed that one."

"You certainly did," I reply, glaring sarcastically down at Slatter on his knees, who beams a kind of dumbstruck, sorry-looking expression in reply. The bottom of the wardrobe is full of rolled-up banknotes fastened tightly by elastic bands; the impressive horde topped by a transparent folder of what looks like documents of some sort. "Looks like you've been busy, Michael. Talk me through it." I try not to sound too angry; Pork Chop whistles a dazed sigh.

"Who says porn don't pay! And there's me thinking I've got it good!" His tone is full of surprise, praising Slatter's entrepreneurial flair.

"The fives are wrapped in bundles of one hundred pounds, the tens in two-fifties, and the twenties in five-hundreds," Slatter explains, pointing to row upon row of what looks like small cylindrical money barrels packed tightly and incredibly uniformly, their coloured denominations of blue, brown-red and purple morphing into a tinted smudge of what I can only describe as an expensive ink palette of bruised flesh. So, this is what several years of trading in child porn looks like. I think of the countless lives ruined and lost to form this twisted montage of our most beloved heritage, icons of incredible sacrifice and personal achievement: The Duke of Wellington, Florence Nightingale and Shakespeare rolled and fastened, reduced to nothing more than a currency in which to trade misery. I wonder, in a similar amount of time, will my game look any different?

I guess not!

"There is twenty thousand, six hundred pounds," Slatter adds, pre-empting my next question.

"Well done you." I congratulate him. "And the folder?"

"They are my identification documents: Passport, birth certificate, driving licence, National Insurance confirmation, banking details, credit card account details, proof of employment, P60 tax documents, the usual." Slatter hands me the see-through plastic wallet.

"Best hang on to it," I say, handing the wallet back. "You never know!"

"Thanks." Slatter packs it into the sports bag along with his stash.

"And don't forget the box of cash on the bed and any other valuables that you wanna take. C'mon, we ain't got long." I hold the sports bag open while Slatter tips the shoebox of loose banknotes in to cover the money rolls and plastic wallet, their crisp sound like that of falling autumn leaves heralding a change in season. "Oh, and leave the books, magazines, photos, tapes, etcetera; they're stopping here," I add, emphasising my point, aware that the hour and twenty minutes I allocated is almost up. "And while we are on the subject of money, what about bank accounts and savings?"

"There should be no more than a few hundred in my current account. I can empty that at a cashpoint. Regarding my savings, well, they're safe in a Swiss account."

"A Swiss account?" I snap.

"Yeah, it was easy to set up."

"In Switzerland?" I'm unable to contain my surprise.

"Didn't I say?"

"No, you fucking didn't," I shout.

"To be honest, I'm amazed more people don't have one. I had it set up a couple of years ago, a direct debit straight from my current account. All it required was one visit to Geneva to verify my identity, give my fingerprints and set up the account password. There was very little fuss involved," Slatter chirps, as though this secretive edge to his world and the whole life-changing scenario is business as usual, just another normal Saturday morning in the extraordinary life of Michael Slattery.

"Fingerprints?" I ask.

"Oh yes, it's amazing. As well as your usual security protocols, like verifying your ID, account number and password, your account is biometrically locked," Slatter explains to my quizzical squint. "It is a type of light-sensitive scanner you put your hand on, similar to a mini photocopier, that takes a digital image of your hand, selecting just the fingerprints and key markings on your palm, which are unique to any one person. This means it can only be accessed in person and not remotely. Cool or what?"

"It sounds pretty cool. But it also sounds like you have a lot invested in this account." Slatter nods.

"I do. But everything is above board," he says confidently.

"That maybe so, but you are not. And if you're not, neither is your money or anything you are connected to. It also means it is traceable. The police will find the trail eventually, but for now, what the police will find Monday is someone in possession of child porn, not evidence of someone who distributes it and profits from its sales. That in itself will buy you precious time. So, is this Swiss account of yours lucrative, or is it just a holding account?" I'm intrigued.

"In the long term it can be very lucrative as long as you don't swap from one saving policy to another, incurring penalty costs."

"And your policy – is that working out the way you hoped?"

"More or less; it's early days," Slatter says nonchalantly. "Though I had an initial stroke of luck when I opened the account in mid-May '89 in that the Swiss franc was at its highest exchange rate it had been for a while, making the opportunity much more affordable." Slatter coughs to clear his throat. "You see, in order to qualify for the top rate of interest, your first deposit had to be a minimum of fifty thousand Swiss francs, which in pounds and pence brought the price down to just a little over seventeen and a half thousand pounds. In banking terms, it was an absolute steal; the bank was reputable, the saving policy cast iron, and so I decided, because I was using cash only in my day-to-day life, each month via a direct debit I would transfer ninety-five percent of my total salary. I'm paid on the twenty-eighth of every month, and on the first working day of the following month, the money goes out. It couldn't be easier," Slatter explains with a shrug of his shoulders. "Like I said, I knew this day would come."

"And I am a man of my word. We are here to help, and that is what we are going to do. I'm not here for your money; I am here for you," I pat him on the shoulder.

"Spoken like a true romantic hero," Slatter jokes. I leave him checking the contents of the sports bag, muttering an inaudible itinerary over and over.

With Slatter busy finishing up in the bedroom, I take Pork Chop aside for a quiet chat. "Right, after we are finished here, Slatter will spend the day with you," I explain to his frustration.

"I thought you were going to take care of him. He is your recruit," says Pork Chop, with a show of hands.

"And your comrade!" My retort is just as biting as Pork Chop's irritation. "Don't forget that! It's just that some other business needs my attention. I need to make some calls and do some prep for next week." I lie about having to make some calls. The calls had already been made before I left Croatia and the prep was sorted. Everything was ready to go on my say-so. Yes, a call has to be made but that is all in hand. I can do that tomorrow or the day after and still fulfil my obligation. Right now, I need some space and time alone to think and ready myself for the night ahead.

"And what's so damned important?" Pork Chop sneers.

"Mr and Mrs Childs and their two remaining children – that's what!" I say, trying to remain civil, annoyed that such an important instruction had been questioned.

"Of course. The mess Dan left us," Pork Chop acknowledges.

"You mean, left me!" I correct Pork Chop's slight inaccuracy. "I dunno. It could work out as a kind of blessing in disguise; a test pilot, for want of a more apt description; a precursor to what I'm trying to achieve in Croatia."

"You're talking about *apok*," says Pork Chop.

"Yes, I am. I want to use the child's family as an example, an advertisement to springboard *apok*'s potential. Their story has the perfect narrative: Betrayal, a string of heinous crimes, revenge and the meting out of justice," I explain. "Just as you exacted your justice on your family."

"I get it, I really do. Dan was a mess, and he deserved what he got. I understand there has to be a reckoning. So have you figured out how you're going to do it?" asks Pork Chop.

"I think so. But for now, I need you to take care of Slatter. Take him out of the city, anywhere; I'm not bothered as long as it's somewhere discreet. He needs to be kept preoccupied and, above all, happy."

"Got it!" Pork Chop whispers.

"Have you finished yet?" I shout towards the bedroom.

"Yes, I have!" Slatter's emphatic response is shouted back. Seconds later, he walks out to greet us, wiping his brow as if to emphasise the effort he has made.

"Good! Put your bag over there by the door with the others, then take a seat," I say. "Porky, give it a once-over." I nod towards the bedroom. His butler-like demeanour is already in motion before I have finished my sentence. "Michael, have you got your flat keys?"

"Yes. Everything is on there." He produces a paltry-looking keyring, its scant contents resembling a metallic chicken's foot.

"Toss 'em over." I beckon and catch the keys one-handed. "You're not gonna be needing these anymore," I gloat, looking at the meagre bunch of four assorted keys: Two standard house keys for Yale door locks, one brass and well worn, the other cheap steel, the kind you get cut as a copy; a larger, sturdier key that I assume is for a more substantial mortise lock; and a small dainty key, the type one might use to unlock a suitcase or a metal carrying case. I try it in the lock of Slatter's prized video container. It fits like a glove. I flick the latch and lift the lid; the moment takes me back to when Neil and I first encountered its damning contents.

"The bedroom's clean. We're good to go," Pork Chop announces, walking back into the lounge. "I'll go 'n' fetch my car, pull up on the drive," he suggests.

"Good idea. I'll come down to the front door with you, check the coast is clear," I say, ushering Pork Chop out of the flat and down the stairs. "As soon as you two are gone, I'm gonna plant the books, mags, photos and tapes so they are easy to find come Monday's raid."

"I would," Pork Chop agrees. "Easier the better. That rabble in vice couldn't organise a piss-up in a brewery, let alone find and collate crucial evidence. Some proper police work will do 'em good." Pork Chop suddenly pauses to wipe his hand across his lower jaw in deep contemplation. "Anyway, fuck 'em! I'm no longer one of *them*, haven't been for a while."

"Feels good, doesn't it, to finally let go and be free," I say, patting his back. He nods gently in reply. Pushing our luck on borrowed time, I let Pork Chop go to fetch his car and re-join Slatter on the sofa. On Pork Chop's swift return, he clicks his fingers, virtually tugging Slatter off the sofa to help him with the bags. "Oh, by the way, I nearly forgot your bag of goodies; the stuff I got for the girls later," Pork Chop mocks, placing the carrying case I had left on the back seat of his car the night before right on the indented spot Slatter has just vacated. "The girls!" He reiterates, nudging Slatter.

"I haven't forgotten," Slatter replies, grinning from ear to ear. "Anyway, if getting laid is my cure, I'm looking forward to a long and fulfilling course of treatment," he adds to my and Pork Chop's 'coming of age' jibes about popping his cherry.

I bid my two recruits *au revoir* till later, reminding them both to be at Slatter's old flat, the one he used to share with Neil, by five o'clock. I run through a shopping list of bags of ice, at least two bottles of champagne – Moet, preferably – tequila, limes, a saltshaker, and whatever tipple gets Slatter in the mood. I don't know why, but on hearing the front door slam downstairs and Pork Chop's Escort drive off, knowing the Turners will arrive any second, I can't help but sit here, close my eyes and savour the silence. There is a lot to be said about quietness, the calm before any storm; it is simply a tranquillity like no other with a noise all of its own, as if time itself is accelerating towards you; a force so all-consuming that it traps, as though you're treading across a bog of thickest tar, your every effort, despite its vigour, never enough to avoid destiny's hurtling charge running you down. My mind momentarily floats back to many a night spent rambling endlessly on patrol, longing for the noises of the creatures that cruise the inky black and the inevitability that destiny always brings. But that's there and I am here with a job to do. I'll be back there soon, but in the meantime, I need to give my dear Slatter a reputation worthy of my second recruit. I jump up, rifle through the cardboard box, and pull out a tape labelled 'girl and boy in bath'. I remember seeing a camcorder on the dressing table in the bedroom. I fetch it, along with a jack lead, and insert the tape into the camcorder, plugging one end of the jack lead into the camcorder and the other end into the back of the TV, ready to play. From the metal tin I pick out the one with 'Congo' scrawled across it and push the large cassette into the VHS player below the TV, a JVC front-loader with surround sound capability. It's a flashy bit of kit, the video player being automatically activated on inserting the cassette. I press the button on the far left of the display panel to turn it off and return both the metal tin and the cardboard box back to their hidey-hole behind the dresser, along with the photos, picking a random handful to place under Slatter's pillows, making sure not to fit the hidey-hole's covering board but just lean it up against the wall, showing enough of a gap that it can easily be detected. The magazines I put in the bottom section of the wardrobe, again not placing the covering piece of veneered panel correctly. To top it off I fetch the carrying case from the sofa and take out the tin of neatly wrapped coke in its little cling-film parcels; anything to add an extra layer of confusion. I unwrap one and sprinkle the fine white powder over the bedclothes and on the coffee table in the lounge, or the seating area as Slatter called it, using a couple of grams to create the false impression that he likes to party, even going so far as to cut some of the coke into a rudimentary line for effect. Happy that the scene is set, I walk through the flat again from room to room, from wall to wall, checking and double-checking, scrutinising every detail, mentally ticking them off till an inward voice tells me *that's enough, let's go*. I pick up the dossier and put it in its original wallet holder before stowing it in the outer zipped section of the carrying case. Again, I check I have everything, that I have done everything: My final act is to leave Slatter's keys on the arm of the sofa before shutting the door behind me.

Chapter 11
What It Is to Be Bad

Not that the world needs more monsters, just a different kind; a physical reminder to those who think they are in charge. And regarding psychopaths, well, what can I say? It's time for my unveiling…

From at least two miles away I see it, a dark funnel swirling, tapering down over the roof tops like an alien craft coming in to land. Yet you just know this is no friendly visitation. Even from a distance you sense its menace, a visible paradox that to all onlookers is no more than a freak occurrence, something ornithologists would probably attribute to erratic weather conditions, or the electromagnetic effect given off by nearby pylons. But to me it is a hundred-feet-tall neon sign unveiling the beginning of a new era. Far-flung specks I knew to be thousands of jet-black crows spiral in a steady descent; my eyes are for a second theirs, gliding through the air looking down as the murder of crows caws my intent to a world which is going to wake up tomorrow to exactly that – a bloody day of glorious murder.

I sit in the front passenger seat as Dad drives me to yet another drop-off point. The ominous whirlwind looms large over the passing roof tops as though denoting my coming of age, a kind of good-luck message sent by an anonymous well-wisher, the kind that has clout over Mother Nature. Pretending it's the gods favouring my fortune, I symbolically tip my hat by way of a broad smile towards the magnificent gesture.

But in the whirlwind's shadow, the world outside changes, the way a sudden shock can take years off a weak and undeserving soul, ravaging purity to something wretched in seconds. Houses turn suddenly derelict, with gardens wildly overgrown and cars left abandoned to rust, forming random climbing apparatus for devil-like imps to clamber over. People mope aimlessly in rags, glaring as we pass by, their eyes dim and sunken and their black, gaping mouths emitting screams of pained purgatory. They wave for help in our wake with a look of impending doom, that look of disease and decay that the barely living have, unaware they are already dead, waiting to be put out of their misery in the vain hope it will be some magical cure.

During the short journey I say nothing except 'thanks' and 'see you later' as Dad waves before driving off. He knows that far-away look and concedes any last-minute questions he may have. I let him go, better for not knowing and not wanting to know, nodding my appreciation for his discretion. Wherever this journey takes me, I fear I am heading down an ever-narrowing tunnel towards an ever-darkening world, a place grim and forbidding. Not that I'm scared of the dark or what may lie within. My fear is that I am going to enjoy it.

I once looked up the definition of evil. It read: Profoundly immoral and wicked; profound immorality and wickedness, especially when regarded as a supernatural force. This niggling curiosity coincided with one of my dad's friends, Sidney, a cut-throat businessman of his day and habitual old-school cynic, telling me before I set out for the Cotswolds, "If I can give you any advice, my boy, it is this: In all that I have done, I have learned there are only two types of pain: The type which makes you strong and the type that is considered useless, which makes you suffer." He went on to emphasise that he got where he is today because he has no time for uselessness. I remember replying, "Neither do I!" Thinking about it, nor has anyone else, for what is uselessness except the bane of most people's issues, a blight that most would do anything to be rid of?

But in retrospect, this characterisation describes my present state of mind perfectly… *"I am it, as it is me, as we are one together"* the voice of my hippy friend chirps. "Embrace the love you have for *it* and what *it* has for you," he preaches, every word resonating like the chimes of a ghostly grandfather clock, his hippy philosophy – just go with the flow, man, and everything will be fine. But fine for who? Me, them, everyone, no one – who?

In conversations I have with myself, I ask, "Do you ever feel imprisoned by your own thoughts?" And a voice from nowhere replies, "What do you mean? In the way they govern, or in how they overwhelm?" – "I guess both!" I say back, at which I am always left hanging, the ethereal airwaves falling deathly quiet, as if there is no answer to give. I knew I had this weird propensity for wishing violence on those I don't like, but to consider myself evil – never in a million years would I think such a terrible thing! But as I don my black leather gloves and insert the key into the lock of Neil and Slatter's old flat, it is all I can think about. Is this what the colonel recognised when he took me hunting?

"I tried to shoot you, you know," the colonel told me afterwards, as we walked back to his chateau. I didn't reply. I just nodded. Surprised, I guess. "When you were about to shoot the first boy, I had you in my sights. I tried twice with the Marlin, the bullets refusing to fire on both occasions. That rifle has never failed me, ever, and neither has the ammunition I use. I ejected them and scratched crosses on the shell casings. I then emptied the rifle of ammunition and reloaded it with only the two bullets that would not fire. And those were the two bullets that you fired to kill my dear old adversary. How this is possible, I cannot explain. But what it does tell me is that you are destined for greatness." I checked the shell casings in my pocket. They both had crosses scratched into them. The colonel's words coined a very fruitful visit. God, how I can still recall every detail of that fateful day. Those faces will never leave me. But what amazed me most about the orchard, was how those three boys on initially seeing the colonel and me, smiled, beaming from ear to ear, their hysterical sobbing and agonised howls for 'Mama' and 'Tata' stopping as though we were the miracle they had been crying out for, albeit for a few blissful seconds.

Is this, this murderous extreme, what is now expected of me?

Am I evil, a monster in the making, or have I always been this way, as defined by my new game's underlying ethos? *Apok* can take any individual, give them a choice of weapon and it will guarantee to reveal the monster within. I guess over the next several hours I'll find out.

***

Not wanting to alert the neighbours any more than I have to, I push the front door to, slowly and deliberately until the latch clicks with a slight echo into its deadlock position. The smell hits me first, then the sun's searching light as I stand amid dozens of illuminating rods, breathing in an enclosed, dank odour of emptiness and neglect, the feeling not that dissimilar to the isolation of a late summer's forest glade. The warm dusty rays lance through the small hallway from the south-facing main lounge, a glow from the kitchen adding to the musty light. The doors have been left wide open, I assume by a previous visitor to help circulate the trapped air. I dump my bag in the kitchen, on the nearest work surface, leaving my gloves on, and proceed to check each room, drawing the curtains as I go. The drapes throughout are of burnt orange colour and unlined; once drawn, the cheap, thin fabric transforms the flat into a rich golden nicotine brown. Taking a moment's solace, I watch shadows creep, crawl, and grow from corners and recesses like gloomy mould spreading along seams and cracks in the amber glow. The moment, which should have provided a brief respite, instead sends a slight chill down my spine; I give a short burst of nervous laughter at dismissing God's pitiful sun and all the pathetic souls who take comfort from it. *His* kind are not invited – not to this party. This party is 'members only' – a strictly private affair. The only attendee not officially listed is the dark that underpins every shadow in every corner, behind every door, its presence like a mandatory guest of honour impatient for the main event.

    The flat's interior is pretty much as Neil described; all of the downstairs and upstairs carpet has gone, plus the kitchen linoleum. I've been here before, so I know the layout. As soon as you enter, the kitchen is on your immediate left, with the main lounge straight ahead. The hallway is a spacious square shape, the stairs situated on the right behind the front door as you open it. Downstairs, just hard surfaces remain, the lot stripped back to the sealed concrete slab, and upstairs there is nothing but bare boards and the odd protruding nail. I can tell by dried water marks that both downstairs and upstairs floors have been recently mopped, and by the bathroom toilet there is a pristine, untouched loo-roll adorning an adjacent holder. The kitchen too, though sporting a little dust, looks clean, even inside the cupboards, which means someone is still keeping an eye on the place. I'm not worried. The chances of bumping into them are minimal, but it is something I have got to consider; whoever it is might come knocking. I head upstairs, trying to be quiet, but the bare floorboards can't help but creak under my weight, the noise amplified tenfold in the flat's barren interior. Again, upstairs offers a simple layout. The stairs lead to a small landing. Directly at the top and to the rear of the property is the bathroom; next to it on the left is the main bedroom; along the landing is a second, smaller bedroom overlooking the front; and at the end of the landing is a tiny box-room. In both front and rear bedrooms, I find a lone mattress tipped up onto its side, leaning up against one of the walls. The mattress in the front bedroom I drag into the rear. Kicking the other mattress over onto the floor, I place the one I have just dragged in directly on top to create a more substantial and comfortable base on which, I hope, Slatter will soon lose his virginity and, with any luck, enjoy it. I mean, what virgin wouldn't with man-eater Mandy on the case? She'll eat him alive, or then again, it could end up that he eats her. You never know with addicts; he's been underground for a while. There's a lot of pent-up angst bottled up in there, and Slatter's got something to prove. Addicts are like that, always wanting to show off that they are in control and how deep they are willing to go in order to demonstrate their point. Either way, tonight's going to be Michael's night, the girls my way of celebrating his genius.

Downstairs in the main lounge, I find the armchair and sofa, but also a low oblong coffee table that Neil forgot to mention; the three items of furniture are like a piece of abstract art in the empty space. The room is a handsome size – a little over twenty feet wide, the width of the entire property, by fifteen feet deep; a large shoebox that on one side, if I hadn't already drawn the curtains, would look out through dated steel-framed windows that span the lounge's entire width, onto a concrete-slabbed parade of padlocked roller-shutters. The off-licence and the betting shop are the only small businesses left, like two greedy cockroaches biding their time, happy to feed off scraps.

I arrange the sofa as strategically as the spartan room allows, longways on as you walk in, about a third of the way across the lounge with the coffee table perfectly parallel within an arm's length, and the armchair – my chair – in a central position on the opposite side, facing it. I try the armchair out for size; it's comfier than it looks, but as soon as I begin to settle, I'm up and pacing the room like a confined beast, half bored and half buzzing with anticipation, circling the carefully sited furniture, knowing that even though the scene is set, there is still something missing. Around and around I go, my frustration building, the missing item like a forgotten answer to an easy question that's on the tip of my tongue. A mirror! Of course! On what else are the girls expected to cut their lines of coke? There's one in the bathroom, oval-shaped with a decorative fluted edge, an Art Deco relic, its silvering beginning to flake, the speckled effect eerily ageing my reflection as I prise it off its supporting shell-clasps. But for some unknown reason the face I see scares me. I flinch away in sudden fright. I dare not look back, but, like a naughty child who is told not to, I do, out of the corner of my eye, again and again, drawn to its wraith-like countenance and piercing gaze. It is a look of the Devil, of obsession and intense wrath.

Join us, comes a deep moan through the glass, a strange voice that seems to circumnavigate the bathroom's close confines, lapping up the amber hue, its power enough to ruffle the Psycho-esque plastic shower curtain and whistle a hurried exit. And just like that, the Devil in the mirror is gone, leaving an obsessed 'me' staring back at my angry self. The clasps prove more difficult than I thought, needing to be twisted 180 degrees rather than prised off. But remove the mirror I do, managing to keep it fully intact with the minimum of noise, and there it is in pride of place, centre stage on the table. I fetch my bag from the kitchen and place it by the armchair for peace of mind. Unnerved by the reflection, I start pacing again, trying to decipher the message, wondering if it's just the pressure getting to me, playing tricks on my mind. Or is it like the crows who were lined up by the hundreds on every available perch waiting to greet me on my arrival and the shadows that creep and crawl throughout the flat? I don't know. But something wants to gate-crash my plans; something that was with me in the Cotswolds and followed me to Wales, then Croatia. Come to think of it, that never-feeling-quite-alone sensation has been with me ever since I can remember. Something I could never quite put my finger on but was always there and, I guess, that I have been questioning subconsciously all my life. It was worst during my teens. I would have episodes where I got lost in a place I called 'the hole'. It was like a fight with the innermost recesses of my mind as I tried to fathom what the hell was happening, my every sense struggling, digging myself deeper, the dark like quicksand, until the surface world was nothing more than a small round moon far above in a starless subterranean sky. But climb out I did. Each time I would awaken in a cold sweat, snapped from its ethereal clutches. But whatever was cruising through my mind also made the jump to my corporal domain. It always happened when I was alone, walking home either from playing football in the local park or from a friend's house. I'd be followed. Not by anything I could identify; it was more like a disturbance in the air that would travel through bushes and trees alongside my path, never to be seen. At night, *it* would get bold in *its* pursuit, resembling something of definite substance and purpose, a predator bounding beyond the streetlights' reach to a sound of snapping twigs and rustling leaves, hot on my heels as I hurried along, scared out of my wits.

However, it was being at home in the day that really put me on edge. I'd see flashes of dark figures reflected in mirrors, in windows or through half-open doorways, nanosecond glimpses of something or someone trying to make contact. That, I didn't mind; it always happened at a distance, and I had time to react. But in the shower, there was no time, no escape; everything would start off normally, and every time I would fall for its ruse and lapse into the same routine. I'd pull the shower-curtain across, close my eyes and let the warm water cascade over my head into my eyes and ears, the immediate intimacy of close-running, splashing water shutting off all outside sound. I would have time to relax, wash and let my body soak, and then when I was at my most vulnerable, I would feel a cold breath glancing off my shoulder and a deathly touch on my back or lower leg. At that instant I'd freeze, shivering, knowing *it* was within inches, ready to pounce and rip me apart, only to find nothing once I'd washed the soap from my eyes. Hence inwardly I was an unusually anxious teenager. It wasn't like having an imaginary friend that you could talk to and perhaps have it talk back. It was odd; each time something happened I would question my own sanity, playing the scene back over and over, dissecting and analysing the pros and cons. I so much wanted to be Harvey, a whimsical, happy-go-lucky fellow who was at peace with his imaginary six-foot-tall rabbit despite his family thinking he was quite insane. I wouldn't have minded being insane if only I'd had the support to begin with. But then again, unlike Harvey, I wasn't at peace with my imaginary friend. I was haunted and confused, with a fear of the unknown that was always there just out of sight. Even on patrols this past month, I could feel *its* presence keeping tabs on me. But now, in my new role, I see *it* differently; *it* feels different and sounds different, like some kind of whispering affinity-cum-reassurance; an invisible talisman guiding my every waking step and infiltrating my sleep. In the day, *it* is an angel; however, at night, *it* remains a terrible demon, despite *its* best intentions.

"I think tonight's the night I'm going to find out what or who you really are," I say, turning around, my eyes darting, and ears tuned for a reaction. "I know you're here," I add in a whisper. If anyone could see or hear me, they'd think me a crazy man, like a vagrant in the street talking to them-selves, drunk on a higher calling, trying desperately to conjure up something out of nothing.

So what if I am talking to myself? So what if someone can see me – what do they know? Nothing! That's what! Are they me? Can they see what I see? Do they know what I know? No, of course, they don't. Yes, in some respects I might be crazy; that's what crazy people do, see things, hear things, feel things – strange shapes and forms they can't explain, ghosts and monsters and things that go bump in the night. In yester year I would have been ripe for the loony bin, carted off, branded mad, a heretic or worse. But that's what happens when you want to teach the world a lesson.

There lies the fine line between genius and insanity.

Who says absolute clarity can't lie in the ramblings of a madman?

I'm sure tonight will go without a hitch. It should do. I have planned meticulously. I'm also sure I will get to go back to my beloved Croatia to fight in the forthcoming war. I'm sure that after the war, the men in white coats will come to take me away, the powers that be exercising their right to reply. All because the warmongers will be facing a greater fear than that which they have already created.

Liberation through social freedoms, that is the power-brokers' worst nightmare, the anomaly which always slips through the net. They know that we, the people, are more than capable of deciding our own future. It is that tipping point when the pen is no longer mightier than the sword. They know that revolution is nigh, that we are ready to burn it all down, despite the cost.

War is almost upon us, and I shall lead by example, not fearing death or any repercussions or means of reparation. My time spent with the men in white coats will be my penance. Something is telling me that in spite of whatever darkest hellhole they throw me in, I will always have a friend by my side. A part of me is looking forward to it.

I am going to let this war be the future model of all wars to come. To quote my hippy friend, *"I am it, as it is me, as we are one together."*

***

I wonder if Noah dreamed before the flood about what it would be like to see millions drown. If he did, would it be like an aid worker foreseeing millions starving, both knowing that when it does happen for real, they will, at least in part, be unable to save them. The one certainty each day brings is my dreams. Today, my dreams are dark, probably due to the sense of occasion. In a blackened landscape, scorched as time's cruel whisper reduces bones to sand, a void between dystopian empires, I sit on my mock armchair throne laughing. If at my very first interview in the Cotswolds, I was sold this most turbulent of experiences based on what I know now, would I still have signed up? Would you, knowing where it will end up? It is one thing to be plucked from obscurity, but quite another to have one's macabre curiosities turned into reality. If I could speak to Noah, it would be to tell him that God moves in mysterious ways, just like genocide has many guises. Yet I sit with purpose, like a shaman who aspires to a condition of power, a most pure and holy form, before making my profound personal transition. Female shamans are believed to be the most powerful, and I believe the most effective transition can be achieved by using powerful women in the crossover ritual. Mandy and Sharon are shaman figures in their own right, bewitching men without so much as having to flutter a single eyelash. Men become putty in their hands, malleable and docile slaves catering for every whim and obeying without question every spell. Their female supremacy in the modern male environment is unparalleled.

It is this dynamic essence I hope to absorb and harness during the ritual, that and what Slatter has to offer, thereby completing this stage of my evolution.

The amber-gold atmosphere lends the scene the desert's cleansed feel; the drawn curtains create an amazing apocalyptic vista, the glowing material a divide between me and an uninvited world soon to be excluded from the rest of its future yet wholly included in its downfall.

Again, like a recurring déjà vu, I find myself at the centre of a storm. The desert void suddenly transforms and whips up into a frenzy of people around me; a cityscape travelling at a million miles per hour, yet I can't move a muscle. It's like I'm stoned, watching other dopers chain-smoking between fixes, hyper in trying to shake off the DTs.

One big mad rush to nowhere! A craziness where nothing seems to matter. My mind goes *clunk-click* like an old photographic slide projector. I view from my armchair scenes of factory production lines curing world hunger. They process severed limbs recycling and pressing them into edible shapes. The sound of the stamping machines changes to the whir of chainsaws. In a tropical rainforest, I see families upon families of orang-utans, crushed and smashed beneath piles of logs, having fallen from their treetop nests, only to stockpile another warehouse of unwanted furniture, as the *clunk-click* of my mind's projector flashes by a quick series of images. The pictures show shoppers in a mall stampeding over one another's bloodied corpses, fighting, and wrestling each other to the ground, for no other reason than to be first through the *hallowed* doors. The follow slides delve into people's homes, their lives revolving around state-sponsored TV as they gorge on edible shapes and lounge on cheap furniture.

It's a horrific vision of indifference, of people easily manipulated and even more easily pleased. It is a place of microwave ready-meals and plastic living, where everything is on-demand at the click of a button. An obese, diabetic populace, disconnected and disenfranchised, learns to dumb down life's expectations; the subterfuge is a master class in slashing the value of today's remaining moral virtues.

The old order has had its day. This is a brave new world demanding a brave new outlook, but from what I saw last night in the bars and clubs, there is no one to deliver it. Young people aren't bothered about the future; they're too stuck in the here and now, already beaten into submission. They just want to forget, to drink, fuck, do drugs, fight, and *party till it's 1999*, anything but relive the day-to-day, week-to-week treadmill that is their humdrum routine. Even though last night was all about my business with Pork Chop and getting the girls on board, I so desperately wanted to find and join in with the young generation, my generation, celebrating their vibrant youth. Instead, I found a generation lost and numb to ambition, success measured daily, not in the long term; a town of herded sheep, everyone with the same self-destructive idea, as if they have somehow decided *'trying is futile, what's the point'?* Forget innovation, forget progress, forget pushing new boundaries, you won't find it here. And so, amongst the booze and pills, the seeds of a wasteland are sown. I can hear my hippy friend now. "It sounds just like the '60s, dude, free love, and free living. We didn't care either, man, just a little weed here, a tab of LSD there, dossing in squats with no one telling us what to do, our only hassle the pigs and rednecks. Hell! Life was good. You should try it. As long as you love what you do, everything will work out. It's like we hippies always say: *All you need is love, love; love is all you need*." He is right in that I love what I do – I'm devoted to it. But there again, I'm not trying to defeat water cannons and riot police with brightly coloured flowers and by blowing kisses. And though I admire the likes of Mahatma Gandhi and Martin Luther King Junior for their methods of non-violent protest and incredible fortitude, the methods I am going to employ will be as far from peaceful as you can get. We have to start again. There's no other way. It's a crying shame, but this is where we are. The glitzy consumerist neon world we see as the pinnacle of humanity's success is the slippery slope, an unobtainable perfection built on lies; it is why the youth of today have given up and why, as a species, we no longer seem to care. We have become complacent and ever more invasive, taking our world's resources for granted. How long till there's not enough food or water? How long till we are at each other's throats? How long till we are past the point of no return and things really won't matter?

Which begs the question: How long do we have?

I mean, what are we waiting for? The next big asteroid? A natural phenomenon to take charge of resetting our collective path? Does this mean God was right in deciding our fate when he had Noah build the ark and then flooded the world? Is this what humankind wants, to begin again at whatever cost, even if it does threaten our extinction? Is this why nothing seems to matter in this throw-away, easy-come-easy-go world we have created? Is this why we just want to throw it away, because we can and it's the easiest thing to do – to do nothing and be indifferent? So, in our present state, it doesn't matter that the world's wealthiest 1 percent have equal to, if not more than, the remaining 99 percent combined, or that I killed those kids in the orchard, or that Croatian police units are secretly killing hundreds every week. If that is so, then I guess it doesn't matter who shot John F. Kennedy, or if man actually stepped onto the moon, or that science is closer to curing cancer, or that if humankind keeps growing at its current rate, our total population will reach an unprecedented ten billion by the year 2050, if not sooner. If this is the case, my question is: What would social freedom mean to the ten billion of 2050 compared to the five point three billion who inhabit the world today? What can the generation of the 1990s teach the generation of tomorrow?

Like I said, the only thing that does seem to matter is: How long do we have?

And the answer, considering we live in a world of such disparity, is…not long.

***

A knock at the front door snaps me to, or so I think, my mind still not free, caught in a dream's nightmarish wake as grotesque faces and horrible claw-like hands press through every surface, the floors, walls, and ceilings stretching and creaking and moaning as what I can only describe as creatures from another dimension try their best to break through into ours. *Tap-tap-tap.* There's the knock again. Three definite raps of the knuckles. Now I am awake. The creatures and their alien shapes slowly sink back into the building's structure as I open the door, the sudden burst of daylight like an acid-bath to them, like salt to slugs. Though I know the creatures are lurking just beneath our world's surface, cruising their hellish shallows, waiting for yet another chance to pull me under; the surrounding air is electric to the point where I almost forget to breathe.

With an almighty exhale of 'here goes', I quickly usher Slatter and Pork Chop in and shut the door behind them, remembering just in time not to slam it. As soon as the door closes, the plan kicks in like it's part of my DNA. *Its five o'clock; time to get this show the road,* a voice inside my head yells.

"Keep us waiting, why don't ya?" Complains Pork Chop jovially. I shrug in response.

"You made Michael carry all of the shopping," I remark, trying to wind Pork Chop up, first eyeballing him square-on, then looking at Slatter, who is struggling with a bulging supermarket carrier bag in each hand.

"Fuck him! He's the new guy. Anyway, FNGs always carry the shopping, you know that," replies Pork Chop with a wry snigger. I reciprocate with a slight giggle, acknowledging his chipper mood, glad to see that emotionally he seems to have pulled through last night's final test and, on the surface at least, there seems to be no lingering side-effects. He's done well. Killing kids can be rough, whether it's accidental or for pre-meditated revenge. Shit like that weighs heavy on the mind, whatever the reason.

"And how are you, Michael?" I ask.

Slatter nods, smiling. "Okay," he says, exuding a calm aura of ease, as if he knows that is exactly what I want to see and hear. It is a very clever response from someone who knows they are still being vetted. It's succinct in meaning and submissive in tone, yet his voice is firm, conveying all the reassurance I need.

"Glad to hear it," I say. "Put the bags in the kitchen, will you? It's through that door…there," I point out the way. Slatter, in his readiness to please, squeezes past me to deposit the bags before I even have a chance to finish my sentence. "Come, I need to talk to you and Porky."

Slatter follows me into the lounge. He sits next to Pork Chop, who is already nestling on the sofa like a fidgety rooster shuffling its backside till comfy. "It's a bit musty," he moans, patting down the cushioned seats in mock disgust.

"So would you be if you'd been left to fester in a damp flat for weeks on end." I wanted to keep this part of the conversation serious; I wasn't in the mood for his tit-for-tat banter.

"We know some folks back in Croatia like that," Pork Chop quips sarcastically.

"Don't we just!" I give a dismissive flick of my wrist. A signal that Pork Chop knows very well means "shut the fuck up" when I'm about to talk. "Anyway, first things first…"

"Sorry, boss," Pork Chop murmurs, bowing his head. Slatter immediately gets the hint.

"Did you get what I asked for?" I ask.

"Yeah, and more besides, thanks to Michael," says Pork Chop in a low, subservient tone.

"And…?" I say, inviting an explanation.

"I got what you said, as per instructions: Ice, tequila, champagne, lemons and limes, saltshaker, and a four-pack of lager for Michael here," Pork Chop says, going from patting the sofa to patting Slatter's thigh in a friendly show of harmony. "Plus, the stuff Michael suggested, due to the flat being empty 'n' all: Some Tupperware beakers with a matching dish and plate, a kitchen knife to slice up the lemons and limes, some nibbles, cheesy cheddars, chip-sticks and assorted flavoured crisps, and a dry-wall hammer."

"What the fuck's a dry-wall hammer?" I ask.

"Well, that was my idea. It's the closest thing to a hatchet-axe thing I could find."

"It's just like your typical hammer, a steel shaft with a nylon-vinyl grip, but instead of a claw or ball pein on the opposite side of the hammer head, it's a sturdy blade, similar to that of an American Indian's tomahawk," Slatter explains, helping out his new partner in crime.

"I see," I pause. "And why might you have bought this particular item?" I ask Pork Chop, staring directly into his eyes, this time genuinely intrigued, because I haven't explained the finer details of *apok* to him, and I'm the only one who knows. At least, I don't think I have.

"It was in Zagreb a month or so ago when I was soaking up a little R&R. We were tired, hadn't slept properly for days and the pivo chased down with some slivovitz knocked us for six. We were tripping, joking around like fools, telling each other stupid stories of our childhoods, and I don't know why, but you loosened up in a way I had never seen before. That's when you told me about *apok* and the choice between a knife, axe or pistol, and how these are the tools that will release the monster within. I thought you'd be glad…"

Pork Chop's voice tails off, unsure of my reply. *Is he going to be angry or more philosophical?* I can see it in his face; his whole demeanour suddenly tenses.

"Sorry, mate, I'd completely forgotten," I say, not angry at all but weirdly apologetic and genuinely surprised. How could this have slipped my mind? I remember the bar, the before and after, even ordering the initial rounds of drinks, yet the rest is a blur, like a radio that is trying desperately to tune in, back and forth across the narrowest of bandwidths. The booze is a chink in my armour, a weakness that I must control. "Michael, would you mind going into the kitchen and giving us a minute? Thank you."

Slatter gets up and leaves the room only to be heard in the kitchen pottering, probably unpacking what he and Pork Chop have bought.

"I just thought with Michael popping both his chastity and killing cherries, he might progress beyond the knife…" suggests Pork Chop, shrugging.

"To the axe!" I complete his sentence.

"Something like that…yeah."

"We'll see," I say. "But with Michael we need to take baby steps, okay? For a calm person I see a lot of rage in there. A man stuck in his past and a boy desperate to move forward, two contrasting yet closely connected souls striving to fill in the gaps that the other one leaves in order to become one. In essence, he is the reverse of me, a storm turned inside out, where a private storm rages on the inside as everything on the outside appears peaceful, unaware that he could erupt at any second. You see, Slatter is the older, more mature personality; a person whose angst and genius relishes the dark side of humanity. Whereas Michael is the younger, more juvenile half, his social awareness as naive as it is undeveloped. Hence the rage that burns is a frustration born out of shyness – that and an inability to relate. I should know – it takes one to know one. But I learned to overcome and control my deficiencies. The person that is both Slatter and Michael hasn't." After being perched attentively with elbows on knees to support his jutting chin, Pork Chop slumps back to puff a long exhale, eyes rolling as he ponders my analysis. He knows, like I know, that the dual personality of Slatter and Michael is in transition as Pork Chop, and I are in transition. The three of us are coming together at this critical time to form a critical mass – a mass that is more than ready to explode and show the world who we really are.

"Hey, Michael, you can come back in now." I deliberately aim my voice at the lounge door, just loudly enough that I am not shouting, and he can hear me.

And, just like he left, an unhurried Slatter noiselessly pushes the door open to rightfully retake his seat at the table. "Right, then; you two listen up and listen carefully. I need to go over what happens after," I explain. "That is before we have a few drinks, okay? For obvious reasons you will both have to commit my instructions to memory. Is that clear?"

Pork Chop is instantaneous in answering "Yes, of course."

Slatter, however, remains an impassive picture of pure concentration, happy to grunt an acknowledgement under his breath, as if to say, 'Get on with it'.

"From here, you will fill up with fuel and drive directly to Dover without stopping. It will reduce the likelihood of anything untoward happening. For instance, in recent months there has been a steep increase in the number of cars being stolen off motorway service station car parks. Needless to say, though the traffic will be light, keep to the speed limits and, above all, no crashes. A crash means police involvement, regardless of if you're already a copper. Plus, you don't want the car searched; not with your baseball bat, the cash and all those drugs in your boot."

Pork Chop gives a firm nod.

"Once at Dover, Porky, you will purchase a suitable day return ticket for your car and two passengers to Calais. Give a cover story that it's a booze run for a fellow officer's retirement party or something, and you drew the short straw at having to do the fetching and carrying. You know the drill, and remember, use your original passports when buying the tickets. That is imperative. And…" I pause, waving my finger, "when talking to either the salespeople in the ticket office or any of the border officials, come across as a team, two friends eager to get over to France, leaving the country together, in the same car together. That part is crucial – okay?" I pause to gauge their reaction, my last comment reiterating loud and clear that this is a one-way trip with absolutely no route back. As of Monday, both will be deemed 'persons of interest' concerning the events of this weekend. Although both already know this, I think it might be best if I give them a minute for the first instalment of the plan to sink in; the concept of never coming back to the UK is still new to them and it's a lot to take in, especially when combined with the added pressure of seeing the plan through without fault.

Slatter and Pork Chop, their expressions brimming with steely determination, nod towards me, then at each other. It's the reaction I want.

"Not a problem," replies Pork Chop. "We'll be fine. Anyway, on day passes, if border control does flag you up as a risk, if you're going out, they usually organise it, so you are stopped on your way back in," he chips in with his expertise.

"Nice one, Porky. That's good to know. Makes sense, really. People bring contraband into the country, not take it out. What do you think, Michael – you good with that?" I glance at Slatter.

"Yeah…I'm good." He smiles.

"Now, once on the ferry, you will have to leave the car. You are not allowed to stay with the car in the cargo area during transit. But at least it will be safe there. Act as most ferry-goers do when wanting to kill an hour or so; go to the main bar on the upper level and get yourselves a drink. Weather permitting, go out onto the open deck, but if not, sit at the stern end of the bar and use the toilets within ten minutes of buying your drinks. In either scenario, you will be approached" – I look at Pork Chop – "by someone who has seen you before – a Croatian. He's a friend, though the two of you have never met. His password will be 'no prisoners – death to all – spare no one…"

"Of course, it will," interrupts Pork Chop, smirking.

"After the man has identified himself, he will specify a certain vehicle which you must follow on leaving the ferry. This will be your security escort all the way to Geneva. You'll take a diagonal route across France via Reims, Dijon and Mâcon, bearing left to Bourg-en-Bresse and then the Swiss border. Once in Switzerland, your escort will take you to a secure location where another man and a medical team will be waiting. Just remember, while you are on the ferry, this man will be your only contact. You will act natural but talk to nobody else – only officials if, and when you have to. Is that understood?" Both Pork Chop and Slatter nod emphatically. "Good. Because once you're on French soil and out of Calais, heading south down the A26/E15 toll road, and are under the protection of your security escort, you're safe. As it stands, I am the only one in this whole process who knows your real identities. As for everyone else involved, well, they couldn't give a fuck who you are. Trust me when I say they answer to a higher power, which means that even if they did, nothing would be said. Plus, once Michael has made his withdrawal from his account in Geneva, you are to destroy your real identity documents immediately. That is non-negotiable, okay? However – and this is a big 'however'" – I use my index and middle fingers on both hands to emphasise the inverted commas – "to fully utilise the respite that the secure location will provide, after you both have established new accounts in a different bank under your new identities, which, I might add, are already in the process of being made up – Michael, yours still requires photographs, but that'll be done as soon as you arrive at the secure location – it is my intention to stage your deaths, or at least give the impression you are both dead. That is, once the Swiss authorities find your car."

"What? How?" asks Pork Chop. "My car?"

"You didn't think you'd get to keep it, did you?"

"I dunno what I thought," he answers. "I guess not."

Slatter can't help but giggle at Pork Chop's dismay.

"You're a copper, for fuck's sake! Think about it," I snap in disbelief to his petulant comment. Boys and their toys. I don't fucking believe it. *Child!* My inner voice growls, surprised at Pork Chop's impertinence and outright stupidity.

"B-but…" Pork Chop stutters. He has a tendency to do that when flustered.

"But nothing!" I counter like a frustrated mom at the school gates on a brat's first day. "Just look at it as though I'm adding yet another layer to the mystery."

"It's exciting" – chirps Slatter – "not to mention impressive. Sophisticated, even."

"You see, Michael's got the right idea."

"Kiss-ass!" Blurts Pork Chop.

"No choice," says Slatter, still grinning at Pork Chop.

"But that's exactly it; there is no choice, not for any of us. Don't you see? We are locked in this together, and together is the only way we will see this thing through." My tone is now definitely that of the schoolteacher. "You just need to let me do this my way. Trust me and everything will be okay."

"I do trust you. Of course, I do," says Pork Chop. "I mean…yeah, fuck the car! I don't know what I was thinking." He waves his hand as if to say 'forget about it'; it signifies a stern self-rebuke at having made one seriously cringe worthy lapse of judgement.

"It's okay, mate. But it is only a car, and it is expendable, just like your wife and family, come the moment of truth, as was Michael's job and his cosy, closeted life when he walked out on it earlier today. Sacrifices have to be made, but the rewards are like nothing you could ever imagine. You are heading for greatness, my friends. Never forget that," I say with fanatical reassurance.

"I know, and I'm grateful," Pork Chop replies, with Slatter nodding wholeheartedly.

"Okay, then. Enough said; let's get back to the plan."

I bow my consent to what I know is his unquestionable loyalty. I pause briefly, checking, as a conductor often does, that my orchestra, albeit just two, is up to the task before commencing what is probably the most intricate part of this particular concerto. "The secure location is a staging-post, a place to change vehicles. It also offers a certain amount of privacy, hence the theatrics. It takes time and patience to stage two deaths and get the scene exactly right, to make a car appear abandoned and ransacked after, let's say, a drug deal gone wrong. They happen across Europe all the time. The bullet holes have to be in the right place, the trajectory spot on, as though they were fired through the front windscreen by an advancing assailant; something fast, dramatic and unforeseen. Not to mention the blood splatter inside the vehicle's cabin to simulate heavy bleeding attributed to massive chest and abdominal trauma. The idea is to have blood bags on you, line them up with the bullet holes, and then burst them to make it look as real as possible, as you, sitting in the car, pretend you've been shot. Recoil at the imaginary bullets and squeeze your blood bags as you, Porky, wipe your bloody hands over the dashboard, steering-wheel and doorhandle and you, Michael, release your seatbelt and partly open your door. The interior needs to reflect your panic and final moments of anguish and a sudden, violent death. It's got to look like you were unable to get out of the car. I want it to look as much like an execution as possible, as though you were set up – y' know, ambushed. And don't worry about the choreography; the Croatian is an expert. Plus, the medical team will assist if necessary, so you create a believable blood trail. Then, from your seated positions, acting dead and covered in blood, you'll be carefully hauled by the medical team from Porky's car onto the ground. There your clothing and body will be thoroughly searched and dragged to a waiting van, all of which must be replicated to the nth degree, enough to satisfy any investigator that this has happened to two freshly shot bodies."

"But if it's meant to look real, that will take a lot of blood – our blood!" says Slatter, his calm exterior beginning to waver.

"Exactly! Authenticity is of the utmost importance. The forensic evidence found in and around the car at the secure location must come from you, and yes, in order to achieve this, I will need you both to donate a certain amount of blood. The DNA must be a perfect match. There's no way around that; an irrefutable link must be established between Porky's home address, that of your wife's friend" – I glance at Pork Chop – "and whatever they find at Michael's flat and in here. It can only work if all of the separate locations tie in together and, equally, are corroborated by any existing records. I want the link, in the eyes of the law, to be beyond any reasonable doubt."

"You're setting us up," Michael says sharply, narrowing his eyes ever so slightly and giving them a cruel edge.

"Only to set you free. You'll be yesterday's news before y' know it."

"I don't think it will be quite that easy, but I get what you're saying."

"Look, I'm being straight with you, as I hope you'll always be straight with me. We're going to be partners; there's no room for ambiguity. Between the three of us, trust is our only currency going forward. Yes, it is unknown territory, but that's the deal. Like you said, you have no choice, considering the mess you have gotten yourself into. This is your one and only chance to escape. If you're having second thoughts, tell me now."

"And have you kill me with the hatchet I bought you? No thanks! It's just that I have a phobia of needles and giving blood. The thought of doing it freaks me out, that's all," Slatter explains, folding his arms into a defensive posture, probably regretting that he has divulged more than he intended to.

"That's no problem; your phobia will be expertly catered for. A twelve-hour window has been allocated in which to achieve this. Two to three pints of blood is perfectly doable in that time. It will be a piece of cake, you'll see," I raise my eyebrows. "So whaddaya say? You still in?"

"Of course, I am. Forgive me" – Slatter blurts out nervously – "and I'm sorry for mentioning the hatchet-hammer thing. I didn't mean to," he jabbers, the thought of having a cannula inserted into his arm clearly unsettling him.

"You don't have to worry, Michael. But just so you know, being killed with a hatchet does hurt. It hurts an awful lot, and it's messy – oh Christ, is it messy! But the frightful horror of the pain and mess…" I pause to eyeball Slatter, "boy, does it pale in comparison to the time it takes for you to die! That, my friend, requires real effort; you work up a sweat smashing in someone's head. You've seen that Congo video – they ain't no overripe watermelons them savages are hacking. Breaking into someone's head is like breaking into concrete; you have to smash it up bit by bit, hitting it again, again, again and again. The job isn't done until the head is no more. If you can picture that, you can appreciate death by hatchet ain't quick, and it certainly ain't pretty! Now that, my friend, is a phobia worth having, wouldn't you agree? Because that is the very essence of *apok*."

I make my allegory purely rhetorical, not requiring an answer or any form of acknowledgement, just an intrinsic understanding that if you fuck up, the next person to have their brains dashed across the floor could be you.

"Now imagine that fear multiplied by a thousand, by hundreds of thousands extending throughout an entire country. Now hold that image in your minds. That is where *apok* is going to take us," I pause, searching the two expressions across the table. Quizzical looks soon turn to a widening of the eyes, then pained grimaces. "Scary, isn't it?"

***

After the lads tell me about their day, strolling around Packwood House and picnicking at Baddesley Clinton, making the most of the good weather and what normality they have left, I let Pork Chop go to fetch the girls. He takes an amended list of candles and matches; perhaps we could do with another bottle of plonk. I suggest red, a nice Côtes du Rhône AOC or a Rioja Tempranillo, something to go with the nibbles, a corkscrew, and soft drinks for him to sober up on, as I know him too well. He will have a few drinks at least, despite the long drive down to Dover. Coppers! They're all alike, spoilt at having it so cushy for so long. But these days, with the new breed of self-righteous do-gooder coming through the ranks, the kind that will sell out their own kin for a foot up the ladder, that's all by-the-by. I need Pork Chop alert, on top of his game, not half-cut.

"Thought I was going mad for a second there," I say, walking into the kitchen. "All of a sudden I turned round, and you weren't there."

"Sorry…just want to keep myself busy, I guess," Slatter says, pouring a bag of ice into the empty washbasin, one of those cheap stainless-steel, all-in-one, sink-and-draining board types of indicative of council tenancies. "I find it best if you have a base layer of ice creating a bank around the edge for the bottles to rest on," he continues, positioning the champagne and tequila with the utmost of care, and then the beer cans, as if they were ticking time-bombs. "Then pour the remaining ice over the top, trapping them between the two layers. Remember to put the plug in, of course," he adds with a raised eyebrow.

"Are you okay?" I ask.

"A little nervous."

Slatter arranges and rearranges items to millimetre precision.

"I can tell."

I look at the plate, dish, knife, then the dry wall hammer centrally positioned on the counter, leading away from the sink in order of size; placed behind them, spanning equal length against the wall tiles with equal space between them, are the lemons, limes and saltshaker. Its exactness makes me smile.

"One of my first drill instructors said to me not long after starting, 'If you're afraid, don't do it. If you do it, don't be afraid'."

"Genghis Khan," Slatter replies.

"What?" I snap unintentionally.

"It's a famous quote by Genghis Khan," Slatter elucidates. "It means that whatever you decide, there is no need to worry. Just believe in yourself and everything will be all right."

"You see how good you are; you've just solved your own problem." I nudge his arm. "Chill out. I believe in you, so you believe in me when I say everything is going to be okay."

"Hmmm!" He murmurs in response. "You know I wouldn't really do anything to kids," he adds, his eyes wide in trepidation. "You do know that?"

"I know," I reply. "Loneliness can be cruel like that. It can make your mind wander till up is down and down is up, and bad is good and good is as evil as evil can get. Not every escape route leads to the Promised Land."

"I've been living for so long looking over my shoulder, like someone with one foot perpetually in prison," Slatter says, his expression one of sad bewilderment. "When you arrived, I thought I was finished. A part of me still does."

"This time tomorrow you'll be wondering what all the fuss was about. You're twenty-four hours away from the rest of your life; a glorious life that you will enjoy in glorious surroundings. Trust me," I say with a smile.

But I know what he means. Loneliness grabs you. It drags you down to its level below the surface, where there's no air to breathe except darkness, a thick, malevolent soup that becomes your only sustenance, inducing you into a crazed, hallucinogenic alternate state where, all of a sudden, the madness makes sense. I remember my first time, staggering through plumes of dust, ducking the terrifying whoosh of RPG rounds, punch-drunk and dazed by successive explosions, my ears ringing, deaf to the dirt kicking up about me. My gun was blazing, the brass piling up around my boots, only for the panic and craziness to switch inexplicably to a bedroom where a little girl, a daughter I haven't even got, whispered "Daddy, Daddy, wake up" and tapped me on my face, hers barely visible in the gloom. I lifted the duvet and the girl climbed in, hugging me for all she was worth, complaining of ghosts in her room and under her bed. "But there are no ghosts; grown-ups don't believe in them," I whispered back. "Why, Daddy?" She answered tenderly. "Because it's always children who tell us they're real" – I replied softly – "Am I not real, Daddy?" She said into my ear, her hug shifting from around my shoulders to a tight grip of hands around my throat. "Am I not real, Daddy?" She said again. "Am I not real?" Her voice was deep and gravelly, getting louder and louder, her grip tighter and tighter. "AM I NOT REAL?" I woke eventually, still tossing and turning in a cold sweat and short of breath, afraid of what might be under my bed, not daring to look in case the face of the demon girl was staring back, a red-eyed, razor-toothed succubus who, if it saw me, would crawl out from amongst the stored bed-linen and blankets, slathering and gnashing its chops before grabbing me and pulling me in. But on other occasions the demon girl did crawl out, using its talon-like claws to drag its gnarled, bent body along the floor, and every time it did, I ran like a petrified rabbit; an adult reduced in a millisecond to a silly child that chose the same hidey-hole, the pantry, a walk-in cupboard under the stairs that led off the kitchen. And every time, scrunched up in the dark with my head tucked into folded arms, knowing the pantry door couldn't be locked, I'd hear the eerie scrape of the girl as she clawed her way step by step down the stairs, along the hallway and into the kitchen, cackling a kind of muted, choking laughter, the kind demons do when they are about to feast, clawing at the pantry door. "I'm here, Daddy; please let me in," it would tease. And as the door handle turned, I would wake, bolt upright, screaming. I have different dreams these days. I can't say I miss the girl much, though it is like jumping out of the frying pan into the fire. A new set of demons have replaced the old ones, driven by a warped sense of adventure set against war's pending romance of bloody mayhem, the monsters queuing up for a taste of what's to come. Resurrecting the girl sends a shiver racing down my spine. It's amazing how fear works, the speed at which it regresses the mind and soul to a time when you were most vulnerable. I see her now, the girl, sitting at the bottom of the stairs in the hallway, just as I used to not that long ago – "I'm gonna get you, I'm gonna get you," she cackles, chomping her teeth and clawing the walls, licking wildly at the air, crazed, chasing phantom flies, her lizard-like tongue reaching as far as the back of her neck.

I look at Slatter, then at the girl and back to Slatter. He shrugs, as if to say 'what' and I shrug back – "It's nothing."

The girl is gone in a flash to re-join the ether from which she came, her spirit exiting with shrill grotesqueness to thrash and fade amid the amber shadows.

"You alright?" asks Slatter.

"Yeah, I'm fine."

I feel quite the opposite, gripped, all of a sudden, by an overwhelming sense of claustrophobia, as though I'm hemmed in tight by a surrounding horde I cannot see, but that I know edges ever closer. Every surface in the flat gets closer, pushed by evil; a thousand glaring eyes, for the Beast is hungry. Whatever this thing is, it's not waiting for darkness to fall like I thought it would. It's coming right now.

Looking around the flat, I move from kitchen to hallway to lounge and back to Slatter, watching its drab wallpaper peel and the not-so-white paint flake from the ceiling like confetti as the floor, like every other surface, sheds its skin to bare its soul. It glows taking on a strange transparency like golden glass; an invisible demarcation where one dimension ends and another begins, with all manner of Hell's spawn pressed up against its restraining force-field.

Wow! To call this a house of horrors really doesn't do it justice.

Is this what folks see on their way to hell?

If it is, it's pretty spectacular. I thought I'd be afraid at finally seeing what it is that has been haunting me for all these years, but now that the moment is here, without fanfare or ceremony, its timing as callous and abrupt as it is inconsequential during the hours of daylight, any trepidation I might have had vanished the very second I saw them – and to think I hesitated. "Please, please forgive me!" I plead under my breath to the creatures that now encompass my position from every which way – front, back, left, right, above, and below, looking in as I look out, the golden glass box totally immersed in hells finest. Slatter glosses over my bewilderment, oblivious to the phenomenon as though the manifestation, like the girl, is for my eyes only.

I tap my feet as though testing ice on a frozen pond and walk tentatively in a tight circle above a monstrous sea of teeth and claws that squirm and writhe like eels. Slatter looks on quizzically, wondering what the hell I'm doing.

"This is unbelievable," I whisper, hoping my inner voice will add to the sheer marvel of this extraordinary sight. "And you can't see this," I remark, trying to get Slatter's attention. He squints a disinterested reply, adjusting and re-adjusting the items on the kitchen counter, his anxiety about the day's magnitude, about what is being asked of him, beginning to show. Just one item moved one millimetre means all the items have to be moved one millimetre to fall back in line; the sweat on his brow, the steadfast grimace, the slow, deep breaths are all indications that he might fall into a relapse. But I also see the creatures react to his despair. Slatter wasn't built for this. He said as much this morning. So why am I surprised to see the strain take its toll? Pressure for him is the worst conceivable torment. His inner turmoil pulls this way and that, fracturing his façade, exposing the vulnerable child beneath. I decide it's best for Slatter to get some rest. "You're tired, mate. C'mon, it's been a big day; perhaps the biggest. How about you go upstairs and have a nap? How does that sound?" I send him upstairs with a can of lager to lie down. "It's the second door on the landing, the one after the bathroom. I'll come up and wake you when they arrive," I call after him as he climbs the stairs, the creatures in the walls licking their fangs at every laboured step. Alone at last, I can't help but stare and gawp at the creatures, a menagerie of monsters so implausibly grotesque and cruel in design. I take a sharp intake of breath and our consciousnesses merge. I know they want it as badly as I do, like the rest of the world does, and the gods, who by revealing their impatience have drawn a line in the sands of time to say enough is enough. Both sides of the eternal divide are finally willing to admit their failings and work together to pull the plug on the current status quo. Today will be the spark that burns down the forest. Humanity will never be as complacent again. It can't – if it wants to survive. The gods won't let it. This show of force is self-evident that *they* approve. I've just got to live up to my end of the bargain and show them what I'm made of. Or else I'll be in hell with them.

Whatever deal was struck in *Jahannam* on that fateful night, this is it. *It* has looked after my needs, now I must cater for it.

The hallway arcs with blue-white discharge, the power generated between us palpable; the air is heavy with electricity, my clothes prickly to the touch, the small space a microcosm of raw energy as two universes unite. The fusion is blinding, igniting a core rage the ripple effect of which will leave no stone unturned or person unaffected. Whether the powers that be class this as a possible extinction levelling event or a serious pandemic, the kind every century endures at some point, nothing will ever be the same again.

I hear it in the creatures, how they roar and screech, gagging for it, chomping at the bit, frustrated, furious at why it hasn't already happened and why humankind let the world get this bad before doing something about it. They know, like I know, that this is way overdue, yet despite their snarling dissatisfaction they are here in all their horrifying magnificence to celebrate the inception of humanity's earthly reign coming to a close, the blackest of Satanic Masses paying their respects, waiting for the seventh seal to be broken so they can bear witness to the dawn of a new, darker beginning. And I, for one, don't intend to disappoint. It's my neck on the line as well. I will break that seal right here in this tiny arena before hell's nobility, bringing down the eternal divide for good so human and demon-kind can fight it out in a hell on earth that will in time bring an end to both a failed epoch and its creators. The demons are here to enforce the level playing field that humans for millennia failed to provide.

The moment of truth is here – it is now. It's time to live the dream. I can see it, a people's movement sweeping from house to house, street to street, empowered by Madame Guillotine's rallying cry, 'Vive la révolution!' And long live *apok*, its mandate daubed in blood for all to see: "No prisoners – death to all – spare no one!"

For we are entering uncharted territory: Humankind must burn if it wants to survive.

***

Waiting for Pork Chop to return, I hear a couple shouting and children crying further along the row of flats. The noise comes from out of the blue. Another voice enters the verbal affray a few seconds later, yelling even louder for them to "keep the fucking noise down."

I head towards the noise and go to the kitchen window, where I peer out of a gap in the curtains, cursing. I hate the sound of social weakness, especially that born out of ignorance. A string of profanity is echoed by another and another like an abusive cluster-bomb indiscriminately releasing its bigoted and deeply malicious payload, hit after hit, xenophobic shouts leading to racist exchanges till there isn't anyone in the block that hasn't been affected by the vile outburst. But once said, it can't be unsaid; the damage is done and the animosity assured, because when you let hatred out of the bag, you can't just wave it off as a silly mistake and stuff it back in. It doesn't work like that – it never has! Once out, it will do anything to stay out. It's a monster, just like the creatures in the walls, floors and ceiling, all jostling and fizzing to the exchange outside; the anger and malevolent intent excite them, whetting their appetites. Their gazes soon turn to me, and every horrible, glaring face seethes its murderous impatience, reiterating their displeasure at being made to wait.

"Don't worry," I say to them. "You'll soon be fed."

And why not?

They deserve their place at the banquet, to feast on our kind. They are the gods that once were and shall be again, impossible beings made possible, living deities that I intend shall walk our earth once more.

It's a radical move, not quite cutting off the head to cure the headache, but it comes pretty damn close.

I'm done with past and present mistakes, with watching the polar ice caps melt and global warming shift weather patterns to decimate crops and flood entire regions, sending world hunger and natural disasters soaring to biblical proportions. It's as though humankind, after biting the apple, has come full circle back to the time of Genesis, still lost to naked ambition, fighting for its very survival, even though there are those already picking through the post-mortem of our brief history upon this planet.

Such is our faith!

If cynicism was a virtue, we'd be laughing.

But instead of His fury, we get His indifference. God is bored with the effort of scheming our demise. He prefers to let us destroy ourselves, drowning not in tumultuous torrents but in a cesspool of our own industrial and technological success, a kind of perverse role reversal of King Midas's curse, where everything we've touched over the last century, land, sea and air, is turning to shit, poisoned to the brink of futility. Only now we don't have a Noah to save us. God in His apparent apathy is denying us even that. Not that anyone cares enough to act. And there lies the shame of who we've become. I mean, the all-powerful *1 percent* doesn't care. They consider themselves above it, thinking they'll somehow outwit nature's revolt, where society's lower tier, the remaining *99 percent* – that is, you, me and everyone we know, the operational strata of the working classes – will be left with the problem of solving the impossible. But it is those who have already given up, who can't be bothered and blame others for their misgivings, that are the main catalyst for spreading the disease. They prefer to drink, fight, and voice their drunken dissent, self-absorbed in petty squabbles, while their children hunker down with hands clasped over ears, dreaming of a better, safer future. If monsters can smile, then I am seeing hundreds drool with glee at the pervading negativity from outside. The creatures will feed. Of that, I am sure. But be patient, my friends. Though listening to the debacle out yonder, if I haven't already been convinced a thousand times that what I am doing is right, the fervent spite and wanton hate which typifies the human condition never fails to cement my resolve. Even the planet itself is crying out for this to end. It's the only decent thing left to do.

I stay at the kitchen window, leaning over the counter, curtain-twitching, looking out to see where the next shouts might come from. People-watching has always been a rather decadent and guilty pleasure of mine, and in years to come it might be as treasured as seeing a rare animal on safari. Standing here scanning the neighbouring flats, I wait for the psychopath inside me to pipe up and take control; the inner, nagging voice, that eggs me on, giving me my power. Not that it takes much. Where is he, my alter ego whose addiction longs for chaos? His only desire is to wrap me up in that certain realm of self-gratification amid the sights and sounds of hurt and suffering.

What is taking him so long? He should be here by now. These are his kind of people, self-deprecated and downtrodden, the expendable kind, cannon-fodder, packed like vermin in their rat-runs, out of the way and out of mind.

Looking back, I don't know how I got by without him, for he is my strength, my vision, my rage. Our souls are a meeting of fire and fire; he is the missing piece of a conundrum that has plagued my entire adolescence to adulthood, a puzzle that took a journey of self-discovery from the Cotswolds to Wales then Croatia to solve before I finally saw where I fitted in to this barmy world. It was a journey from something infinitesimal to something very different indeed, an experience not so much about myself but about a much bigger, wider picture in which I am integral. But in view of this bigger picture, my path of self-discovery, the skills, knowledge, and maturity I have gained, has been – how can I put it? – more of a mercy mission, learning how to put the morally weak out of their misery. Moving forward, this is how I see it, but on a grand scale; a scale worthy of the Great Flood, worthy of God taking notice.

Academics have repeatedly said that the world is run by psychopaths, but they have neglected to point out that the psychopaths currently holding the reins have never actually come across the real thing; a similar scenario to religious leaders and their god.

I have often wondered what would happen if they did meet, deities by their very divinity being so hard to please, let alone impress.

And thinking of gods, I turn my mind to the creatures. Of course, they will feed – not that the world needs more monsters, just a different kind; a shock reminder to those who think they are in charge. And regarding psychopaths, well, what can I say? It's time for my unveiling.

The era of diplomacy and indecision is over.

Chapter 12
Such Is My Vile Impiety

Can you feel it, can you feel it, can you feel it…

The knock at the door, a single lightly weighted tap, echoes through the flat like the inevitable pop of an executioner's pistol. The sudden crack in the still air transports me to Saigon during the infamous 1968 Tet Offensive to watch Lém, a Viet Cong prisoner, being summarily shot in the head. Its sound is that of destiny calling and history in the making. Fate has finally pressed 'Go'. This is it! The girls are here. This is what it has all been leading up to. Like a legendary sprinter, I'm up and off the armchair and at the front door in two seconds dead, my right hand, though slightly sweaty on the palm, ready to twist the small latch. I know that when I open the door, I will set in motion a chain of events that will eventually alter the path of humankind indelibly. This the actual point of no return, a blinding, split-second spark of two critical masses coming together for the first time. The bomb and the detonators are finally in the same place ready to be primed. The prophecy of the second coming is imminent as the planets suddenly align, an instant, brilliant flash signalling to the gods the dawn of a long-awaited divination. And when the world comes seeking answers – and they will – I'll gladly tell them it all started right here, right now! Like Lém, I want the death of society as we know it to be witnessed and documented for future peace and prosperity, a matter of public record to stand as an indictment of *our* failings, which will hopefully, once and for all, galvanise the masses to break the cycle that for so long has threatened every man, woman, and child the world over. As I have said and will keep on saying, out of the ashes *we* will rise.

In other words, I am going to enjoy being cruel so I can truly relish what it is to finally be kind. And with this in mind, I beam a deep and contented smile, whisper "que sera, sera", thumb the latch downwards and let the weight of sheer female audaciousness, push the door open.

"Hiya, Andrew," Mandy purrs, giving me a quick peck on the lips. Her sultry elegance hasn't waned one iota since last night. She hands me a heavy polythene shopping bag of what looks like two bottles of wine and some cans.

"There was no need to bring your own," I say, surprised.

"I didn't. It's his." She raises her eyebrows with an exasperated sigh as Pork Chop squeezes past, carrying two more shopping bags.

"How ya goin' babe?" Chirps Sharon excitedly, following her sister's lead. The flat goes from deathly silence to exuberant liveliness and the clip-clop of high heels in the blink of an eye.

"Carry on in, girls," I say, showing them into the main lounge. "Take a seat. I'll be with you in a sec."

"Is it clean?" Sharon asks, pawing the arm of the sofa.

"Of course, it's clean." I grin reassuringly. "The place may look sparse at the moment, but that's the whole point of inviting you over."

"Just sit down, sis," interjects Mandy, her soft tone like that of an appeasing dog-handler.

"I'll be back with some champagne – how's that?" I say. Sharon's smile grows and Mandy nods.

I backtrack in haste to the kitchen so as not to keep the girls waiting too long. I find Pork Chop unpacking the last of his bulging shopping bags.

"There's the stuff you asked for," he says, pointing to the bag I'm carrying. "Two bottles of red wine, some cans of Coke and a corkscrew."

"Thanks, mate. And the candles?" I place the bag Mandy handed me beside the stuff Pork Chop has already unpacked.

"They're here." He prods the other bag. "Proper church candles. Y' know, the big chunky ones. I wasn't gonna settle for any of those spindly votive-prayer things. They don't last ten minutes. These are straight off the altar; top notch, made from paraffin wax. They'll last all fucking week. Hence what's-her-face had to carry your bag, which, by the way, also has the matches in somewhere," Pork Chop says wearily. "And to save any argument, before you ask, I got both a Côtes du Rhône AOC and a Rioja Tempranillo. Wow, who stacked the crisps and things into a perfect pyramid?"

"Michael did. He was stressed. I guess that is what he does to cope." I point to the exactness of the other items.

"At least he's neat." Pork Chop quips. "Could be worse," he shrugs.

"Yeah, it could be," I murmur, thinking it had better not be. "Did you get anything else?" I add, *'cos last time you bought me a surprise fucking hatchet*, though I don't say that out loud.

"No. That seems to be the lot," answers Pork Chop, a note of sarcasm hinting that there isn't a dry-wall hammer in any of the bags.

"You're a good man. Thanks," I say in a slight rush to open the champagne. I fill two Tupperware beakers till they are nearly overflowing. "Sorry about the wait, girls," I announce, walking back into the lounge.

"I should fuckin' hope so!" Sharon cackles sardonically, which in turn causes Mandy to chuckle.

"So, when are we going to get a tour?" Asks Mandy.

"Yeah…when?" Sharon adds.

"Let's have a drink first; celebrate our new partnership. There's no rush. I've got plenty of champers and some tequila," I take my place in the armchair.

"Champagne slammers!" Sharon blurts. "Remember them, Mand? Magaluf!"

Mandy shakes her head. "How can I forget?" she sighs. "Tequila topped with cheap fizz in tumblers. Cover the glass with your palm, slam it on the bar, then down in one – lethal! Mind you, we were goin' at it. That was one crazy night."

"Off your tits crazy, y' mean!" Sharon laughs, her eyes wide, as if to emphasise how crazy it really was. "I don't believe we actually did it!" she adds with an air of mystery.

"Did what?" I ask, intrigued.

Mandy waves away my enquiry as soon as the words leave my mouth, the gesture a clean swerve around the subject. "What goes on in Magaluf stays in Magaluf," she purrs, an index finger held over her luscious red lips. "To be honest, I still don't know how we survived," she puffs in mock consternation, her remark more of a cautionary note towards her sister to perhaps take it easy tonight instead of going all out. But who's Mandy kidding? They're party girls, here on the pretext of free champagne and coke and a lifestyle they have been dreaming of since they left school. Of course, they're going to go all out – it's what they do. It is exactly why I chose Mandy; the girl simply can't help herself. Her sister was an unexpected, but very welcome, bonus.

"Bloody good night though, eh, Mand?" Sharon says. Mandy gives a deep, reflective nod.

"Do you wanna do the candles before we get too comfy?" I say in a low voice towards the kitchen, aware that the girls' boisterous mood, which is likely to continue, has already alerted the flats on either side to our presence.

"Roger that. Will do," I hear Pork Chop reply, in a reciprocated low tone.

"Mandy, Sharon, we just need to keep it down a tad," I say.

This time it's my turn to put my index finger over my lips to demonstrate the point while Pork Chop dashes to and from the kitchen with lighted candles. He places six large, squat hunks of opaque wax on the coffee table, two at both ends and two in the middle, their glow somewhat cancelled out by the late show of amber sunlight coming through the curtains.

"Why?" Sharon whispers sharply, disgruntled at having been told to quieten down. "I thought you said this flat is yours!"

"Neighbours aren't dodgy, are they?" adds Mandy, raising her eyebrows yet again. I mentally cross my fingers, hoping that the row I heard earlier is not preparing for Round Two.

"No – none of that," I say, rolling my eyes for effect, "but for now, while it's still early days, I would like to keep the neighbours at arm's length, keep 'em guessing – y' know, a low profile 'n' all that. Unnecessary interference at this stage is the last thing we want, especially in my line of business. Anyway, it will give you girls some breathing space to settle in – you know what I mean."

"Sure thing. We want this to go as smoothly as you do."

Mandy's response is a telling indicator of how serious she is and how well she has taken the bait.

"Is that why the curtains are drawn?" asks Sharon. "And what's with the candles?" she shrugs her shoulders. "It's still daylight!"

"To get us in the mood, I think," Mandy whispers to her sister.

"Come on, Porky, get in here an' charm these women. They're getting restless," I joke as Pork Chop comes waltzing in from the kitchen waving a half-empty bottle of Moët. "Any more for anymore?" he chirps.

"How about topping me up?" Sharon says, offering up her plastic beaker.

"Don't mind if I do, sweetheart. There you go."

Pork Chop flirts back, filling her beaker to the brim. "And how about you, gorgeous?" he asks Mandy.

She nods, leaving her beaker on the table. Pork Chop fills it in situ, then takes a sip straight from the bottle. "You can't beat a drop of the good stuff," he says with a satisfied 'aahhhh'.

"No, you certainly can't," I say, watching the girls lap up every second. Their eyes squint ever so slightly on each refill. I notice that look of ruthless desire as they relish how close it seems this lifestyle is to becoming reality.

"I know you introduced yourself when you picked us up, but what do you do?" Mandy asks Pork Chop, the question a little out of the blue but not entirely unexpected.

"You mean what role do I play regarding the business?" Pork Chop replies. She nods. "Shall I tell her?" he says, looking over at me.

"Yeah, go ahead – why not?" I give Pork Chop a knowing wink, telling him to say it like it is.

"I'm a policeman," Pork Chop announces, the moment an absolute jaw-dropping classic, his voice one of utter sincerity.

"What the fuck?" Sharon snaps. "Y' better fuckin' not be!" She bites instantly at the revelation. Mandy's feline eyes widen to their fullest extent, her sister's involuntary response bringing them both to the edge of their seats.

"Well, he certainly sounds like one!" Mandy's sixth sense right on the money.

"That's because I am a real policeman. Detective Sergeant Darren Space from vice at your service," he says jovially. The girls eyeball me, shaking their heads in muted disbelief. "And before you ask, you needn't worry; because of my job title, plus the position it holds, it means that I look after all of the business's security. I make sure it operates trouble-free – meaning no police interference, no rival gangs, no unnecessary violence, no surprise arrests, just a calm, relaxed work environment," he explains, his mellow tone like that of a masseur selling a spa treatment accompanied by the tranquil harmonies of whale music.

"He's for real?" Asks Mandy, pointing at Pork Chop.

"Oh yeah…Detective Space is very real. Show 'em your ID." I gesture towards Pork Chop. He reaches for his pocket and hands Mandy a small leather wallet.

"Fuck me!" Mandy snarls quietly, as she opens it up. I put up a show of hands to suppress her restrained yet understandably surprised retort.

"But let me assure you that Porky here is as dedicated to the business as I am. His loyalty is not in question," I insist to a slightly displeased Mandy.

"You let him call you Porky? But you're a copper! Or you're meant to be," exclaims Sharon, changing tack, sounding perplexed.

"It's my nickname. My friends call me Pork Chop, hence Porky," Pork Chop explains.

"Some fucking nickname! Sounds like they're taking the piss if you ask me."

"I was the one who chose it."

"Fair enough." Sharon sighs, pulling a face and holding up a hand of conciliation.

"Okay" – interjects Mandy – "we've established your security." She points to Pork Chop. "And you're our manager, so to speak," she adds, pointing to me. "So who's the money? A business like this requires money."

"I'm glad you asked, 'cos the moneyman you'll meet later. To his close associates, he's known as Michael. But since you girls are new on the scene, I think it's best if you keep it more formal and call him Slatter," I explain.

"Is he a millionaire?" Sharon asks unashamedly.

"You could say that."

Her smile broadens and she giggles excitedly.

"See, told ya we would be quids in," she whispers across to her sister, unable to contain herself.

"Is there room for a small one?" Pork Chop asks the girls. "We don't do small ones, do we, Mand?" Jokes Sharon.

"Come on, PC Plod. Come and make us safe," Mandy quips, patting the vacant seat cushion between her and Sharon, inviting Pork Chop onto the sofa.

Pork Chop in a flash dives in, wiggling his arse as if bedding down. "Let me be the meat in your sandwich." He laughs, his humour met with a predictable response.

"You wish," comes Mandy's snap reply.

"He fucking does an' all." Sharon laughs, nudging Pork Chop in a friendly half-embrace.

"But tell me this, girls," I say, looking at both Mandy and Sharon in turn, trying to build up my delivery as I reach into my bag for the tin of cocaine wraps. "What head of security do you know who can come up with treats like these?" I pause to count – "One…two…three…" spilling the tin's entire contents across the large oval mirror on the count of four; my is trick met with the same sudden gasp and rapturous applause as that from a couple of kids at a birthday party watching me pull a rabbit from a hat.

"A totally awesome one," Sharon squeals, giving Pork Chop a huge hug.

"The best kind," Mandy says, offering Pork Chop a peck on the cheek.

"Well, what can I say?" Pork Chop sighs, his smug satisfaction beaming from ear to ear as he slumps back to a healthy slug from the upturned champagne bottle.

I watch the three of them exchange light-hearted banter, a kind of getting-to-know-you small-talk. Their conversation, free and easy, reminds me of better times, of boozy bank-holiday pub lunches and lazy afternoons, trying to forget we had work the next day. They were happy days, learning how to string out a beleaguered wage, but string it out and get merrily drunk I did – we all did, though days like that were few and far between. The sentiment therein, the treasured memories of friends and good times had, is almost not deserving of what is around the corner.

Aware that it will be getting dark in about half an hour, I let Pork Chop and the girls get properly acquainted. Anticipating an attack of the munchies, I ferry in the nibbles: A bowl full of cheesy cheddar squares, the big packet of chip-sticks and assorted crisps, together with another bottle of Moët and the Rioja Tempranillo for myself.

Sharon's the first to dive in. "Prawn cocktail!" she cries, grabbing a packet of crisps. Pork Chop, only milliseconds behind her, opts for chip-sticks as Mandy unwraps her first gram of the night.

"Ahhhhhh!" she purrs softly, offering a second nailful up to her other nostril. Robotically, she rubs what is left of the tiny parcel around her teeth and gums with her index finger and slumps back next to Pork Chop, the two of them totally chilled, grazing on chip-sticks and sipping champagne to the adjacent sound of Sharon's hungry chomping. I decide to check on Slatter. Thinking he'll be where I sent him, in the main bedroom, I suppose was asking too much. The room is empty, but for an empty beer can, which I pick up, the ring-pull rattling around inside. I note the indented mattress, a long-ways trough from top to bottom. He was here, so where's he gone? It's not like he can go far. He's tied to the upstairs, for God's sake; there's nowhere to go! There is a teeny-weeny boxroom and a small bedroom at the front of the flat, an airing cupboard, and a main bedroom and bathroom at the rear, all of which are clear. I've checked twice!

So where is he?

All I can think is that the creatures have him trapped inside the walls, a coup to show me who is really boss. But even they wouldn't dare upset the natural order; there is protocol to be observed, a process to be followed. I've missed something; I know I have – but what? He has to be in the kitchen. But I passed the kitchen, and if he was there, I would have seen him. Just as I'm about to go downstairs, Pork Chop starts to come up with the girls in tow.

"Mind your step, ladies," he says, with a helping hand. "Thank you, Porky. You're a gent," I hear Mandy murmur.

"You all right, Andy? Didn't see ya there," he chirps up at me. "Thought I'd give Mandy and Sharon a quick look around before it gets dark; let them get a feel for the place."

"Good idea. Come up," I reply, getting out of their way.

When they reach the top, I pull Pork Chop to one side. "You could've run this by me before showing them around," I whisper into his ear. He shrugs his indifference.

"Didn't know it would be such an issue."

"Well, it is! Slatter's gone AWOL, which means he's up here somewhere, but not, if you see what I mean." We look at one another for a second in disbelief. "I know how implausible it sounds, but that's the situation," I say, trying my utmost not to be overheard by the girls.

"I'll keep an eye out." He shrugs again, his expression of *how hard can it be?* As sarcastic as if he'd actually said it out loud. "And if I find him?" He asks, his sarcasm still very apparent.

"Then do your best. Say that he's our mystery millionaire, anything as long as the girls buy it," I say with a heavy sigh.

"Is everything okay, boys?" Mandy asks.

"Yes, of course. I've just been pointing out to Porky budgets for decorating and possible flooring solutions. Y' know, carpet, different fabrics, durability, wear and tear for the hall, stairs and landing, for example, and laminate for the kitchen; just suggestions for you to discuss while you're looking round." I leave them to amble from room to room and wait on the landing while they mooch and talk about colour schemes and wallpaper versus vinyl silk emulsion, new curtains, and furniture.

"I'm excited. Are you, Mand?" I hear Sharon squeal, her exuberance naive and distinctly juvenile, the kind of happiness I find quite endearing, like a kid at Christmas. "It's gonna be good, sis," comes an equally jubilant reply.

Retiring out of sight into a room they have already viewed, I linger like a fanatical fisherman, quiet and statuesque, obsessed with catching the prize carp he knows is nearby. I watch from the tiny gap created by the hinge between the doorjamb and the half-open door of the front bedroom as the girls begin their descent downstairs, closely chaperoned by Pork Chop. The girls seem more than satisfied, chattering on about their plans, asking Pork Chop about what lampshades go with what furniture and which bathroom suite would look best. His knowledge of interior design is all but exhausted. Happy that everyone is finally downstairs in the lounge, I emerge from my hiding place, treading lightly, listening for anything out of the ordinary. Slatter suddenly appears from behind the door of the main bedroom.

"Where the fuck have you been?" I growl, angry but incredibly relieved.

"Have you ever thought this place is haunted?" Slatter says, looking around.

"Why? What have you seen?" My heart skips a beat, afraid that he has seen one of the creatures.

"I haven't seen anything. But if you just stop for a sec, you can feel it – a kind of negative electricity," Slatter explains. "I woke too soon," he jabbers. "Got scared and hid in a cupboard. Thought I was being watched," – he adds – "by something in the walls."

"What cupboard – where?" I say.

"It's built in; hard to see. The previous owners wallpapered over the door to blend it in."

"It won't be long now. Just keep it together for a little while longer, okay? Then you'll get what I promised," I say with a reassuring pat on the arm.

With that said, I leave a rather timid Slatter sitting on the top step of the stairs, looking frit, his frame withdrawn, as I go down to retrieve the second shopping bag of candles. Taking one for the kitchen, I put it on the draining board beside the ice-filled sink, light it and go back up to the main bedroom, handing Slatter another can of beer on my way.

"Get it down you," I say, not waiting for a response.

Wanting to at least make the main bedroom look a little more appealing than the lowest-scoring hovel in an Eastern European rough-sex guide, I place the remaining five candles at equal distances from one another around the makeshift love nest of the two stacked mattresses, approximately a metre away because of the naked flame. One I put centrally at the top, one on either side, roughly in line with someone's shoulders if they were to lie on it, and two at the foot of the bed, so they almost formed a five-pointed star. As a final gesture, I do my best to puff up the top mattress to rid it of Slatter's imprinted outline, finding it hard to believe that Mandy didn't pass comment on what or who had made such a large dent. Grateful for small mercies, I breathe a sigh of relief and make my way back down to Pork Chop and the girls, patting Slatter on the back of his shoulder as I pass him. "Not long now, mate," I say; he gives a slow nod in reply. He hands me a small bottle with a teat-pipette screw lid.

"What's this?" I ask.

"It's gamma hydroxybutyric acid."

"What?" I don't have a clue what I've just been given and why.

"GHB – it's a date rape drug, a clear liquid, odourless and tasteless. A couple of drops in a drink will make 'em drowsy and docile-like, easy to handle," he explains in his soft, matter-of-fact way. "They do sound kind of feisty," he adds, smiling. *You don't know how feisty,* I feel like saying back to him. But, like me, he wants nothing else except to get on with it. I just hope he can handle what he's letting himself in for. Being afraid of ghosts is one thing but walking amongst demons is quite another. For tonight is going to be one hell of an eye-opener.

***

I still find it incredible how in only a few minutes twilight can plunge an innocuous space into something so brooding and full of menace. But this is the power of the dark. It causes people like Slatter to question their own bravery, their sense of what is right and wrong and what is real and what is not, their sanity neither here nor there. The only thing of relevance is the dark, which slowly, but surely, becomes all-encompassing, getting ever darker, more intimidating, and scarier, sapping strength and resolve till you can no longer see yourself, just an infinite blackness, and all you can hear is the sound of the creatures within. Again, the shadows deepen to creep outwards from the hallway's corners, the way evil does when it senses a foothold somewhere new. Like a phantom slick, it flows upwards, against gravity, across walls and over each step. The gloom rises, its deluge relentless, a fight you will never win. The once-amber gold of the late afternoon is now fast diminishing in the dwindling light. The church candle I lit in the kitchen is Slatter's only beacon to guide him. Buddha says three things cannot be long hidden: The sun, the moon and the truth. I get what Buddha is saying in that I see it as light and dark, good versus evil. Everyone who has ever lived or shall live has no choice but to surrender themselves to both sets of conditions, therefore revealing the truth of each and every person.

In other words, it doesn't matter what you do, where, when or even how; the truth will always prevail, for better or worse. As I see it, truth is the only constant inevitability we have; it's an undeniable force that can never be outrun or avoided, like death, haunting our every day. If I'm to look at today, the sun's transparency has shown us who we really are, and now the moon, under its dark, secretive cloak, is allowing us to be who we really are. The truth is in our subsequent unveiling. *Be brave my friend,* I say inwardly, looking up from the bottom of the stairs towards Slatter. *You're going to need it.* I know he'll pull through; the dark has taken a liking to him, hence why would it have revealed its presence earlier, especially before nightfall? That's rare; it hates daylight. The creatures hate it even more. A sudden surge of laughter yanks my attention towards the lounge and the intoxicating current of mirth and silliness emanating from the half-open door, but the frivolity is far too coherent for my liking. The girls are taking too long, and the sun has almost set. Their alcoholic tolerance and the buzz from the coke, as ironic as it sounds, are acting like a reprieve in the face of death's snarling impatience. Now the sands of time are against me. To get the gods on my side, I promised the creatures a feast, a boast of my intent and good will towards them to the extent of parading the sacrificial pair not inches from the invisible barrier that separates us. And as I contemplate what to do next, precious seconds of the few minutes I have left continue to slip silently away into the shadows. Time is like a leak that cannot be plugged, and it's as though it's me wasting away, my essence pouring into the gloom and filling the air, making everything all around get darker as I get weaker, the scent of my fear teasing the creatures who watch my every move. I want so much to accelerate the process and use the GHB Slatter gave me, but it's not the narrative I wish to leave. I know that if I do, the drug will show in the pathologist's toxicology report. The results are fast, my outcome guaranteed. But then the authorities would know that someone had purposefully drugged the girls and their deaths were staged. That fact alone would decimate the ambiguity crucial to my plan's success. I want the police left with 'what ifs' and 'maybes', not certainty.

Plus, there is the question of why Slatter had this drug in his possession. Why did he have it so readily to hand? I've got this horrible nagging doubt in my mind that I may have misjudged his character. I thought I had him tagged, but this not only contradicts my hypothesis, but it also blows it clean out of the water. Pork Chop was right. The dossier screamed sexual predator and much worse. And though I need his incredible intellect and expertise going forward, I am eager to know who exactly have I recruited: Michael, someone I see as dependable and hard-working, or Slatter, the dark flipside; a twisted fetishist who craves violent sex. Like Buddha says, the truth cannot be long hidden. Anyway, it's too late to argue the toss now; the day's light is all but gone, the creatures are growing ever more relentless, and, come what may, once the dark of nightfall is here, they will expect to be fed. Pork Chop said he had used sux, succinylcholine, a rapidly acting depolariser, on his family. I wonder if he's got any left. It would be perfect. A 100 mg IV dose is enough to depolarise every muscle in the body of a 70 kg man in twenty to thirty seconds, so in rough approximation, I guess a 50 mg IV dose will be sufficient, judging by the girls' bodyweight, to achieve more or less full paralysis in the same amount of time. The bonus of sux, providing the dose is kept on the side of caution, is that it keeps the victim awake and still able to feel pain. Plus, it is very difficult to detect because its metabolites are all naturally occurring molecules, the same as what is already present in our bodies. This is due to how it's so quickly broken down by enzymes in the blood. Why didn't I think of this earlier? I pocket the GHB and go into the kitchen. I see that the second bottle of Moët has been taken from the sink, along with a few more packets of crisps and the pack of cheesy nibbles.

"Come on, you're missing all the fun," cackles Sharon, waving me in to rejoin the party. "We're on slammers and shots. Though it's not the same in plastic cups," she adds, covering her cup with her other hand, lifting it slightly, slamming it hard on the table and necking her drink in one gulp, only to shake her head and exude a low, protracted growl as the sudden shock of hard liquor hits, going down her throat.

"Hope you don't mind. We started on the tequila." Pork Chop giggles.

"I can see," I reply, scanning the clutter of Tupperware and mess on the table, the plate of lemon and lime wedges next to a half-eaten bowl of cheesy nibbles and a couple of cups on their sides next to the saltshaker. An empty Möet bottle rolls beneath the table, the second Möet bottle, together with the opened tequila, on top, its cap missing for some reason and a litter of cling-film and screwed up bits of paper everywhere. The mirror is speckled with tiny white dots and smeared by fingers licked to mop up any spillage. The girls, by the looks of it, have got into their groove, the debris clear evidence that they must have sniffed at least three or more grams a piece. At this rate, if left to their own devices, they'll be buzzing into the early hours, whereas I have only a couple of minutes before the building starts to creak with the impatient moans of a thousand demons raring to be set free.

"C'mon, mate." Pork Chop beckons. "Wanna try?"

He smiles, offering me the bottle of tequila as though expecting a well-done pat on the head for getting the party started. The table, sofa and floor are a messy muddle of discarded wrappers, packets, and crumbs. Spilt crisps and snacks have been trodden into the floor's hard surface. But instead of my OCD getting twitchy, I'm overridden by an overwhelming appreciation of this *au naturel* party aesthetic. I couldn't wish for the scene to have panned out any better. It's perfect; just how I want it to be found.

"I'm good, thanks. I'll stick to my wine," I reply. "By the way, I've sorted out upstairs," I add with a wink, pushing the champagne bottle towards him. "Waste not, want not," I say to his glowing approval.

"Good!" Pork Chop reaches for the champers. "One less thing to worry about, eh!"

"Yeah, thank God. But there's one more thing." I beckon and he leans towards me. "You got any sux left over from last night?" I whisper directly into his ear. My query is met by raised eyebrows. But despite this obvious reservation, he nods all the same.

"Yeah…I got some," he murmurs, his tone like that of an FNG questioning his first-ever direct order. "You sure?" I nod and pat his arm to confirm my decision is final. "It's in the car. Want it now?" He asks.

"If y' could. An' I want it ready to go." He gets up off the sofa and leaves the flat.

"You two fallen out or something?" Jibes Sharon, her sarky tone immediately picked up on by Mandy.

"Yeah…is everything okay?" Adds Mandy, exchanging a quizzical glance with her sister.

"Everything's fine. And no, we haven't fallen out," I snipe, mirroring Sharon's sarcasm for comedic effect. "It's part of my big surprise, if you must know."

Mandy lets out a loud, protracted 'oooh'. "Get you; first the job, then the flat, and now a big surprise!" She jokes, her tone coming across as a dig, half sounding me out and half mocking my too-good-to-be-true string of delights.

I sit back in the armchair, hoping that I haven't overplayed my hand; the cogs are turning once more behind those pretty blue eyes. Mandy narrows her gaze, beaming that intuition of hers like a sonar-cum-lie-detector, waiting for her sixth sense to echo back a confirming ping that something is up.

For a brief second, I tense. *What can she see?* The voice in my head screams, unsure if I've been rumbled or not. My brain, not waiting for the rest of me to catch up, runs through a worst-case scenario of grabbing the champagne bottle and bludgeoning both girls to death. *Let's see if your sonar intuition can pick up that!* My inner voice snarls.

The room suddenly falls quiet, and an awkward stand-off ensues, the two of us momentarily lost, stuttering over how best to move forward rather than being stuck for words. But just as the pause in conversation is becoming too noticeable, bordering on outright uncomfortable – I disguise my lean towards the table, my hand reluctantly, though steadily, beginning to reach for the neck of the weighty champagne bottle – Sharon saves the day. "It fuckin' better be okay!" She blurts out, her remark as dry and callous as Mandy's was derisive. But the intervention, as rude as it is, has the desired effect of snapping Mandy from her train of thought.

Despite my relief, I seethe at Sharon's take-take-take mindset and her apathetic ethos. I'd hoped the mention of the surprise would have generated a genuine spark of appreciation, a step forward, not this unsavoury derision and the spoilt, bratty 'it fuckin' better be okay' attitude. I know they're excited by the yarn I have spun, but if it were true, all of a sudden it is as if everything – the job, the flat, even the surprise – is somehow not enough, as though it would be never enough, always falling short.

Yet a part of me is perfectly happy to dismiss this momentary lapse so that I, along with Mandy, can squint my disdain Sharon's wrecking-ball of an approach to everything she touches, like involuntary Tourette's, unable to help herself.

"Yeah, fuck you." I snigger, holding my hand up to my mouth, daring to say it, though the words are barely audible under my breath, their every syllable a long-awaited release of absolute contempt. My inner voice, however, reacts by yelling the sentiment, jubilant in screaming it to the rafters. *I don't care. You're as good as dead, as dead can be,* the voice in my head growls, frothing and spitting, positively apoplectic on hearing such insolence.

I keep up the small talk, my tolerance waning. I picture smashing the girls' faces in, then retrieving the dry-wall hammer and knife from the kitchen to cleave open their skulls and gut them like fish. *Fuck the plan,* the voice hollers. *Fuck it, fuck them, fuck everyone,* it shrieks, the uncontrollable banshee inside finally fed up, baying for blood and gore and horror and everything else that comes with it. The creatures are suddenly rabid, thrashing with a cacophony of gnashing teeth and scraping claws. The building creaks to the monsters within.

So, this is what it sounds like and what it feels like. The girls are oblivious to the power of the maelstrom whirling about them. My God! It's here! This is what I have been waiting for. The feeding frenzy has begun.

The gods are watching.

The time has come.

I must pay my dues for *their* protection and favour.

The walls, floor, and ceiling, like before, suddenly turn transparent. The creatures pressed up to the invisible divide are agitated. Their patience, like mine, is boiling over to an infinite roar on the inside, whereas on the outside we sit at an even simmer, our combined fury so volatile that it sends trace arcs scooting randomly across the room. The air is thick with electricity, and the smell of impending death is palpable. I don't know what is holding the creatures back.

Not seconds later, Pork Chop returns, barging in to give me the thumbs-up.

A lot happier now that every last piece of the puzzle is in place, I slump back in the armchair, moulding myself to its comfy cushions, and watch Pork Chop enjoy playing his part to absolute perfection, as though there had been no interruption whatsoever. After quickly allaying any qualms the girls had, he gets straight back into the swing of things, grinding salt onto the back of Mandy's hand. She licks it off, then quickly downs her double shot of tequila in one, biting on a lime wedge to mock applause from her sister.

"Wow! Way to go!" Pork Chop cheers. "You up for another?" He turns to Sharon.

"Oh, go on," she chirps. Pork Chop pours a roughly measured splash of tequila into her cup, hardly letting her finish speaking, and crudely powders her hand in salt, cheering her on. "Drink! Drink! Drink!" He insists, and Sharon duly gulps down the cup's contents, the wedge of sharp citrus offering little respite to the liquor's toxicity.

Sensing the shadows suddenly deepen around the room's edge and the building's noises beginning to escalate, I feel the creatures nudging me closer to the edge of hell's precipice.

Go on, if you dare, goad the building's creaks and groans. *Of course, I dare,* my mind's voice yells in reply.

I lean forward to drum-roll my fingers on the edge of the coffee table. "Right then, folks," I announce. "With no further ado, it's time for tonight's big surprise." My words, like the proclamation of a prime-time Saturday night game-show host, get the undivided attention of both Mandy and Sharon, now leaning towards me as if to reply, *okay then, Mr Big-Shot, show us what ya got.* Even Pork Chop is suckered in, tipped forward, his face racked with anticipation, knowing this is the unscripted part of the evening – the fun part!

I reach into my bag and pull out the larger see-through plastic parcel of cocaine, unfolding it to the girls' amazement. Their bottom jaws get lower and lower until *voila!* – one square polythene re-sealable bag, the type you save food in and store in the fridge or freezer, except in this case it contains a Class A narcotic that I know the girls will do anything for. Holding the paper-thin plastic bag by the corner between forefinger and thumb, I swing it gently to and fro; the girls are mesmerised and, for a second, totally speechless.

"Is that what I think it is?" Mandy pipes up after a long exhale.

"For fuck's sake, Mand, I've never seen so much," exclaims Sharon.

"It is, Mandy. One hundred grams of ninety percent pure cocaine commanding a street value of up to forty pounds per gram. The best on the market, and the same stuff you've been sampling." I nod towards the empty wrappings littered across the oval mirror.

"Wow! Four grand," Sharon murmurs as though dazed. Her eyes are like saucers, the candlelight dancing across their glistening sheen; *the girl with kaleidoscope eyes,* unable to comprehend that the pot of gold at the end of her rainbow is actually dangling not four feet from her nose.

"Yes, Sharon. Four thousand pounds' worth. Looks good, doesn't it?" I swing the bag, goading the desired response. The coke, unbeknown to both her and Mandy, is nothing but an expensive prop for the forensic guys in vice.

"Yes," both girls purr in synchronised decadence, hypnotised to the point of blindness in their shared gluttony and a vision of shameless living.

"And what's more…it's yours" – I say, placing the bag on the mirror – "to enjoy or cut up and re-sell, I'm not bothered," I add, my sales pitch complete. The deceit is so simple, I can't help but beam the most devilish of smiles. Both lambs to the slaughter, gullible and stupid; as easy as hooking frogs at a kiddies' funfair. In fact, now I think of it, too easy.

"It's ours!" Mandy replies, her remark not exactly a question, more of a shocked response to something quite unexpected.

"Yep!" I say nonchalantly as though it doesn't matter, the monetary value of the bag irrelevant compared to the happiness of my two new employees. "And it'll be here waiting for you." I pause, to let my last comment sink in. The girls' captivated gaze switches from the coke to me. Mandy gives me a knowing yet quizzical glare, as if to say, 'am I meant to be going somewhere?' And there it is again, another shot fired across my bow, that defensive, street-smart sixth sense, you have to be so careful of – an Achilles heel as much as it is a gift, giving rise to an explosive nature, a total personality role reversal whose outcomes are almost impossible to predict, let alone contain. I continue to smile, the pretence making my cheeks ache, and the girls, by their expressions, are unsure how to respond.

"It's nothing, Mandy," I reply softly, trying to avoid any possible backlash. "Porky just needs to discuss something with you upstairs."

"You mean slip her something upstairs, more like," interjects Sharon bluntly. "Don't worry, Mand, I'll hold the fort down 'ere." She cackles, shuffling to adjust her little black dress.

Pork Chop ignores the jibe with a roll of his deep brown eyes; he has a look that tends, in the candlelight, to be both sinister and cunning, the way a wily old fox hoodwinks a chicken into thinking it is not a fox.

"Shall we?" Pork Chop stands up, offering a chivalrous hand to Mandy. Mandy, accepting the courteous gesture, gets to her feet, corrects her black lycra mini-dress, pulling it haphazardly down over her black stocking tops, and turns to leave the room arm-in-arm with Pork Chop, but as she does so, she gives me a sly but scathing frown. She hates that I know her so well and know that she has done far worse for much less.

"Oh, and don't forget the champers." I hand Pork Chop the bottle, reminding him of my expectations with a stern gaze.

Sharon and I listen to the slow clip-clop of Mandy's stiletto heels, our eyes glued to her sound from our respective seats, each step a seductive wooden click as they climb the stairs and make their way across the bare floorboards into the rear bedroom, directly above us. There they stop – I guess on reaching the double layer of mattresses. Sharon, still staring upwards, sticks out her bottom lip as though her uncomplicated intellect is trying to calculate whether she's missing out on something special, or maybe she's simply dejected at missing her sibling. To distract her, I let her pick up the bag of cocaine. She weighs it in each hand in turn, ogling the white powder, tipping the bag one way then the other, the coke like sand inside an hourglass counting down the last remaining minutes of a fairy-tale she still thinks is going to happen.

I guess ignorance is bliss in Sharon's domain. At least she has that to cling to – not that I or the creatures will care, come the moment.

***

In my peripheral vision, I get a glimpse of movement, of shadow on shadow crossing the hallway; a brief silhouette is highlighted in the faint flickering candlelight coming from the kitchen. There was no noise or descending footsteps on the stairs, so it must be where he hid after I left him perched at the top of the stairs, now eager to make his entrance. Taking advantage of Sharon's pre-occupation with the bag of coke, I get up and stand by the curtains to draw her line of sight in the opposite direction to the lounge door, allowing Slatter to slip in unnoticed. But much to my surprise, he stands for a brief second right behind Sharon in the flickering orangey-yellow light, like a voyeur in a backstreet brothel perving over the female flesh he intends to abuse, before silently backing himself into the shadows on her blindside. The gloom welcomes him with open arms.

Now that Slatter is here and ready, I need Pork Chop, who, by the length of time he is taking, is obviously enjoying himself upstairs. I ply Sharon with another shot of tequila. Without batting an eyelid, she places the coke back on the oval mirror and necks her drink in one.

"Ahhhh!" She growls, reaching for a wedge of lemon. "So what now?" She blurts out in her usual brazen manner. "You gonna fuck me? Is that what you want?"

"No, not me; I'm just the man with the plan," I reply. She shrugs as though to say "Well, who then?" Knowing full well, like Mandy, that that much coke only has one kind of price tag – your heart, body, and soul. "Remember that guy Mandy asked about, the man with the money?" I say.

"Ah-ha," she says with bated breath.

"It's him." My persona somehow defaults automatically to that of the game-show host for the big reveal.

"And you told him about me?" She shrieks, bubbling with excitement.

"Yes, I did," I say, nodding. "In fact, I paid him a special visit this morning to tell him all about you and how special you are." I emphasise the word 'special', its significance changing Sharon's demeanour from a cheap imitation of her more glamorous sister to someone who might actually think that they too are worthy to be a princess in waiting.

"Oh my God – you're kidding; you must be. Please tell me you're not – please! – Please!" Sharon shrieks again to my shaking head, the realisation dawning on her.

"No, I'm not," I reply.

"I'm going to meet a millionaire," she squeals. "I mean, he is a millionaire, isn't he? You said he was," she babbles, clapping her hands, unable to contain herself, giddy on the booze and a dream so close she thinks she's already in it.

"I'm pretty sure he is – yeah," I say, trying to eke out the conversation, hoping Pork Chop will hurry up. "I know he's looking forward to meeting you."

"Really?" She asks in a high-pitched squeak, pointing to herself in a kind of joyous disbelief.

"Yes, really!" Comes a third voice from behind the sofa as Slatter steps out of the shadows. "I've been waiting for this moment all my life."

"Sharon, meet Slatter, and Slatter, this is Sharon," I say, seizing the initiative to make the introductions.

"Hi," Slatter says nervously. "Delighted to meet you. And please call me Michael; all my friends do." The added remark was a nice improvisation to smooth over his entrance.

"Wow! You're actually here. Are you really a millionaire?" Asks Sharon, whispering her unabashed nosiness.

"I feel like a millionaire, so…yeah!" Slatter replies, taking a seat next to her, his face rosy and beaming in the yellow-orange hue of the candles, like all his Christmases have come at once.

Just then, a tirade of one person's heavy footsteps pounds across the ceiling and down the stairs, its brusqueness taking all three of us by surprise. Our eyes follow the noise.

"Sorry, that took so long," pants Pork Chop, flinging open the lounge door.

"Quick, grab her!" I say. The order is an immediate gut reaction to Sharon turning away from me to look at Pork Chop as he bursts into the room. With her guard down, I launch myself like a sprinter out of the blocks to cover the few steps to the sofa. I wrap the palm and fingers of my outstretched left hand tightly around Sharon's mouth and grab her nearest arm with my right as Slatter, in a flash, gets with the programme, straddling her thighs and taking hold of her remaining free arm.

"Porky, do it now. Use the left arm. Find a vein and do it fast," I snap, well aware that speed is the key to not leaving any unnecessary bruising. Pork Chop, in a concise demonstration of his well-seasoned abduction skill-set, takes her left arm out of my grasp to straighten it and taps hard on the inside of the forearm.

"God, your sister takes some fucking," Pork Chop moans to Sharon, the affront enough to stir a last-ditch effort and force Slatter and me to shift position and strengthen our combined hold on her. I glare into Pork Chop's brimming face, willing him to keep his ill-timed comments to himself. Despite Sharon's wriggling, my concentration is all on my number one recruit, who carefully hovers the micro-bore needle over a pronounced snaking line of blue vein. I feel the relief of a bright red plume spurting into the syringe's clear suxy solution, indicating he hit the blood vessel perfectly the first time. After twenty seconds, I feel Sharon's taut, clenched frame go limp and I release the hand covering her mouth. After a further fifteen seconds, I, Pork Chop and Slatter carefully position her paralysed, yet totally awake body, lengthways on the sofa.

"Good work, gents," I say with utter relief. "Michael, you were Johnny on the spot, pinning her down like you did. Well done."

"Don't mention it," says Slatter, grinning like a Cheshire cat, his eyes on the prize, fixed firmly on Sharon.

"So, what you waiting for?" I ask. I'd thought he'd be all over her first chance he got.

Slatter shrugs, sucking on his bottom lip and his face slightly tilted downward. He shuffles awkwardly. A shy demeanour suddenly replaces his sinister grin, and it hits me. I completely forgot he is still a virgin. How stupid of me. Of course, as far as sex is concerned, he is still a boy whose prudish idea of romance, despite the depraved act he is about to commit, is nothing more than two people sharing an intimate moment.

"She's all yours, mate. Crack on," I say in an attempt to spur him on. "Oh...and by the way, you are here to have sex with her, not beat on her or kill her – is that clear?" Slatter nods, and, feeling happy that he understands this, I drag Pork Chop out into the hallway and close the door behind me to give him the privacy that he is too shy to ask for.

"How's Mandy?" I ask Pork Chop.

"Just like her sister, good for at least half an hour or more," Pork Chop says. I nod in acknowledgement. "But Christ, did she faff about, wanting to try most of the karma sutra before I was able to get her face down. Stuck her in the base of the hairline at the top of the neck just below the ridge of the skull. It's not impossible to trace, but I used a hair follicle to disguise the point of entry, so it will need a well-trained eye."

"Is she ready and prepped for when Slatter goes up?" I ask, not that I need to check Pork Chop's due diligence.

"Yeah, she's ready, but it's sloppy seconds, I might add. So I don't want him moaning," Pork Chop quips, nudging my arm.

"Understood." I allow myself a wry chuckle. Though my inner psycho, purist that it is, is still at odds with how sex seems to grease the wheels of violence. The rape and pillage, it isn't me, but I feel it is going to be a key feature in the war to come. How can it not be? Rape has been used as a weapon for millennia. If you cannot kill them all, then breed them out – a strategy as brutal as it is crass, but one that has been hailed by kings and queens alike, for its devastating and long-lasting effects. And it is this impression I am always left with when observing those in combat roles, that when presented with an opportunity, the urge to fuck, in whatever capacity, far outweighs the urge to kill.

Yet here I am with Pork Chop, the two of us a most reluctant audience, standing in a dank, dark hallway waiting, listening to the inaugural shuffling sounds of an inept sexual novice as he navigates his way around a woman's body, first whispering his intentions and then, in his newfound euphoria, offering an overwhelming yet eerie academic description of how she tastes and feels, panting and groaning and grunting throughout what appears to be a most bizarre encounter.

Quicker than I thought, a breathless Slatter emerges, dressed only in his boxer shorts, the candlelit doorway framing an otherwise unremarkable physique with little if no defining quality and poor stamina. Pork Chop smirks, almost laughing out loud, and gives me a look, as if to say, "that's computer geeks for you."

"You okay?" I ask. Slatter nods exuberantly, like one of those stupid mascot dogs you see on the back shelf of a car bobbing its dumb, grinning head up and down, nineteen to the dozen, through the rear window. "Well, if you're okay, we're okay, eh Porky?" I add as Pork Chop, and I shepherd him back into the lounge.

I hadn't expected the unceremoniously shameful sight of Sharon spreadeagled across the sofa, her dress wrenched up around her waist, legs akimbo and breasts exposed. I've seen this kind of horror before, so I don't know why this time is any different. I suppose listening to the intimacy of the event unfold didn't help; it reinforced all the reasons why I am so hardwired to abhor rape. That, and the fact that Sharon is collateral damage, an unintended by-product of my plan, a true victim in that sense, even though I do despise her brazen superficiality. Mandy was always the real target. But if my plan works, there are going to be a lot more like Sharon and the kids in the orchard; unintended casualties that I will be accountable for. In hard times, shit happens; you either embrace it, make a friend of it, or get out and run as fast as you possibly can away from the horror that is surely not far behind.

It's little things like this that highlight the chinks left in my armour, the things which I must iron out if I'm to see my plan through to fruition.

I've got to toughen up, that's for sure.

Looking down at Sharon and the awful state in which Slatter left her, I hail to the room's four walls and to the grotesque horde I know is salivating, looking in. *The first of the night is about to be yours,* my inner voice croons softly. As if the gods know their cue, the floor, ceiling, and walls reveal the creatures within, their pupils dilated as black as black can be at the fresh meat on offer.

"Porky, reach into my bag by the armchair and get one of those syringes filled with heroin." I wave my hand and point. "Now take the cap off the needle, place the cap on the mirror and insert the needle into Sharon's left arm, using the exact point of entry you made when you injected the Suxy."

Pork Chop, without saying a word, follows my instructions implicitly. He kneels in position and prepares the syringe, places the cap on the mirror and squirts a brief jet of the heroin solution through the needle to expel any trapped air. He then extends the arm nice and straight, inserts the needle and waits, his thumb poised over the plunger, ready to press and send Sharon to hell and beyond.

"Now, wait until I give the command to inject," I say, training my gaze on Sharon's fixed, expressionless gawp. "By now, you've guessed your fairy tale job of living the high life isn't going to happen. What is going to happen instead is that you are going to die in the most horrible way I can think of," I explain to a pair of glaring eyes, windows into a petrified soul trying to come to terms with what I have just said. I watch a single tear slowly roll down her cheek, the only sign of her overpowering fear, which by now must be unbearable. "But that I'll leave for my final and biggest surprise of the night. It's nothing elaborate, just an idea I've had. But if it works – and I'm not saying it will, but if it does – now there, it could be said, is a stroke of genius, especially in its wickedness. Thing is, I need help on this one, and I don't mean from these two fine fellows, for this particular surprise requires a special kind of help – one that can only come from a special kind of someone, or rather something, who, like my millionaire friend here, once I had told him about you, was literally chomping at the bit to meet you. I just don't know if the god or gods in question are watching. If they are, if they can see what I see…trust me when I say that if the gods like what they see and come through in granting my wish, in a couple of minutes that ten millilitres of pure heroin ready to shoot into your arm will seem like a blessed relief compared to the inconceivable suffering you are about to endure."

Let her be eaten from the inside out. Let her stomach and lungs fill with fly larvae. Let them multiply to occupy every airway, every intestine, every tube, and vessel. Let her body writhe to their vile rhythm till she can take no more and the vileness spills from every orifice; such is my wish, and such is my impiety. Please, oh great one, whoever you are, she is the first of my offerings to you and your legions,

my inner voice pleads to the ether, hoping the ether will respond. My head trips to disco fever and my foot taps to the Jacksons – *can you feel it, can you feel it, can you feel it?*

Slatter is standing close to my side. I grip his arm, sensing his nervousness. "Just give it a minute" – I tell him – "and don't be frightened by what you see," I add, trying not to be drowned out by the music filling my head – *now tell me! Can you feel it, can you feel it, can you feel it?* – The climactic crescendo building. "Porky, you ready?"

"Ready when you're ready, boss."

"Then be ready as of now," I say, unsure what I have ordered and how poor Sharon will be served up. Half-anticipating the spectacular, attributing my expectations to that of wild superstition and stories embellished by Gypsy folk and their garish, bald-faced showmanship, I wait for Sharon to suddenly explode and spew a vile torrent of maggots and blood-strewn guts across the room and for the creatures to feast upon her. But instead of something extravagant designed to wow, I get a masterclass in raw subtlety. Sharon's abdomen swells and rises as though in seconds she is eight months pregnant, only for the swollen bulk to deflate. Her torso, neck and limbs twitch spasmodically as her stomach's contents spread like a flash flood down through the digestive tract and up her slender throat, its girth visibly thickening, forcing the jaw to widen before spilling a mouthful of white, wriggling larvae.

"Jesus Christ!" Mutters Pork Chop, turning his head away from the writhing mass now pouring from Sharon's mouth, nose, and ears and from between her legs. All three of us try to refrain from gagging at the fetid reek, an instantaneous air-burst due to a horrid, squirming soup of rotten bile, gastric juices and fresh faeces forced out by the sheer volume of larvae being emitted from Sharon's every orifice.

"What the fuck!" Whispers Slatter, pointing as one lone maggot emerges from a tear duct, closely followed by another, then another and then another. Sharon's pupils are dilated black as death's dark door, desperately seeking out the last of the fast-fading light. Her fear and revulsion are as palpable as it gets when you are acting out the final few seconds of your worst possible nightmare. I tell Pork Chop to inject her, and he does without reply. He gets to his feet, then steps back, leaving the empty syringe hanging precariously, the combination of the needle lodged at an angle in the vein and the plastic syringe's slight but significant weight lifting the prominent blood vessel almost out of the skin, like a cable snagged by an anchor hauled to the surface.

I feel the drug course its way through the dying girl as I feel the ether respond, allowing the creatures to leap forth and rejoice at the sacrifice; the stampede of demons from their domain into ours is like the deepest, purest breath of super-charged hypersonic oxygen. In a nanosecond, I have already dubbed it the king of fixes, an energising hit that has no equal and enough punch to wake the dead and empower the monster that dwells within my own dark confines.

I had always assumed that, once released, the creatures would run amok. Yet these things, as grotesque and merciless as they are, have somehow channelled themselves into me. The smack of their transition is like a tumultuous fanfare of trumpets, of pounding bass drums, like a blinding light and a millennium of screams and shouts and the roar of something not quite human. Everything is packed into several enthralling seconds of pure ecstasy.

"How is that even possible?" Pork Chop whispers, anxious at being the first to break the silence.

"But that's just it," answers Slatter. "It isn't!"

I glance at Pork Chop trying to join the dots – the times bullets have swerved my position or shrapnel fails to hit me and my inexplicable rise as a warrior – this young upstart far beyond his years, whom he follows without question. At how I embrace fear and horror, not only as if we're the best of friends, but as if we are family.

Slatter is simply gob smacked. He looks at me lost for words.

"That maybe so, Michael, but I needed you both here to witness it, all the same," I say, smiling, happy they are seeing what I can and that I now have proof I am not dreaming. But although they cannot see the monsters, I now know that they are real and not the twisted product of a delusional mind or, even worse, of someone who has clearly gone mad.

"You okay to go upstairs?" I ask Slatter.

But as soon as I ask, what I can only describe as a faint apparition of something monstrous and truly frightening transfers itself from my body to his; a minotaur-esque creature with snapping, snake-like tentacles rams its viciously pointed head into his now-heaving chest. The demon is gone in a flash, now nothing but a brief flicker of flame in the new host's eye.

"You good to go?" I ask again.

"Yes, I'm good to go," replies a confident and born-again hard mentality I hadn't seen before, but which, by the grace of the gods, is there now.

"Then you had better make your way up to tonight's star attraction, hadn't you?" My tone is as deliberate as it is sarcastic, though not to insult, more to prompt Pork Chop into taking my lead, which he does in a heartbeat, guiding Slatter into the hallway and up the stairs.

"I'll look after him." Pork Chop's words float down from the darkness above, together with the sound of tentative footsteps disappearing behind a closing door and the reassuring rustle of Pork Chop pitching up to take watch on the landing.

"That's m' boy," I whisper, not singling either of my new recruits out for praise, yet I smirk when I realise the sentiment's unintentional efficiency in that it applies to both, one in his role to overcome and adapt, and the other in his duty to protect. Smug as a bug, I turn and swoop to grab my wine before the inching carpet of larvae reaches it. With a full beaker in one hand and the half full bottle in the other, I shove the armchair, kick by kick, across the lounge to the farthest corner to escape the wriggling range of the maggots and take solace in the dark, delicious fruits of my labour. From the comfort of my chair, I take a hefty slug of wine and look back across the room, but instead of Sharon, I see the sad sight of a junkie girl, a hopeless chancer fresh out of luck, her mascara run and lipstick smudged, draped across an old sofa before an altar of her own making, her life, like her dress, thrust aside, trashed and defiled, her legacy, if any, reflecting the cheapness of the fix that choked her, a sight common under many a flyover amongst the pop-up cardboard communities of the junkie homeless. If I could have framed the scene, I would have called it *The Maggot Feast,* a Dali-esque *The Last Supper* turned on its head, a depiction of youth's fatalistic duality: The callous decadence of today's couldn't-give-a-fuck generation made apparent by death's inevitable entourage of outright ugliness. But who will see its magnificence except a smattering of police officers and forensic experts? Sometimes, I think the work I do is wasted if there isn't a higher purpose to all of this. Still, I will sit here quietly, drink my wine, and wait patiently for Slatter to finish.

I feel my body relax with the warming alcohol and the wine's rich berries, peppery tobacco and vanilla smoothness, the opulent taste of a job well done. From the corner's dark recess, I watch the phantom monsters swim through the air with graceful menace, creature's unknown to the animal kingdom; bipedal devil-like plesiosaurs, vaguely similar to the genus *Homo*, like mythical beings retaining the grotesque features of archaic beasts just like the minotaur that entered Slatter. They are aberrations of what should not be; they have thrived in hell's parallel dimension and, resurrected, are amongst us once more, their sheer awesomeness a perfect coming together of Jurassic supremacy and a truly evil mind. The creatures swoop suddenly to rise, then plunge, flying straight into Sharon's body, through the sofa, then through the floor and back out into the ether only to come whooshing back via a wall or the ceiling. The dashing demon-flock is locked in some ritualised dogfight. Their party-piece, like a flow of electrons recharging as they pass through the cells of a battery, is to rush through me, their new host, with jaws open wide, bellowing roar after exhilarating roar. The hits, like bullets from a machine-gun, zap into my chest, lighting me up and electrifying the air around me, transforming it into some kind of alien menthol energy, an outer world gas exciting every nerve, every sinew from head to toe, yet cooling my reactions to something just above inert. It's weird, but as each creature hits, I expect to be knocked clean through the wall, smashed and carried along by the hurtling monsters, yet incredibly my body offers no reaction. My skin doesn't even sense so much as a quiver at the tumultuous frenzy. In fact, compared to how I should be feeling, I feel next to nothing – no fear, exhilaration, impact, or evisceration, just the unwinding boozy warmth of wine and pride, as though my subdued celebration has come at the expense of not being able to switch off. I have spent months – years – worrying about this very moment. After the event you always look back and wonder what all the fuss was about. But in this case, I know what the fuss was about and, more importantly, what it has already cost and what is still required, especially as the night of sacrifice is still young.

According to the Old Norse religion of the Vikings, sacrifice is necessary in order to be on good terms with the gods and ensure you're favourably treated regarding weather, fertility or luck in battle. These rituals, called *blót* sacrifices, were human sacrifices where Norse folk would revel in heated, drunken celebration, the meat and beer of the feast blessed by the magnate, a pagan priest. Toasts were first made in honour of Odin, then to 'king and victory'. Afterwards, cups would be replenished and promptly emptied for Njörd and Frej in the hope of securing a prosperous and peaceful future. Then the revelling throng, once more with full cups, would empty them with a personal pledge to undertake great exploits – for example, sailing to raid distant lands and taking on the inevitable battle with foreign armies – and finally, toasts were made for kinsmen resting in burial mounds and those in Valhalla.

A tradition, for tonight at least, I intend to live up to and hopefully in time pass on, cometh the call to war by the dreaded gods, patrons of its dire necessity and their equally feared birth child, *Apok*.

***

Sleepy and lost amongst the ether's absurd vista, finally at rest after the creatures' feeding frenzy, the empty wine bottle and cup long discarded, my mind floats through an endless space and the wildest of dreamscapes, that teems to the call of Cthulhu. The Great Old Ones emerge from dark horizons.

For it is quite the sight to be amongst them, like staring into a realm of gods, of legends past rising from their ancient slumber to begin where they left off. And this is where I think I am – at the start of a well-trodden path about to embark on someone else's quest. One that was never finished; my first step begins where my predecessors were so rudely interrupted.

"Boss! You awake?" Comes a voice to ruin my dreamy bliss. "Boss, wake up," it says, determined and impatient. "Please, boss!" It says again, its tone changing from questioning to pleading; a familiar voice that I know, gods or no gods, will not stop until I answer.

"Yeah, I'm awake. Whaddaya want?" I sound hoarse. My mouth is dry from the tannin of the wine. I don't want to open my eyes. I'm pissed off at having my time with the Great Old Ones cut short.

"We've got a situation," Pork Chop says, his voice jittery.

"Is that *you* have a situation, or are you quoting the 'royal we', as in *I* have a situation?" I ask, the gruffness in my tone shifting to annoyance.

"No. I mean *we* have a situation, as in both of us," Pork Chop says.

"So, has Michael finished?"

"Yeah, Slatter's finished all right," puffs Pork Chop, showing his obvious displeasure with an exaggerated sigh of exasperation.

What the fuck? Porky's properly narked, plus he used the name Slatter with such disdain, not Michael – why? They were getting on so well. What the hell's going on? Now I'm intrigued.

"What's the time?" I ask, rubbing my eyes and stretching.

"Nearly ten," says Pork Chop matter-of-factly.

"Blimey, that's flown." I get to my feet to stretch some more. "So, tell me what's the situation?"

"I think it's best if you take a look for yourself," Pork Chop replies, shaking his head.

"Surely it's not that bad," I say to Pork Chop's continuing puffs and irritated pants.

I follow him out into the hallway and up the stairs, the creatures circling like horrid vultures, able to sniff out the gore and horror blindfolded.

"You'd best prepare yourself," says Pork Chop as I push the bedroom door open.

Oh…my…fucking…God!

"Wow!" I cough, the shock catching my breath, as my eyes adjust to what is lying before me.

"Wow – indeed!" Murmurs Pork Chop.

Pork Chop was right; nothing could have prepared me for what I am seeing, chiefly because I didn't think Slatter had it in him. Clearly, I was wrong. I won't be making the same mistake again. No wonder Pork Chop has reverted back to calling Michael Slatter, the name of a monster, his Mr Hyde to Michael's Jekyll. The term defines a fiend, someone or something cowardly and depraved, and the kind of horror reserved for dark basements, shaped out of abusive childhoods and pent-up, malignant rage. Before properly entering, I look back over my shoulder at Pork Chop, who merely shrugs, his frustration all too apparent at me placing too much trust too soon in an unknown quantity. But what he doesn't get, let alone appreciate, is that this is what I am after. I want the darkness of Slatter rather than the level-headedness of Michael. I want his dark alter ego to excel and show me what he is capable of. It is about the ultimate expression of true freedom and taking those initial steps towards a lifestyle without limits in an environment that will actually let you.

Pork Chop should have grasped that. I'm surprised; after all, isn't that what happened last night when I gave him carte blanche to kill the family of his wife's so-called lover and his own family, too? I mean, creativity can't be micro-managed. Once the outlet has been fashioned, so to speak, you just have to let them run with it, like any creative process. Or could it simply be a re-manifestation of Pork Chop's initial dislike of Slatter bubbling up to the surface, tired of making the effort to remain repressed?

I dunno, my inner voice sighs, hoping that a seasoned police detective and an academic who loves paedophilic and violent sex films can make it work. Once inside, I scan the room rapidly over and over, the way a three-dimensional printer builds up an image, line by line, layer on layer, before committing it to memory; then I walk slowly forward till I am only a foot away from the bottom-left candle.

The scene, unquestionably macabre, is a horror show to scare even the most stalwart and determined of adversaries; certainly, it's a fate exceeding any misdemeanours I ever accused Mandy of. Yet, seeing her brutalised body enthuses me, reinforcing the faith I have put into Slatter. The 'situation', as Pork Chop put it, has turned out to be a lot better than I expected. I look down at the two stacked mattresses and the awful sight which lies upon them. I don't know why, but when I came up the stairs, I did at least expect to see Mandy one last time, similar to how I found Sharon. A part of me will be forever in love, not wanting to lose that trademark sexiness that she made look so effortless, exuding from her every pore, as though for her it was the only way to be. Instead, though the figure bears her vague shape, all I can see is an obscene menagerie of the most grotesque abuse, of torturous mastication, flesh ripped and torn away as if eaten by some rabid animal. I see her fingers chewed to uneven lengths, clumps of hair pulled so hard it has separated scalp from skull, her brow, cheekbones and jaw, pounded till swollen and her nose bitten clean through to the cartilage. Her features are misshapen, grossly disfigured and her once-voluptuous smile has been smashed to a crooked fissure. Standing here, following the wretched trail down her clawed neck to her ravaged breasts and unrecognisably ruined genitalia, I feel strangely humbled. I can't help but be excited at what I have unleashed. This morning, Slatter, though depraved in mind, was meek and mild, nothing more than a hapless introvert; the demon, it seems, is the difference between that and the crudest savagery. I move around to get a better look into the eyes of a battered, bloody soul, the shock of their exposed roundness only accentuated more by the eyelids having been removed or, more aptly, gnawed away. These eyes not twenty-four hours ago could part young men willingly from their hard-earned money. They could sing like angels. Mandy will always be remembered as a siren of the modern world, the sexiest, most sultry of grifters singing the way all sirens have sung since time immemorial. Boy, did the passing sailors love her for it, being fleeced of wages and valuables by someone so lustfully wanton, the irony being that for those sailors it was probably the highlight of their night and something to be talked about for many nights to come. Yet now, for all the beauty they once held, Mandy's eyes are nothing but fixed portals into a darkening hell. Her pupils unable to hide in their open, fleshy sockets, the surrounding tissue nibbled away to the brow, flicker nineteen to the dozen. Her body, similarly afflicted, fits spasmodically as though subjected to sub-zero temperatures, shivering violently. It's hard to fathom that she is still alive under all that horror, the hundreds of penetrating teeth marks and the bite-size chunks mauled over and spat out. I note the blobs of chewed skin and fat stuck to the radiator and to the adjacent wall, rinsed of their goodness till palest pink, signs of a grisly fulfilment in gratifying the craziest of hungers, for I know, now the monsters are amongst us, that it is no more than hell demands. A demon will always shock in showing you its voracity, a level of viciousness that you thought could never possibly exist, yet which does to those possessed by hell's fury.

For the moment I dismiss making eye contact with Slatter. He stands, smeared red, in the dimness of the far corner like a plump, naked doppelganger, his rounded features rendered sinister by the flickering candlelight. I glance over at him clenching his fists and gritting his teeth, his seething resentment of my and Pork Chop's intrusion palpable. It is like looking at a whole new person; his mind is still caught in the moment, lost in realising his fantasy of tasting human flesh. It is the strongest I have seen him, this overt show of anger and glaring confidence. It is a million miles away from what he was this morning.

The demon steps from his body and, like a puppet that has just had its strings cut, Slatter's whole demeanour slumps. The upright self-belief is gone, leaving a submissive figure with hands clutched between his loins like a chastised schoolboy, nervously fumbling; the contrast is everything I could have hoped for. The demon stands before him, almost motionless as if getting its bearings, looking around the room till its gaze fixes upon mine, and in a flash, it rushes straight for me. I brace myself, then flinch, but, like before, there is no impact. I laugh again at its absurdity, at the laws of physics being broken, proving that the stuff of make-believe is more believable than people might think.

But, unlike my dear Pork Chop, when speaking to or about Slatter, I will continue to call him Michael in the knowledge that Slatter is in there, and thriving, just below the surface.

Though I am mesmerised at the difference only one demon can make. Just imagine if I release them all…

For they are the essence of *apok*, the conduits of man's inner rage and of the monster we all tell ourselves is not there. I take a deep breath, more out of blessed relief than anything else, and smell the evaporated wax and burning wicks. The delicate waft is strangely seductive with feral undertones; the room's orange hue lends it and what is left of Mandy a Mediterranean glow, a tinge of the weirdly exotic, of spells cast, the colours and aromas alive with witchery. Her naked body resembles da Vinci's *Vitruvian Man*, splayed with ritualistic intent, the head and torso central, arms flung out and legs spread, the line of the head and each limb pointing with uncanny accuracy towards the five candles completing a pentagram, her agonised flesh, its vertices and defining structure. Suddenly, from all around, the creaking strain of another dimension pressing hard against ours fills my mind. It feels like an ancient ship trying to dock; its hull groans and ropes rasp in opposition to its alien moorings. Afraid that either Pork Chop or Slatter might make a run for it, I look quickly at both of them to gauge their reaction, hoping they stay strong. But they are blissfully unaware of the walls, floor and ceiling turning a glassy black with a ruckus of ghouls stretching back as far as the eye can see in every direction. There are even more than there were earlier, all baring fangs and claws, jostling impatiently, waiting for the gateway to open. The creatures, on seeing the star in all its grotesque yet perfect proportions, surge forward to press against the invisible divide. The noise of the creaking ship heightens with the pressure of the excited monsters in all their hideous forms as they drool over and ogle the pentagram's satanic magnificence and erupt in a terrifying roar of unified celebration. As the hellish cheer subsides, I cannot help but seize the moment of their approval. The lads look on, perplexed, in an otherwise deathly quiet room, watching me turning ever so slightly clockwise, a step at a time, bowing courteously as I go and in turn receiving the creatures' snarling endorsement on behalf of a much greater power.

"What the hell...?" I imagine Pork Chop saying from the bemused look on his face.

"I've done it!" I whisper to myself. Of all the variables that could have gone wrong, none have. Everything, just like I dreamed it would, has turned out fine. I'm exactly where I want to be – under the gods' scrutiny on the first rung of *Jacob's Ladder* with *His* blessing to proceed.

Give me war, I beseech you, oh Lord, my inner voice pleads, in over-exuberant solicitation. *You will not regret it.*

In the blink of an eye, the creatures vanish, and I feel a sudden warmth within me.

"C'mon, gather your clothes. We're going." I motion for Slatter to hurry.

"Y-y-yeah, right away," he stutters fretfully, picking up a neatly folded pile only to drop a trail of socks, pants, and a shoe. "So s-s-sorry!" He adds, faltering once more, as I send him back, pointing out the things he has dropped.

"Hey, you need to calm down – don't worry. You're not in any trouble," I say, stopping him in the doorway. "Look, I said it was your night and that you could do what you wanted – and you did. Good for you. You didn't hold back, and I like that. You took us by surprise, that's all. Seems like you have more Congo in you than you were letting on," I say to a newly minted monster. His wild expression and slack face betray a layer of mixed, yet raw emotion etched deep into his psyche. But I see it as my comrades will, as someone who has truly crossed over, when horror becomes more friend than foe. Slatter now has the thousand-yard stare, that unmistakeable look of dissociation, a kind of strange peace, a respite in the form of a virtual void where the madness can no longer touch you yet will remain, as though indelibly tattooed, to scar forever so that you bear that all-too-distinctive signature as if inked by the Devil himself.

Slatter, without looking at me, whispers a barely audible "thank you" – "It's okay," I reiterate as he disappears down the stairs. "Blimey, it's like having a kid," I remark.

Pork Chop laughs, rolling his eyes. "He just needs a few minutes to chill, that's all."

"I know," I say. "He's done well, as have you."

"Cheers, mate." He acknowledges my appreciation by simply tipping his head, then points towards Mandy. "What about her?"

"She's paid her dues. You can inject her now." Pork Chop nudges past me to kneel at Mandy's right arm. Minding the candle's flame, he finds a suitable vein, sticks in the needle, presses the plunger and, just as he did with Sharon, leaves the syringe in situ, its fatal payload spent, as Mandy's spasmodic trembling quickly becomes deathly stillness. Pork Chop gets to his feet, takes a step back and together we watch over her in mock prayer as she slips into the dark ether, my mind somehow still connected. I feel her cross over from light to dark, the tip of Leviathan's tentacle dragging her down into the inky blackness. The asphyxia, claustrophobia and panic are so stifling that I sense her choke and convulse; the incredible spasm and sudden nausea spew bile, blood and lung tissue, a wretched slick trailing out into the abyss – the calling card of a stranded soul, struggling and frightened beyond belief. A trail for the predators to home in on as she watches the patch of light from where she entered get further and further away.

The first bite comes from nowhere, a whoosh of razor-sharp teeth tearing off a chunk of lower leg or maybe just a foot; she can't tell in the pitch black. Another set of gnashing jaws hits, then another and another, all from different angles, all taking their pound of flesh. The sickly-sweet smell of fresh blood and gore engulfs her. It is everywhere as she screams louder than she has ever screamed before, knowing the creatures are there merely feet away, ready to finish the job and tear her soul apart. I don't know how, but I find myself inside Mandy's head, living the insanity of having just lost her limbs; stumps of shredded flesh and splintered bone move off involuntary brain impulses alone. The terror is surreal, the trauma off the scale, as phantom legs battle the downward current in vain and hands, she no longer has to try desperately to feel for the mutilation she cannot see. The searing pain is enough to tell the story and send her to the brink of unconsciousness, drifting in and out; her dreadful screams, like in space, do not travel, their sheer awfulness deafeningly silent and her despair utterly gut-wrenching. She thinks that this is it, the end, that it can get no worse, that her ordeal at its penultimate stage and that death will soon come, albeit in a frenzy of sharp teeth. But our link is a one-way channel. I cannot communicate with her. If I could, I would tell her, "Now the *dark* has you, your suffering won't end here – this is the beginning!" Just like the god that is the *dark* itself, an infinite and eternal being, so will your suffering be infinite and eternal, for the soul of man is the dark's ambrosia and our fear its nectar, as though we simply exist like a farmed delicacy, a caviar or foie gras of sorts, to feed *it* and *its* kind.

Feeling like I am being dragged down as well, I snap out of the trance and shake the disorientation from my head. "So that's what it is like from the outside looking in," I mumble to myself. Mandy's plight sparks a vague recollection of being chased by unknown creatures in a not too dissimilar dream-like hell.

"Whaddaya say?" Asks Pork Chop in knee-jerk fashion, thinking he's missed something vital.

"Nah, it's nothing." I wave away his interest. "Just thinking aloud. Why don't you see to Michael while I finish up here?" I add, searching for inspiration to at least partially mask the state of Mandy's tortured body, like I did downstairs with Sharon when I conjured up those maggots.

"Back in Croatia, we let the rats finish them off – remember?" Pork Chop laughs and I nod in acknowledgement as he goes out onto the landing. On leaving, he throws me a knowing look. *You're going to do it again – aren't you*, his eyes easy to read. I listen to him descend the stairs to where Slatter is sitting on the bottom step and hear their muffled voices as Pork Chop adopts the role of a squad leader, helping his new comrade dress and sort himself out.

"That's it – rats!" I whisper. My thought pings out into the ether in a heartbeat, and I hope the gods will grant me one more favour.

Excitedly, I wait. The silence electrifies to the point where it makes the hair on the back of my neck stand on end. I try to be patient.

I don't hear it at first, a low rustling, its volume slowly, but surely, building underneath the floor, something fast and soft moving and scraping and making haste. My ears prick left and right and my head swivels at the tiny sounds like an owl trying to determine a field mouse's exact location in the dead of night. The noise's supple daintiness makes a sudden change of pace, develops into a definite scratching that circumnavigates the room eagerly behind the skirting-boards. I spin at the horrid, yet subtle clamour, following what I assume are tiny, clawed feet scurrying, the demon spirits propelling them, their appetites as ravenous as they are relentless in gathering intensity. The now-hurried vociferousness converges at the shadowy base of the room's four corners, as though the floor and walls cannot hold the pressure any longer. Then, after a few seconds of plaster cracking and wooden boards creaking, from the corners' gloomy recesses a plague of darkest ebony spills to scamper in their multitude, jumping onto the mattresses the way salmon leap to overcome obstacles when returning to their spawning grounds. The rats jostle and collide like four riptides coming together, clambering across one another, knocking over the candles, the melted wax splashing and flames extinguished with the brief crackle of singed fur and pained squeaks. In seconds, the rats are swarming all over Mandy's bloody corpse, nuzzling and sniffing, inspecting, then gorging. The only visible parts are her hands and feet. And with that, I am done. I check the candles are properly extinguished and shut the bedroom door behind me. With my hand still on the door handle, I pause for a moment, suddenly aware of a glad, strange light breaking across my face like dark sunshine, a kind of cold happiness, symptomatic of malice aforethought and everything that is tainted unholy. But it is happiness all the same, and I take it for the positive it is. Though it is not the jumping up and down, shouting for joy type of happiness I thought it would be, just a modest inner glow of knowing I pulled it off and the sense of a job well done as I stand on the shoulders of giants. Its reward is akin to having life's judge and jury hail me as their new, undisputed king of murderers, applauding as my crimes are universally acquitted by the Devil's court, so I may go free with impunity to murder again.

    I chuckle at the irony; my own private fanfare announcing to the gods the latest hero to grace their sinful fold. I descend the stairs towards where Pork Chop and Slatter are waiting.

    "You guys good to go?" I direct my question at Pork Chop.

    "Yeah, we're good," he replies. "He's had an ice wash." Pork Chop giggles. "Got that blood off his face, neck and hands. Like I said, we're good."

    "Is that right, Michael? You okay?" I ask Slatter directly.

    "Yes, I'm good," he murmurs, his meek response typical of someone who has just come out of their particular closet, though I am picking up, via a host of anxious mannerisms, a distinct feeling that he still thinks he has done me some wrong in letting go like he did, and thus might be in line for some form of punishment.

"Look, Michael, there's no need to sweat it. Believe it or not, you did good. Like I said to you upstairs, it was your night to shine, and you did. There's no shame in that. At some stage we all go through it. You did tonight what I did in an orchard several weeks ago," I explain. Slatter silently mouths "You what?" I hold up a hand. "It's too long a story for now. I'll tell you when we next meet up. But in a nutshell, it's how people like us evolve. Our transformations involve no chrysalis or restful metamorphosis. We are born again out of blood and violence, as if it is the only way our DNA, knowing nothing else except life's wild extremes, can best adapt and prepare us for those kinds of challenges. Yes, it feels weird, almost awkward, for your secret to be out in the open. We, by our very nature, are considered abnormal; we're despised. That is why we hide, albeit in plain sight. But most significantly, it is because we are feared. Always remember that, because when you walk out of that door," – I continue, tapping my index finger on the front door – "that's when everything we talked about – your dreams, my dreams – that's where it all starts, as soon as you take the first step. So, from now on its chin up, chest out and act like you mean it. I'm not after arrogance; I just want to instil a little confidence, or more accurately a sense of self-belief I feel is lacking. You know what I mean?"

"Yes, I do, and thank you," replies Slatter sincerely.

"Don't mention it," I say, as we shake hands. "I'll admit it takes a bit of getting used to, taming the monster within, but you'll get there once you're amongst other monsters." I wink and smile, my inner voice carrying on the conversation – *'cos that, my friend, is what you have signed up for. That is apok: No prisoners, death to all, spare no one!*

"Now listen up; this is important. Once you leave here, there's a chance we won't see one another for a while," I say.

"How come?" Asks Pork Chop with a hint of concern.

"Hopefully, the outbreak of war, for one thing," I pat Pork Chop on the shoulder, and he reciprocates with a nod as if to say, "Oh, yeah, I'd forgotten about that!"

"And if that's the case, I expect there to be a lot of fallout; widespread disruption and confusion, not to mention violence. Plus, there's no telling how it might go. Travel in-country might be difficult or nigh on impossible at times. It is just a risk we will have to work around, I'm afraid."

"See what you mean," acknowledges Pork Chop.

"Anyway, as far as you two are concerned, it's the Russians, not the Croats, that are calling the shots on your future plans. They're running security, even if they have got the Croats doing all the donkey work. Now, the Croats are no-nonsense, as you know," – I say to Pork Chop, who confirms with a single nod – "but the Russians are on a whole different level. Be very polite is my advice. And never, ever question their authority. Apart from those two rules, they are very easy to get along with; very generous and very accommodating. And what's more, they are looking forward to meeting you." My comment generates smiles of approval all round. "My guess is that they will most likely have you in Bratislava for a short time, possibly Pécs in southern Hungary and Celje in Slovenia before bringing you to Croatia. You know, help to set up shop, so to speak, regarding the business side of *apok*; logistics, supply routes, security measures and protected lines of communication, that sort of thing," I explain. "Is that okay?"

"Yeah, no prob. Sounds like an adventure, but where are you gonna be?" asks Pork Chop, that note of concern returning.

"In the thick of it, fighting, I hope," I reply to two pairs of raised eyebrows. "Hence, I don't know where I will end up. From here I'm heading straight back to base at Vojarna Tuškanac, then onto Vukovar. All I can tell you is that it's a promise I've made, and one which I must keep. Do you trust me?" An awkward pause ensues as both Pork Chop and Slatter slowly nod.

"You know we do," Pork Chop confirms.

"Yes, absolutely," adds Slatter.

"Good…and thank you. It means a lot." My sentiment, as rare as it is, is sealed with a firm handshake, the kind men do before embarking on the challenge of their lives. "Now, have you had a final check around the flat?" I change the subject.

"Yes, I have," Pork Chop fires back, his tone positively brimming with smug satisfaction. "I took the bag, the one you left lying on the floor," – he smirks – "and set the works – that is, all the drug paraphernalia you asked for – out on the table. The heroin in the syringes was cooked up using that very equipment, plus I emptied the sachet of citric acid and left it screwed up nearby to complete the picture, which ties in with the level of authenticity you're after."

"Nice touch. And what about the drinks?" I ask, looking into the kitchen, the stainless-steel sink, its plug pulled, empty but for melting ice.

"As regards the leftover booze, I poured it down the sink. That included the two beer cans, the tequila and, I'm sorry to say, your other bottle of red. The empties, including the cork and wrapping off the wine bottle, I placed randomly with the tin and the remaining coke wraps on the floor by the sofa. It will add to the story we want that room to tell – a frenetic party atmosphere – and exaggerate the possible number of people involved. And as for the ice, it will be gone in an hour or so," – he explains, mentally ticking off his to-do list – "Oh, and what about the dry-wall hammer? You want me to get rid of it?"

"Leave the hatchet. I need it for something." I raise my hand to stop any questions.

"Okay," concedes Pork Chop, knowing better than to ask a second time. "Right, then; the soft drinks I'll take for our journey, and the black bag which had your stuff in, and the plastic carrier bags from the supermarket I will take and bin en-route. Now, I take it you want to leave the corkscrew, knife and fruit where they are on the kitchen counter?" His query is more rhetorical than anything.

"Yeah, might as well," I say. "It lends a more organic, more natural feel. Whaddaya think?"

"I agree."

"Yes, definitely adds dimension," Slatter chips in, nodding wholeheartedly.

"Well, then, that's it; time for you two to hit the road," I say. The three of us exchange hugs and congratulatory pats on the back.

"It's been one hell of a weekend. I can't believe it is actually over." Pork Chop laughs in exultant release.

"I know! And this is just the beginning," I reply, the two of us grinning like madmen.

I can see all over Pork Chop's face that he is desperate to know how I left it with Mandy, but that's a conversation for another time. To properly explain the rat thing, I would have to start with the maggots and how I call to the gods, as insane as it sounds, to summon them. And then I would have to come clean about who I am. It's hardly your run-of-the-mill conversation, and for something so fantastical, it would take too long to explicate, to break down into its constituent parts in order for it to be more easily absorbed and digested. I haven't the time; not tonight. The only person I have ever told, in a roundabout way, who I might be is Dan – not that I think Porky Chop or Slatter couldn't handle it. It's just that Dan and I, for a while anyway, were on the same wavelength. He had this dumb but knowing smile, a kind of half-crazed darkness that never left him, as though there was nothing to think about – he simply got it. I saw the way he used to look at me. It was if I had the power of life and death over him, like he was constantly in awe of something, a force that we both knew existed but were unable to clarify.

I remember him something he said once, when we had returned from an ill-fated patrol somewhere deep in the boonies southeast of Vinkovci after our point-man had tripped a claymore. We were lying in our bunks sipping a well-earned pivo. "That was some extreme shit, my friend. You see him come apart?"

"Yeah…I saw it," I replied. A man shredded to a bloody blur in one deafening split second, followed by the awful screams of the dying and injured behind him.

"So why'd ya take his place?" Dan asked.

"Why'd ya think? It's not as if anyone else wanted the gig," I joked.

"It's not as if there was anyone else who could!" Dan giggled back as we laughed at yet another hapless nobody that no one seemed to know or care for. "You're one way-out, crazy dude, y' know that? You ain't like us," he added. I nodded in acknowledgement.

"I don't know how to put it." I paused to check with myself if I should continue, and I did, telling Dan what he wanted to hear and what his insidious smile had always reflected. "It's just that when I'm out front, I feel invincible, like I know nothing earthly can touch me, as though I am not of this world."

"You mean born of a jackal 'n' all that shit," Dan quipped, but nonetheless he was eyeing me up.

"Something like that."

"Well, you've got the luck of the Devil, I'll give you that." He chuckled, sitting up, his usual smile gone, as if he was about to say something that he'd always wanted to say but the timing had never been quite right. "I don't know if the others can see it, but you're a scary guy, Andy. God help whoever crosses you, that's all I can say. God fucking help them!" In my entire life that is as close as I have got. The subject is subliminally taboo. Each time it is broached, I can't quite bring myself to admit the impossible. If I got into it now, we would be here all night, and though I am finished here in the flat, I am not finished with what I have to do outside. Yes, the ritual was a success, and I'm thrilled to have had the chance to demonstrate this new power invested within me with such emphatic and dramatic effects. However, it is not enough. The ritual's success may satisfy the gods for now, but they, like me, will need convincing of my longevity and that I can use this new power of mine on a larger scale, in a totally unpredictable environment with no guarantee of the outcome. And I need that to happen tonight. This acid test will double up as a miniature test pilot, for want of a better description, for this experiment will determine what *apok* is going to look like when I go back to Croatia.

Chapter 13
Saturday Night's All Right for Carnage

It's weird watching someone you don't know mutilate their own child. It has this detached creepiness about it that is so impersonal and yet incredibly intimate, making you feel awkward, like a peeping Tom that's been invited into their voyeuristic safe haven to oversee the most private of private affairs…

I let Pork Chop and Slatter go. I don't know why, but I'm in a strange mood; the kind where you don't want something to stop. I'm not one for outward emotion, but tonight feels different, and though the guys need to get going, a part of me wishes they could have stopped, despite it being imperative that they get out of the country on the six o'clock ferry. If they had stopped, we would probably have talked for hours, checking and re-checking the plan, and joked about how I can conjure up maggots and rats and monsters they cannot see. We would have been three happy killers putting the world to rights in a way only killers can, our addictions soaking up every second of what the night had to offer, our spirits soaring, the chat incessant and animated, reliving the past hours, keeping the celebration going. But what I wanted most and was not able to do was to be truly honest. I wanted them to know what was going to happen in explicit detail. I wanted a frank conversation about what was to come, not the vague overview that I ended up giving. Reassuring the troops overtook my need to impress them; my inner voice was quashed by the reason and sensibility of my role as leader. I needed the lads confident and inspired, not scared, and riddled with uncertainty. Still, I wanted so much to revel in the horror to come and how Vukovar will descend into a hell on earth. I wanted Pork Chop and I, two fully blooded brothers who have been there, seen it and done it, to wax lyrical into the early hours, telling Slatter of the joys of what he is letting himself in for.

"It's gonna be a bloodbath" – I would have proclaimed – "a slaughter!"

"You reckon?" Pork Chop would have replied excitedly.

"Yeah, I do. And if I know the Croats like I think I do, then it'll be worse than anyone can imagine. You know what they're like. They'd rather fight to the last man and destroy Croatia in the process than give the Serbs an inch." I would have shrugged my shoulders like some movie tough-guy giving it the big John Wayne hard sell. We would have laughed and joked at how war would send everyone east of Osijek into panic mode, sparking sporadic violence and reprisals, a catalyst that would manifest itself into a living nightmare of tit-for-tat sectarianism, turning neighbour against neighbour and ultimately brother against brother.

"And this is how it starts…" I would have said, baiting my audience on purpose, heightening their interest in the rest of my story. And with the scene set, I would have gone on to explain how I was told once that the Bible is a collection of fantastical stories, the first of these stories being Genesis, where a beautiful world was created; a world that now has to be re-created. And just like God did with his world in Chapter 1, I would have relished describing my magnum opus and how I intend to create mine, rewriting a new chapter for a new dawn. I'd declare my promise to the gods and to the people of the world of a new beginning, a brave new world crafted from the chaos of the old. I'd have laid down my strategy, baring my soul in a selfless act of full transparency. Like it says in Job 1:21, *the Lord gave, and the Lord has taken away*, but as a self-appointed creator in waiting, I'm proposing taking away in order to give. The price for such a gift is astronomical and will have to be earned. New worlds in this era of hyper-inflation don't come cheap. Humankind is way past the point of striking a bargain. I wanted to explain the mathematics of my plan, the total cost, the numbers involved and the equation to which this all relates. I wanted so much to tell them how I am intending to save our planet and bring it back from the brink. I wanted Pork Chop and Slatter to know the vital importance of their roles. I wanted to stress the significance of *apok* and how it will bring about the change needed to ensure the continued survival of our species. So that they not only know but fully appreciate the enormity of the experiment and the fact that they will, for a time, be running *apok* and its business without me and will be wholly responsible for its reputation. But more importantly, I wanted to properly explain to Slatter how *apok* unlocks the mind, and how experiencing horror up close is like being hit simultaneously with all the answers you have ever wanted out of life, a hit so powerful it supersedes life itself, like reaching what Buddhists call enlightenment. I wanted it to be a time of reflection, an opportunity for him to give his take on how the evening unfolded and for us to talk through the sequence of events, a kind of post-op coping session to help him figure out and interpret the experience. I wanted us to go through everything from when he first introduced himself to Sharon and her subsequent rape, right the way through to what happened with Mandy, when he finally let go and his inner monster took over. And with that fixed in his mind, I wanted both Slatter and Pork Chop to realise how each paying participant in *apok*, regardless of background or circumstance, when returning to their home and society, will automatically, as an unwitting host, spread the evil they have travelled so far to find. Like a virus, it will contaminate all they touch. I wanted that conversation so much. I wanted to reveal the mechanism of *apok* in its wider, more fluid form and introduce Pork Chop and Slatter to the creatures that will carry its message like a plague to infect every man, woman, and child.

Instead, I watch proudly as my two new best friends saunter off along the dimly lit walkway towards the stairs that leads down to the shuttered units below. Slatter exudes a slight swagger, that irrepressible sense of elation you get when you feel you can't cruise any higher and you know there ain't no one who's gonna rain on your parade – not tonight! I should know what it looks like. I had it after my first night patrol, that indestructible buzz fizzing through my veins, affecting every movement; even the way I exhaled had attitude. It felt like I had grown ten feet tall walking back into camp, and this is exactly how Slatter feels now, for he is a man whose fear is gone, who knows his friends have his back and will do right by him regarding the deal he has struck. I'm truly happy for him, as now he can really begin to live. In the gloom below I follow their footsteps crossing the car park, two dark figures barely distinguishable against the tarmac's black surface. Pork Chop's car beeps, the indicators blink three times, and the interior light simultaneously pings into life, shedding light on two newly christened killers about to embark on the adventure of their lives.

Watching the RS Turbo fire up and drive away, my mind turns to *apok* and a conversation I had at the Vojarna Tuškanac military base before leaving for the UK. I didn't know his name or anything about him; you never bothered with most FNGs. He was just one of those faces I had seen around and spoken to on several occasions, typical in that he seemed forever lost, unsure if he had bitten off too much in going to Croatia; a fragile soul trying so hard to keep up with those around him. I don't why he stood out from the crowd. He was of average height and build, his appearance having no real redeeming features to speak of.

For all intents and purposes, he was a stranger amid a wash of strange folk. Yet stand out he did. I guess that's why I chose him, this affable stranger, someone of a similar age to myself whose presence I found oddly compatible and by the same token comforting. He was still capable of civilised dialogue amongst the deluge of Europe's cast-offs, and it's my guess he felt the same.

We had the kind of conversation you have with a newbie, an exchange of pleasantries about nothing in particular; this encounter was no exception. Still, I was surprised when I saw him standing with a few others by the main gate, all with their kit bags by their sides. Just by the look of them, the way they shuffled their feet with faces lowered, scared, and embarrassed, unable to make eye contact, I knew they were waiting for the bus to the station, the first leg of their homeward journey and the much-needed detox before re-joining normality; their dark tourist fantasies were over. There is no shame in catching the bus. Plenty do, especially younger recruits, two-pint wonders giddy on adolescent bravado, wanting to fight the world after a couple of bottles of pivo, only to be brought crashing down to earth by horror's cruel, random touch.

The affable stranger, sad and gaunt, looked like he couldn't wait to get going. He was clearly out of his depth in what he thought should have been the making of him. Yet when I stared into his teary eyes, I knew, as he knew, that his plan had backfired spectacularly. His dreams of conquering manhood had been shattered and the pieces would haunt him forever. It was a tragic, horrid nightmare about how three friends died; one in particular, a late arrival, as wet behind the ears as you can get, who on that initial day had been issued with his weapon, a Zagi sub-machine gun.

"There were no rifles or AKs left, so they gave him a Zagi. He loved it; couldn't stop cleaning it," the guy said. "But the damn thing just went off."

My stranger friend, with tears rolling down his cheeks, went on to explain how the four of them had been in their room a few nights before, readying their kit for the following day, chatting shit, telling jokes, and discussing who was going to buy the beers later that evening, when without warning a clatter of automatic gunfire ripped through their tiny living quarters. His friend, who had been cleaning his new gun, frantically juggled the discharging weapon in a blind panic as thirty-two 9mm rounds spat forth to engulf the modest twelve-by-twelve room in what would have been three or four seconds of pure hell followed by the inevitable but horrible screams of the mortally wounded trying to plug their punctured, bloodied bodies with their fingers.

"Just get home" – I told him – "and promise me you will never think of coming back."

He nodded a pale and drawn reply. He had the hunched frailty of an old man, as if those few horrific seconds had sapped the youth from his once-vibrant core. He was just like the rest of the sorry bus queue, distressed, no longer who they used to be inside, their mental fortitude smashed to smithereens, wishing with what rational thought remained that they had never made the trip in the first place.

Accidents were rife and skilled supervision in scant supply. Veterans had a saying: Keep your shit wired tight at all times. In other words, no mistakes: If in doubt – ask! The Zagi, a cheaply made SMG synonymous in its simplicity to the British Stun-gun of World War II, was renowned for its continuous discharge of the magazine, with no way to stop it once the trigger had been pulled. Yet someone from the armoury, probably knowing full well the gun's pitfalls and that the recipient was a total novice, had given the poor lad this problematic weapon to use.

"People coming over don't get that you can die out here," the guy sobbed. "And the real war hasn't even started yet. Then it will be cut-throat – they die, or you die," he continued, pointing towards me. "I mean…who's gonna come over for that?" His whimpering voice tailed off in nervous laughter. The demons inside were already eating away at whatever semblance of normality he had left.

I know what my stranger friend meant. Modern conflict is hard to describe to the average layperson. They don't understand that when a grenade is thrown into an enemy foxhole, the results can be swept up into a sack. Many struggle with the concept, because of its sheer abhorrence; in a split second a living human being can be reduced to a pile of smoking body parts. It is too obtusely grotesque for those in civvy street to appreciate, as though refusing to accept its existence is protection enough against the horror you know is out there.

Like it or not, everyone who catches the bus takes the horror with them like a warped keepsake of their brush with death – the tortuous fever of nightmarish insomnia.

As I look out into the punctuated darkness to the streetlights beyond and the flats around me, I realise that my stranger friend, this person I didn't know and will never see again, was right – who would come to such a hellhole? Only the clinically insane would sign up for such a mission. And there are already plenty of them to go around. You can't sell an adventure on the probability of being killed. Killing amidst the thrill of a war zone, yes! Killing is what *apok* is all about – the realism and intensity – but dying in the process, no. *Apok* and its guardians will have to protect its participants, similar, I guess, to how it works on safaris, where older, infirm animals are selected for their slowness, or at bullfights where the bull's horns are blunted to lessen the odds of the matador being gored. It may seem unfair, but I had a practice run with the Austrian. I set the scene and put the odds in the client's favour, so he got to tell his friends and boast of his exploits. Our brand will be strengthened by the very people who vow to return to their favourite theme park.

Now that's what you call authenticity, the kind of corroborating evidence of provenance a product like *apok* needs. Sell that and the rest will take care of itself.

***

The streets visible to me are all but empty, the night, almost by definition, signalling a curfew to those who prefer to stay snuggled up inside their tiny castles. The paranoid breed of 'see no evil, hear no evil, so there is no evil' are glued to their TVs, practising their daily ritual of fending off a centuries-old curse with latter-twentieth-century technology. Yet still these people in their gross hypocrisy return to a god whose name, every minute of every hour, they take in vain and whose existence they deny, hopelessly fickle, praying for daybreak and respite from the dark and the creatures it unleashes.

Leaning on the balcony rail of the outside walkway, I briefly close my eyes, take a deep breath, and listen to the noises of a world apart, of distant footsteps and boisterous chatter, the echo of pounding feet running in an alley and youthful shouts getting closer. The wash of traffic is ever present, coming in waves, punctuated by a car's sudden acceleration and the screeching of tyres. I compare the sound of night-time suburbia to that of competing televisions, both the blueish light and the sound of people's best-loved dramas emanating from behind locked doors, those inside hunkered down, trying their level best to drown out the outside menace. During my time in Croatia, I came to appreciate that noise is different in the dark. It has that knack of never failing to make your eyes dart and put your senses on alert. It is somehow louder and has a harsher tone, something primordial and unadulterated that allows it to travel as though it has a mystical energy. It can outrun whoever's in earshot, giving it a power that is quite innocuous during the day but reigns supreme after nightfall. It has that rare superiority over us, like the ultimate apex predator you cannot see, possessing the ability to make our imaginations run amok and make us fear the worst despite having a tangible grip on reality. For something that is a part of our every day and so simple, the dark will always remain the definitive pressure test for determining human frailty, because if you think a situation cannot get any worse, imagine that same terrible situation but in the dark. In the daytime we forget, taking the reassurance light provides for granted. But at night the rules of engagement change, exposing a new classification of haves and have-nots where money is not a factor: Those who are fearful of the night's inhabitants and those who are not. In fact, in my experience, the bleaker someone's prospects, the hungrier they are and the more fight they have. Survival is second nature; it lessens any fear they may feel when faced with an adversary. Take someone who is at rock bottom, for example, and potentially you have the most dangerous, most unpredictable person you will ever meet.

On a street level, fear is society's clear divide and where decades of peace have taken us, with our collective safety net layered thick on a mass indoctrinated apathy; it's a kind of elaborate pretence that we kid ourselves will last forever. This comfy living is today's status quo, the new untouchable holy trinity: God bless our father, capitalism; the son, the ever-faithful consumer; and the holy spirit of money. But most importantly, the sounds of the night air and the chills they bring are how the minority have managed to outwit the majority. Light and dark have been split in people's perceptions, and this is how fear has been propagated.

But if the blaring TVs of the meek and frightened versus the howls of today's lost generation is the collective noise of peace, of decades of what the politicians call progress, then it is a noise I despise; a noise of weakness and the slow death of a species. It is a noise that cannot be allowed to continue. In suburban Zagreb, for instance, there is parity in what you hear, though the sounds are not so much 'drink and be merry' but 'get pissed and destroy!' It is the noise of anxious people forced to embrace uncertainty as they come to terms with the upheaval that waits. That is the noise of the future; a unified roar and the sound of those who will do anything to survive. But survival extends to the bigger picture, to the powers that be and *apok*. It is the pep talk those on the bus get before reaching the station, the instruction to keep their mouths shut, the words 'ships' in the phrase 'loose lips sink ships' relating to family members. A profile is handed to each person detailing their respective genealogical data, the names and addresses a sledgehammer of a reminder that *they* know who you are and where to find you. But survival also means continued existence. The world still needs people. I may be, in the short term, proposing a global wave of indiscriminate genocide, a plan to reduce humanity, but I am certainly not suggesting total annihilation. For Armageddon isn't the end and was never intended to be. It is, in fact, and has always been meant to be interpreted as a new beginning, a chance to start over with the right mix of the right people, a reworked, re-envisaged version of Noah's vision. For in the modern day, the only formula that does work is one that contains a little bit of everything, or, as my mom would say, 'Everything in moderation, my dear'. It is a common answer that solves our common problem: Moderation. It is the square root of man's total greed divided by the planet's overall populace; a universal parity which exists in theory only; a God equation if ever there was one.

The powers that be know this and have done for millennia. They've been scared to let go ever since the relatively simple maths that solves the human condition came to light; the holiest of grails that no one with influence ever seemed to care for. History tells us that, and in recent decades, events have only reiterated that nothing has changed. But, knowing their secret, I for one am not scared to lift the lid off the jar once and for all like the ancient Greek poet Hesiod described: A gift from Zeus was left in Epimetheus' care, a jar that contained evils, toil and illness, the lid of which I lifted when I released the creatures. But, let's face it, this is where generations of poor choice and indecision leave you, grasping at straws with hopes dashed, desperately trying to cling onto whatever optimism there is, however tenuous. So, imagine being presented with one such jar, its contents a total lottery of godly gifts, unsure if the gifts are all good or all bad or a mixture of both. The gamble is a kill-or-cure scenario that will, if successful, solve the current crisis and all future crises in which we as a species find ourselves – would you open it?

And what's more, would you open it knowing that once the contents were unleashed, there would be absolutely no going back, the path to salvation a one-way ticket via the darkest hell? In the not-too-distant future, that's where humankind will end up anyway. You see, in restoring balance, there is no one party that will allow total annihilation. Everybody needs somebody. The gods need humans to worship them, and humans need gods to favour them. The world leaders and politicians need voters, and the voters are lost without rule.

Financiers need industry, industrialists and entrepreneurs need a workforce to generate finance, and the workforce in turn wants nothing more than to have a purpose, live well and please the gods and those higher up the food chain. It's the way of the world, a whole El Niño effect all on its own; it's the weather pattern of weather patterns that keeps everyone in check and the world turning. But even though this set of circumstances I describe, albeit with a much-reduced populace, sounds like business as usual, a micro version of our macro dilemma, the strategy employed, by its very definition, will separate the wheat from the chaff, which in turn will provide our future with the right mix of the right people who are willing to pull together and pool our global resources in order to move forward. The rest, as my method dictates, are surplus to requirements.

Evolution is the only diktat for a species that wants to prevail. The maths – and believe me, I've run through the numbers – supports no other findings. But to humans, evolution means revolution; out of the ashes, we are reborn. Such drastic change comes no other way. And to that end, I also believe we are at the stage where individual choice has to be taken from our conscious self and our destiny placed into that of our inner monster, the only part of us that can overcome the hurdles in order to survive by any means necessary, ensuring that, as a species, we live on. Hence the forthcoming war in Croatia will be my test pilot; a revised version of natural selection; an experiment in how to indiscriminately fashion a brave new breed for a brave new world. I chose the mission statement for *apok*, the mechanism of this process: "No prisoners – death to all – spare no one." It is a fitting mantra for the task ahead, and one easily remembered if you enjoy killing. But for the bigger picture, I was unsure of a suitable slogan, so I settled for a quote from Voltaire which in my mind embodies my vision – "It is forbidden to kill, therefore all murderers are punished unless they kill in large numbers and to the sound of trumpets." In other words, if everyone kills and kills and kills again, everything should be okay. I mean, how else are you expected to make a serious dent in a global populace of five point three billion, a number that is rising by four to five births per second, exceeding all previous forecasts, a number that is showing no signs of slowing down? Six billion is forecast for the year 2000, seven billion in 2010, eight in 2020, and so forth. But in the end, won't it be ironic if Armageddon is the by-product of wholesale industrial and technological innovation, that and trying to feed and water the workforce those advancements have made redundant?

Our planet may seem limitless, but it can only cater for so many.

If recent history has taught us nothing else – 'Computers, machines, the silicon dream' – it comes at a price, and that price is us. We will fall foul of the oldest rule of thumb there is: Out with the old and in with the new. Our demise will be considered as clinical as that. Or it could be interpreted as nature, the most ancient of gods, re-calculating our decades of interference and teaching us a lesson in why you should not meddle – showing us the cost of rearranging the natural order of things. Machines, knowing human fallibility as it is, would decide our fate in a nanosecond if they could. Nature, however, like the Croatian people, has learnt to bide its time harnessing that greatest of strategies, the art of patience and cunning passed down the generations. But how long is too long? They say strike while the iron's hot. In the meantime, if the gods favour war, as I hope they will, *apok* will be there, ready to steer the course. It will be a litmus test to kick off a new way of thinking – order via chaos. Chaos is the true birthmother of everything we hold dear; in the same way, chaos is the rightful mother of my demon throng and all demon-kind, the mightiest of she-devils. Chaos will stop at nothing to create a hell on earth, in which to draw out and nurture the inner monster that dwells within us all. For we are entering wondrous times! All hail to the gods, and may destiny, the slave of all that is divine, yield to Valhalla and the war-cry of its warrior faithful. All hail to *apok*, the new god of sex and horror, for the thrill of bloody battle and the spoils of glorious and hard-won triumph, and hail to those in the fray, who will fulfil the prophecy and fight to the death for the honour of being allowed to start over in the new world.

***

Back in the flat, preferring my efforts to be found how I want them to be found and not burnt beyond recognition like an accident, I snuff out the candles on the coffee table using an ice cube from the sink. I start with the furthest one and quickly work my way towards the door, being careful not to tread on any migrating maggots. Footprints of squished larvae would be a tell-tale sign, for sure, that someone has already visited the scene. I toss the watery piece of ice onto the floor, having already extinguished the candle in the kitchen. Still, I hesitate in the gloom, my legs all of a sudden like lead. It's as if a wave of emotion, that feeling I almost never have, is keeping me here, as though it, like me, doesn't want tonight to end. Taking my time, I stand in the hallway and turn to catch one final glimpse of Sharon lying on the sofa, the front door wide open, the meagre light from the walkway lights and the moon only reaching her still, grey feet. The rest of her is in total darkness. But the fact that I can see her is enough – more than enough. I know that the larvae inside her are eating their way out and another squirming mass are burrowing their way in. I think of how she will appear come morning; a riddled infestation, stiff with rigor and hideously pockmarked, the flesh turned grey and yellow, cratered, and peppered with tiny reddish-purple sinkholes. The true horror of her ordeal will be reflected in devoured eyes of writhing creamy white and a wide mouth that screams, fixed in darkest death, a spewed river of foul plague. I nod with deepest sincerity my appreciation towards Sharon, then cast my gaze upwards and spare a final thought for the sexiest girl that ever was. "It's been a pleasure, girls – sweet dreams," I murmur, pulling the lounge door to, knowing that as soon as it is shut, I'm leaving Sharon and her sister for the night to work its black magic and claim them both. For they are now condemned to hell's darkness, shrouded by the black of night. Their respective rooms contain something worse than the worst imaginings, an inescapable horror of horrors – my gift to the creatures in the hope they serve me well. Before I leave the flat, I grab the dry-wall hammer off the kitchen counter and slam the front door shut behind me. Its sudden bang is deliciously indicative of the threat, anger, and malice to which the dark alludes. The noise echoes off the surrounding buildings, its wave a sonic boom sending a message through concrete and brick to those within range: I am here at last, and what's more, so is *apok*!

    I study the building's architecture and layout. It has an L-shaped footprint of thirteen two-up, two-down flats comprising one larger corner plot and six dwellings extending out at ninety degrees to one another, all situated on top of a host of small commercial units, all empty and locked up except for the off-licence and betting shop. Looking around, I wonder which flat contains the couple I heard shouting earlier, whose children cried in fear, and where the intervening voice that yelled at them to "keep the fucking noise down" was. I can hear them now, the string of profanity echoing like a scar in time, playing over and over, the shouts, the screams, the crying an aberration in what was otherwise just another day. It brought the dilemma of night into the light; the perpetrators were quickly dismissed in favour of turning a deaf ear and maintaining a trouble-free life. The offended shrank back, withdrawing unnoticed, and the offenders crawled back under the rock from whence they came like the cockroaches they were. I bet the creatures could find them. They're good at wheedling out insects from hard-to-reach places. But they are already gone, like spectral bloodhounds hot on the trail sniffing out any trace of human pessimism, to exploit whatever frailties they find. Excited that the evening's entertainment isn't yet over, I feel the creatures jostle and fizz, their appetites whet once more and attuned to the heavy whiff of malicious intent.

I haven't known the creatures long, but I do have an inkling of their train of thought, of how they do what they do. They twist doubt into suspicion, which generates hate and anger, which eventually manifests as rage, its malignance a lightning-fast cancer. By now it's racing through every flat infecting each family, person by person, an instantaneous chain reaction that will reach every cubic inch of breathable air, sparing no one. I literally feel the atmosphere change. There's a disturbance in the natural flow of things like an abrupt calm between storms. Something about it is reminiscent of cordite – its smell and unique acrid taste, its faint stinging touch on the skin after a burst on full-auto. In my mind, the clinking of brass shell casings chimes as they fall at my feet. The flats are quiet for a few minutes, the silence crackling as though inexplicably charged, a lit fuse fizzing away towards a myriad of hidden bombs.

Unsure of what is going to happen, I listen, straining, almost impatient, wanting the calm to be shattered. I turn my head left, then right, then turn my body in a full three-sixty till my ears pick up shouts and what I think is the sound of breaking glass from the direction of the off-licence.

An instinctive compulsion takes over, and I decide not to wait. With my drywall hammer in hand, I walk to the nearest door and knock. A man in his early thirties answers. He stands there barefoot and scruffy, his messy hair filtering down via bushy sideburns into a wispy, unkempt beard. He's wearing a creased T-shirt and a pair of baggy cargo shorts.

Before the man can say or do anything, I grab him by the hand and watch a demon stride through his torso to disappear inside him. The sudden hit makes him jolt with the electric smack of possession. His eyes glaze over, and a supercilious grin falls like a shutter over an otherwise crazed expression.

"Could you fetch me a long sharp knife from the kitchen?" I ask with the familiarity of an old friend. His gaze is kind and agreeable, as though we are sharing a private joke, the kind that runs deep like a secret oath he has been waiting to fulfil all his life. This moment ties us both to the first step of *apok*.

"Sure, but I don't keep it in the kitchen," he replies nonchalantly as he turns to disappear from whence, he came. He's happy to oblige this stranger on his doorstep, someone he sees as posing no threat whatsoever. Not caring if the knife is in the kitchen, in the bathroom or under his bed, I don't question it, and in less than a minute he returns to hand me what I least expected. I can only describe it as a Japanese ceremonial long knife or short sword. The blade is approximately eighteen inches of razor-sharp, exquisitely fashioned steel. "Is that okay?" He asks softly.

"Yes, that'll be more than fine," I answer, feeling the weightiness of the blade, its handle of tightly bound red cord lending a balance and feel that is just begging for its first kill. I hand him back the knife and duly present the dry-wall hammer, which he holds aloft in awe, as though it is not the weapon, he sees but the impending trophy of a severed head. His gaze then switches to lock onto my own.

"You have in your hands a knife and a hatchet, the first and second weapons of choice available to participants in *apok*. The third and final choice is a gun, which I do not have, hence the choice. And as dramatic and gladiatorial as they look, I'm glad I have no gun to give, because just by looking at you it's obvious that these two weapons were clearly made for you," I explain. His eyes are soulless, glazed and yet oddly manic, as though receiving devilish instruction from elsewhere. His dilated pupils flicker erratically to the random dot-dash bleeps of some nightmarish Morse code. "The rules of *apok* are simple: No prisoners, death to all, and spare no one. Do you understand?" I stipulate the main criteria and the man reciprocates by nodding slowly. "Then what are you waiting for? Go an' get 'em!" I say, smiling. The man suddenly turns to lunge towards a woman coming out of the lounge behind him into the hallway.

"What the hell's taking you so long..." The woman's voice tails off in a violent groan and winded exhale. The knife plunged deep into her stomach pushes her back through the doorway she just walked out of. The man chops at her face and head, carrying on long after she's fallen. The pastel lounge carpet is soon sprayed a glorious red. In the manic rush he leaves the knife stuck in her midriff and the hatchet embedded in her forehead and dashes upstairs. I follow. At the top, he stops abruptly when he sees a little girl, who I presume is his daughter. She looks cute, as little girls should, in her sky-blue nightie dotted with flowers, weary at having been disturbed, rubbing the tiredness from her eyes. For a second, towering over her, he looks down, a father smiling sympathetically at his cherished little love, then in one diabolic movement he grabs the girl's fragile sleepy head, twists it hard with a swift crack and brushes her to one side over the stairs' precipice, forcing me to dodge the limp body as it goes tumbling past to end scrunched up at the bottom. A horrible cry adds to the madness; a boy, no more than fifteen, screams, charging along the short landing to collide with his father in a clumsy, half-hearted rugby tackle, terrified beyond belief and spurred on by what I can only assume is the sheer shock at just having seen his sister so coldly dispatched. The two struggle in a frenetic clash, the lad in floods of tears, bordering on hysteria. He blindly flails, kicks and punches only to be beaten down by his dad's superior strength and dragged into the bathroom. His head is smashed into the porcelain basin, then his lithe frame is flung face-up over the side of the bathtub arched back. The frenzied ruckus suddenly abates but for the frantic gasping of the monster leaning over his prey.

"What now?" A voice of insanity snarls, a truly horrid voice, the kind that needs no grotesque face to scare. Its sheer gravitas is enough to give you goose bumps. It's as gravelly and thick as it is unearthly, totally atypical of a husband or father, more befitting the monster the demon creature has revealed. The man is no longer a man, but grossly misshapen and twisted in his madness.

"You know what to do," I reply. "You've always known what to do."

Again, I can't help but smile, waiting for the penny to drop, as the demon and I exchange an intense sharing of minds, glaring into one another's aspirations and nightmares till finally I see the monster within the man smile back. The monster, not the man, is at last in full control. My gaze guides his hand to reach for an electric toothbrush, the unlikeliest of horrors but one which, whenever I am at my very lowest, never fails to ruin my sleep. The man, his chest still heaving with the exertion, tightens his grip on the boy's neck and jaw, before pulling the brush-head off the toothbrush with his teeth, spitting it out vehemently with a thrash of the head and an exaggerated growl to expose the needle-like steel spindle underneath. Holding it aloft, brandishing it like a weapon the way an executioner might show off his axe, he thumbs the button, producing an instantaneous buzz. The sudden whirr is the signal for his hand to drop and begin work. He jams the vibrating spindle into the tear duct, laughing out loud as he labours against the connective tissue, crudely gouging around the socket and discarding the bloody eyeball before starting work on the next. It's weird watching someone you don't know mutilating their own child. It has this detached creepiness about it that is impersonal and yet incredibly intimate. You feel awkward, like a peeping Tom who has been invited in from your voyeuristic safe haven to oversee the most private of private affairs. Stepping out of the bathroom, I leave the monster to butcher his son and wait at the bottom of the stairs next to the girl, her slight frame hideously crumpled and complexion already pallid. Her still, tired eyes stare in stark disbelief. This will be the third family that has died this weekend, but probably not the last if I decide to reschedule my visit to Dan's parents for tomorrow. I mean, what is there to say about Dan except that he used to be both mine and Pork Chop's closest 'oppo'? We arrived in Zagreb together, trained together, went on patrols, and lived through firefights together. But unlike Pork Chop, who was more of a visitor, flitting back and forth to the UK, Dan stopped with me, the two of us seeing each other through thick and thin, and therefore in seeking my own solace I considered him a brother. He preferred to be called Dan because whenever he was in trouble as a kid, which according to him was most of the time, his parents would yell 'Daniel, do this…' and 'Daniel, don't do that…', but always 'Daniel' something or other, his name bandied about with the same contempt as the most vile of profanities. Hence his childhood was an unhappy one and Croatia, when the opportunity came, was the outlet he had always craved.

You see, the last time I saw Dan before eventually catching up with him, was when he too was waiting to catch the bus, head bowed with the other poor unfortunates. But unlike the rest, who had chosen to be there and had no shame in catching the bus, burnt out and damaged, their emotions in tatters, Dan had no choice. He was told to leave. His childish bullshit and exaggerated exploits had finally lost the respect of his comrades, and what tipped the balance was his liking for young girls, something the Croats were not willing to overlook. There had been rumours, though nothing substantiated. Sexual crime was becoming rife, and for the police trying to quell its growing popularity it was like handing out speeding fines at the Grand Prix. Even murder had to be blatant and overly violent so the charges could stick; day by day the judicial grip on society was slipping to a point where the plight of the badly beaten, raped and missing were all but forgotten in the face of everything else that was going on. But we all knew there was no smoke without at least a little fire. His willingness to leave and accept that walk of shame was almost an admission of his guilt – and perhaps the degree to which his crimes extended. I heard later that he did well to get out in one piece. However, I knew then, as a foreign national, that if these allegations were confirmed by the Croatian authorities and corroborating evidence did surface linking Dan to them, evidence verified beyond reasonable doubt, the Croats would never let it go. They would do to him as they had done with others, and hunt him down like a dog, to the ends of the earth if necessary. He didn't know it, but he was in way over his head. The gossip that circled his subsequent absence was as malicious as a toxic loan accruing an exorbitant rate of interest. In the same way as a bad debt can spiral out of control, hyper-inflating to render whatever is actually owed no longer enough to settle the balance, the aggrieved parties were left wanting a lot more than was originally taken.

All I can say is that Dan should've stayed to face the music, as tough as it was, because being out of sight, to the Croats, meant you were forever in their minds – the one that got away, blighting an otherwise spotless record. For the Croats it was a matter of the utmost pride. As for Dan, it was more dangerous him not being there than if he had decided to come back. At least then he could have gone out with a little dignity. The boys would have respected that, made it as painless as it had to be. But the thing is, he didn't, and what you never, ever do is leave a gang of psychopaths hanging. You simply don't! At the time I remember quoting to Dan, "Keep your friends close, but your enemies closer," knowing the tactics employed by our Croatian hosts. It is like the mafia say: The person sent to kill you, will be someone you already know, and they will come bearing smiles. Hence you never see it coming. Hell, I've seen it where some don't even hear the shot! But then, that's the deal when you sign up – you sign your life over to your commanders and your soul to the Devil. As catch-22 dictates, you have got to be holding one hell of a hand if you think you can break the rules of this pact. Even in my short time, I've seen them stupid enough to try their luck thwarting fate, the high priestess poker god she is, always slam-dunking whatever cards they've had with an ace high, five of a kind, a *royal flush* sending them straight to hell. That is what Dan failed to realise, that the odds were fixed. And there was something else he didn't know – that I am one of those *they* call upon when someone oversteps their remit.

As if I didn't already have enough to do!

But in all fairness, where does it stop? When considering the rape of a child or the act of infanticide, add sentiment in the heat of the moment and what has that debt risen to?

I know if it were my daughter, I'd kill 'em all – mom, dad, siblings, aunts, uncles, cousins; I'd wipe out the whole fucking bloodline, every last motherfucking one!

Like the saying goes, "You don't dance with the Devil if you're not willing to dance his steps."

It is the dance we killers do when paying homage to the business of death, a business that never ceases to amaze me in how its customers can quickly stack up, the workload overwhelming for an even more depleted and scarcer skill-set.

Outside the flat, I hear the outcry demanding those same skills; the familiar turbulence of discontent and affray, angry words escalating into heated shouts and slamming doors, running arguments and the thud of pounding feet, trying both to escape and to join in the fight. Shrieks of dread compete against the catcalls and yelling of those chasing them down. The creatures, I take it, are managing to re-ignite the earlier dispute and spread the word. The purge, by the sounds of it, is already underway, its intensity taking hold. The urge of the oppressed and downbeat is too enticing to pass up, though the bullies will do their best to suppress the rising insurgence. In that context, it is a revolution the creatures and I are offering, the chance to finally right wrongs and let all that pent-up aggression out and enjoy a freedom like never before. To the underdog it will be like an unbottling of happiness, hope, achievement, inspiration and aspiration all at once, a sense of what the most magnificent of butterflies must feel the moment it emerges from its drab chrysalis. It will be like breaking through the wall from the Eastern block to the West, an instant transition from rationed black, white and grey to luxurious colour and a deluge of the exotic, euphoria to the introvert, the subdued and the many who have been repressed. It will be a no-brainer, the addiction immediate and the effect like nothing else that the world has to offer.

Imagine that all of a sudden you were empowered to rid yourself of all those niggling issues that would otherwise go unpunished. If you could…would you?

I know I would!

But, given the opportunity, would you follow me out into the night, into the affray to fight and, if need be, kill, knowing that on the flipside, despite the risks, you would finally be free of the fear and doubt that had held you back for so long?

Well…would you?

I listen again to the outside ruckus beckoning like an unavoidable summons – "You started this shit; you wanted it" – cries the mêlée – "so you can damn well get out here and fucking do it!" The momentum is building, its voice getting louder, angrier, more powerful, no longer asking me to join it but demanding I join it. The creatures are relentless in baiting and fuelling the fire; the whole cacophony is cheering on the violence. I sneer at the intolerable haste to question my delay and the insinuation implied. How dare they accuse me of anything but living up to my end of the bargain!

"Fuck 'em!" I growl. "If violence is all they want, then violence is what they'll get," I say to the girl next to me, as if trying to seek counsel in her cold dead eyes. I'm looking for reassurance that I'm doing the right thing in making the gods wait as I prepare myself mentally for the big finish.

For a moment, staring into the girl's fixed gaze as the once-mesmerising blue irises gradually ice over to a pallid opacity, I try to picture the utter confusion outside and the insanity brutally etched deep on peoples' faces. No doubt they're overcome with the shock and sheer exhilaration of doing battle with whatever they managed to grab from the kitchen drawer or the toolbox, their thoughts instinctively drawn to that of something else, something primal and deranged. The attack is sapping yet relentless; the red mist transforms neighbours into strangers and friends into foes as life, without any warning whatsoever, gets tipped upside down and dragged out under the moon's merciless gaze. The latest wave of killers is being born, able to stand on two legs and hit the ground running – the most savage of savage beasts, desperate for their moment of madness, if but a fleeting glimpse. This collision of fate is accelerating the unnoticed and the most insignificant to the dizziest of heights.

But that is the beauty of spontaneity: By catching people unawares it standardises the starting point for everyone, with no time to prep, only react, favouring no one and therefore providing a level playing-field. The instruments of the task are as crude as they are inclusive and accessible, and the fight to survive as brutally honest as it is medieval. This is the parity I am after.

Though why my ability is still in question is beyond me. I feel like a rat for the gods to toy with. My existence is a never-ending sequence of tests, sadistic jokes at my expense, as cryptic as they are cyclic bullshit, each time dumping me back at the beginning, the process trying its utmost to strip my sails of wind. It's not so much aiming to thwart me, more applying the brakes, creating a period of rest before the mayhem, even though the storm outside continues.

But as the dead girl stares back, although her purple lips don't stir, from the dark depths I hear the soft death-rattle of a voice. "Don't mistake nerves for feeling sorry for yourself," croaks her ghost, the words gurgling up through her twisted oesophagus.

Judging by what the evening has already delivered, I half expect the sweet little thing to stand and slap my face, yelling for me to 'snap out of it' and 'pull yourself together' as if I can still save her, and somewhere in my mind she does exactly that, despite her bones being beyond repair and her smile stained with blood.

But staring into those dull eyes, I know I'm on the brink, seconds away from sliding back to square one, where once again I'll be trapped in the abyss to tread blindly in the thick darkness, submerged in a tar-pit going nowhere fast, not exactly drowning, but not managing to get to the surface either. I'll be stuck in a no-man's-land of subdued panic, scrabbling and clawing like mad at the dense void, my mind blank, burning with pure rage.

It's sobering to think that this is what it all boils down to, proving my worth in close-quarters hand-to-hand combat; no guns or grenades, just what's at hand – that and an iron will to do whatever it takes. Perhaps I do feel nerves. Maybe the pressure is finally getting to me, where before it was lost in the romance of how the night unfolded – the creatures revealing themselves, the girls arriving, the party atmosphere, the sex, the sacrifice and the outcome, everything perfect, like an unrehearsed wedding going without a hitch. But nerves are good. That's one of the first things the instructors at Vojarna Tuškanac tell you; they keep you sharp and, more importantly, keep you alive. Sorrow, on the other hand, is for those who are no longer alive, like the girl, whose cautionary note – beware of feeling sorry for yourself – can be fatal in the doubt it harbours and the hesitation it creates. Hence this end-point assessment to see if I have what it takes when facing mortal danger in its most raw and primitive form. There is no other way to prove myself. The gods know my history and, in particular, know how I avoid bullets and shrapnel or rather, how they avoid me. But if they already know this, then the real question they want answering is: Will the same thing happen to someone's plunging blade?

To be honest, I don't know.

But in the next few minutes I'm going to find out.

Having delayed long enough and not wanting to disappoint, I get up and go into the lounge. The room, like the hallway, stinks, but even more so; the girl's mother's body is lying amid a mess of spilt Chinese takeaway, beer cans and an upturned ashtray, the butts still smoking on the carpet and the TV blaring the finale of some late-night chat show or other, although there's no one left alive to watch it. The knife and hatchet are difficult to pull out. I have to use my foot as leverage, first against the chest to release the knife embedded to the hilt in the stomach, then on the neck to gain better purchase on the hatchet, its blade similarly wedged deep into the forehead.

Back in the hallway, I release the latch and let the front door swing open to rest against the little girl's bent legs, glad, as I take a deep breath, of the cool night air and its menthol freshness diluting the deep-seated odour of poor living. With it comes the vociferous flood of wild noise, like a tsunami smashing through the flat. The intoxicating call to arms instantly synchronises my mood to that of its chaotic rhythm as I step back, get ready and brace myself for the onslaught.

***

I stare into the darkness beyond the open doorway. The noise is gut-wrenching and getting closer. For the first time since I can remember, I am out of options, cornered like a press-ganged gladiator who's about to grace the sands of the arena. I feel sick with nerves as the incoming roar swells in anticipation. The gods are poised for my introduction as the demon creatures guide their hosts, drawing them ever nearer.

I can only liken it to being tied to a set of tracks, knowing a train is somewhere out there and will soon come smashing through like the raucous din that precedes it.

I ready myself, adopting a squat martial arts stance, set to pounce, the knife clenched in my leading left hand and the hatchet slightly raised, geared up to strike, in my right.

In the light of the doorway, figures flit past like fleeing antelope, one unexpectedly hitting the door frame and ricocheting off into a dazed heap inside the hallway. Their pursuer skids to a halt, glaring first at me, then at the weaker calf singled out from the herd, stunned, and hurt, with a horrible craziness in her eyes, drooling and laughing, hysterical with a hunger like no other. Just when I think she won't, in a split second the mad woman, as her inner monster reveals itself, pounces, diving on top of her quarry. "You fucking bitch! You fucking bitch!" She screams over and over, grabbing handfuls of hair to smash the face of her victim, a younger woman, repeatedly into the foot of the kitchen door frame where it meets a corner of the wooden skirting-board. Teeth, gums, and nose cartilage crunch as the woman flies into a rage like a crazed witch. Instinctively I step forward and swipe the young woman's attacker. The hatchet catches her across the cheek bone, and I raise it to chop again as two men rush in. I stab at the front runner and twist the knife with a swirl of my wrist as I pull it from his midriff. Falling on his side, he howls in pain, and I strike his wingman through the face with the hatchet, its blade driving down through the top lip and slicing his bottom jaw in two, but there's a third hanging on his coattails. He catches me unawares and out of position, with my weight on my weaker front foot. I try to turn towards the unexpected blur in my peripheral vision, but he's too fast. We clash, his frantic grappling blocking the freedom of my arms, the moment fraught; somehow, I turn him, gain the upper hand, push back and chop wildly at his chest, ducking a last-ditch flailing arm to bump into another oncoming body, a sizeable bulk bellowing its war-cry. This guy is solid, leading with his shoulder. His mighty tattooed arms grab me and force me backwards. It feels like being hit by the proverbial train; the impact sends my mind into a spin as I pray for my adrenaline to spike. My arms are locked in his. In the close crush, unable to see this giant's face, I shake my head, feeling the rasp of heavy stubble rake my skin and his teeth skirt my cheek. I'm trying to avoid him biting my nose and ears; his laboured breath is rank, his exertions spewing a trail of saliva across my face. I'm alarmed at how he can wrestle with such competent ease, indicating a degree of specialist training; despite a lack of obvious fitness, his vice-like grip tightens. I jerk to twist my hips and wince, his knee missing my groin only to find my ribs. Again, and again his right knee slams into my floating rib, each hit on the verge of breaking bone, making it harder for me to breathe. But whatever I do, I can't move; however hard I try to wriggle or shift my weight, he's got me. All I can do is crane my neck. I head-butt once, twice, three times…his grip loosens…a fourth time – whack! – His nose splits and I crouch down. Unable to gain a firm footing, I trip and fall. The floor is alive with a shifting, bloody mess, out of which arms extend with reaching fingers to claw my clothes as if trying to drag me down into their bleeding mire. I heave myself from the red, viscous bog and clamber across a body; it's the witch, her face glaring, cut clean through like a hideous, gaping scream hissing bloody spittle. She grabs me, clinging to my trouser belt. On my elbows and knees, with the giant's heavy blows beginning to rain down on my back, I can only hammer the butt of the knife into her eye. Again and again, I pound; the eye socket caves in, and I cut away at her fingers, freeing myself, lashing out at the other grabbing hands around me. I slice digits and forearms with my knife like a scythe harvesting wheat. The sudden jolt of someone else joining in the assault surprises me, coming in from my flank kicking and stamping; my kidneys are already throbbing from the giant's weighty fists. The blows make me rock to and fro, slipping and sliding on the bodies underneath me. I try to lift my head to look for an opportunity, but I can't; the onslaught is a terrible blitz pinning me down. I know that if I do take a solid blow to the head, it's all over. Stuck, I shuffle around curled up like an armadillo, with nothing to lose and just enough manoeuvrability to hack and stab at anything at floor level. I seek out feet, ankles, and calves; my blade finds the giant's Achilles tendon and suddenly he's bellowing in anguish, and we are rolling in the gore together. Everything is seen through a reddish, agonised haze. I'm struggling against the odds. I push, parry and block, exhausted, my arms numb, the adrenaline peaking at last, juicing me up. My eyes twinkle, reflecting the flash of Japanese steel, and I hear the thud of my hatchet finding solid bone. The frenzy is over. A lucky strike was the difference between us. For a precious couple of seconds, I see myself on top, pushing with all my might the long, sharp blade into the big man's mouth. His shovel-like hands try desperately to pull it out; like someone losing a tug of war, the blade slips through his fingers till they're severed, falling like fat sausages around his neck as I twist the blade and drive it through his large bovine tongue and into the back of the throat. I'm lost for a second in euphoric respite. Then I snap to and turn to the man who is kicking me, a weasel-like, sinewy figure of diminutive stature with stab wounds on his lower legs. As I get to my feet, he shuffles awkwardly back until he comes to rest against the dead girl at the bottom of the stairs.

"I suppose it would be cool to say, 'there's one I prepared earlier'." I point at the girl with my knife. The giant's blood drops off its blade. "If only to heighten the tension and scare you some more. But if I did, I'd be lying. The monster that did this atrocity is still upstairs. I don't need to scare you any more than you already are – do I?" I add. The weasel acknowledges me, shame-faced – "No!" He croaks, shielding his face with a defensive palm as I bring the hatchet full swing over my shoulder to slice clean between the middle fingers down through the hand to the wrist.

"Ahhhhh! Fuck! Fuck! My fucking hand!" He squeals in sheer disbelief. He probably thought he was going to get off lightly. He clutches at the two flapping pieces of hand, his whole body shaking violently, the crotch of his denim jeans abruptly darkening to leak a growing pool of urine.

"Fuck your hand and fuck you!" I snarl, flicking the knife's tip hard against the side of his neck to open up the jugular vein, turning to see who else is left. Not wanting to leave anyone alive, I stand above the first man to attack me, whose chest I chopped. His gasping, dying body lies blood-spattered and trampled. Looking down, I see nothing more than an animal that needs to be put out of its misery, so I hack through his ear into the head till the pallid pink of brain spills out. Expecting him to scream, he bizarrely makes little noise, if any. Just a sudden grimace and pained murmur in farewell and it's over. Then there's the young woman, a hapless victim, semi-conscious, choking on her own teeth and bits of gum, her whole face puffed out, her nasal cavity ripped apart and grotesquely exposed, the mouth unrecognisable, the lower jaw destroyed, and front upper palate shattered into a hideous concave dent. Her incisors protrude from the blood-smeared woodwork of the kitchen doorframe.

I bend down and rest the knife's blade across a pronounced neck vein, undecided whether to put her down or not. She's no threat, never was, just cannon fodder for the creatures to do with as they please, the kind of collateral damage you hope can be avoided yet always expect. But still, who would want to live on after such devastation and undergo the long road to recovery – the constant agony, the never-ending operations, the painstaking rehabilitation – and still be nowhere near what you once were, forever disfigured, a freak to some and pitied by the rest?

So, what's it to be? What is the lesser of two evils? I know what the gods would have me do. They would have me kill her – a quick thrust to the base of the skull, sever the brain stem, job done. But from the human perspective it's damned if you do and damned if you don't. A second's pain and restful peace, or leave her to squirm in agony and endure a lifetime of hurt?

Either way, it is not for me to decide – not this time.

Fate will see if she pulls through or not.

Happy to leave the monster upstairs, I exit the flat. I know that to the right, the walkway leads to a dead end. Left is my only real option, towards the corner of the building's big L-shaped footprint and the only set of stairs down to ground level. It's that or jump. Deciding I want no one behind me when I do go for the stairs, I head right, hacking down the first person I come across with a single downward swipe, not knowing if they are male or female, friend, or foe. Their presence is no more than a smudged silhouette, an obstacle I need to overcome. There's another! I feel their hands and their hurried breath upon me. I duck, push, stab, hack, and they're down. Another chop makes sure they stay down. A third silhouette turns to run away, jumping over the walkway's end into dark empty space rather than hanging around for me to give chase. I thank him or her, whoever it was, for the brief respite as I quickly swivel one-eighty towards the only direction left for me. I take stock, resting against a patch of rough brick and assess the damage to my own body, checking for cuts and areas of acute pain, allowing the red mist time to properly evaporate so I am clear in mind and vision.

But before I even consider what lies ahead and the affray blocking my path, I notice the surrounding blackness closing in. The gods and their hunger are so palpable and their desire so impatient that the night sky parts to let the dark bare its fangs and claw-like talons. Gargantuan in stature, the night vista is blacker still against their gleaming brilliance as huge eyes of the crudest jet shine to glare with cruel intent. The gods have let their mightiest of beasts off its leash. It knows I'm more than up for the challenge. I know it won't accept failure as an option. And here *it* comes to cheer me on – my biggest fan. Just as night follows day, I know the dark will descend. Its presence is imminent. Just as I know I will shine oh so brightly under God's luminescence if I'm to survive when immersed in the heart of the Devil's bosom, for it is the highest and most perilous of high wire balancing acts. I will only get one attempt. After I am done here, win or lose, I know there will be no escaping its clutches; the dark will come for me and it will claim me, as it will try to claim everyone else – one final test to see if the gods have chosen well.

But first I must get through the affray.

I study the walkway, scanning its every inch. I diligently note its width – approximately four to five feet. The flats are on my left and a steel balustrade topped by a continuous rail, which stands just over three feet high, on my right. I scrutinise every detail, the brick to window to door ratio, their spacing, and, once the fighting starts, places to rest, staging points to make for and the danger points – places to avoid getting held up. I look at the height of the kitchen windows, the already-broken glass, even the slight protrusion of the windowsills, and, of course, the steel railing, anything that might be a factor in my reaching the stairs. But to reach the stairs, I must run the gauntlet of terror, its length made up of the width of three flats and a further dash through a narrow passage that leads to the front of the building and the exiting stairway, a total of seventy feet or more.

Blocking this path is the affray, a body of people about forty deep, a rabid horde that I hoped would be less in number. They're hell-bent on bludgeoning one another into oblivion, yet it seems all eyes are upon me, the mêlée preferring to unite rather than take their chances as individuals; a wise move on their part, but one I neglected to cater for. I thought this particular scenario would be impossible. Yet there they stand, shoulder to shoulder, jostling and swaying like meadow grass on a summer's eve, no more than twenty feet away, their seething eagerness fixed on my slightest movement. They glare wildly and I stare back at them. All of us stand ready, poised to charge.

But as I wait for one of them to make the first move, in the other wing of the building there is no rest for the wicked. I can hear the cries of anguish behind closed doors, barricaded to contain the suffering. Suddenly the noise of breaking glass draws my eye up to a high window and a shower of glittering, tiny stars surrounding a blanketed bundle. I watch the loosely wrapped layers plummet to the cries of a baby falling. There is an abrupt silence when it reaches the hard concrete some thirty feet below.

Curious as to what might follow, I stay glued to the spot, monitoring the adjacent fracas despite my own pressing concerns, with one eye on the forty-or-so-strong mêlée front of me, while the other tracks this latest development under the walkway's dim yellow light. With distant shouts and bangs, the fracas erupts, the splintering crash of breaking wood and brawling bodies spilling out of the flat below to a dulcet soundtrack – *'cos Saturday night's alright for fighting, get a little action in. Fighting goes without saying* – says my inner voice with a shrug – *but carnage, now there's the future.* The feral rush of figures tearing at one another, screaming, and yelling obscenities, cheered on by neighbours, men, women and children alike, for small gains, their manic aggression an *end of days* delirium.

I know my own fight for survival is coming at any second. I can feel it. From nothing, the electricity that I have got to know so well starts to grow. The air is charging, the anticipation accelerating, the itchy feet, the nervous shuffling, that sound building. An infectious, malevolent hum grips all, directing those in the affray to lock into mortal combat, a fight to the death. A sea of makeshift clubs are raised with a glint of ruthless steel to salute a worthy opponent: The gods, demons and creatures happy with their choice.

I nod my appreciation and don the hood of my sweatshirt like the Reaper hiding my face of death, for as of now, I have no fear and no feeling. I consider myself already dead.

How else are you meant to face such insurmountable odds?

Wanting to go out in style, I think of all the top athletes I have seen and get down into a starting posture as though readying myself on a set of blocks at the beginning of the Olympic 100 metres sprint final. What it must be like to be the fastest man on earth, the very best of the best in your discipline, hailed by all and doubted by none.

In my mind I hear the tell-tale click of the hammer on the starter's pistol. My legs tense, elevating my posture slightly, and my feet dig in for good purchase. That beautiful sound opens up my adrenal gland like flicking a nitro switch to boost an engine, that instant flood of epinephrine a psycho's wet dream. I raise the long knife in my left hand while steadying myself with my right, the hatchet firmly in my grasp.

Bang!

Go!

I sprint, they charge, we crash; we come together with a clash of steel on steel, a deafening roar, a sudden heat, a claustrophobic crush, the splash of blood, the hideous screams of the injured and dying, the glorious noise of battle all around. I duck, lunge, swing, thrust and stab, twisting and turning and swiping and hacking. I know I'm hurt; the mêlée is wild and frenetic, lashing out, beating me. My pain is numbed by the wake of bleeding bodies behind me and fuelled by the frenzied mayhem still in front.

"NOW I'M HAVING FUN!"

Adrian Lee Baker lives in a small village outside Ashby-de-la-Zouch, Leicestershire. He is fifty-three years old, married to Angela and has two daughters, Phoebe and Milly. His occupation is in teaching and works as a lecturer and trainer-assessor in further education. He likes country walking, mountain biking and is a Second Dan in the combat sport of kick-boxing. It has always been his ambition to write and have something published. He is an avid fan of both books and films, especially of the sci-fi and horror genres, and latterly, dark fantasy. Hence his writing style reflects the darker side of life. Favourite books include *Nineteen Eighty-Four*, *A Clockwork Orange*, *Heart of Darkness*, *Dracula*, *Naked Lunch*, and *Fear and Loathing in Las Vegas*.